W9-CQL-164

SF   THE NEW AWARENESS

9.95

THE NEW AWARENESS

THE NEW AWARENESS

religion through science fiction

edited by Patricia Warrick and
Martin Harry Greenberg

DELACORTE PRESS / NEW YORK

Manufactured in the United States of America

First printing

Library of Congress Cataloging in Publication Data

Warrick, Patricia S   comp.
        The new awareness.

        Bibliography: p.
CONTENTS: Primitive religion: Sambrot, W. Night of
the leopard. —The power of the religious vision: Moorcock, M.
        Behold the man. —Religious institutions, past:
Miller, W. M., Jr. A canticle for Leibowitz. [etc.]
        1. Science fiction. 2. Religions—Juvenile fiction.
    [1. Science fiction. 2. Religions—Fiction. 3. Short
    stories] I. Greenberg, Martin Harry, joint author.
                        II. Title.
        PZ5.W23Ne   [Fic]   74-22631
                ISBN 0-440-05989-5

Excerpt from "Man Against Darkness" by W. T. Stace: Copy-
    right © 1948, by The Atlantic Monthly Company, Boston,
    Mass. Reprinted with permission. Reprinted with permission of
    Mrs. W. T. Stace.
"Night of the Leopard" by William Sambrot: Reprinted by per-
    mission of Curtis Brown, Ltd. Copyright © 1967 by William
    Sambrot.
"Behold the Man" by Michael Moorcock: Copyright © 1966 by
    New World SF and Copyright © 1968 by Michael Moorcock.
    Reprinted by permission of the author and Henry Morrison,
    Inc., his agents.
"A Canticle for Leibowitz" by Walter M. Miller, Jr.: Copyright

To Scott, Kristin, and David
and
to Kari and Katie

CONTENTS

Religion is
the vision of something which
stands beyond, behind, and within
the passing flux of immediate things;
something which is real, and yet waiting
to be realized; something which is a remote
possibility, and yet the greatest of present facts;
something that gives meaning to all that passes,
and yet eludes apprehension; something
whose possession is the final good,
and yet is beyond all reach;
something which is the
ultimate ideal, and
the hopeless
quest.

—ALFRED NORTH WHITEHEAD
in **Science and the Modern World**

PREFACE

This book contains a collection of science fiction stories that serve as a vehicle for exploring the fundamental questions asked by various religions. The book purposely does not provide answers; the hope of the editors is that out of the dialogue the reader carries on with the ideas of the stories, he will develop his own answers. Self-created answers are, finally, the only sustaining answers.

The organization of the stories, however, does contain a shaping pattern. It is the belief that man's increasing knowledge about the universe leads him to new levels of technical complexity, but also to new levels of self-consciousness or awareness. With this new awareness he is in the process of moving forward to new levels of integration—integration within himself, and integration with men and nature outside himself. There will be more diversity as man becomes aware of himself as a unique individual; but, incorporating this diversity, more unity as he realizes he is also a social being who benefits from loving cooperation.

To move in this direction, he needs both science and religion, disciplines that can no longer ignore each other. Each serves a similar function: to help man shape his universe enough to make it comprehensible. Religion has its poetic or intuitive language, using myths to express its images of the universe. Science uses hypotheses and models. To ask which is true is a meaningless question. Each is a different way of perceiving the cosmos, of shaping reality. A better question to ask is: Does the myth or model function? Does it provide a guide that makes life meaningful and significant?

In the last part of the twentieth century we are beginning to recognize that the scientific model functions very well in describing and controlling the material world. However, it does not give meaning to the human spirit. We seem ready now to move to the complexity of holding two views at once—both the scientific and the religious. The fundamental law of ecology is that everything is related and relevant to everything else. All the great religions through history have also expressed this same law.

THE NEW AWARENESS

INTRODUCTION

I

What is religion? Does it have a function in a technological world? What is man's place in the universe described by modern science? Where is God? How is God to be understood? Why does man exist? What is his purpose? These are the questions man asks today as he struggles to identify himself in the restless, mechanized environment that technology has created for him.

The questions about the nature of God, man, and the universe are eternal. Man, unique in his sense of wonder and curiosity, has from his beginning explored the mystery. Earliest man, who lived by hunting, created answers he expressed in stories of animal spirits and the marvelous powers manifested in the world around him. Later man, who lived by farming,

1

shaped myths of planting and the seasons to light his existence in the mysterious cosmos.

With the advent of the industrial revolution, a new kind of man was born—one whose world was shaped by science, industry, and technology. Today, technological man in the twentieth century must ask again these perennial questions about meanings. The answers must be new answers for men manipulating enormous power through their machines, for men threatening their fellowmen with atomic destruction, for men traveling through the heavens to the moon and beyond. Religion must be reexplored.

Good science fiction utilizes the concepts and equipment of contemporary science and technology. It is, as a result, uniquely able to examine technological man in his search for meaning. Science fiction need not limit itself to what man and his thought systems are now, but can consider his potential and offer models for talking about man and God in the future. The stories in this anthology explore some of the perennial questions of religion from new vantages.

Man seems to be unique among all living creatures on this planet in that he has self-awareness; he is conscious of his own being and conscious that he will die. He, alone, has the imaginative capacity to relate to the universe in a sense of cosmological wonder. One of his strongest concerns is to make this universe coherent and meaningful. The apparent meaninglessness of modern life pushes him to make the search for a purpose his first concern. The theologian Paul Tillich says "everything which is a matter of unconditional concern is made into a god." Man's unconditional concern

today, then, is to search for meaning in the universe—
to search for God.

The search, which anthropologists tell us seems to
be carried on by all peoples—from primitive to present
times—has yielded a rich store of answers. They have
been formalized into a variety of religious systems—
Christianity, Hinduism, Buddhism, Judaism, Muhammadanism—whose likenesses are greater than their differences. They all answer the question of the *creation* of
the universe. They describe a *Godhead* that is the ultimate power and ground of being. They explain the
appearance of this divine form on the Earth in some
kind of incarnation—Jesus in Christianity, Buddha in
Buddhism, for example. They suggest that, while reality is represented by this world, there is also another
world of reality—*a super-natural world*. This other
reality may be experienced directly by humans through
mystical experiences, with gifted individuals being
more easily able to touch the divine ground. They usually become the prophets and teachers of the religion.
Prayer and *meditation* are the paths to be followed in
seeking the joy and power of the divine. *Rituals* celebrate and beseech the divine. Because the Godhead
creates, controls, and gives meaning and order to the
universe, the faithful have the security of knowing they
share that same order and meaning in their world. As
God created order out of chaos in the universe, so man
can create order out of chaos in his life. Those actions
that contribute to order he calls *good* and *moral*; those
contributing to chaos are *immoral* and *evil*. Man's religion, then, gives him a moral code, a desired standard
of behavior.

II

Early man—with the emergence of self-consciousness —must have seen himself as existing in a world filled with mysterious forces, both marvelous and threatening. He would have differentiated very little between the natural and the supernatural world. In his everyday world he lived with the gods. He saw spirits in trees and in rocks. His concern for the burial of his dead indicates he felt man also possessed a spiritual self. Anthropological and archaeological studies conclude that man has always been a religious creature. It is one of his unique qualities. He has a capacity for *transcendence*; his mind rises above and goes beyond the limits of his physical world. He has the unique ability to erect mental pictures of what is not in his immediate physical sight. When these mental pictures lie beyond the natural world, they become supernatural images and are called myths. These ideals of what might be, in their ultimate form, are his gods, or the irresistible power that draws man to transcend himself, becoming more than he otherwise could have been.

Primitive man moved toward a divine ground that helped him survive in the face of starvation, disease, such mysterious and threatening forces as lightning, winds, and volcanic eruptions. He practiced hunting rites, planting rites, and many other rituals to protect himself against an awesome and often unpredictable Nature. His religious structures functioned to sustain him in his greatest anxieties—starvation and disease. Religion was concerned not with moral problems but with survival problems. Only after the problem of the survival of life has been solved can religion turn to moral concerns.

Primitive man had a limited conception of the universe. He knew that power exists in the universe, and that to live and succeed, he must have some of that power. This universal power might be personified in ghosts and spirits. *Animism* is the term used to describe his view that spirit beings inhabit most natural objects—plants, trees, animals, clouds. The world around him was spiritually alive.

Let us move from the primitive religions to the religions of more complex societies that have developed written language and have begun to keep written records. The religion that has most directly influenced our Western culture is Judaism. The ancestors of the Jewish people were seminomads who roamed through the lands of the Middle East about 2000 B.C. The Book of Genesis contains the history of the founding fathers, Abraham, Isaac, Jacob, and Joseph. About 1300 B.C. the towering leader, Moses, led the Jews out of slavery in Egypt. Moses, who formulated and refined many of the religious concepts of his people, declared: "Hear, O Israel, the Lord our God, the Lord is One." These words mark a new awareness in religion, called monotheism, which held that there are not many gods (polytheism) but only one. The books of the Old Testament demonstrate that the Jews' primary concern was with living in harmony with God's will. Their life was primarily religious, grappling with problems of law and morality—how should man conduct himself and his society so that his behavior was acceptable and pleasing to God?

When we move to the time of medieval Christianity, we find man's self-awareness and -knowledge had continued to expand, but he was still a religious man. He had continued to restructure his cosmic images, and now they were much different from those of primitive man. He saw himself in a fixed, static world, a spherical cosmos with Heaven above, Hell below, and man midway in a great chain of being. He owed his allegiance to the spiritual God of Light above, but the God of Darkness below, the Devil, tempted him through his lust for sex, drink, and the physical life of the senses. The Earth lay at the center of the universe, with the stars and sun rotating around it, and man was the final masterpiece of God, who had accomplished the creation in 4004 B.C.

The medieval universe, according to the Christian world view, was a fixed, closed universe where specific answers were provided for the haunting cosmic mysteries. If an individual followed the codes prescribed by the Holy Catholic Church, he would be rewarded with eternal salvation; the sinner faced a searing eternity in Hell. Perhaps the strongest element of medieval Christianity was its certainty. It saw God as the "First Cause," who created and gave purpose to the cosmos. Everything, including man, was a part of a cosmic plan. Even if man could not understand all of it, nevertheless the design existed. The Church, the earthly structure to carry out God's plan, could prescribe with confidence how the true believer ought to behave. Having followed the requirements of the Church, he could rest in the certainty that he was in harmony with God's will. His life in this world might be bleak and short, but he had the comfort of knowing he would be eternally rewarded in a future heavenly life. The meaning and purpose of life was clear. In this brief life, man prepared himself for a future existence.

III

Twentieth-century man lives with no such certainty. The Renaissance produced a new cosmic view. In the late fifteenth century the old Ptolemaic earth-centered universe was replaced by the awareness of the Polish astronomer Copernicus, who declared that the Earth and other planets revolved around the sun. Other scientists, like Galileo and Newton, contributed insights that eventually destroyed the old image of the benign universe governed by spiritual laws. Galileo and Newton, paradoxically, were like most early scientists; they were religious men who had no intention of destroying the structures of the Church. This happened almost as an accidental by-product of the scientific method. W. T. Stace, in "Man Against Darkness," explains that:

> The founders of modern science—for instance, Galileo, Kepler and Newton—were mostly pious men who did not doubt God's purposes. Nevertheless they took the revolutionary step of consciously and deliberately expelling the idea of purpose as controlling nature from their new science of nature. They did this on the ground that inquiry into purposes is useless for what science aims at: namely, the prediction and control of events. To predict an eclipse, what you have to know is not its purpose but its causes. Hence

science from the seventeenth century onwards became exclusively an inquiry into causes. The conception of purpose in the world was ignored and frowned on. This, though silent and almost unnoticed, was the greatest revolution in human history, far outweighing in importance any of the political revolutions whose thunder has reverberated through the world.

For it came about in this way that for the past three hundred years there has been growing up in men's minds, dominated as they are by science, a new imaginative picture of the world. The world, according to this new picture, is purposeless, senseless, meaningless. Nature is nothing but matter in motion. The motions of matter are governed, not by any purpose, but by blind forces and laws. Nature on this view, says Whitehead—to whose writings I am indebted in this part of my paper—is "merely the hurrying of material, endless, meaninglessly." You can draw a sharp line across the history of Europe, dividing it into two epochs of very unequal length. The line passes through the lifetime of Galileo. European man before Galileo —whether ancient pagan or more recent Christian —thought of the world as controlled by plan and purpose. After Galileo, European man thinks of it as utterly purposeless. This is the great revolution of which I spoke.[1]

Modern man, as a result of this revolution, finds himself in a dilemma of despair. He is a product of scientific thinking that does not ask *why* but *how*. Science explores the causes of physical phenomena and accepts only answers that can be verified experimentally. Science has never claimed either to have proved or disproved the existence of God. It has felt that this is a question whose answer cannot be verified experimentally, and that, therefore, it lies outside the field of inquiry of science. Almost by default, then, the question of the purpose of the universe and the purpose of man has been dropped. Yet to live without answers to the why of existence is to live without meaning. To accept the view that his life and death are totally without purpose drowns man in despair.

The science that unintentionally robbed man of the security of his medieval world did something else. It gave him increasing knowledge and increasing power. The ultimate power that knowledge has released is the power of thermonuclear explosion. Man now has at his disposal power for unbelievable destruction. Formerly, foot soldiers carrying guns were limited to small acts of destruction. Planes carrying atomic bombs are not. This awesome power forces man to recognize that he now has new responsibilities. If mankind is to survive and give its members the chance to lead creative lives of fulfillment, we must learn to establish a world community of harmonious interaction.

Modern man, besides struggling to orient himself in a world apparently without meaning, clutching in horror his weapons of total destruction, has yet another anxiety. After science came technology, which implements the concepts of science. Since science deals with the material world, the products of technology are material. In an avalanche they pour out over modern man, besieging him to engage in an orgy of consumption. That part of his nature which is nonphysical is neglected, again almost by default, because it is easier to supply material than spiritual needs. Instead of becoming an active, creative, loving individual, he becomes a passive consumer destroying the world around him with pollution. Other men, instead of being fellows to whom he can relate in the fulfillment of a harmonious community, become competitors with whom he must struggle for material goods. More and more, society asks him to be nothing more than a passive consumer of goods.

These, then, are the two most perplexing problems facing man today: (1) How does he find a meaning in life that allows him to explore and fulfill the full potential of *Self*? (2) How does he establish a true *Community* of men, both within nations and among nations, that will preserve Mankind and his Earth?

IV

Man's quality of *transcendence*, his ability to move beyond the chaos that threatens to engulf him, is alive today as it always has been. His self-awareness allows him to study his present dilemma and formulate questions that need to be answered if he is to escape the morass of material struggle threatening to engulf him. And once having asked the right questions, he is remarkably inventive in formulating answers. He begins to realize today that technology gives him the potential of creating almost any environment and life-style he wants. He is freed of the limitations of the natural world as earlier man never was. With this new freedom to become, he discovers he must ask again: What should be man's purpose? Is there a universal purpose with which he needs to live harmoniously? He needs religion as much as he ever has, but because he has new problems today, he must create new answers with new images and models. Religion is being remade again as it has been remade in the past. As one author suggests:

> Man creates for himself a divine master who proceeds to teach man new ways, out of which emerge new cultural forms, which in turn require men to adopt new forms of consciousness. But men with new consciousnesses are new men and new men need to declare the old gods dead and to create new and more appropriate gods to go with their new consciousness and their new needs, and so on. It follows that a death-of-God era is also a god-building era . . . : our own time is one of the most religious periods of all history, a time in which god-building is taking place at a dizzying pace.[2]

The idea that man's concept of God will change seems at first startling and perhaps disturbing. But upon reflection it becomes even more disturbing to think that man's concept of God might not change. God is spirit, nonmaterial. To talk about the material, man erects images and myths, drawing from the concrete world around him. Images of shepherd and flock are meaningful to a nomadic people. They lose meaning for a technological people who have never seen a shepherd. As theologian Paul Tillich describes it, the myth is broken. The spiritual meaning for which the image stood is lost. The broken myth must be replaced with a fresh one.

The mathematician and philosopher Alfred North Whitehead describes the universe as process.[3] All matter is in motion, constantly in the process of becoming. Newton's earlier physics, which described a fixed point in space at a specific time, has been revised to incorporate the awareness that no such static condition exists. We can only describe a field and the probability of where matter will be at a given moment. Matter and time are a continuum, constantly flowing.

Man, as a part of the universe, is also in motion. He is always becoming something he has not been before. It is not easy, therefore, to define what man is. But the most prominent aspect of the direction in which he moves is clear. He is evolving through more and more complex levels of consciousness. The awareness of a caveman is not the awareness of a space man.

The complexity of the knowledge accumulated by science in the twentieth century is staggering. There is nothing in the observable physical world that provides us with a model or an understanding of the realms to which scientific exploration leads us. We are now exploring the universe at its extremes. We understand rather well the middle ground of the immediately apparent world around us, and now turn to study—at one extreme—the distant stars and heavenly bodies and—at the other extreme—submicroscopic particles. Physicist Erwin Schrödinger explains the difficulties we experience as our "mental eye" tries to penetrate where it has not seen before: "We find nature behaving so entirely differently from what we observe in visible and palpable bodies of our surroundings, that *no* model shaped after our large scale experiences can ever be 'true.'" This new universe that we try to conquer is not only "practically inaccessible, but not even thinkable. Or, to be precise, we can, of course, think it, but however we think it, it is wrong; not perhaps quite as meaningless as a 'triangular circle,' but much more so than a 'winged lion.' "[4]

Man can now do what he cannot comprehend. Consider the moonshots we observe by television: the miraculous power of the rockets in takeoff, the complexity of the computers that instruct the spaceship as it journeys moonward. We observe what happens, but most of us cannot understand exactly how it happens.

Clearly, then, man with a more complex consciousness of the material world is ready to construct a more complex awareness of the spiritual world—is indeed constructing it now. James Joyce, the twentieth century's finest novelist, seemed to understand this. In *A Portrait of the Artist as a Young Man* he pictures Stephen Daedalus, as the novel ends, flying off to create a new conscience for his race. Some of the aspects of that new conscience that humanity is now building begin to appear already. Our televised sight of our planet from space—a blue-and-white spherical unity in the dark void—gives man a new vision of himself. Mankind is one, a single organism living on his host the Earth. The view of Earth from space is different from the view of Earth from Earth, and man needs a new religious vision to express it.

Some of the values this new vision must contain are explored by biologist Bentley Glass in *Science and Ethical Values*. He explains that

in the evolutionary progression from simpler forms to the most complex, life has passed through a hierarchy of levels of organization. Among the organisms of today we can readily discern all these same levels of organization. From the molecular level we pass to the cellular level. Cells are grouped into differentiated tissues and organs. The organs make up the body of a complex individual, such as a human being, but the levels of organized life do not stop here. Individuals collectively form a population belonging to a single species. All the populations coexistent in a single area form a community. The communities of the earth are interknit to constitute a great biome.[5]

We can see the image of this great biome, or interlaced life web, in the pictures of our planet sent from the moon. Earth is indeed a spaceship carrying life through the heavens.

All life is mutually dependent. As the single-celled animal evolves into a more complex one, groups of cells specialize to perform particular functions that contribute to the survival of the whole. In an analogous way, individuals organize themselves into a social order, mutually dependent upon one another. Man is the only animal that has achieved this banding together to make a real society. Glass continues,

> Only in human society do we find specialized individuals basing their skills on learning rather than instinct. . . . The values inherent in cooperation and coordination, promoted so blindly but so perfectly on the level of the cell by the chemical organization it possesses . . . must in the society which is based on learning be imposed by force or

be nurtured by conscience. Religion that exalts these values, that "all men are brothers," and invokes the force of human kindness and brotherly love to cement these bonds, clearly plays a great part in the preservation of this type of society.[6]

Survival of humanity, then, depends on man's being able to extend his awareness beyond his individual needs to the needs of the whole social organism that lives on its host Earth. Man must learn—finally—to define himself not in terms of his nation, or race, or culture, but in terms of himself and his relationship to all his fellowmen in the world organism and beyond that to the whole universe. The cooperation that produces harmony in the social organism leading to its survival is good; that which disrupts it is evil.[7]

V

Religion has the task of defining man and the universe again in terms of the new complexities and of new awareness of the twentieth-century space age. Religion needs to develop new and imaginative symbols to convey the enlarged morality technological man must have to survive. Man must redefine a belief system that holds as the highest good a harmonious and sustaining relationship of (1) man with *all* his fellowmen, and (2) man with his physical environment.

The nineteenth century had a great faith in progress toward a utopian society, but unfortunately progress was understood largely in terms of material goods. Nature was seen as some kind of hostile force, and the "conquest of Nature" became a primary objective.

Today, according to biologist René Dubos, the "one credo of technology which has been accepted practically all over the world is that nature is to be regarded as a source of raw materials to be exploited for human ends rather than an entity to be appreciated for its own value."[8] But this destruction of the natural world for the sake of immediate material advantage becomes self-defeating. Man is part of the natural world. To destroy it is to eventually destroy himself.

Aldous Huxley, a futurist, pointed out in 1963 that man's exploitation of nature threatens "through erosion, through deforestation and soil exhaustion, through the progressive pollution and depletion of water resources, to render further human progress . . . difficult, perhaps in a relatively short time impossible —even [though] today the essential wickedness of man's inhumanity to Nature remains unrecognized by the official spokesmen for morality and religion." He concludes: "Man, the species, is now living as a parasite on the earth. Intelligent parasites take care not to kill their hosts; unintelligent parasites push their greed to the point of murder and, destroying their own food supply, commit suicide."[9] Man must become wise enough to preserve his natural environment if he is to survive.

Nature must be made sacred again, as it was held sacred by primitive men. We must recreate a religion of Nature that claims a mysterious and marvelous divinity for all God's creation of life, not merely for life in human form. All life on our planet sustains and enriches all other life. Insect, plant, tree, bird, man—all matter is divine, is to be cherished, not destroyed. The Apollo missions to the moon revealed the barren, gray surface of a lifeless body. The other planets in our solar system are apparently equally lifeless. By contrast, how marvelously rich and lovely is the green and blue planet Earth. It truly is a magic garden blooming in abundant life, a Garden of Eden unique and sacred among the planets. Religion must declare this divinity of Nature.

Second, religion must provide a vital vision to energize each man on Earth to live in a harmonious and sustaining relationship with all his fellowmen. We know, in abstract terms, that a world community of men is right. But we do not yet have the images and symbols that, united in a religious system, would enable us to create in the real world what we now only wistfully dream of in our hearts. This new religious view must be a vision that can go beyond such diverse religious systems as Buddhism, Christianity, Muhammadanism, and Hinduism.

Economically, we are moving toward one community as world trade increases. Intellectually, scientists and thinkers in all parts of the world exchange ideas. Television and communications systems unite us in a kind of "global village." More and more, we are in contact all over the Earth in many ways. How can we make this contact creative, not destructive?

As all the groups of cells and organs in the human body cooperate to maintain the life of that body, so must all groups of people cooperate to preserve the body of life on Earth. But we will not become united until we have a forceful image to shape that becoming. We need a space age myth, and it is religion that can create the electrifying images to light our new awareness of the unity of all life.

VI

The collection of science fiction stories that follows provides a means of looking anew at religion, from its beginnings far back in the unrecorded past to its possible directions in the future. At first glance, some of the stories may appear shocking or sacrilegious. They are not intended to be. Their use is aimed not at belittling religion, but at providing a means to think about it in a fresh and creative way. The oft-told religious stories are just that—stories told so often that the reader has a conditioned response rather than genuine and fresh thoughts about them. These science fiction stories move the reader to a new view, which hopefully will be a stimulating view. They give him the opportunity to discover a new sense of how religion functions to give meaning and value to men's lives.

Science fiction seems a natural vehicle for exploring religion today in a scientific and technological age. It is the literature that attempts to portray and interpret the ideas and effects of science on society. It shows man traveling through space, looking at the universe from new vantage points. It is rich in imaginative alternatives and a sense of wonder. It can revitalize older ways of thinking that have become complacent and stale. It can stimulate us to create new images of ourselves and our relationship to the universe.

Actually, science and religion, as biologist René Dubos points out, have similar origins and are evolving toward similar goals. "Both the myths of religion and the laws of science, it is now becoming apparent, are not so much descriptions of facts as symbolic expressions of cosmic truths."[10]

Anthropologist Carlos Castaneda suggests this same idea in his widely applauded *Journey to Ixtlan*. In this book he presents the remarkable old Indian sorcerer and teacher, Don Juan, who says that we see the world as we have been trained to see it. From the time we are born, we are told to see the world in a particular way, and so we do. We are "hypnotized" by our culture. Our modern scientific stance has conditioned us to see reality in a particular way, and we confuse our way of seeing with the truth itself. Don Juan says we could just as well be trained to "see" it another way. Different cultures at different times have seen reality with a lens different from the scientific looking glass. Science, he notes, looks only to understand what it sees, and this limited way of looking robs us of an awareness of the rich mystery of the world. He argues for a "double perception of the world, which allows the opportunity for seeing what we are ordinarily incapable of perceiving."[11]

His mystical view, Don Juan says, gives him a fuller vision: "For me the world . . . is stupendous, awesome, mysterious, unfathomable; my interest has been to convince you that you must assume responsibility for being here, in this marvelous world, in this marvelous desert, in this marvelous time. I wanted to convince you that you must learn to make every act count, since you are going to be here for only a short while, in fact, too short for witnessing all the marvels of it."[12] Don Juan goes on to argue for an enlarged vision: "Change your idea of the world. That idea is everything, and when that changes, the world itself changes."

Our idea of the world needs to contain the "double perception" of Don Juan. We can perhaps—as we explore religious concerns through science fiction—take a step toward learning that double perception. Religion and science have for too long been seen as separate cultures. It is not a question of which is "true." Both are necessary symbolic ways of perceiving in the twentieth century. The myths of religion can give us a belief in ourselves as a world family of loving individuals. The laws of science can give us the technology that—used creatively—can lead to the fulfillment of the religious image.

The new view we must create and use is not simple. Mankind has, with his accumulating mountain of knowledge, climbed to new awarenesses that make it impossible to accept simple answers. Complex problems are surmounted only with complex visions. The narrow simplicity of either/or choices will no longer serve; both must be encompassed. Man must learn to balance himself in the creative tension of apparent contraries. From this dynamic harmony we can hopefully discover a vision of the value of sacred life on a blessed planet in a mysterious and awe-inspiring universe. This vision of what is of the highest value is the vision of God.

[1] W. T. Stace, "Man Against Darkness," *The Atlantic Monthly*, September, 1948, p. 54.

[2] Harvey Wheeler, "The Phenomenon of God," *The Center Magazine*, March/April, 1971, p. 23.

[3] Ruth Nanda Anshen, ed., *Alfred North Whitehead* (New York: Harper and Brothers, 1961), p. 131.

[4] Erwin Schrödinger, *Science and Humanism* (London: Cambridge University Press, 1951), p. 26.

[5] Bentley Glass, *Science and Ethical Values* (Chapel Hill: The University of North Carolina Press, 1965), p. 12.

6 *Ibid.*, p. 27.

7 *Ibid.*, pp. 32–34.

8 René Dubos, *A God Within* (New York: Charles Scribner's Sons, 1972), p. 204.

9 "Has Man's Conquest of Space Increased or Diminished His Stature?" in Robert M. Hutchins and Mortimer J. Adler, eds., *The Great Ideas Today* (Chicago: Encyclopaedia Britannica, Inc., 1963), p. 24.

10 Dubos, *A God Within*, p. 255.

11 Carlos Castaneda, *Journey to Ixtlan* (New York: Simon and Schuster, 1972), p. 72.

12 *Ibid.*, p. 107.

1

PRIMITIVE RELIGION

Night of the Leopard
WILLIAM SAMBROT

"Night of the Leopard" explores the religion of a tribe of primitive people in Africa. A religion is a set of symbols and images and beliefs relating man to the ultimate conditions of his existence. The conditions of a primitive people's existence are vastly different from those of twentieth-century technological man. Man, unlike animals, does not passively endure the conditions of his existence, but attempts to control and direct them. Primitive man lived closely with Nature. Animals, trees, water, sun, wind, fire—these were the elements of the natural world in which primitive man lived, and he knew this world contained mysterious power that could nourish him or threaten him. He felt deities or spirits occupied animals and plants, giving them life, and he held this life-force in awe and reverence. Because he also possessed life, he recognized a spiritual kinship with Nature.

It was the function of his religion to aid him in feeling he had some control over the power of the Nature around him. The *shaman* was the man in the tribe who was gifted in communicating with the spirits in and above Nature, pleasing and directing them so that the tribe could better survive. He had secret knowledge of magic that could be used with the spirits. Often the spirits were seen as opposing and warring forces—the forces of Good or Light facing the forces of Evil or Darkness.

"Night of the Leopard" portrays an encounter of the religion of the modern world, Christianity, with a primitive religion in a primitive culture.

Oturu, the witch doctor, controls his primitive tribe through his knowledge of magic. Religion and magic have in the past understandably gone hand in hand. Religion aimed at explaining enough of the universe so that man felt some security in it. When facts were limited, superstitions sprang up. When real power to control was not available, magic was used. Oturu is the village medicine man who knows the secrets of black magic. He is a huge, muscular man who radiates power. His glittering eyes discharge hypnotic control. Because he believes in his magic and the natives also believe in that magic, it works. He can cause a "voodoo" death among his people because they believe he can. They are fearful of his power, and he utilizes this fear to control them.

Father Everett, a Christian mission priest, and Eunice, a young American, are devout Christians who bring their religion to confront Oturu and what they believe is his evil. It is a violent struggle to the death between Oturu's black magic—symbolized by the ugly gleaming idol called an obeah—and what Father Everett believes is the superior magic of his religion and the Christian cross. The struggle is carried on in the night, when the wind moans in the trees and spirits roam.

The story is a study of the conflict between an early religion and a later one, but it is also a study of the process of modernization today in the underdeveloped or Third World. In this modernization, numerous vested interests are threatened by change. Among them are witch doctors and medicine men, who traditionally have enjoyed the power and status associated with the healing arts. Modern medicine and its representatives —doctors, nurses, and wonder drugs—threaten this traditional status because the witch doctor cannot successfully compete with modern medicine. Thus, modernization is a very complex process involving much more than merely bringing the fruits of modern industry and technology to underdeveloped countries. It involves a change in the world view or religious system a people have erected to make their world understandable. As a result, modernization can be a very disruptive and painful process.

Night of the Leopard
WILLIAM SAMBROT

The trouble started the moment we set foot inside the village of Koluma.

There were four of us, members of the Peace Corps, who'd been sent to the new African nation of Sierra Leone: Jacob Tannenbaum, a bearded pre-med from NYU; an expert oboe player, jazzophile with a complete catalogue of everything Thelonius Monk had ever done. There was Michael Fallon from Oregon State, a B.A. in Forestry; redhead, freckled, a dead-ringer for a youthful Arthur Godfrey. There was Eunice Gantly, a B.A. in Sociology, a beautiful Negro girl born in Oakland, California, a grad of U.C., at Berkeley.

And lastly, there was myself, Bob Metzger, with an M.A. in Math, if you please, and fully aware I'd never use any part of it in the village of Koluma, deep in an indigenous rain forest near the Guinean-Liberian border. Kono-tribe territory. Far beyond the railhead, where primitive Africa really took over. Bush country.

We knew, as well as six weeks' briefing could tell us, just what we were getting into. We knew that Koluma lay in the heart of a country of festering swamps, plateaus, and remnants of immense rain forests. A country where rain exceeded ten feet—when it rained. A country where children have one chance in four of living to maturity. Where the women begin aging at fourteen and die of unremitting childbirth and labor before they're forty. Where trachoma, frambesia, elephantiasis and the tsetse fly are the norm. Where the tribal chiefs still exercise feudal life or death power.

A breathtakingly beautiful country, where the superstitions of a thousand generations hold the natives in
unbreakable thrall: where they fear to walk the forest
at night because God is a leopard who eats their souls
and mangles their bodies—and the witch doctor his
earthly representative. Only he roamed the night—in
many forms.

The witch doctor. They didn't tell us much about
him, at the briefings, back at the big clean U.C. campus
in Berkeley. But we learned of him in a hurry—and his
power—the hard way, the moment we stepped foot in
Koluma.

In Sefadue, the last town of any size before hitting
the bush country, we were met by Father Everett, a
Maryknoll priest. An American, he ran a tiny mission
not far from Koluma. He'd spent thirty years in the
bush, struggling to bring a ray of light into the primeval
darkness of that area. A lean, gentle-eyed man, he and
his grizzled old Negro assistant, Job, had walked out of
the bush to volunteer us his services.

He smiled, shaking our hands, and holding Eunice's
hands in both his for a long time, he studied her intently. "You have strength," he told her. "Do you
know, I believe you sprang from a Nilotic-Hamitic an-
cestry. I'd almost swear—Masai."

She laughed, her deep throaty laugh, her brilliant
eyes sparkling. "Straight Mississippi, Father," she said.
"For over two hundred years, now."

"I meant—before that," he said gently. "They know
the lions of Africa—the Masai—even here," he said.
His sunken eyes probed our faces, measuring our
bodies. "You are beautiful souls," he said. "I've forgotten how wonderful a young healthy body can be.

You've all had your shots; you know about the malaria here?"

We groaned in unison, and Father Everett smiled his brief melancholy smile. Job helped us with our gear; we had a miniature caravan of two used but serviceable jeeps, piled high with our possessions—two years' worth.

Job was aptly named; he suffered every imaginable woe and pain, but worked indefatigably; meanwhile keeping up a stream of conversation in a broad if broken English accent. Sierra Leone was for many years a British protectorate; many of the colony natives speak a passable brand of English. Others use pidgin only. In the bush country, they speak their own language.

We moved out, heading northeast, through vast open savannahs, still thick with game; over burnt-out grasslands, moving up and east, through second-growth bush country, and finally, plunging into the indigenous rain forest which extended from here hundreds of miles east into Guinea and Liberia.

Narrow trails, barely wide enough for the jeeps, were our only roads. This was truly primitive country. And as we bumped along, Father Everett told us what to expect in Koluma.

"The first person you must meet in your village will be Oturu—he's the chief and the village medicineman."

"The local witch doctor?" I smiled.

He gave me a sharp look. "He's the reason I wanted to meet you—to prepare you for him." He spoke seriously. "Don't make the mistake of under-rating him. He's of the Mende tribe; he's been to school in Free-

town and speaks excellent English. But juju—magic—
is his real business. His villagers fear his powers with a
superstitious awe—and he works on their fears ruth-
lessly. The man's an utter despot."

We stared at him, somewhat skeptically, and he
said, "He's very opposed to your coming—and you can
understand why. You represent another kind of magic
—one which could topple him. So I strongly urge you
to do nothing which could give him reason to—to
harm you—or your cause."

"He's what's wrong with Africa," Eunice said hotly.
"He's educated; he knows what he's doing is detri-
mental to his own people. He's a common crook,
sponging off their superstitious fears, keeping them in
abject misery and ignorance for his own gain." Her
dark eyes flashed. "He's despicable. You can bet your
bottom buck I'll do everything I can to topple him."

Father Everett seemed distressed at her outburst.
"You don't understand," he said. "His powers are real
—very real. He—" he glanced toward Job in the next
jeep "—he's rumored to be a ranking chief of the
Tongo Players—an outlawed group. Human leopards.
To even mention them is tabu to the natives. To see
one after dark means death to them—and many have
died that way—mauled and torn to bits."

Eunice looked askance. "You sound as though you
believe that rubbish, Father."

He hesitated, looking troubled. "It's not important
what I believe," he told her. "I—I'm white, from a
different world. What is important is that these people
do believe, and with an unshaken belief rooted in time
immemorial. *They believe*—and so things happen to
them which go beyond explanation."

He told us, as the jeeps bumped along and shadows lengthened, how their entire lives were ruled from birth to death by the makers of medicine—good or bad. Their unshakable belief in the powers of the witch doctor: that he could wither an eye, an arm, or even stop their hearts from beating, if they incurred his displeasure.

Father Everett told us of the natives' belief in black magic; how evil ones could lie in their huts at night, while their spirit rose to fly great distances. Of their terror of these evil ones who had the power to change their forms, to become alligators, baboons, and, most feared, leopards. Roaming the night, feasting on human victims.

We reached Koluma as the low-slanting rays of the sun pierced the tall trees. It was a scattering of huts underneath the gigantic flower-hung trees, like an open sewer in the midst of paradise. The smell was overpowering, and for the first time I realized the seriousness of the job we'd so blithely undertaken six weeks ago.

Every inch of ground about the huts was piled with offal, crawling with maggots, swarming with flies. Scrawny pigs rooted in the garbage, tick-infested chickens pecked and scurried underfoot. Flea-ridden curs snarled and yapped over tidbits, while everywhere the children tumbled, picking up dirt-encrusted scraps, eating them with apparent relish. Children with swollen stomachs, rickety legs, open sores, running diseased eyes. Ribs showing, teeth missing. Mothers, barely in their teens with breasts already withered, dangling grotesquely. Men stood about on one leg, the other cocked up against their inner knee, like meditative storks, gaping lackadaisically, the soles of their feet pitted with yaws.

We gazed about, silent. There were tears in Eunice's eyes.

The jeeps stopped before a great Yairi tree. Underneath the tree was a crudely carved image of a potbellied creature with the head of an animal, but the arms and legs of a human. Cruel claws extended from the fingers and toes of the idol, and a long tail drooped behind it.

Flies buzzed blackly about the image, and piled up before it were putrid bits of flesh, decayed vegetables, fish-heads and spoiled fruit. From the tree dangled bits of glass and metal—obviously offerings to the village deity.

"That would be his obeah," Eunice said bitterly.

"The leopard god," Father Everett said. "And that hut next to it belongs to Oturu, the witch doctor."

We got out of the jeeps, and, as we moved toward Oturu's hut, I noticed the villagers remained at a distance instead of swarming around as we'd expected. I looked at Father Everett. "They don't seem very glad to see us, Father."

He nodded shortly. "They're not."

A man stepped out of the large hut near the obeah. "Oturu," Father Everett murmured.

He was tall, and strongly built, lighter than the others—nearly as light as Eunice. He came close and I saw then how really big he was. I'm six two and he towered a good half foot over me. He approached us, and at a curt word from him the villagers who'd surged forward, now faded back respectfully.

He was dressed plainly, in sun-faded khaki shorts, a

sleeveless cotton shirt, his long muscular arms bulging the armholes. A cord around his neck held two curving yellowish tusks—the incisors of a great cat. He radiated controlled power. His eyes glittered as he raked us with a keen glance, lingering longest on Eunice.

We stared at him, fascinated. Eunice had cool disdain on her face—but—I saw the flickering in her eyes; a brief hint of fear she suppressed immediately.

Father Everett said something, obviously ceremonious, in a slow guttural tongue, but Oturu gave him a cold look of thinly concealed hatred, cutting him short with a burst of harsh language. His voice was deep, vibrant with power.

"What does he say?" Eunice asked.

Oturu looked at her, and his eyes burned. "I told the white father that I've thrown the bones," Oturu said in an incongruous British accent.

"A form of divination," Father Everett said, "which shows your presence here is not welcome."

"The bones say there will be much sorrow to the people if these Americans remain here," Oturu said.

Eunice laughed aloud, a hard ringing contemptuous sound. The villagers murmured, drawing closer.

"I can understand how our presence here might be bad medicine for you—but it can only bring good for these people." She put her slim hands on her hips. "We're here at the request of the government in Freetown. We have their invitation in writing to settle in here, to live with the people and aid them in any way we can." She leaned forward, eyes snapping. "We didn't come seven thousand miles just to go back because your bones say we're bad medicine."

Oturu's thick brows drew together, but his voice was

controlled as he rumbled, "I have no more to say. The bones never lie. If you stay, the wrath of our grandfather, the leopard, will be terrible."

"I do not fear your leopard," Eunice said, projecting her voice so that those in the crowd who might understand English would certainly hear her. She whirled, took a lipstick from her pocket and with two rapid strokes she drew a brilliant red cross on the protruding pot-belly of the obeah. The villagers, watching intently, gave a gasp and fell back.

Eunice turned to face them, her aristocratic features boldly challenging. "Since when does the daughter of the lion fear the leopard?" She threw off her jacket and stood before the obeah, tall, strikingly beautiful, and I saw Father Everett bow his head. An excited rumble passed among the villagers.

Oturu impaled Eunice with eyes that seemed suddenly dusty. She shrank back imperceptibly, but returned his look bravely.

"Now there will be many souls eaten," he said. "Theirs—" he gestured toward the villagers "—and yours." He stalked back into his hut.

Seconds later the villagers had melted from sight; only the pigs grunted on the little square. Even the curs had slunk away as though scenting a brewing storm.

That night, we sat around the small fire, while the wind moaned in the towering trees. Before the obeah, the bits of metal and glass jangled. And suddenly the dim paleolithic figure of Oturu loomed there. In the flickering light, he seemed to be carrying a large stick, or club, draped with fur, and a small bag that rattled. He pointed the stick in the direction of the hut Eunice occupied alone, and his harsh gutturals were faintly audible to us.

He bent over the miniature altar before the obeah, stamping his feet, gesturing, rattling his bag. When Oturu was through, he walked away, and suddenly, from the depths of the dark forest, we heard the weird coughing grunt of some animal.

"Leopard," Job whispered.

Father Everett rose and walked quickly to the obeah. We saw him take something from the little altar. When he returned, his face was like carved stone in the firelight.

"What was that all about?" Tannenbaum asked uneasily.

Father Everett held up a small object. "It is evil," he said, after a long moment. "A juju—an offering of a soul to placate the leopard god."

We studied the object. It was a crude doll-like figure, with tiny curved thorns, like miniature claws, piercing the eyes, the heart, and the loins. The molded clay face was unmistakable.

"Eunice," I said.

"Yes," Father Everett said. Abruptly he tossed the object into the fire, and strode toward Eunice's hut. He knocked, and in a moment, vanished inside.

And finally, Tannenbaum, the pre-med (here, in this remote rain forest, his beard dark against his white face, NYU another planet, almost), Tannenbaum suddenly rose, kicked angrily at a log lying askew, and went into our hut. A few moments later his battery-operated phonograph began booming out, a swinging Thelonius Monk bit; chaotic, richly melodic, as only the Monk can play—but somehow right, here with the stars obscured by immense trees, bending close, the strange scents and sounds of the African forest. Here, after all, was the genesis of such music. And it, too, was a form of magic—but good magic.

The next morning Father Everett left us, clasping us each in a brief warm hug. And it was after he'd gone that I saw Eunice was wearing a heavy silver crucifix against her honey-colored neck. There were shadows under her eyes.

The villagers avoided us that day, although we began the first of the many simple, easily-imitated improvements we'd planned for the village—a deep, wide, sheltered latrine, with a pile of soft loose earth and hand-carved paddle-shaped shovels with which to throw loose dirt into the latrines after use. Primitive, but effective, sanitary cover.

For the next two nights, although we watched until long into the night, we spotted no one under the Yairi tree—but found each morning another crude figure of Eunice, pierced with thorn-claws. And daily, Eunice, strained-looking, moved about among the women, observing their way of life, saying nothing, aware that they were waiting to see the outcome of her clash of wills with Oturu. Her crucifix, like a magnet, drew their frightened glances. ·

But Tannenbaum got the first breakthrough. Or rather, Thelonius Monk, with an assist from Lester Young and Charlie "Bird" Parker. On the third day, with still no souls having been eaten, the villagers relaxed their attitudes. Tannenbaum drew a sizeable collection of thoughtful appreciative listeners to his canned jazz concert.

One old man in particular, with an open running

sore on his wizened leg, hopped about and clapped in rhythm. His ulcerated leg was plastered with a disgusting poultice of ground-up bones, mud, spittle and other unmentionables, liberally sprinkled with flies.

Tannenbaum, emerging from changing records, saw the old man and beckoned for him to come closer. Cautiously, the oldster came nearer, and Tannenbaum looked at the leg. He shook his head gravely, then pushed the old man onto a log and stretched the leg out. The old man cast an anxious glance toward Oturu's hut, but when Tannenbaum began cleaning the ulcer, the old man submitted quietly. I saw he was looking over Tannenbaum's shoulder. I turned. Eunice stood there, smiling, the heavy silver crucifix at her neck winking softly.

That night the wind arose again; the moon, nearly full, scudded from tree to tree. And even though I waited up for hours, peering toward the obeah, I didn't see Oturu—or anyone else. But later, much later, we heard the wild screams from the deep woods, just beyond the village.

And in the morning, the body of the old man Tannenbaum had treated was found, on the edge of the deep forest. It was terribly mutilated and mauled, apparently by a leopard. The leg that had been neatly bandaged was torn completely off.

All that day, the villagers stayed in their huts; the body of the old man, straw-shrouded, lay before the obeah. Oturu was not to be seen. We prowled the forest outside the village area, rifles ready, but to our untrained eyes, nothing was visible.

That night, as quietly as he'd left, Father Everett

returned, slipping into the village with Job, his assistant. He went directly to Oturu's hut.

We were waiting for him, when he came out, but he gestured for us to wait, and he went into Eunice's hut. He was there a long time, and when he came out, his face was grave; and pale.

"Oturu says the old one's soul was eaten by the leopard god for submitting to the white man's magic." He ran a tired hand over his face. "Of course there'll be more of this unless Eunice—and you—leave. That bit of information was revealed to him by his faithful bones."

"But—we just can't walk out on these people now," I protested. "There must be something we can do to stop this."

He meditatively fingered the heavy black crucifix he wore, then he said in a low voice, "Job tells me that the tracks of an enormous leopard lead from the scene of the kill into the village—and disappear. The villagers know this and they're in mortal terror, poor souls. They say it's a spirit-leopard."

We looked at one another. "Listen," I said urgently, "I'm a damned good shot, if I do say so—I made expert in the Marine Corps. I don't know too much about them, but don't leopards always come back to their kill? Let's buy a goat or a pig from someone here, kill it and put it in the same spot. I'll get up a tree with my big flashlight, and—"

Father Everett shook his head. "This leopard will never be caught that way." He stopped and looked beyond us.

We turned. Eunice stood in the doorway of her hut,

and I saw again how terribly drawn and exhausted she looked. I noticed for the first time she wasn't wearing her silver crucifix. Her neck looked oddly vulnerable, without it. She nodded slowly to Father Everett.

He took a deep breath. "I'll need one of your rifle bullets," he said to me. "You have a good flashlight?" I nodded. He turned to Fallon and Tannenbaum. "Tonight, please stay in your huts—no matter what you might hear in Eunice's hut—or elsewhere. This is a job for just two of us." He was very sad, and solemn when he said, "Nothing must be done to frighten the—the leopard off."

I brought him one of my .375 magnum bullets—300 grains of killing power—and he tucked it into his palm, not looking at it. He said to me, "Stay away from Eunice's hut. I'll come for you—and your rifle—the back way. Until then—God be with you." He walked away and went into Eunice's hut. In a few minutes we heard muffled tapping sounds. Nothing else . . .

Father Everett and I crouched beyond the obeah, down the twisting trail that led into the rain forest, near the spot where the old man had been so cruelly killed. We stood motionless behind the smooth bole of an immense Yairi tree while the brilliant moon dappled the forest floor, and shadows swam like underwater images. We waited, looking not toward the forest—but back, toward the village.

Earlier, Father Everett had tapped at the back of our hut and whispered for me to follow. I'd gone out the tiny rear window, wiggling carefully, handing out my rifle and flashlight. I heard a click as Father slid

back the bolt and slipped in a bullet, then he rammed it
home. And afterward, we'd made our way in a circle,
skirting the entire village, to take up our place on the
forest edge.

We waited. The jungle roared; and suddenly, all
sound stopped. There came a rending noise from the
village and Father Everett gripped my arm. I sensed he
was shifting the flashlight, bringing it up, ready to snap
on.

I waited tensely, blood pounding in my head, and
then we heard it, a yeowrring, a coughing grunt or two,
and the sound of soft scuffling, as though some large
creatures were rolling in the leaves. More sounds, and
then the eyes, glowing, greenish—two pairs of eyes.

Abruptly the flashlight was a blazing beacon, and
Father Everett was roaring in my ears, "The big one.
The big one. *Shoot now, for the love of Jesus Christ!*"

Two leopards crouched there, transfixed in the
bright light, enormous, their pelts glowing softly, the
huge spots brilliant in the beam, feral eyes like nothing
I've ever dreamed in my worst nightmares, unblinking,
wide, glaring. And the immense male, mouth wide
open, huge incisors glistening wetly, red tongue lolling
out, lips drawn back in a sneer.

It coughed, crouched; I brought the rifle up and
without conscious aim fired. The heavy recoil jarred
me back. In that same instant the great leopard gave a
scream that could only have been human, reared back,
crashed down, thrashed around, coughing, yowling,
snapping in ferocious rage.

The smaller leopard spun, bounded away, and the
light was snapped off. We stood there, blinking,

blinded, while the awful snapping coughing sounds continued, as the animal fought to live. And finally, a grunt, a sigh, a diminishing sound of thrashing—a thump—and stillness. And from beyond, in the direction of the village, a terrible scream, shrill, high, impossibly higher, then it died.

The light came on again and Father Everett went crashing back down the trail. I followed him, gun at the ready. When I reached the clearing, near the obeah, I found Father Everett kneeling on the ground, holding Eunice in his arms. Her rich skin was an unbelievable ivory, her eyes rolled completely back in her head.

"Take her back to her hut. Whiskey, if you have it," he said hastily. "Circulation. Rub her well." He stood up and made a quick little gesture over her with his hand—the sign of the cross. Then he rushed off back down the trail, still carrying my flashlight.

I picked her up—she was surprisingly light for such a tall girl, and staggered back with her to her hut. Nothing moved in the village. I put her down on her pallet and bustled about, getting her some medicinal alcohol, trying to pour some down her throat. She coughed, opened dull eyes, obviously deep in shock, and while I rubbed her, she talked.

"It was just like the other three times I told you about, Father," she whispered, looking at me with glazed eyes, thinking I was Father Everett. "That tugging, that feeling that I must go—must go. But before —I had the crucifix, and I resisted. This time— This time—" She closed her eyes and her voice went on, while I listened, horror chilling me, despite the heat and humidity:

She had awakened (Eunice murmured, while I rubbed her wrists and massaged her shoulders) aware that the full moon was shining through the little window. The hot heavy night of Africa swept over her, full of sounds, voluptuous scents. She stretched deliciously and glided off the bed and to the window. *He* was out there, on the edge of the forest, calling her—calling her.

With a sudden unpremeditated movement she lunged at the small opening. It burst open with a rending of rotten wood and in an instant she was outside, looking back at the small hut, bathed in the flood of cold pearly moonlight. Somewhere beyond the village, in the velvet blackness, an animal coughed, a sound she instantly recognized.

There in the trees she saw the green eyes glowing at her, the slow gentle twitching of a long powerful tail, then the sinuous step by step of an immense leopard approaching.

She waited, watching this great soft-stepping creature that came nearer and nearer. She felt no fear; no surprise to note that she had claws, that she was on all fours, and enfolded in rich spotted fur. No surprise at all. She looked deeply into the eyes of the huge male leopard and she knew him.

He was next to her, rubbing his muzzle against her shoulder, breathing softly in her ear. He became more insistent, and suddenly angered, she crouched on her haunches and brought up a paw in a quick slashing motion to the leopard's muzzle. Her claws raked down one side from ear to shoulder in a lightning gesture. The leopard yeowrred with pain, bounding back.

But in an instant it was next to her again, rubbing against her, oblivious of the bright red streak of blood that marred its stunning spotted fur. She purred, a deep soft rumbling sound, half acceptance, half warning. They turned, and shoulder to shoulder, heads swinging right and left, accepting the fact that they were creatures of the night, and supreme; that soft things awaited them to be torn and rendered, with salty blood theirs for the taking—together they ambled into the dark forest.

"And then—and then," her eyes opened, Eunice winced, clutched at me, fell back, her hands squeezing at her forehead. "There was a light, a bright light. And a sound—a voice, a terrible roaring voice— And I ran. I ran—and it hit me—it hit me—" She wrenched out from under my hands, clasping her breasts, gasping with great pain.

"I woke up," she panted. "And—it must have been the dream again—only, it was so real. And I was—I was outside." She got up on an elbow, peering at me, puzzled.

"Bob? I thought— Father Everett?" She looked around, and at that moment the brilliant beam of my flashlight came into the room. She sat up, terror glared from her eyes as she looked into it. She fumbled at her neck, feeling for her missing crucifix, and the beam snapped off.

"It's all right, Eunice." Father Everett stooped over her, bringing with him the scent of incense, of forest mold—and of fresh blood. "You've just had a terrible nightmare—you mustn't worry. It's over."

"That dream—the one I told you about—it came

again, Father," she murmured, suddenly sleepy. "I thought—" She was asleep, then, making little gasping sounds as she breathed.

"I'll need your help for just a little bit more, Bob," Father said to me, taking my arm. I reached for my rifle but he restrained me. "You won't need that—not anymore."

We went back down the twisted trail, the bright beam of the light picking out huge flowers, pallid, unnatural looking. We were silent until we approached the spot where I'd shot the animal.

"Is it dead?" I said, although I knew it was.

"Yes," he said grimly, "the beast is dead."

It was lying up against the bole of a tree, the eyes half open, glittering in the flashlight, and then my heart gave a fearful leap; the hairs on my neck stood up and I shivered with a terrible chill. It was no leopard lying there, blood still oozing from a big hole in the chest where that 300 grains had gone in and expanded inside. It was Oturu.

He lay there, lips skinned back in a death grin. He was wearing a magnificent leopard skin, the head of the animal just behind his own, the great mouth open, yellow incisors gleaming wickedly, a red tongue, stiff, lolling out. The forelegs of the animal had been tied to his own arms, and the animal's leg skins tied to his own legs; the claws dangling, menacing, needle-sharp. The long tail coiled behind, life-like, seeming still to twitch.

"My God—it's impossible. I couldn't have made that kind of a mistake. It was a *leopard* I shot. Not a man in a skin. I saw it—them. Two of them. A big

leopard and—and—" I stopped. I looked at Father
Everett. He was holding his heavy crucifix again, and I
noticed there was blood on his robes.

"That dream—Eunice told me about her dream. But
it wasn't a dream, was it, Father? It was real. *She was
the other leopard.* Oh God! How can it be?"

He held the light away from us, and his grave face,
peaceful now, was reflected strongly in the subdued
rays. He looked at something he held in his hand,
something curiously flattened and battered that reflected the flash beam.

"You can choose to believe one of two things, Bob:
That you were a prime participant in a struggle between the forces of light and the dark forces of evil that
still bind Africa with chains so powerful they can reach
back over two hundred years—to a girl born in
America, of undiluted African blood." His hand
clenched tight around the misshapen object. "A girl so
courageous—so filled with love, she was willing to risk
her immortal soul to help break those chains."

He looked piercingly at me. "Or—you can believe
that what happened here tonight was all a ghastly but
perfectly understandable mistake." He cleared his
throat. "After all, an old villager *was* mauled and
killed hereabouts by a leopard last night. We *were*
hunting it—and Oturu had the bad luck to be prowling
in the immediate area—wearing an outlawed leopard
skin—at night."

"But—the other leopard. There were two of
them—"

"Call it—coincidence," he said softly. He put a hand
on my shoulder. "Whatever you choose to believe, only

remember this and be comforted: a great evil has been eradicated here and a village set on a path that leads only one way—upward, out of primeval darkness."

"I—I don't know what to believe, Father. I'm only sure of one thing—this is Oturu's body. He's dead—and I shot him." I looked down at Oturu, grinning starkly in death. "The villagers believed he was invulnerable."

"Only against the common forms of death," Father said. "They also believe that when their witch doctor is out in the spirit, a stronger spirit can kill him—using certain magic amulets—a silver bullet, for example."

I started, and then reached for the dully gleaming lump of metal he was holding. I examined it closely. It wasn't the remnants of an ordinary .375 magnum bullet.

"It's silver, isn't it?" I stared at him. He nodded. I remembered the tapping sounds that came from Eunice's hut earlier in the night, and suddenly I had the complete picture. "This was Eunice's crucifix—the one you gave her that first night."

"Yes," he said, "her one protection against the beast. She gave it to me to use. Offering herself as the lure." He rolled it in his fingers. "But it can be recast. When the villagers learn what happened here tonight they'll expect Eunice to be wearing it again. For their sakes, I hope she will: They need her kind of magic."

He tucked the battered silver bullet into a pocket, then said, "We'd better get started carrying the body back. It's best to put it in his hut before daybreak—for various reasons."

I nodded and stooped to take Oturu's shoulders, and I saw the still-glistening blood on a long thin curving scratch down the side of his face and neck, continuing down onto the dark skin of his broad shoulder. A scratch as though made by a big angry cat with sharp claws.

Then again—it might only have been a thorn scratch —which is what I choose to believe . . .

2

THE POWER OF THE RELIGIOUS VISION

Behold the Man
MICHAEL MOORCOCK

"Behold the Man" is one of the most brilliant of that body of science fiction stories exploring religious themes. It is a very complex story, and a very daring story. You will have a strong response as you finish it—regarding it either as a very powerful, very beautiful story, or as a shockingly irreligious story. As is true for all great literature, it can be read again and again, with new insights appearing each time, as you work down through the multiple levels of meaning.

"Behold the Man," a story about man and Christ, demonstrates what good science fiction can do uniquely well—combine fact and imagination. It is solidly grounded in fact. The portrayal of the religious and political situation in Palestine at the time of Christ is very accurate. But it looks at the story of Christ from a fresh and unique point of view, with the creative imagination of author Michael Moorcock leading us to a new awareness of the power of the Christian symbols as we finish the story.

"Behold the Man" is the story of Karl Glogauer, a modern man living in confusion—without any real meaning in his life. But he is unwilling to settle for a meaningless, empty life. Although he admits, "I am just a man," he pushes to explore the full possibilities of what it means to be that man, and he senses that man has more potential than he has limitations. Karl is torn between the materialism of science—which demands evidence before anything can be accepted as truth—and the mystical need to find more meaning and truth than can presently be proved by science. He is modern man in search of a soul despite the fact that science is not willing to admit he has one. In his search, he experiences a kind of rebirth, as the opening symbol of the story tells us. His time machine, as he travels from modern London to Palestine at the time of Christ, is like a giant womb, and he is born anew as he crawls from it.

The central conflict of the story is between reason and intuition as ways of knowing truth. Science holds that only through logic (inductive and deductive reasoning) can we arrive at a reliable hypothesis. The experiments that lead to an hypothesis must be repeatable by anyone with the necessary equipment, or the hypothesis is not acceptable. Religion, on the other hand, has always held that truth can be revealed by intuition—knowledge mystically received in a flash of insight without the use of reason. Since the intuitive insight is the unique experience of one individual, it is not repeatable, and therefore is not verifiable, according to the methods required by science. The revelation of the prophet must be accepted on faith. Karl Glogauer represents one pole of the argument—mystical insight—and his wife Monica the other—logical thought. For her, science has become a kind of god who can solve all problems, and she viciously attacks Karl, who yearns for the added dimension he feels religion can bring to his life. Science can never answer the question of why, he argues, and he feels he must know why. The debate between husband and wife is bitter. Monica, pure reason, cannot understand Karl's feelings because she has buried her emotions under an iron shield of logic.

"Behold the Man" is the story of a man who goes on a quest for meaning. His quest is completed when he finally experiences the fulfillment of doing what he had always sought to do as a psychiatrist—help people. The miracle of rebirth is possible because he has a myth to follow as a guide in transcending his old self. With his last words, as well as his last courageous act, he answers Monica's taunt that religion is nothing but an escape for the weak. Only a very strong man, inspired by his vision of what he can become for the sake of others, could have done what he does.

In the end, the intuitive insight of the Christian vision has been verified by Karl's experiencing of it. Christ's experience, recorded in the New Testament, has been repeated by Karl in a unique and subjective way. Perhaps, the story seems to suggest, the ways of science and religion are not so opposed as Monica believes. The scientist's hypothesis, although verified by experimentation, may be first born of intuition; and the religious experience is indeed repeatable.

Behold the Man
MICHAEL MOORCOCK

He has no material power as the god-emperors had; he has only a following of desert people and fishermen. They tell him he is a god; he believes them. The followers of Alexander said: "He is unconquerable, therefore he is a god." The followers of this man do not think at all; he was their act of spontaneous creation. Now he leads them, this madman called Jesus of Nazareth.

And he spoke, saying unto them: Yea verily I *was* Karl Glogauer and now I am Jesus the Messiah, the Christ.

And it was so.

I

The time machine was a sphere full of milky fluid in which the traveler floated, enclosed in a rubber suit, breathing through a mask attached to a hose leading to the wall of the machine. The sphere cracked as it landed and the fluid spilled into the dust and was soaked up. Instinctively, Glogauer curled himself into a ball as the level of the liquid fell and he sank to the yielding plastic of the sphere's inner lining. The instruments, cryptographic, unconventional, were still and silent. The sphere shifted and rolled as the last of the liquid dripped from the great gash in its side.

Momentarily, Glogauer's eyes opened and closed, then his mouth stretched in a kind of yawn and his tongue fluttered and he uttered a groan that turned into a ululation.

He heard himself. The Voice of Tongues, he thought. The language of the unconscious. But he could not guess what he was saying.

His body became numb and he shivered. His passage through time had not been easy and even the thick fluid had not wholly protected him, though it had doubtless saved his life. Some ribs were certainly broken. Painfully, he straightened his arms and legs and began to crawl over the slippery plastic towards the crack in the machine. He could see harsh sunlight, a sky like shimmering steel. He pulled himself halfway through the crack, closing his eyes as the full strength of the sunlight struck them. He lost consciousness.

Christmas term, 1949. He was nine years old, born two years after his father had reached England from Austria.

The other children were screaming with laughter in the gravel of the playground. The game had begun earnestly enough and somewhat nervously Karl had joined in in the same spirit. Now he was crying.

"Let me *down!* Please, Mervyn, stop it!"

They had tied him with his arms spreadeagled against the wire-netting of the playground fence. It bulged outwards under his weight and one of the posts threatened to come loose. Mervyn Williams, the boy who had proposed the game, began to shake the post so that Karl was swung heavily back and forth on the netting.

"Stop it!"

He saw that his cries only encouraged them and he clenched his teeth, becoming silent.

He slumped, pretending unconsciousness; the school ties they had used as bonds cut into his wrists. He heard the children's voices drop.

"Is he all right?" Molly Turner was whispering.

"He's only kidding," Williams replied uncertainly.

He felt them untying him, their fingers fumbling with the knots. Deliberately, he sagged, then fell to his knees, grazing them on the gravel, and dropped face down to the ground.

Distantly, for he was half-convinced by his own deception, he heard their worried voices.

Williams shook him.

"Wake up, Karl. Stop mucking about."

He stayed where he was, losing his sense of time until he heard Mr. Matson's voice over the general babble.

"What on earth were you doing, Williams?"

"It was a play, sir, about Jesus. Karl was being Jesus. We tied him to the fence. It was his idea, sir. It was only a game, sir."

Karl's body was stiff, but he managed to stay still, breathing shallowly.

"He's not a strong boy like you, Williams. You should have known better."

"I'm sorry, sir. I'm really sorry." Williams sounded as if he were crying.

Karl felt himself lifted; felt the triumph. . . .

He was being carried along. His head and side were so painful that he felt sick. He had had no chance to discover where exactly the time machine had brought him, but, turning his head now, he could see by the way the man on his right was dressed that he was at least in the Middle East.

He had meant to land in the year 29 A.D. in the wilderness beyond Jerusalem, near Bethlehem. Were they taking him to Jerusalem now?

He was on a stretcher that was apparently made of animal skins; this indicated that he was probably in the past, at any rate. Two men were carrying the stretcher on their shoulders. Others walked on both sides. There was a smell of sweat and animal fat and a musty smell he could not identify. They were walking towards a line of hills in the distance.

He winced as the stretcher lurched and the pain in his side increased. For the second time he passed out.

He woke up briefly, hearing voices. They were speaking what was evidently some form of Aramaic. It was night, perhaps, for it seemed very dark. They were no longer moving. There was straw beneath him. He was relieved. He slept.

In those days came John the Baptist preaching in the wilderness of Judaea, And saying, Repent ye: for the kingdom of heaven is at hand. For this is he that was spoken of by the prophet Esaias, saying, The voice of one crying in the wilderness. Prepare ye the way of the Lord, make his paths straight. And the same John had his raiment of camel's hair, and a leathern girdle about his loins; and his meat was locusts and wild honey. Then went out to him Jerusalem, and all Judaea, and all

*the region round about Jordan, And were baptized
of him in Jordan, confessing their sins.*

(Matthew 3: 1–6)

They were washing him. He felt the cold water running over his naked body. They had managed to strip
off his protective suit. There were now thick layers of
cloth against his ribs on the right, and bands of leather
bound them to him.

He felt very weak now, and hot, but there was less
pain.

He was in a building—or perhaps a cave; it was too
gloomy to tell—lying on a heap of straw that was
saturated by the water. Above him, two men continued
to sluice water down on him from their earthenware
pots. They were stern-faced, heavily-bearded men, in
cotton robes.

He wondered if he could form a sentence they might
understand. His knowledge of written Aramaic was
good, but he was not sure of certain pronunciations.

He cleared his throat. "Where—be—this—place?"

They frowned, shaking their heads and lowering
their water jars.

"I—seek—a—Nazarene—Jesus. . . ."

"Nazarene. Jesus." One of the men repeated the
words, but they did not seem to mean anything to him.
He shrugged.

The other, however, only repeated the word Nazarene, speaking it slowly as if it had some special significance for him. He muttered a few words to the
other man and went towards the entrance of the room.

Karl Glogauer continued to try to say something the
remaining man would understand.

"What—year—doth—the Roman Emperor—sit—in Rome?"

It was a confusing question to ask, he realized. He knew Christ had been crucified in the fifteenth year of Tiberius' reign, and that was why he had asked the question. He tried to phrase it better.

"How many—year—doth Tiberius rule?"

"Tiberius?" The man frowned.

Glogauer's ear was adjusting to the accent now and he tried to simulate it better. "Tiberius. The emperor of the Romans. How many years has he ruled?"

"How many?" The man shook his head. "I know not."

At least Glogauer had managed to make himself understood.

"Where is this place?" he asked.

"It is the wilderness beyond Machaerus," the man replied. "Know you not that?"

Machaerus lay to the southeast of Jerusalem, on the other side of the Dead Sea. There was no doubt that he was in the past and that the period was sometime in the reign of Tiberius, for the man had recognized the name easily enough.

His companion was now returning, bringing with him a huge fellow with heavily muscled hairy arms and a great barrel chest. He carried a big staff in one hand. He was dressed in animal skins and was well over six feet tall. His black, curly hair was long and he had a black, bushy beard that covered the upper half of his chest. He moved like an animal and his large, piercing brown eyes looked reflectively at Glogauer.

When he spoke, it was in a deep voice, but too

rapidly for Glogauer to follow. It was Glogauer's turn to shake his head.

The big man squatted down beside him. "Who art thou?"

Glogauer paused. He had not planned to be found in this way. He had intended to disguise himself as a traveler from Syria, hoping that the local accents would be different enough to explain his own unfamiliarity with the language. He decided that it was best to stick to this story and hope for the best.

"I am from the north," he said.

"Not from Egypt?" the big man asked. It was as if he had expected Glogauer to be from there. Glogauer decided that if this was what the big man thought, he might just as well agree to it.

"I came out of Egypt two years since," he said.

The big man nodded, apparently satisfied. "So you are a magus from Egypt. That is what we thought. And your name is Jesus, and you are the Nazarene."

"I *seek* Jesus, the Nazarene," Glogauer said.

"Then what is your name?" The man seemed disappointed.

Glogauer could not give his own name. It would sound too strange to them. On impulse, he gave his father's first name. "Emmanuel," he said.

The man nodded, again satisfied. "Emmanuel."

Glogauer realized belatedly that the choice of name had been an unfortunate one in the circumstances, for Emmanuel meant in Hebrew "God with us" and doubtless had a mystic significance for his questioner.

"And what is your name?" he asked.

The man straightened up, looking broodingly down

on Glogauer. "You do not know me? You have not heard of John, called the Baptist?"

Glogauer tried to hide his surprise, but evidently John the Baptist saw that his name was familiar. He nodded his shaggy head. "You do know of me, I see. Well, magus, now I must decide, eh?"

"What must you decide?" Glogauer asked nervously.

"If you be the friend of the prophecies or the false one we have been warned against by Adonai. The Romans would deliver me into the hands of mine enemies, the children of Herod."

"Why is that?"

"You must know why, for I speak against the Romans who enslave Judaea, and I speak against the unlawful things that Herod does, and I prophesy the time when all those who are not righteous shall be destroyed and Adonai's kingdom will be restored on Earth as the old prophets said it would be. I say to the people, 'Be ready for that day when ye shall take up the sword to do Adonai's will.' The unrighteous know that they will perish on this day, and they would destroy me."

Despite the intensity of his words, John's tone was matter of fact. There was no hint of insanity or fanaticism in his face or bearing. He sounded most of all like an Anglican vicar reading a sermon whose meaning for him had lost its edge.

The essence of what he said, Karl Glogauer realized, was that he was arousing the people to throw out the Romans and their puppet Herod and establish a more "righteous" regime. The attributing of this plan to "Adonai" (one of the spoken names of Jahweh and meaning The Lord) seemed, as many scholars had guessed in the 20th century, a means of giving the plan extra weight. In a world where politics and religion, even in the west, were inextricably bound together, it was necessary to ascribe a supernatural origin to the plan.

Indeed, Glogauer thought, it was more than likely that John believed his idea had been inspired by God, for the Greeks on the other side of the Mediterranean had not yet stopped arguing about the origins of inspiration—whether it originated in a man's head or was placed there by the gods. That John accepted him as an Egyptian magician of some kind did not surprise Glogauer particularly, either. The circumstances of his arrival must have seemed extraordinarily miraculous and at the same time acceptable, particularly to a sect like the Essenes who practiced self-mortification and starvation and must be quite used to seeing visions in this hot wilderness. There was no doubt now that these people were the neurotic Essenes, whose ritual washing —baptism—and self-deprivation, coupled with the almost paranoiac mysticism that led them to invent secret languages and the like, was a sure indication of their mentally unbalanced condition. All this occurred to Glogauer the psychiatrist manqué, but Glogauer the man was torn between the poles of extreme rationalism and the desire to be convinced by the mysticism itself.

"I must meditate," John said, turning towards the cave entrance. "I must pray. You will remain here until guidance is sent to me."

He left the cave, striding rapidly away.

Glogauer sank back on the wet straw. He was without doubt in a limestone cave, and the atmosphere in the cave was surprisingly humid. It must be very hot outside. He felt drowsy.

II

Five years in the past. Nearly two thousand in the future. Lying in the hot, sweaty bed with Monica. Once again, another attempt to make normal love had metamorphosed into the performance of minor aberrations which seemed to satisfy her better than anything else.

Their real courtship and fulfillment was yet to come. As usual, it would be verbal. As usual, it would find its climax in argumentative anger.

"I suppose you're going to tell me you're not satisfied again." She accepted the lighted cigarette he handed to her in the darkness.

"I'm all right," he said.

There was silence for a while as they smoked.

Eventually, and in spite of knowing what the result would be if he did so, he found himself talking.

"It's ironic, isn't it?" he began.

He waited for her reply. She would delay for a little while yet.

"What is?" she said at last.

"All this. You spend all day trying to help sexual neurotics to become normal. You spend your nights doing what they do."

"Not to the same extent. You know it's all a matter of degree."

"So you say."

He turned his head and looked at her face in the starlight from the window. She was a gaunt-featured redhead, with the calm, professional seducer's voice of the psychiatric social worker that she was. It was a voice that was soft, reasonable and insincere. Only occasionally, when she became particularly agitated, did her voice begin to indicate her real character. Her features never seemed to be in repose, even when she slept. Her eyes were forever wary, her movements rarely spontaneous. Every inch of her was protected, which was probably why she got so little pleasure from ordinary lovemaking.

"You just can't let yourself go, can you?" he said.

"Oh, shut up, Karl. Have a look at yourself if you're looking for a neurotic mess."

Both were amateur psychiatrists—she a psychiatric social worker, he merely a reader, a dabbler, though he had done a year's study some time ago when he had planned to become a psychiatrist. They used the terminology of psychiatry freely. They felt happier if they could name something.

He rolled away from her, groping for the ashtray on the bedside table, catching a glance of himself in the dressing table mirror. He was a sallow, intense, moody Jewish bookseller, with a head full of images and unresolved obsessions, a body full of emotions. He always lost these arguments with Monica. Verbally, she was the dominant one. This kind of exchange often seemed to him more perverse than their lovemaking, where usually at least his role was masculine. Essentially, he realized, he was passive, masochistic, indecisive. Even his anger, which came frequently, was impotent. Monica was ten years older than he was, ten years more bitter. As an individual, of course, she had far more dynamism than he had; but as a psychiatric social worker she had had just as many failures. She plugged on, becoming increasingly cynical on the surface but still, perhaps, hoping for a few spectacular successes with patients. They tried to do too much, that was the trouble, he thought. The priests in the confessional supplied a panacea; the psychiatrists tried to cure, and most of the time they failed. But at least they tried, he thought, and then wondered if that was, after all, a virtue.

"I did look at myself," he said.

Was she sleeping? He turned. Her wary eyes were still open, looking out of the window.

"I did look at myself," he repeated. "The way Jung did. 'How can I help those persons if I am myself a fugitive and perhaps also suffer from the *morbus sacer* of a neurosis?' That's what Jung asked himself. . . ."

"That old sensationalist. That old rationalizer of his own mysticism. No wonder you never became a psychiatrist."

"I wouldn't have been any good. It was nothing to do with Jung. . . ."

"Don't take it out on me. . . ."

"You've told me yourself that you feel the same—you think it's useless. . . ."

"After a hard week's work, I might say that. Give me another fag."

He opened the packet on the bedside table and put two cigarettes in his mouth, lighting them and handing one to her.

Almost abstractedly, he noticed that the tension was increasing. The argument was, as ever, pointless. But it was not the argument that was the important thing; it was simply the expression of the essential relationship. He wondered if that was in any way important, either.

"You're not telling the truth." He realized that there

was no stopping now that the ritual was in full swing.

"I'm telling the practical truth. I've no compulsion to give up my work. I've no wish to be a failure. . . ."

"Failure? You're more melodramatic than I am."

"You're too earnest, Karl. You want to get out of yourself a bit."

He sneered. "If I were you, I'd give up my work, Monica. You're no more suited for it than I was."

She shrugged. "You're a petty bastard."

"I'm not jealous of you, if that's what you think. You'll never understand what I'm looking for."

Her laugh was artificial, brittle. "Modern man in search of a soul, eh? Modern man in search of a crutch, I'd say. And you can take that any way you like."

"We're destroying the myths that make the world go round."

"Now you say, 'And what are we putting in their place?' You're stale and stupid, Karl. You've never looked rationally at anything—including yourself."

"What of it? You say the myth is unimportant."

"The reality that creates it is important."

"Jung knew that the myth can also create the reality."

"Which shows what a muddled old fool he was."

He stretched his legs. In doing so, he touched hers and he recoiled. He scratched his head. She still lay there smoking, but she was smiling now.

"Come on," she said. "Let's have some stuff about Christ."

He said nothing. She handed him the stub of her cigarette and he put it in the ashtray. He looked at his watch. It was two o'clock in the morning.

"Why do we do it?" he said.

"Because we must." She put her hand to the back of his head and pulled it towards her breast. "What else can we do?"

> We Protestants must sooner or later face this question: Are we to understand the "imitation of Christ" in the sense that we should copy his life and, if I may use the expression, ape his stigmata; or in the deeper sense that we are to live our own proper lives as truly as he lived his in all its implications? It is no easy matter to live a life that is modeled on Christ's, but it is unspeakably harder to live one's own life as truly as Christ lived his. Anyone who did this would . . . be misjudged, derided, tortured and crucified. . . . A neurosis is a dissociation of personality.
>
> (Jung: Modern Man in Search of a Soul)

For a month, John the Baptist was away and Glogauer lived with the Essenes, finding it surprisingly easy, as his ribs mended, to join in their daily life. The Essenes' township consisted of a mixture of single-story houses, built of limestone and clay brick, and the caves that were to be found on both sides of the shallow valley. The Essenes shared their goods in common and this particular sect had wives, though many Essenes led completely monastic lives. The Essenes were also pacifists, refusing to own or to make weapons—yet this sect plainly tolerated the warlike Baptist. Perhaps their hatred of the Romans overcame their principles. Perhaps they were not sure of John's entire intention. Whatever the reason for their toleration, there was little doubt that John the Baptist was virtually their leader.

The life of the Essenes consisted of ritual bathing three times a day, of prayer and of work. The work was not difficult. Sometimes Glogauer guided a plough pulled by two other members of the sect; sometimes he looked after the goats that were allowed to graze on the hillsides. It was a peaceful, ordered life, and even the unhealthy aspects were so much a matter of routine that Glogauer hardly noticed them for anything else after a while.

Tending the goats, he would lie on a hilltop, looking out over the wilderness which was not a desert, but rocky scrubland sufficient to feed animals like goats or sheep. The scrubland was broken by low-lying bushes and a few small trees growing along the banks of the river that doubtless ran into the Dead Sea. It was uneven ground. In outline, it had the appearance of a stormy lake, frozen and turned yellow and brown. Beyond the Dead Sea lay Jerusalem. Obviously Christ had not entered the city for the last time yet. John the Baptist would have to die before that happened.

The Essenes' way of life was comfortable enough, for all its simplicity. They had given him a goatskin loincloth and a staff and, except for the fact that he was watched by day and night, he appeared to be accepted as a kind of lay member of the sect.

Sometimes they questioned him casually about his chariot—the time machine they intended soon to bring in from the desert—and he told them that it had borne him from Egypt to Syria and then to here. They accepted the miracle calmly. As he had suspected, they were used to miracles.

The Essenes had seen stranger things than his time machine. They had seen men walk on water and angels descend to and from heaven; they had heard the voice of God and His archangels as well as the tempting voice of Satan and his minions. They wrote all these things down in their vellum scrolls. They were merely a record of the supernatural as their other scrolls were records of their daily lives and of the news that traveling members of their sect brought to them.

They lived constantly in the presence of God and spoke to God and were answered by God when they had sufficiently mortified their flesh and starved themselves and chanted their prayers beneath the blazing sun of Judaea.

Karl Glogauer grew his hair long and let his beard come unchecked. He mortified his flesh and starved himself and chanted his prayers beneath the sun, as they did. But he rarely heard God and only once thought he saw an archangel with wings of fire.

In spite of his willingness to experience the Essenes' hallucinations, Glogauer was disappointed, but he was surprised that he felt so well, considering all the self-inflicted hardships he had to undergo, and he also felt relaxed in the company of these men and women who were undoubtedly insane. Perhaps it was because their insanity was not so very different from his own that after a while he stopped wondering about it.

John the Baptist returned one evening, striding over the hills followed by twenty or so of his closest disciples. Glogauer saw him as he prepared to drive the goats into their cave for the night. He waited for John to get closer.

The Baptist's face was grim, but his expression softened as he saw Glogauer. He smiled and grasped him by the upper arm in the Roman fashion.

"Well, Emmanuel, you are our friend, as I thought you were. Sent by Adonai to help us accomplish His will. You shall baptize me on the morrow, to show all the people that He is with us."

Glogauer was tired. He had eaten very little and had spent most of the day in the sun, tending the goats. He yawned, finding it hard to reply. However, he was relieved. John had plainly been in Jerusalem trying to discover if the Romans had sent him as a spy. John now seemed reassured and trusted him.

He was worried, however, by the Baptist's faith in his powers.

"John," he began. "I'm no seer. . . ."

The Baptist's face clouded for a moment, then he laughed awkwardly. "Say nothing. Eat with me tonight. I have wild-honey and locusts."

Glogauer had not yet eaten this food, which was the staple of travelers who did not carry provisions but lived off the food they could find on the journey. Some regarded it as a delicacy.

He tried it later, as he sat in John's house. There were only two rooms in the house. One was for eating in, the other for sleeping in. The honey and locusts was too sweet for his taste, but it was a welcome change from barley or goat-meat.

He sat cross-legged, opposite John the Baptist, who ate with relish. Night had fallen. From outside came low murmurs and the moans and cries of those at prayer.

Glogauer dipped another locust into the bowl of honey that rested between them. "Do you plan to lead the people of Judaea in revolt against the Romans?" he asked.

The Baptist seemed disturbed by the direct question. It was the first of its nature that Glogauer had put to him.

"If it be Adonai's will," he said, not looking up as he leant towards the bowl of honey.

"The Romans know this?"

"I do not know, Emmanuel, but Herod the incestuous has doubtless told them I speak against the unrighteous."

"Yet the Romans do not arrest you."

"Pilate dare not—not since the petition was sent to the Emperor Tiberius."

"Petition?"

"Aye, the one that Herod and the Pharisees signed when Pilate the procurator did place votive shields in the palace at Jerusalem and seek to violate the Temple. Tiberius rebuked Pilate and since then, though he still hates the Jews, the procurator is more careful in his treatment of us."

"Tell me, John, do you know how long Tiberius has ruled in Rome?" He had not had the chance to ask that question again until now.

"Fourteen years."

It was 28 A.D.—something less than a year before the crucifixion would take place, and his time machine was smashed.

Now John the Baptist planned armed rebellion against the occupying Romans, but, if the Gospels were to be believed, would soon be decapitated by Herod.

Certainly no large-scale rebellion had taken place at this time. Even those who claimed that the entry of Jesus and his disciples into Jerusalem and the invasion of the Temple were plainly the actions of armed rebels had found no records to suggest that John had led a similar revolt.

Glogauer had come to like the Baptist very much. The man was plainly a hardened revolutionary who had been planning revolt against the Romans for years and had slowly been building up enough followers to make the attempt successful. He reminded Glogauer strongly of the resistance leaders of the Second World War. He had a similar toughness and understanding of the realities of his position. He knew that he would only have one chance to smash the cohorts garrisoned in the country. If the revolt became protracted, Rome would have ample time to send more troops to Jerusalem.

"When do you think Adonai intends to destroy the unrighteous through your agency?" Glogauer said tactfully.

John glanced at him with some amusement. He smiled. "The Passover is a time when the people are restless and resent the strangers most," he said.

"When is the next Passover?"

"Not for many months."

"How can I help you?"

"You are a magus."

"I can work no miracles."

John wiped the honey from his beard. "I cannot believe that, Emmanuel. The manner of your coming was miraculous. The Essenes did not know if you were a devil or a messenger from Adonai."

"I am neither."

"Why do you confuse me, Emmanuel? I know that you are Adonai's messenger. You are the sign that the Essenes sought. The time is almost ready. The kingdom of heaven shall soon be established on earth. Come with me. Tell the people that you speak with Adonai's voice. Work mighty miracles."

"Your power is waning, is that it?" Glogauer looked sharply at John. "You need me to renew your rebels' hopes?"

"You speak like a Roman, with such lack of subtlety." John got up angrily. Evidently, like the Essenes he lived with, he preferred less direct conversation. There was a practical reason for this, Glogauer realized, in that John and his men feared betrayal all the time. Even the Essenes' records were partially written in cipher, with one innocent-seeming word or phrase meaning something else entirely.

"I am sorry, John. But tell me if I am right." Glogauer spoke softly.

"Are you not a magus, coming in that chariot from nowhere?" The Baptist waved his hands and shrugged his shoulders. "My men saw you! They saw the shining thing take shape in air, crack and let you enter out of it. Is that not magical? The clothing you wore—was that earthly raiment? The talismans within the chariot —did they not speak of powerful magic? The prophet said that a magus would come from Egypt and be called Emmanuel. So it is written in the Book of Micah! Are none of these things true?"

"Most of them. But there are explanations—" He broke off, unable to think of the nearest word to "rational." "I am an ordinary man, like you. I have no power to work miracles! I am just a man!"

John glowered. "You mean you refuse to help us?"

"I'm grateful to you and the Essenes. You saved my life almost certainly. If I can repay that . . ."

John nodded his head deliberately. "You can repay it, Emmanuel."

"How?"

"Be the great magus I need. Let me present you to all those who become impatient and would turn away from Adonai's will. Let me tell them the manner of your coming to us. Then you can say that all is Adonai's will and that they must prepare to accomplish it."

John stared at him intensely.

"Will you, Emmanuel?"

"For your sake, John. And in turn, will you send men to bring my chariot here as soon as possible? I wish to see if it may be mended."

"I will."

Glogauer felt exhilarated. He began to laugh. The Baptist looked at him with slight bewilderment. Then he began to join in.

Glogauer laughed on. History would not mention it, but he, with John the Baptist, would prepare the way for Christ.

Christ was not born yet. Perhaps Glogauer knew it, one year before the crucifixion.

And the Word was made flesh and dwelt among us (and we beheld his glory, the glory as of the only begotten of the Father) full of grace and truth. John bare witness of him, and cried, saying,

This was he of whom I spake, He that cometh after me is preferred before me: for he was before me.

(John 1: 14–15)

Even when he had first met Monica they had had long arguments. His father had not then died and left him the money to buy the Occult Bookshop in Great Russell Street, opposite the British Museum. He was doing all sorts of temporary work and his spirits were very low. At that time Monica had seemed a great help, a great guide through the mental darkness engulfing him. They had both lived close to Holland Park and went there for walks almost every Sunday of the summer of 1962. At twenty-two, he was already obsessed with Jung's strange brand of Christian mysticism. She, who despised Jung, had soon begun to denigrate all his ideas. She never really convinced him. But, after a while, she had succeeded in confusing him. It would be another six months before they went to bed together.

It was uncomfortably hot.

They sat in the shade of the cafeteria, watching a distant cricket match. Nearer to them, two girls and a boy sat on the grass, drinking orange squash from plastic cups. One of the girls had a guitar across her lap and she set the cup down and began to play, singing a folksong in a high, gentle voice. Glogauer tried to listen to the words. As a student, he had always liked traditional folk music.

"Christianity is dead." Monica sipped her tea. "Religion is dying. God was killed in 1945."

"There may yet be a resurrection," he said.

"Let us hope not. Religion was the creation of fear. Knowledge destroys fear. Without fear, religion can't survive."

"You think there's no fear about these days?"

"Not the same kind, Karl."

"Haven't you ever considered the *idea* of Christ?" he asked her, changing his tack. "What that means to Christians?"

"The idea of the tractor means as much to a Marxist," she replied.

"But what came first? The idea or the actuality of Christ?"

She shrugged. "The actuality, if it matters. Jesus was a Jewish troublemaker organizing a revolt against the Romans. He was crucified for his pains. That's all we know and all we need to know."

"A great religion couldn't have begun so simply."

"When people need one, they'll make a great religion out of the most unlikely beginnings."

"That's my point, Monica." He gesticulated at her and she drew away slightly. "The *idea* preceded the *actuality* of Christ."

"Oh, Karl, don't go on. The actuality of *Jesus* preceded the idea of *Christ*."

A couple walked past, glancing at them as they argued.

Monica noticed them and fell silent. She got up and he rose as well, but she shook her head. "I'm going home, Karl. You stay here. I'll see you in a few days."

He watched her walk down the wide path towards the park gates.

The next day, when he got home from work, he

found a letter. She must have written it after she had
left him and posted it the same day.

> *Dear Karl,*
> *Conversation doesn't seem to have much effect*
> *on you, you know. It's as if you listen to the tone*
> *of the voice, the rhythm of the words, without ever*
> *hearing what is trying to be communicated. You're*
> *a bit like a sensitive animal who can't understand*
> *what's being said to it, but can tell if the person*
> *talking is pleased or angry and so on. That's why*
> *I'm writing to you—to try to get my idea across.*
> *You respond too emotionally when we're together.*
> *   You make the mistake of considering Christian-*
> *ity as something that developed over the course of*
> *a few years, from the death of Jesus to the time the*
> *Gospels were written. But Christianity wasn't new.*
> *Only the name was new. Christianity was merely*
> *a stage in the meeting, cross-fertilization meta-*
> *morphosis of Western logic and Eastern mysticism.*
> *Look how the religion itself changed over the*
> *centuries, re-interpreting itself to meet changing*
> *times. Christianity is just a new name for a con-*
> *glomeration of old myths and philosophies. All the*
> *Gospels do is retell the sun myth and garble some*
> *of the ideas from the Greeks and Romans. Even*
> *in the second century, Jewish scholars were show-*
> *ing it up for the mish-mash it was! They pointed*
> *out the strong similarities between the various sun*
> *myths and the Christ myth. The miracles didn't*
> *happen—they were invented later, borrowed from*
> *here and there.*
> *   Remember the old Victorians who used to say*

that Plato was really a Christian because he an-
ticipated Christian thought? Christian thought!
Christianity was a vehicle for ideas in circulation
for centuries before Christ. Was Marcus Aurelius
a Christian? He was writing in the direct tradition
of Western philosophy. That's why Christianity
caught on in Europe and not in the East! You
should have been a theologian with your bias, not
a psychiatrist. The same goes for your friend Jung.

Try to clear your head of all this morbid non-
sense and you'll be a lot better at your job.

Yours,
Monica.

He screwed the letter up and threw it away. Later
that evening he was tempted to look at it again, but he
resisted the temptation.

III

John stood up to his waist in the river. Most of the
Essenes stood on the banks watching him. Glogauer
looked down at him.

"I cannot, John. It is not for me to do it."

The Baptist muttered, "You must."

Glogauer shivered as he lowered himself into the
river beside the Baptist. He felt light-headed. He stood
there trembling, unable to move.

His foot slipped on the rocks of the river and John
reached out and gripped his arm, steadying him.

In the clear sky, the sun was at zenith, beating down
on his unprotected head.

"Emmanuel!" John cried suddenly. "The spirit of Adonai is within you!"

Glogauer still found it hard to speak. He shook his head slightly. It was aching and he could hardly see. Today he was having his first migraine attack since he had come here. He wanted to vomit. John's voice sounded distant.

He swayed in the water.

As he began to fall towards the Baptist, the whole scene around him shimmered. He felt John catch him and heard himself say desperately: "John, baptize *me!*" And then there was water in his mouth and throat and he was coughing.

John's voice was crying something. Whatever the words were, they drew a response from the people on both banks. The roaring in his ears increased, its quality changing. He thrashed in the water, then felt himself lifted to his feet.

The Essenes were swaying in unison, every face lifted upwards towards the glaring sun.

Glogauer began to vomit into the water, stumbling as John's hands gripped his arms painfully and guided him up the bank.

A peculiar, rhythmic humming came from the mouths of the Essenes as they swayed; it rose as they swayed to one side, fell as they swayed to the other.

Glogauer covered his ears as John released him. He was still retching, but it was dry now, and worse than before.

He began to stagger away, barely keeping his balance, running, with his ears still covered; running over the rocky scrubland; running as the sun throbbed in the sky and its heat pounded at his head; running away.

But John forbade him, saying, I have need to be baptized of thee, and comest thou to me? And Jesus answering said unto him, Suffer it to be so now: for thus it becometh us to fulfill all righteousness. Then he suffered him. And Jesus, when he was baptized, went up straightway out of the water: and, lo, the heavens were opened unto him, and he saw the Spirit of God descending like a dove, and lighting upon him: And lo a voice from heaven, saying, This is my beloved Son, in whom I am well pleased.

(Matthew 3: 14–17)

He had been fifteen, doing well at the grammar school. He had read in the newspapers about the Teddy Boy gangs that roamed South London, but the odd youth he had seen in pseudo-Edwardian clothes had seemed harmless and stupid enough.

He had gone to the pictures in Brixton Hill and decided to walk home to Streatham because he had spent most of the bus money on an ice cream. They came out of the cinema at the same time. He hardly noticed them as they followed him down the hill.

Then, quite suddenly, they had surrounded him. Pale, mean-faced boys, most of them a year or two older than he was. He realized that he knew two of them vaguely. They were at the big council school in the same street as the grammar school. They used the same football ground.

"Hello," he said weakly.

"Hello, son," said the oldest Teddy Boy. He was chewing gum, standing with one knee bent, grinning at him. "Where you going, then?"

"Home."

"Heouwm," said the biggest one, imitating his accent. "What are you going to do when you get there?"

"Go to bed." Karl tried to get through the ring, but they wouldn't let him. They pressed him back into a shop doorway. Beyond them, cars droned by on the main road. The street was brightly lit, with street lamps and neon from the shops. Several people passed, but none of them stopped. Karl began to feel panic.

"Got no homework to do, son?" said the boy next to the leader. He was redheaded and freckled and his eyes were a hard gray.

"Want to fight one of us?" another boy asked. It was one of the boys he knew.

"No. I don't fight. Let me go."

"You scared, son?" said the leader, grinning. Ostentatiously, he pulled a streamer of gum from his mouth and then replaced it. He began chewing again.

"No. Why should I want to fight you?"

"You reckon you're better than us, is that it, son?"

"No." He was beginning to tremble. Tears were coming into his eyes. " 'Course not."

" 'Course not, son."

He moved forward again, but they pushed him back into the doorway.

"You're the bloke with the kraut name, ain't you?" said the other boy he knew. "Glow-worm or something."

"Glogauer. Let me go."

"Won't your mummy like it if you're back late?"

"More a yid name than a kraut name."

"You a yid, son?"

"He looks like a yid."

"You a yid, son?"

"You a Jewish boy, son?"

"You a yid, son?"

"Shut up!" Karl screamed. He pushed into them. One of them punched him in the stomach. He grunted with pain. Another pushed him and he staggered.

People were still hurrying by on the pavement. They glanced at the group as they went past. One man stopped, but his wife pulled him on. "Just some kids larking about," she said.

"Get his trousers down," one of the boys suggested with a laugh. "That'll prove it."

Karl pushed through them and this time they didn't resist. He began to run down the hill.

"Give him a start," he heard one of the boys say.

He ran on.

They began to follow him, laughing.

They did not catch up with him by the time he turned into the avenue where he lived. He reached the house and ran along the dark passage beside it. He opened the back door. His stepmother was in the kitchen.

"What's the matter with you?" she said.

She was a tall, thin woman, nervous and hysterical. Her dark hair was untidy.

He went past her into the breakfast-room.

"What's the matter, Karl?" she called. Her voice was high-pitched.

"Nothing," he said.

He didn't want a scene.

It was cold when he woke up. The false dawn was gray and he could see nothing but barren country in all

directions. He could not remember a great deal about
the previous day, except that he had run a long way.

Dew had gathered on his loincloth. He wet his lips
and rubbed the skin over his face. As he always did
after a migraine attack he felt weak and completely
drained. Looking down at his naked body, he noticed
how skinny he had become. Life with the Essenes had
caused that, of course.

He wondered why he had panicked so much when
John had asked him to baptize him. Was it simply
honesty—something in him which resisted deceiving
the Essenes into thinking he was a prophet of some
kind? It was hard to know.

He wrapped the goatskin about his hips and tied it
tightly just above his left thigh. He supposed he had
better try to get back to the camp and find John and
apologize, see if he could make amends.

The time machine was there now, too. They had
dragged it there, using only rawhide ropes.

If a good blacksmith could be found, or some other
metal-worker, there was just a chance that it could be
repaired. The journey back would be dangerous.

He wondered if he ought to go back right away, or
try to shift to a time nearer to the actual crucifixion.
He had not gone back specifically to witness the crucifixion, but to get the mood of Jerusalem during the
Feast of the Passover, when Jesus was supposed to
have entered the city. Monica had thought Jesus had
stormed the city with an armed band. She had said that
all the evidence pointed to that. All the evidence of one
sort did point to it, but he could not accept the evidence. There was more to it, he was sure. If only he
could meet Jesus. John had apparently never heard of

him, though he had told Glogauer that there was a prophecy that the Messiah would be a Nazarene. There were many prophecies, and many of them conflicted.

He began to walk back in the general direction of the Essene camp. He could not have come so far. He would soon recognize the hills where they had their caves.

Soon it was very hot and the ground more barren. The air wavered before his eyes. The feeling of exhaustion with which he had awakened increased. His mouth was dry and his legs were weak. He was hungry and there was nothing to eat. There was no sign of the range of hills where the Essenes had their camp.

There was one hill, about two miles away to the south. He decided to make for it. From there he would probably be able to get his bearings, perhaps even see a township where they would give him food.

The sandy soil turned to floating dust around him as his feet disturbed it. A few primitive shrubs clung to the ground and jutting rocks tripped him.

He was bleeding and bruised by the time he began, painfully, to clamber up the hillside.

The journey to the summit (which was much further away than he had originally judged) was difficult. He would slide on the loose stones of the hillside, falling on his face, bracing his torn hands and feet to stop himself from sliding down to the bottom, clinging to tufts of grass and lichen that grew here and there, embracing larger projections of rock when he could, resting frequently, his mind and body both numb with pain and weariness.

He sweated beneath the sun. The dust stuck to the

moisture on his half-naked body, caking him from head to foot. The goatskin was in shreds.

The barren world reeled around him, sky somehow merging with land, yellow rock with white clouds. Nothing seemed still.

He reached the summit and lay there gasping. Everything had become unreal.

He heard Monica's voice, thought he glimpsed her for a moment from the corner of his eye.

Don't be melodramatic, Karl. . . .

She had said that many times. His own voice replied now.

I'm born out of my time, Monica. This age of reason has no place for me. It will kill me in the end.

Her voice replied.

Guilt and fear and your own masochism. You could be a brilliant psychiatrist, but you've given in to all your own neuroses so completely. . . .

"Shut up!"

He rolled over on his back. The sun blazed down on his tattered body.

"Shut up!"

The whole Christian syndrome, Karl. You'll become a Catholic convert next, I shouldn't doubt. Where's your strength of mind?

"Shut up! Go away, Monica."

Fear shapes your thoughts. You're not searching for a soul or even a meaning for life. You're searching for comforts.

"Leave me alone, Monica!"

His grimy hands covered his ears. His hair and beard were matted with dust. Blood had congealed on the minor wounds that were now on every part of his body. Above, the sun seemed to pound in unison with his heartbeats.

You're going downhill, Karl, don't you realize that? Downhill. Pull yourself together. You're not entirely incapable of rational thought. . . .

"Oh, Monica! Shut up!"

His voice was harsh and cracked. A few ravens circled the sky above him now. He heard them calling back at him in a voice not unlike his own.

God died in 1945. . . .

"It isn't 1945—it's 28 A.D. God is alive!"

How you can bother to wonder about an obvious syncretistic religion like Christianity—Rabbinic Judaism, Stoic ethics, Greek mystery cults, Oriental ritual. . . .

"It doesn't matter!"

Not to you in your present state of mind.

"I need God!"

That's what it boils down to, doesn't it? Okay, Karl, carve your own crutches. Just think what you could have been if you'd have come to terms with yourself. . . .

Glogauer pulled his ruined body to its feet and stood on the summit of the hill and screamed.

The ravens were startled. They wheeled in the sky and flew away.

The sky was darkening now.

> *Then was Jesus led up of the Spirit into the wilderness to be tempted of the devil. And when he had fasted forty days and forty nights, he was afterward an hungred.*
>
> (Matthew 4: 1–2)

IV

The madman came stumbling into the town. His feet stirred the dust and made it dance and dogs barked around him as he walked mechanically, his head turned upwards to face the sun, his arms limp at his sides, his lips moving.

To the townspeople, the words they heard were in no familiar language; yet they were uttered with such intensity and conviction that God himself might be using this emaciated, naked creature as his spokesman.

They wondered where the madman had come from.

The white town consisted primarily of double- and single-storied houses of stone and clay-brick, built around a market place that was fronted by an ancient, simple synagogue outside which old men sat and talked, dressed in dark robes. The town was prosperous and clean, thriving on Roman commerce. Only one or two beggars were in the streets and these were well-fed. The streets followed the rise and fall of the hillside on which they were built. They were winding streets, shady and peaceful: country streets. There was a smell of newly-cut timber everywhere in the air, and the sound of carpentry, for the town was chiefly famous for its skilled carpenters. It lay on the edge of the Plain of Jezreel, close to the trade route between Damascus and Egypt, and wagons were always leaving it, laden with the work of the town's craftsmen. The town was called Nazareth.

The madman had found it by asking every traveler he saw where it was. He had passed through other towns—Philadelphia, Gerasa, Pella and Scythopolis, following the Roman roads—asking the same question in his outlandish accent: "Where lies Nazareth?"

Some had given him food on the way. Some had asked for his blessing and he had laid hands on them, speaking in that strange tongue. Some had pelted him with stones and driven him away.

He had crossed the Jordan by the Roman viaduct and continued northwards towards Nazareth.

There had been no difficulty in finding the town, but it had been difficult for him to force himself towards it. He had lost a great deal of blood and had eaten very little on the journey. He would walk until he collapsed and lie there until he could go on, or, as had happened increasingly, until someone found him and had given him a little sour wine or bread to revive him.

Once some Roman legionaries had stopped and with brusque kindness asked him if he had any relatives they could take him to. They had addressed him in pidgin-Aramaic and had been surprised when he replied in a strangely-accented Latin that was purer than the language they spoke themselves.

They asked him if he was a rabbi or a scholar. He told them he was neither. The officer of the legionaries had offered him some dried meat and wine. The men were part of a patrol that passed this way once a month. They were stocky, brown-faced men, with hard, clean-shaven faces. They were dressed in stained leather kilts and breastplates and sandals, and had iron helmets on their heads, scabbarded short swords at their hips. Even as they stood around him in the evening sunlight they did not seem relaxed. The officer, softer-voiced than his men but otherwise much like them save that he wore a metal breastplate and a long cloak, asked the madman what his name was.

For a moment the madman had paused, his mouth opening and closing, as if he could not remember what he was called.

"Karl," he said at length, doubtfully. It was more a suggestion than a statement.

"Sounds almost like a Roman name," said one of the legionaries.

"Are you a citizen?" the officer asked.

But the madman's mind was wandering, evidently. He looked away from them, muttering to himself.

All at once, he looked back at them and said: "Nazareth?"

"That way." The officer pointed down the road that cut between the hills. "Are you a Jew?"

This seemed to startle the madman. He sprang to his feet and tried to push through the soldiers. They let him through, laughing. He was a harmless madman.

They watched him run down the road.

"One of their prophets, perhaps," said the officer, walking towards his horse. The country was full of them. Every other man you met claimed to be spreading the message of their god. They didn't make much trouble and religion seemed to keep their minds off rebellion. *We should be grateful,* thought the officer.

His men were still laughing.

They began to march down the road in the opposite direction to the one the madman had taken.

Now the madman was in Nazareth and the townspeople looked at him with curiosity and more than a little suspicion as he staggered into the market square.

He could be a wandering prophet or he could be possessed by devils. It was often hard to tell. The rabbis would know.

As he passed the knots of people standing by the merchants' stalls, they fell silent until he had gone by. Women pulled their heavy woolen shawls about their well-fed bodies and men tucked in their cotton robes so that he would not touch them. Normally their instinct would have been to have taxed him with his business in the town, but there was an intensity about his gaze, a quickness and vitality about his face, in spite of his emaciated appearance, that made them treat him with some respect and they kept their distance.

When he reached the center of the market place, he stopped and looked around him. He seemed slow to notice the people. He blinked and licked his lips.

A woman passed, eyeing him warily. He spoke to her, his voice soft, the words carefully formed. "Is this Nazareth?"

"It is." She nodded and increased her pace.

A man was crossing the square. He was dressed in a woolen robe of red and brown stripes. There was a red skull cap on his curly, black hair. His face was plump and cheerful. The madman walked across the man's path and stopped him. "I seek a carpenter."

"There are many carpenters in Nazareth. The town is famous for its carpenters. I am a carpenter myself. Can I help you?" The man's voice was good-humored, patronizing.

"Do you know a carpenter called Joseph? A descendant of David. He has a wife called Mary and several children. One is named Jesus."

The cheerful man screwed his face into a mock

frown and scratched the back of his neck. "I know
more than one Joseph. There is one poor fellow in
yonder street." He pointed. "He has a wife called
Mary. Try there. You should soon find him. Look for a
man who never laughs."

The madman looked in the direction in which the
man pointed. As soon as he saw the street, he seemed
to forget everything else and strode towards it.

In the narrow street he entered the smell of cut timber was even stronger. He walked ankle-deep in wood-
shavings. From every building came the thud of ham-
mers, the scrape of saws. There were planks of all sizes
resting against the pale, shaded walls of the houses and
there was hardly room to pass between them. Many of
the carpenters had their benches just outside their
doors. They were carving bowls, operating simple
lathes, shaping wood into everything imaginable. They
looked up as the madman entered the street and approached one old carpenter in a leather apron who sat
at his bench carving a figurine. The man had gray hair
and seemed short-sighted. He peered up at the madman.

"What do you want?"

"I seek a carpenter called Joseph. He has a wife—
Mary."

The old man gestured with his hand that held the
half-completed figurine. "Two houses along on the
other side of the street."

The house the madman came to had very few planks
leaning against it, and the quality of the timber seemed
poorer than the other wood he had seen. The bench
near the entrance was warped on one side and the man

who sat hunched over it repairing a stool seemed misshapen also. He straightened up as the madman
touched his shoulder. His face was lined and pouched
with misery. His eyes were tired and his thin beard
had premature streaks of gray. He coughed slightly,
perhaps in surprise at being disturbed.

"Are you Joseph?" asked the madman.

"I've no money."

"I want nothing—just to ask a few questions."

"I'm Joseph. Why do you want to know?"

"Have you a son?"

"Several, and daughters, too."

"Your wife is called Mary? You are of David's
line."

The man waved his hand impatiently. "Yes, for
what good either have done me. . . ."

"I wish to meet one of your sons. Jesus. Can you tell
me where he is?"

"That good-for-nothing. What has he done now?"

"Where is he?"

Joseph's eyes became more calculating as he stared
at the madman. "Are you a seer of some kind? Have
you come to cure my son?"

"I am a prophet of sorts. I can foretell the future."

Joseph got up with a sigh. "You can see him.
Come." He led the madman through the gateway into
the cramped courtyard of the house. It was crowded
with pieces of wood, broken furniture and implements,
rotting sacks of shavings. They entered the darkened
house. In the first room—evidently a kitchen—a woman
stood by a large clay stove. She was tall and bulging
with fat. Her long, black hair was unbound and

greasy, falling over large, lustrous eyes that still had the heart of sensuality. She looked the madman over.

"There's no food for beggars," she grunted. "He eats enough as it is." She gestured with a wooden spoon at a small figure sitting in the shadow of a corner. The figure shifted as she spoke.

"He seeks our Jesus," said Joseph to the woman. "Perhaps he comes to ease our burden."

The woman gave the madman a sidelong look and shrugged. She licked her red lips with a fat tongue. "Jesus!"

The figure in the corner stood up.

"That's him," said the woman with a certain satisfaction.

The madman frowned, shaking his head rapidly. "No."

The figure was misshapen. It had a pronounced hunched back and a cast in its left eye. The face was vacant and foolish. There was a little spittle on the lips. It giggled as its name was repeated. It took a crooked step forward. "Jesus," it said. The word was slurred and thick. "Jesus."

"That's all he can say." The woman sneered. "He's always been like that."

"God's judgment," said Joseph bitterly.

"What is wrong with him?" There was a pathetic, desperate note in the madman's voice.

"He's always been like that." The woman turned back to the stove. "You can have him if you want him. Addled inside and outside. I was carrying him when my parents married me off to that half-man. . . ."

"You shameless—" Joseph stopped as his wife

glared at him. He turned to the madman. "What's your business with our son?"

"I wished to talk to him. I . . ."

"He's no oracle—no seer—we used to think he might be. There are still people in Nazareth who come to him to cure them or tell their fortunes, but he only giggles at them and speaks his name over and over again. . . ."

"Are—you sure—there is not—something about him—you have not noticed?"

"Sure!" Mary snorted sardonically. "We need money badly enough. If he had any magical powers, we'd know."

Jesus giggled again and limped away into another room.

"It is impossible," the madman murmured. Could history itself have changed? Could he be in some other dimension of time where Christ had never been?

Joseph appeared to notice the look of agony in the madman's eyes.

"What is it?" he said. "What do you see? You said you foretold the future. Tell us how we will fare?"

"Not *now*," said the prophet, turning away. "Not *now*."

He ran from the house and down the street with its smell of planed oak, cedar and cypress. He ran back to the market place and stopped, looking wildly about him. He saw the synagogue directly ahead of him. He began to walk towards it.

The man he had spoken to earlier was still in the market place, buying cooking pots to give to his daughter as a wedding gift. He nodded towards the strange man as he entered the synagogue. "He's a relative of

Joseph the carpenter," he told the man beside him. "A prophet, I shouldn't wonder."

The madman, the prophet, Karl Glogauer, the time-traveler, the neurotic psychiatrist manqué, the searcher for meaning, the masochist, the man with a death-wish and the messiah-complex, the anachronism, made his way into the synagogue gasping for breath. He had seen the man he had sought. He had seen Jesus, the son of Joseph and Mary. He had seen a man he recognized without any doubt as a congenital imbecile.

"All men have a messiah-complex, Karl," Monica had said.

The memories were less complete now. His sense of time and identity was becoming confused.

"There were dozens of messiahs in Galilee at the time. That Jesus should have been the one to carry the myth and the philosophy was a coincidence of history. . . ."

"There must have been more to it than that, Monica."

Every Tuesday in the room above the Occult Bookshop, the Jungian discussion group would meet for purposes of group analysis and therapy. Glogauer had not organized the group, but he had willingly lent his premises to it and had joined it eagerly. It was a great relief to talk with like-minded people once a week. One of his reasons for buying the Occult Bookshop was so that he would meet interesting people like those who attended the Jungian discussion group.

An obsession with Jung brought them together, but everyone had special obsessions of his own. Mrs. Rita

Blen charted the courses of flying saucers, though it was not clear if she believed in them or not. Hugh Joyce believed that all Jungian archetypes derived from the original race of Atlanteans who had perished millennia before. Alan Cheddar, the youngest of the group, was interested in Indian mysticism, and Sandra Peterson, the organizer, was a great witchcraft specialist. James Headington was interested in time. He was the group's pride; he was Sir James Headington, wartime inventor, very rich and with all sorts of decorations for his contribution to the Allied victory. He had had the reputation of being a great improviser during the war, but after it had become something of an embarrassment to the War Office. He was a crank, they thought, and what was worse, he aired his crankiness in public.

Every so often, Sir James would tell the other members of the group about his time machine. They humored him. Most of them were liable to exaggerate their own experiences connected with their different interests.

One Tuesday evening, after everyone else had left, Headington told Glogauer that his machine was ready.

"I can't believe it," Glogauer said truthfully.

"You're the first person I've told."

"Why me?"

"I don't know. I like you—and the shop."

"You haven't told the government."

Headington had chuckled. "Why should I? Not until I've tested it fully, anyway. Serves them right for putting me out to pasture."

"You don't know it works?"

"I'm sure it does. Would you like to see it?"

"A time machine." Glogauer smiled weakly.

"Come and see it."

"Why me?"

"I thought you might be interested. I know you don't hold with the orthodox view of science. . . ."

Glogauer felt sorry for him.

"Come and see," said Headington.

He went down to Banbury the next day. The same day he left 1976 and arrived in 28 A.D.

The synagogue was cool and quiet with a subtle scent of incense. The rabbis guided him into the court-yard. They, like the townspeople, did not know what to make of him, but they were sure it was not a devil that possessed him. It was their custom to give shelter to the roaming prophets who were now everywhere in Galilee, though this one was stranger than the rest. His face was immobile and his body was stiff, and there were tears running down his dirty cheeks. They had never seen such agony in a man's eyes before.

"Science can say how, but it never asks why," he had told Monica. "It can't answer."

"Who wants to know?" she replied.

"I do."

"Well, you'll never find out, will you?"

"Sit down, my son," said the rabbi. "What do you wish to ask of us?"

"Where is Christ?" he said. "Where is Christ?"

They did not understand the language.

"Is it Greek?" asked one, but another shook his head.

Kyrios: The Lord.
Adonai: The Lord.
Where was the Lord?
He frowned, looking vaguely about him.
"I must rest," he said in their language.
"Where are you from?"
He could not think what to answer.
"Where are you from?" a rabbi repeated.
"*Ha-Olam Hab-Bah . . .*" he murmured at length.
They looked at one another. "*Ha-Olam Hab-Bah,*" they said.
Ha-Olam Hab-Bah; Ha-Olam Haz-Zeh: The world to come and the world that is.
"Do you bring us a message?" said one of the rabbis. They were used to prophets, certainly, but none like this one. "A message?"
"I do not know," said the prophet hoarsely. "I must rest. I am hungry."
"Come. We will give you food and a place to sleep."
He could only eat a little of the rich food and the bed with its straw-stuffed mattress was too soft for him. He was not used to it.
He slept badly, shouting as he dreamed, and, outside the room, the rabbis listened, but could understand little of what he said.

Karl Glogauer stayed in the synagogue for several weeks. He would spend most of his time reading in the library, searching through the long scrolls for some answer to his dilemma. The words of the Testaments, in many cases capable of a dozen interpretations, only confused him further. There was nothing to grasp, nothing to tell him what had gone wrong.

The rabbis kept this distance for the most part. They had accepted him as a holy man. They were proud to have him in their synagogue. They were sure that he was one of the special chosen of God and they waited patiently for him to speak to them.

But the prophet said little, muttering only to himself in snatches of their own language and snatches of the incomprehensible language he often used, even when he addressed them directly.

In Nazareth, the townsfolk talked of little else but the mysterious prophet in the synagogue, but the rabbis would not answer their questions. They would tell the people to go about their business, that there were things they were not yet meant to know. In this way, as priests had always done, they avoided questions they could not answer while at the same time appearing to have much more knowledge than they actually possessed.

Then, one sabbath, he appeared in the public part of the synagogue and took his place with the others who had come to worship.

The man who was reading from the scroll on his left stumbled over the words, glancing at the prophet from the corner of his eye.

The prophet sat and listened, his expression remote.

The Chief Rabbi looked uncertainly at him, then signed that the scroll should be passed to the prophet. This was done hesitantly by a boy who placed the scroll into the prophet's hands.

The prophet looked at the words for a long time and

then began to read. The prophet read without compre-
hending at first what he read. It was the book of
Esaias.

> *The Spirit of the Lord is upon me, because he*
> *hath anointed me to preach the gospel to the poor;*
> *he hath sent me to heal the brokenhearted, to*
> *preach deliverance to the captives, and recovering*
> *of sight to the blind, to set at liberty them that are*
> *bruised, to preach the acceptable year of the Lord.*
> *And he closed the book, and gave it again to the*
> *minister, and sat down. And the eyes of all of them*
> *that were in the synagogue were fastened on him.*
> (Luke 4: 18–20)

V

They followed him now, as he walked away from Nazareth towards the Lake of Galilee. He was dressed in
the white linen robe they had given him and though
they thought he led them, they, in fact, drove him before them.

"He is our messiah," they said to those that inquired. And there were already rumors of miracles.

When he saw the sick, he pitied them and tried to do
what he could because they expected something of him.
Many he could do nothing for, but others, obviously in
psychosomatic conditions, he could help. They believed in his power more strongly than they believed in
their sickness. So he cured them.

When he came to Capernaum, some fifty people followed him into the streets of the city. It was already
known that he was in some way associated with John

the Baptist, who enjoyed huge prestige in Galilee and
had been declared a true prophet by many Pharisees.
Yet this man had a power greater, in some ways, than
John's. He was not the orator that the Baptist was, but
he had worked miracles.

Capernaum was a sprawling town beside the crystal
Lake of Galilee, its houses separated by large market
gardens. Fishing boats were moored at the white quay-
side, as well as trading ships that plied the lakeside
towns. Though the green hills came down from all
sides to the lake, Capernaum itself was built on flat
ground, sheltered by the hills. It was a quiet town and,
like most others in Galilee, had a large population of
gentiles. Greek, Roman and Egyptian traders walked
its streets and many had made permanent homes there.
There was a prosperous middle-class of merchants,
artisans and ship-owners, as well as doctors, lawyers
and scholars, for Capernaum was on the borders of the
provinces of Galilee, Trachonitis and Syria and though
a comparatively small town was a useful junction for
trade and travel.

The strange, mad prophet in his swirling linen robes,
followed by the heterogeneous crowd that was primarily composed of poor folk but also could be seen to
contain men of some distinction, swept into Capernaum. The news spread that this man really could foretell the future, that he had already predicted the arrest
of John by Herod Antipas and soon after Herod had
imprisoned the Baptist at Peraea. He did not make the
predictions in general terms, using vague words the
way other prophets did. He spoke of things that were
to happen in the near future and he spoke of them in
detail.

None knew his name. He was simply the prophet from Nazareth, or the Nazarene. Some said he was a relative, perhaps the son, of a carpenter in Nazareth, but this could be because the written words for "son of a carpenter" and "magus" were almost the same and the confusion had come about in that way. There was even a very faint rumor that his name was Jesus. The name had been used once or twice, but when they asked him if that was, indeed, his name, he denied it or else, in his abstracted way, refused to answer at all.

His actual preaching tended to lack the fire of John's. This man spoke gently, rather vaguely, and smiled often. He spoke of God in a strange way, too, and he appeared to be connected, as John was, with the Essenes, for he preached against the accumulation of personal wealth and spoke of mankind as a brotherhood, as they did.

But it was the miracles that they watched for as he was guided to the graceful synagogue of Capernaum. No prophet before him had healed the sick and seemed to understand the troubles that people rarely spoke of. It was his sympathy that they responded to, rather than the words he spoke.

For the first time in his life, Karl Glogauer had forgotten about Karl Glogauer. For the first time in his life he was doing what he had always sought to do as a psychiatrist.

But it was not his life. He was bringing a myth to life—a generation before that myth would be born. He was completing a certain kind of psychic circuit. He was not changing history, but he was giving history more substance.

He could not bear to think that Jesus had been nothing more than a myth. It was in his power to make Jesus a physical reality rather than the creation of a process of mythogenesis.

So he spoke in the synagogues and he spoke of a gentler God than most of them had heard of, and where he could remember them, he told them parables.

And gradually the need to justify what he was doing faded and his sense of identity grew increasingly more tenuous and was replaced by a different sense of identity, where he gave greater and greater substance to the rôle he had chosen. It was an archetypal rôle. It was a rôle to appeal to a disciple of Jung. It was a rôle that went beyond a mere imitation. It was a rôle that he must now play out to the very last grand detail. Karl Glogauer had discovered the reality he had been seeking.

> *And in the synagogue there was a man, which had a spirit of an unclean devil, and cried out with a loud voice, saying, Let us alone; what have we to do with thee, thou Jesus of Nazareth? art thou come to destroy us? I know thee who thou art; the Holy One of God. And Jesus rebuked him, saying, Hold thy peace, and come out of him. And when the devil had thrown him in the midst, he came out of him, and hurt him not. And they were all amazed, and spake among themselves, saying, What a word is this! for with authority and power he commandeth the unclean spirits, and they come out. And the fame of him went out into every place of the country round about.*
>
> (Luke 4: 33–37)

"Mass hallucination. Miracles, flying saucers, ghosts, it's all the same," Monica had said.

"Very likely," he had replied. "But *why* did they see them?"

"Because they wanted to."

"Why did they want to?"

"Because they were afraid."

"You think that's all there is to it?"

"Isn't it enough?"

When he left Capernaum for the first time, many more people accompanied him. It had become impractical to stay in the town, for the business of the town had been brought almost to a standstill by the crowds that sought to see him work his simple miracles.

He spoke to them in the spaces beyond the towns. He talked with intelligent, literate men who appeared to have something in common with him. Some of them were the owners of fishing fleets—Simon, James and John among them. Another was a doctor, another a civil servant who had first heard him speak in Capernaum.

"There must be twelve," he said to them one day. "There must be a zodiac."

He was not careful in what he said. Many of his ideas were strange. Many of the things he talked about were unfamiliar to them. Some Pharisees thought he blasphemed.

One day he met a man he recognized as an Essene from the colony near Machaerus.

"John would speak with you," said the Essene.

"Is John not dead yet?" he asked the man.

"He is confined at Peraea. I would think Herod is

too frightened to kill him. He lets John walk about within the walls and gardens of the palace, lets him speak with his men, but John fears that Herod will find the courage soon to have him stoned or decapitated. He needs your help."

"How can I help him? He is to die. There is no hope for him."

The Essene looked uncomprehendingly into the mad eyes of the prophet.

"But, master, there is no one else who can help him."

"I have done all that he wished me to do," said the prophet. "I have healed the sick and preached to the poor."

"I did not know he wished this. Now he needs help, master. You could save his life."

The prophet had drawn the Essene away from the crowd.

"His life cannot be saved."

"But if it is not the unrighteous will prosper and the Kingdom of Heaven will not be restored."

"His life cannot be saved."

"Is it God's will?"

"If I am God, then it is God's will."

Hopelessly, the Essene turned and began to walk away from the crowd.

John the Baptist would have to die. Glogauer had no wish to change history, only to strengthen it.

He moved on, with his following, through Galilee. He had selected his twelve educated men, and the rest who followed him were still primarily poor people. To them he offered their only hope of fortune. Many were those who had been ready to follow John against the

Romans, but now John was imprisoned. Perhaps this man would lead them in revolt, to loot the riches of Jerusalem and Jericho and Caesarea. Tired and hungry, their eyes glazed by the burning sun, they followed the man in the white robe. They needed to hope and they found reasons for their hope. They saw him work greater miracles.

Once he preached to them from a boat, as was often his custom, and as he walked back to the shore through the shallows, it seemed to them that he walked over the water.

All through Galilee in the autumn they wandered, hearing from everyone the news of John's beheading. Despair at the Baptist's death turned to renewed hope in this new prophet who had known him.

In Caesarea they were driven from the city by Roman guards used to the wildmen with their prophecies who roamed the country.

They were banned from other cities as the prophet's fame grew. Not only the Roman authorities, but the Jewish ones as well, seemed unwilling to tolerate the new prophet as they had tolerated John. The political climate was changing.

It became hard to find food. They lived on what they could find, hungering like starved animals.

He taught them how to pretend to eat and take their minds off their hunger.

Karl Glogauer, witch-doctor, psychiatrist, hypnotist, messiah.

Sometimes his conviction in his chosen rôle wavered and those that followed him would be disturbed when he contradicted himself. Often, now, they called him the name they had heard, Jesus the Nazarene. Most of the time he did not stop them from using the name, but at others he became angry and cried a peculiar, guttural name.

"Karl Glogauer! Karl Glogauer!"

And they said, Behold, he speaks with the voice of Adonai.

"Call me not by that name!" he would shout, and they would become disturbed and leave him by himself until his anger had subsided.

When the weather changed and the winter came, they went back to Capernaum, which had become a stronghold of his followers.

In Capernaum he waited the winter through, making prophecies.

Many of these prophecies concerned himself and the fate of those that followed him.

> *Then charged he his disciples that they should tell no man that he was Jesus the Christ. From that time forth began Jesus to shew unto his disciples, how that he must go unto Jerusalem and suffer many things of the elders and chief priests and scribes, and be killed, and be raised again the third day.*
>
> (Matthew 16: 20–21)

They were watching television at her flat. Monica was eating an apple. It was between six and seven on a warm Sunday evening. Monica gestured at the screen with her half-eaten apple.

"Look at that nonsense," she said. "You can't honestly tell me it means anything to you."

The program was a religious one, about a pop-opera

in a Hampstead Church. The opera told the story of the crucifixion.

"Pop-groups in the pulpit," she said. "What a comedown."

He didn't reply. The program seemed obscene to him, in an obscure way. He couldn't argue with her.

"God's corpse is really beginning to rot now," she jeered. "Whew! The stink!"

"Turn it off, then," he said quietly.

"What's the pop-group called? The Maggots?"

"Very funny. I'll turn it off, shall I?"

"No, I want to watch. It's funny."

"Oh, turn it off!"

"Imitation of Christ!" she snorted. "It's a bloody caricature."

A Negro singer, who was playing Christ and singing flat to a banal accompaniment, began to drone out lifeless lyrics about the brotherhood of man.

"If he sounded like that, no wonder they nailed him up," said Monica.

He reached forward and switched the picture off.

"I was enjoying it." She spoke with mock disappointment. "It was a lovely swan-song."

Later, she said with a trace of affection that worried him, "You old fogey. What a pity. You could have been John Wesley or Calvin or someone. You can't be a messiah these days, not in your terms. There's nobody to listen."

VI

The prophet was living in the house of a man called Simon, though the prophet preferred to call him Peter.

Simon was grateful to the prophet because he had cured his wife of a complaint which she had suffered from for some time. It had been a mysterious complaint, but the prophet had cured her almost effortlessly.

There were a great many strangers in Capernaum at that time, many of them coming to see the prophet. Simon warned the prophet that some were known agents of the Romans or the Pharisees. The Pharisees had not, on the whole, been antipathetic towards the prophet, though they distrusted the talk of miracles that they heard. However, the whole political atmosphere was disturbed and the Roman occupation troops, from Pilate, through his officers, down to the troops, were tense, expecting an outbreak but unable to see any tangible signs that one was coming.

Pilate himself hoped for trouble on a large scale. It would prove to Tiberius that the emperor had been too lenient with the Jews over the matter of the votive shields. Pilate would be vindicated and his power over the Jews increased. At present he was on bad terms with all the Tetrarchs of the provinces—particularly the unstable Herod Antipas who had seemed at one time his only supporter. Aside from the political situation, his own domestic situation was upset in that his neurotic wife was having her nightmares again and was demanding far more attention from him than he could afford to give her.

There might be a possibility, he thought, of provoking an incident, but he would have to be careful that Tiberius never learnt of it. This new prophet might provide a focus, but so far the man had done nothing against the laws of either the Jews or the Romans.

There was no law that forbade a man to claim he was a messiah, as some said this one had done, and he was hardly inciting the people to revolt—rather the contrary.

Looking through the window of his chamber, with a view of the minarets and spires of Jerusalem, Pilate considered the information his spies had brought him.

Soon after the festival that the Romans called Saturnalia, the prophet and his followers left Capernaum again and began to travel through the country.

There were fewer miracles now that the hot weather had passed, but his prophecies were eagerly asked. He warned them of all the mistakes that would be made in the future, and of all the crimes that would be committed in his name.

Through Galilee he wandered, and through Samaria, following the good Roman roads towards Jerusalem.

The time of the Passover was coming close now.

In Jerusalem, the Roman officials discussed the coming festival. It was always a time of the worst disturbances. There had been riots before during the Feast of the Passover, and doubtless there would be trouble of some kind this year, too.

Pilate spoke to the Pharisees, asking for their cooperation. The Pharisees said they would do what they could, but they could not help it if the people acted foolishly.

Scowling, Pilate dismissed them.

His agents brought him reports from all over the territory. Some of the reports mentioned the new prophet, but said that he was harmless.

Pilate thought privately that he might be harmless

now, but if he reached Jerusalem during the Passover, he might not be so harmless.

Two weeks before the Feast of the Passover, the prophet reached the town of Bethany near Jerusalem. Some of his Galilean followers had friends in Bethany and these friends were more than willing to shelter the man they had heard of from other pilgrims on their way to Jerusalem and the great Temple.

The reason they had come to Bethany was that the prophet had become disturbed at the number of the people following him.

"There are too many," he had said to Simon. "Too many, Peter."

Glogauer's face was haggard now. His eyes were set deeper into their sockets and he said little.

Sometimes he would look around him vaguely, as if unsure where he was.

News came to the house in Bethany that Roman agents had been making inquires about him. It did not seem to disturb him. On the contrary, he nodded thoughtfully, as if satisfied.

Once he walked with two of his followers across country to look at Jerusalem. The bright yellow walls of the city looked splendid in the afternoon light. The towers and tall buildings, many of them decorated in mosaic reds, blues and yellows, could be seen from several miles away.

The prophet turned back towards Bethany.

"When shall we go into Jerusalem?" one of his followers asked him.

"Not yet," said Glogauer. His shoulders were

hunched and he grasped his chest with his arms and hands as if cold.

Two days before the Feast of the Passover in Jerusalem, the prophet took his men towards the Mount of Olives and a suburb of Jerusalem that was built on its side and called Bethphage.

"Get me a donkey," he told them. "A colt. I must fulfill the prophecy now."

"Then all will know you are the messiah," said Andrew.

"Yes."

Glogauer sighed. He felt afraid again, but this time it was not physical fear. It was the fear of an actor who was about to make his final, most dramatic scene and who was not sure he could do it well.

There was cold sweat on Glogauer's upper lip. He wiped it off.

In the poor light he peered at the men around him. He was still uncertain of some of their names. He was not interested in their names, particularly, only in their number. There were ten here. The other two were looking for the donkey.

They stood on the grassy slope of the Mount of Olives, looking towards Jerusalem and the great Temple which lay below. There was a light, warm breeze blowing.

"Judas?" said Glogauer inquiringly.

There was one called Judas.

"Yes, master," he said. He was tall and good looking, with curly red hair and neurotic intelligent eyes. Glogauer believed he was an epileptic.

Glogauer looked thoughtfully at Judas Iscariot. "I

will want you to help me later," he said, "when we have entered Jerusalem."

"How, master?"

"You must take a message to the Romans."

"The Romans?" Iscariot looked troubled. "Why?"

"It must be the Romans. It can't be the Jews—they would use a stake or an axe. I'll tell you more when the time comes."

The sky was dark now, and the stars were out over the Mount of Olives. It had become cold. Glogauer shivered.

> *Rejoice greatly, O daughter of Zion,*
> *Shout, O daughter of Jerusalem:*
> *Behold, thy King cometh unto thee!*
> *He is just and having salvation;*
> *Lowly and riding upon an ass,*
> *And upon a colt, the foal of an ass.*
> (Zechariah 9:9)

"*Osha'na! Osha'na! Osha'na!*"

As Glogauer rode the donkey into the city, his followers ran ahead, throwing down palm branches. On both sides of the street were crowds, forewarned by the followers of his coming.

Now the new prophet could be seen to be fulfilling the prophecies of the ancient prophets and many believed that he had come to lead them against the Romans. Even now, possibly, he was on his way to Pilate's house to confront the procurator.

"*Osha'na! Osha'na!*"

Glogauer looked around distractedly. The back of

the donkey, though softened by the coats of his followers, was uncomfortable. He swayed and clung to
the beast's mane. He heard the words, but could not
make them out clearly.

"*Osha'na! Osha'na!*"

It sounded like "hosanna" at first, before he realized
that they were shouting the Aramaic for "Free us."

"Free us! Free us!"

John had planned to rise in arms against the
Romans this Passover. Many had expected to take part
in the rebellion.

They believed that he was taking John's place as a
rebel leader.

"No," he muttered at them as he looked around at
their expectant faces. "No, I am the messiah. I cannot
free you. I can't. . . ."

They did not hear him above their own shouts.

Karl Glogauer entered Christ. Christ entered Jerusalem. The story was approaching its climax.

"*Osha'na!*"

It was not in the story. He could not help them.

> *Verily, verily, I say unto you, that one of you
> shall betray me. Then the disciples looked at one
> another, doubting of whom he spake. Now there
> was leaning on Jesus' bosom one of his disciples,
> whom Jesus loved. Simon Peter therefore beckoned
> to him, that he should ask who it should be of
> whom he spake. He then lying on Jesus' breast
> saith unto him, Lord, who is it? Jesus answered, He
> it is, to whom I shall give a sop, when I have
> dipped it. And when he had dipped the sop, he*

gave it to Judas Iscariot, the son of Simon. And
after the sop Satan entered into him. Then said
Jesus unto him, that thou doest, do quickly.

(John 13: 21–27)

Judas Iscariot frowned with some uncertainty as he
left the room and went out into the crowded street,
making his way towards the governor's palace. Doubtless he was to perform a part in a plan to deceive the
Romans and have the people rise up in Jesus' defense,
but he thought the scheme foolhardy. The mood
amongst the jostling men, women and children in the
streets was tense. Many more Roman soldiers than
usual patrolled the city.

Pilate was a stout man. His face was self-indulgent
and his eyes were hard and shallow. He looked dis-
dainfully at the Jew.

"We do not pay informers whose information is
proved to be false," he warned.

"I do not seek money, lord," said Judas, feigning the
ingratiating manner that the Romans seemed to expect
of the Jews. "I am a loyal subject of the Emperor."

"Who is this rebel?"

"Jesus of Nazareth, lord. He entered the city today . . ."

"I know. I saw him. But I heard he preached of
peace and obeying the law."

"To deceive you, lord."

Pilate frowned. It was likely. It smacked of the kind
of deceit he had grown to anticipate in these soft-
spoken people.

"Have you proof?"

"I am one of his lieutenants, lord. I will testify to his guilt."

Pilate pursed his heavy lips. He could not afford to offend the Pharisees at this moment. They had given him enough trouble. Caiaphas, in particular, would be quick to cry "injustice" if he arrested the man.

"He claims to be the rightful king of the Jews, the descendant of David," said Judas, repeating what his master had told him to say.

"Does he?" Pilate looked thoughtfully out of the window.

"As for the Pharisees, lord . . ."

"What of them?"

"The Pharisees distrust him. They would see him dead. He speaks against them."

Pilate nodded. His eyes were hooded as he considered this information. The Pharisees might hate the madman, but they would be quick to make political capital out of his arrest.

"The Pharisees want him arrested," Judas continued. "The people flock to listen to the prophet and today many of them rioted in the Temple in his name."

"Is this true?"

"It is true, lord." It was true. Some half-a-dozen people had attacked the money-changers in the Temple and tried to rob them. When they had been arrested, they had said they had been carrying out the will of the Nazarene.

"I cannot make the arrest," Pilate said musingly. The situation in Jerusalem was already dangerous, but if they were to arrest this "king," they might find that they precipitated a revolt. Tiberius would blame him, not the Jews. The Pharisees must be won over. They must make the arrest. "Wait here," he said to Judas. "I will send a message to Caiaphas."

> *And they came to a place which was named Gethsemane: and he saith to his disciples, Sit ye here, while I shall pray. And he taketh with him Peter and James and John, and began to be sore amazed, and to be very heavy; And saith unto them, My soul is exceeding sorrowful unto death: tarry ye here, and watch.*
>
> (Mark 14: 32–34)

Glogauer could see the mob approaching now. For the first time since Nazareth he felt physically weak and exhausted. They were going to kill him. He had to die; he accepted that, but he was afraid of the pain that was to come. He sat down on the ground of the hillside, watching the torches as they came closer.

> *"The ideal of martyrdom only ever existed in the minds of a few ascetics," Monica had said. "Otherwise it was morbid masochism, an easy way to forgo ordinary responsibility, a method of keeping repressed people under control. . . ."*
> *"It isn't as simple as that. . . ."*
> *"It is, Karl."*

He could show Monica now. His regret was that she was unlikely ever to know. He had meant to write everything down and put it into the time machine and hope that it would be recovered. It was strange. He was not a religious man in the usual sense. He was an agnostic. It was not conviction that had led him to defend religion against Monica's cynical contempt for it; it was rather *lack* of conviction in the ideal in which she had set her own faith, the ideal of science as a solver of all problems. He could not share her faith and there was nothing else but religion, though he could not believe in the kind of God of Christianity. The God seen as a mystical force of the mysteries of Christianity and other great religions had not been personal enough for him. His rational mind had told him that God did not exist in any personal form. His unconscious had told him that faith in science was not enough.

"Science is basically opposed to religion,"
Monica had once said harshly. "No matter how
many Jesuits get together and rationalize their
views of science, the fact remains that religion
cannot accept the fundamental attitudes of science
and it is implicit to science to attack the funda-
mental principles of religion. The only area in
which there is no difference and need be no war
is in the ultimate assumption. One may or may
not assume there is a supernatural being called
God. But as soon as one begins to defend one's
assumption, there must be strife."
"You're talking about organized religion. . . ."
"I'm talking about religion as opposed to a be-
lief. Who needs the ritual of religion when we
have the far superior ritual of science to replace it?
Religion is a reasonable substitute for knowledge.
But there is no longer any need for substitutes,
Karl. Science offers a sounder basis on which to
formulate systems of thought and ethics. We don't

need the carrot of heaven and the big stick of hell
any more when science can show the consequences
of actions and men can judge easily for themselves
whether those actions are right or wrong."

"I can't accept it."

"That's because you're sick. I'm sick, too, but at
least I can see the promise of health."

"I can only see the threat of death. . . ."

As they had agreed, Judas kissed him on the cheek
and the mixed force of Temple guards and Roman
soldiers surrounded him.

To the Romans he said, with some difficulty, "I am
the King of the Jews." To the Pharisees' servants he
said: "I am the messiah who has come to destroy your
masters." Now he was committed and the final ritual
was to begin.

VII

It was an untidy trial, an arbitrary mixture of Roman
and Jewish law which did not altogether satisfy anyone. The object was accomplished after several conferences between Pontius Pilate and Caiaphas and three
attempts to bend and merge their separate legal systems in order to fit the expediencies of the situation.
Both needed a scapegoat for their different purposes
and so at last the result was achieved and the madman
convicted, on the one hand of rebellion against Rome
and on the other of heresy.

A peculiar feature of the trial was that the witnesses
were all followers of the man and yet had seemed eager
to see him convicted.

The Pharisees agreed that the Roman method of execution would fit the time and the situation best in this case and it was decided to crucify him. The man had prestige, however, so that it would be necessary to use some of the tried Roman methods of humiliation in order to make him into a pathetic and ludicrous figure in the eyes of the pilgrims. Pilate assured the Pharisees that he would see to it, but he made sure that they signed documents that gave their approval to his actions.

> And the soldiers led him away into the hall, called Praetorium; and they called together the whole band. And they clothed him with purple, and platted a crown of thorns, and put it about his head, And began to salute him, Hail, King of the Jews! And they smote him on the head with a reed, and did spit upon him, and bowing their knees worshiped him. And when they had mocked him, they took off the purple from him, and put his own clothes on him, and led him out to crucify him.
>
> (Mark 15: 16–20)

His brain was clouded now, by pain and by the ritual of humiliation; by his having completely given himself up to his rôle.

He was too weak to bear the heavy wooden cross and he walked behind it as it was dragged towards Golgotha by a Cyrenian whom the Romans had press-ganged for the purpose.

As he staggered through the crowded, silent streets, watched by those who had thought he would lead them against the Roman overlords, his eyes filled with tears so that his sight was blurred and he occasionally staggered off the road and was nudged back onto it by one of the Roman guards.

"You are too emotional, Karl. Why don't you use that brain of yours and pull yourself together? . . ."

He remembered the words, but it was difficult to remember who had said them or who Karl was.

The road that led up the side of the hill was stony and he slipped sometimes, remembering another hill he had climbed long ago. It seemed to him that he had been a child, but the memory merged with others and it was impossible to tell.

He was breathing heavily and with some difficulty. The pain of the thorns in his head was barely felt, but his whole body seemed to throb in unison with his heartbeat. It was like a drum.

It was evening. The sun was setting. He fell on his face, cutting his head on a sharp stone, just as he reached the top of the hill. He fainted.

And they bring him unto the place Golgotha, which is being interpreted, The place of the skull. And they gave him to drink wine mingled with myrrh: but he received it not.

(Mark 15: 22–23)

He knocked the cup aside. The soldier shrugged and reached out for one of his arms. Another soldier already held the other arm.

As he recovered consciousness Glogauer began to tremble violently. He felt the pain intensely as the ropes bit into the flesh of his wrists and ankles. He struggled.

He felt something cold placed against his palm. Although it only covered a small area in the center of his hand it seemed very heavy. He heard a sound that also was in rhythm with his heartbeats. He turned his head to look at the hand.

The large iron peg was being driven into his hand by a soldier swinging a mallet as he lay on the cross which was at this moment horizontal on the ground. He watched, wondering why there was no pain. The soldier swung the mallet higher as the peg met the resistance of the wood. Twice he missed the peg and struck Glogauer's fingers.

Glogauer looked to the other side and saw that the second soldier was also hammering in a peg. Evidently he missed the peg a great many times because the fingers of the hand were bloody and crushed.

The first soldier finished hammering in his peg and turned his attention to the feet. Glogauer felt the iron slide through his flesh, heard it hammered home.

Using a pulley, they began to haul the cross into a vertical position. Glogauer noticed that he was alone. There were no others being crucified that day.

He got a clear view of the lights of Jerusalem below him. There was still a little light in the sky but not much. Soon it would be completely dark. There was a small crowd looking on. One of the women reminded him of Monica. He called to her.

"Monica?"

But his voice was cracked and the word was a whisper. The woman did not look up.

He felt his body dragging at the nails which supported it. He thought he felt a twinge of pain in his left hand. He seemed to be bleeding very heavily.

It was odd, he reflected, that it should be him hanging here. He supposed that it was the event he had originally come to witness. There was little doubt, really. Everything had gone perfectly.

The pain in his left hand increased.

He glanced down at the Roman guards who were playing dice at the foot of his cross. They seemed absorbed in their game. He could not see the markings of the dice from this distance.

He sighed. The movement of his chest seemed to throw extra strain on his hands. The pain was quite bad now. He winced and tried somehow to ease himself back against the wood.

The pain began to spread through his body. He gritted his teeth. It was dreadful. He gasped and shouted. He writhed.

There was no longer any light in the sky. Heavy clouds obscured stars and moon.

From below came whispered voices.

"Let me down," he called. "Oh, please let me down!"

The pain filled him. He slumped forward, but nobody released him.

A little while later he raised his head. The movement caused a return of the agony and again he began to writhe on the cross.

"Let me down. Please. Please stop it!"

Every part of his flesh, every muscle and tendon and bone of him, was filled with an almost impossible degree of pain.

He knew he would not survive until the next day as he had thought he might. He had not realized the extent of his pain.

> *And at the ninth hour Jesus cried with a loud voice, saying, "Eloi, Eloi, lama sabachthani?" which is, being interpreted, My God, my God, why hast thou forsaken me?*
>
> (Mark 15: 34)

Glogauer coughed. It was a dry, barely heard sound. The soldiers below the cross heard it because the night was now so quiet.

"It's funny," one said. "Yesterday they were worshiping him. Today they seemed to want us to kill him—even the ones who were closest to him."

"I'll be glad when we get out of this country," said another.

He heard Monica's voice again. "It's weakness and fear, Karl, that's driven you to this. Martyrdom is a conceit. Can't you see that?"

Weakness and fear.

He coughed once more and the pain returned, but it was duller now.

Just before he died he began to talk again, muttering the words until his breath was gone. "It's a lie. It's a lie. It's a lie."

Later, after his body was stolen by the servants of

some doctors who believed it to have special proper-
ties, there were rumors that he had not died. But the
corpse was already rotting in the doctors' dissecting
rooms and would soon be destroyed.

3

RELIGIOUS INSTITUTIONS—
PAST

A Canticle for Leibowitz
WALTER M. MILLER, JR.

Within forty days after the crucifixion of Christ, his followers, inspired by their conviction that he had reappeared to them, were eager to proclaim his message. They traveled about Palestine filled with a real missionary spirit. Most vigorous of all the disciples in this missionary effort was Simon, also known as Peter. He traveled westward through Greece and on to Rome, carrying the message of a new Messiah who had arisen from the dead.

The other outstanding missionary was Paul. Born in Turkey, he was a Jew who went to study in Jerusalem, where he encountered and fought against the teachings of Christianity. Later, in A.D. 35 as he was riding to Damascus, he had the shattering mystical experience he describes in the New Testament, when a light flashed in the heavens, and he heard Jesus's voice speaking to him. He became the most ardent of the missionaries and is credited with the major part in organizing the early Church and developing its theology. From its small beginnings, the religion became a flourishing institution. Both Peter and Paul were killed in Rome about A.D. 65, but their deaths did not stop the growth of the Church in the Middle East and Southern Europe. The growth continued at a phenomenal rate. Constantinople in the East and Rome in the West became centers of the religion.

The Church grew into an institution that united individuals in their religious quest. It developed rituals, prayers, and dogmas that bound men together in a shared experience. The Church offered itself, without restriction, to all. No individual, or class, or nation was excluded. Even sinners were welcomed, and offered forgiveness. Its morality was brotherhood and peace. The Church is remarkable among institutions in its vigor and endurance for almost two thousand years.

After Rome's fall in A.D. 455, Europe lived in a confusion of fighting and political anarchy known as the Middle or Dark Ages. But the Holy Roman Church remained united and strong, and in its monasteries the knowledge of the Roman, Greek, and Jewish cultures was preserved. The Church became the keeper not only of religious knowledge, but all other knowledge. Printing had not yet been invented, so often monks made copies of texts by hand, and surely a simple monk must often have copied material whose meaning he did not understand.

"A Canticle for Leibowitz" is a story of a religious institution in another Dark Age, but one laid in a future time, one which follows a holocaust known as the Deluge of the Flame—apparently some kind of nuclear catastrophe. The scene of the story is the western desert of the United States, and we view the action through the eyes of Brother Francis, who is just seventeen when the story opens. He is young and simple, and there are many things he does not understand about his world. But he does not question the wisdom of those above him and is content to live in ignorance, not knowing. His faith is enough.

Although Brother Francis lives in a future world institution, all the details are those of a medieval abbey. He practices the prescribed ritual of fasting in the desert during Lent while he waits for his vocation to be revealed to him. He believes in relics, surviving fragments from the saints that possess magical power. The institution is authoritarian with a well-defined power structure extending from the Pope at the top to the lowest novice at the bottom. Each must remember his assigned place in the system and follow the prescribed dogma.

The Church in this future time—like the Holy Roman Church in the Middle Ages—is again the preserver of knowledge. But this time it is another kind of knowledge—the knowledge of Science. The population after the nuclear holocaust had turned against the scientist, and in the Age of Simplification, attacked them and burned their writings. The scientists had sometimes escaped by seeking shelter in the monasteries. Leibowitz, an electronics engineer, had been sheltered by the Holy Mother Church, and he eventually founded an abbey. Finally he was discovered and killed, but the abbey remained. Now, ages later, that earlier time is only known in myth and legend. There

are no remains, until the day—as the story opens—
when Brother Francis finds a mysterious relic in the
desert, a metal box that has survived from the age of
Leibowitz. What happens to that box and its finder,
Brother Francis, is the story of "A Canticle for
Leibowitz."

This is a very famous science fiction story, and de-
servedly so. It is full of irony. The reader, of course,
understands more than Brother Francis does. The
relics he brings out of the box are a puzzle to him, but
not to us. In this future world almost everything is
reversed from what we might expect. In actual history,
for the last two hundred years science and religion
have been at each other's throats; in contrast, in
Brother Francis's world the Church has become the
protector of the remains of science, and the electronics
engineer, Leibowitz, becomes elevated to sainthood.

The little monk, Brother Francis, is one of the most
lovable of all characters in science fiction. We know so
much more than he, but we never condemn him for his
lack of knowledge and his cheerful acceptance of his
world. When he first discovers the tin box of relics, he
is thrilled, and he reads without comprehension, but
with reverence, one of the papers in the box, which
contains a list of words: "Pound pastrami, can kraut,
six bagels, for Emma." He works for years patiently
making a beautiful and decorative copy of the blueprint named "Transistorized Control System for Unit
Six-B." He is inspired by the glory of the green vines,
golden fruit, and birds with which he decorates the
copy; and totally unconcerned with the fact that he has
no idea of what it means. His life is fulfilled when—
one marvelous day—he presents his document to the

Pope in New Vatican. And again, as we read the story, we know much more than he, but we do not laugh at his ignorance; rather we wonder if perhaps in his simplicity he might not be much wiser and happier than we. We want to sing a canticle, or song, for Brother Francis.

A Canticle for Leibowitz
WALTER M. MILLER, JR.

Brother Francis Gerard of Utah would never have discovered the sacred document, had it not been for the pilgrim with girded loins who appeared during that young monk's Lenten fast in the desert. Never before had Brother Francis actually seen a pilgrim with girded loins, but that this one was the bona fide article he was convinced at a glance. The pilgrim was a spindly old fellow with a staff, a basket hat, and a brushy beard, stained yellow about the chin. He walked with a limp and carried a small waterskin over one shoulder. His loins truly were girded with a ragged piece of dirty burlap, his only clothing except for hat and sandals. He whistled tunelessly on his way.

The pilgrim came shuffling down the broken trail out of the north, and he seemed to be heading toward the Brothers of Leibowitz Abbey six miles to the south. The pilgrim and the monk noticed each other across an expanse of ancient rubble. The pilgrim stopped whistling and stared. The monk, because of certain implications of the rule of solitude for fast days, quickly averted his gaze and continued about his business of hauling large rocks with which to complete the wolf-proofing of his temporary shelter. Somewhat weakened by a ten day diet of cactus fruit, Brother Francis found the work made him exceedingly dizzy; the landscape had been shimmering before his eyes and dancing with black specks, and he was at first uncertain that the bearded apparition was not a mirage induced by hunger, but after a moment it called to him cheerfully, *"Ola allay!"*

It was a pleasant musical voice.

The rule of silence forbade the young monk to answer, except by smiling shyly at the ground.

"Is this here the road to the abbey?" the wanderer asked.

The novice nodded at the ground and reached down for a chalk-like fragment of stone. The pilgrim picked his way toward him through the rubble. "What you doing with all the rocks?" he wanted to know.

The monk knelt and hastily wrote the words "Solitude & Silence" on a large flat rock, so that the pilgrim —if he could read, which was statistically unlikely— would know that he was making himself an occasion of sin for the penitent and would perhaps have the grace to leave in peace.

"Oh, well," said the pilgrim. He stood there for a moment, looking around, then rapped a certain large rock with his staff. *"That* looks like a handy crag for you," he offered helpfully, then added: "Well, good luck. And may you find a Voice, as y' seek."

Now Brother Francis had no immediate intuition that the stranger meant "Voice" with a capital V, but merely assumed that the old fellow had mistaken him for a deaf mute. He glanced up once again as the pilgrim shuffled away whistling, sent a swift silent benediction after him for safe wayfaring, and went back to his rock-work, building a coffin-sized enclosure in which he might sleep at night without offering himself as wolf-bait.

A sky-herd of cumulus clouds, on their way to bestow moist blessings on the mountains after having cruelly tempted the desert, offered welcome respite from the searing sunlight, and he worked rapidly to finish before they were gone again. He punctuated his labors with whispered prayers for the certainty of a true Vocation, for this was the purpose of his inward quest while fasting in the desert.

At last he hoisted the rock which the pilgrim had suggested.

The color of exertion drained quickly from his face. He backed away a step and dropped the stone as if he had uncovered a serpent.

A rusted metal box lay half-crushed in the rubble . . . only a rusted metal box.

He moved toward it curiously, then paused. There were things, and then there were Things. He crossed himself hastily, and muttered brief Latin at the heavens. Thus fortified, he readdressed himself to the box.

"*Apage Satanas!*"

He threatened it with the heavy crucifix of his rosary.

"Depart, O Foul Seductor!"

He sneaked a tiny aspergillum from his robes and quickly spattered the box with holy water before it could realize what he was about.

"If thou be creature of the Devil, begone!"

·The box showed no signs of withering, exploding, melting away. It exuded no blasphemous ichor. It only lay quietly in its place and allowed the desert wind to evaporate the sanctifying droplets.

"So be it," said the brother, and knelt to extract it from its lodging. He sat down on the rubble and spent nearly an hour battering it open with a stone. The thought crossed his mind that such an archeological relic—for such it obviously was—might be the Heaven-sent sign of his vocation but he suppressed the notion as quickly as it occurred to him. His abbot had warned him sternly against expecting any direct personal Revelation of a spectacular nature. Indeed, he had gone forth from the abbey to fast and do penance for 40 days that he might be rewarded with the inspiration of a calling to Holy Orders, but to expect a vision or a voice crying "Francis, where art thou?" would be a vain presumption. Too many novices had returned from their desert vigils with tales of omens and signs and visions in the heavens, and the good abbot had adopted a firm policy regarding these. Only the Vatican was qualified to decide the authenticity of such things. "An attack of sunstroke is no indication that you are fit to profess the solemn vows of the order," he had growled. And certainly it was true that only rarely did a call from Heaven come through any device other than the *inward* ear, as a gradual congealing of inner certainty.

Nevertheless, Brother Francis found himself handling the old metal box with as much reverence as was possible while battering at it.

It opened suddenly, spilling some of its contents. He stared for a long time before daring to touch, and a cool thrill gathered along his spine. Here was antiquity indeed! And as a student of archeology, he could scarcely believe his wavering vision. Brother Jeris would be frantic with envy, he thought, but quickly repented this unkindness and murmured his thanks to the sky for such a treasure.

He touched the articles gingerly—they were real enough—and began sorting through them. His studies had equipped him to recognize a screwdriver—an instrument once used for twisting threaded bits of metal into wood—and a pair of cutters with blades no longer than his thumbnail, but strong enough to cut soft bits of metal or bone. There was an odd tool with a rotted wooden handle and a heavy copper tip to which a few flakes of molten lead had adhered, but he could make nothing of it. There was a toroidal roll of gummy black stuff, too far deteriorated by the centuries for him to identify. There were strange bits of metal, broken glass, and an assortment of tiny tubular things with wire whiskers of the type prized by the hill pagans as charms and amulets, but thought by some archeologists to be remnants of the legendary *machina analytica*, supposedly dating back to the Deluge of Flame. All these and more he examined carefully and spread on the wide flat stone. The documents he saved until last. The documents, as always, were the real prize, for so few papers had survived the angry bonfires of the Age of Simplification, when even the sacred writings had curled and blackened and withered into smoke while ignorant crowds howled vengeance.

Two large folded papers and three hand-scribbled notes constituted his find. All were cracked and brittle with age, and he handled them tenderly, shielding them from the wind with his robe. They were scarcely legible and scrawled in the hasty characters of pre-Deluge English—a tongue now used, together with Latin, only by monastics and in the Holy Ritual. He spelled it out slowly, recognizing words but uncertain of meanings. One note said: *Pound pastrami, can kraut, six bagels, for Emma.* Another ordered: *Don't forget to pick up form 1040 for Uncle Revenue.* The third note was only a column of figures with a circled total from which another amount was subtracted and finally a percentage taken, followed by the word *damn!* From this he could deduce nothing, except to check the arithmetic, which proved correct.

Of the two larger papers, one was tightly rolled and began to fall to pieces when he tried to open it; he could make out the words RACING FORM, but nothing more. He laid it back in the box for later restorative work.

The second large paper was a single folded sheet, whose creases were so brittle that he could only inspect a little of it by parting the folds and peering between them as best he could.

A diagram . . . a web of white lines on dark paper!

Again the cool thrill gathered along his spine. It was a *blueprint*—that exceedingly rare class of ancient document most prized by students of antiquity, and usually most challenging to interpreters and searchers for meaning.

And, as if the find itself were not enough of a blessing, among the words written in a block at the lower corner of the document was the name of the founder of his order—of the Blessed Leibowitz *himself!*

His trembling hands threatened to tear the paper in

their happy agitation. The parting words of the pilgrim tumbled back to him: "May you find a Voice, as y' seek." Voice indeed, with V capitalized and formed by the wings of a descending dove and illuminated in three colors against a background of gold leaf. V as in *Vere dignum* and *Vidi aquam*, at the head of a page of the Missal. V, he saw quite clearly, as in Vocation.

He stole another glance to make certain it was so, then breathed, *"Beate Leibowitz, ora pro me. . . . Sancte Leibowitz, exaudi me,"* the second invocation being a rather daring one, since the founder of his order had not yet been declared a saint.

Forgetful of his abbot's warning, he climbed quickly to his feet and stared across the shimmering terrain to the south in the direction taken by the old wanderer of the burlap loincloth. But the pilgrim had long since vanished. Surely an angel of God, if not the Blessed Leibowitz himself, for had he not revealed this miraculous treasure by pointing out the rock to be moved and murmuring that prophetic farewell?

Brother Francis stood basking in his awe until the sun lay red on the hills and evening threatened to engulf him in its shadows. At last he stirred, and reminded himself of the wolves. His gift included no guarantee of charismata for subduing the wild beast, and he hastened to finish his enclosure before darkness fell on the desert. When the stars came out, he rekindled his fire and gathered his daily repast of the small purple cactus fruit, his only nourishment except the handful of parched corn brought to him by the priest each Sabbath. Sometimes he found himself staring hungrily at the lizards which scurried over the rocks, and was troubled by gluttonous nightmares.

But tonight his hunger was less troublesome than an impatient urge to run back to the abbey and announce his wondrous encounter to his brethren. This, of course, was unthinkable. Vocation or no, he must remain here until the end of Lent, and continue as if nothing extraordinary had occurred.

A *cathedral will be built upon this site*, he thought dreamily as he sat by the fire. He could see it rising from the rubble of the ancient village, magnificent spires visible for miles across the desert. . . .

But cathedrals were for teeming masses of people. The desert was home for only scattered tribes of huntsmen and the monks of the abbey. He settled in his dreams for a shrine, attracting rivers of pilgrims with girded loins. . . . He drowsed. When he awoke, the fire was reduced to glowing embers. Something seemed amiss. Was he quite alone? He blinked about at the darkness.

From beyond the bed of reddish coals, the dark wolf blinked back. The monk yelped and dived for cover.

The yelp, he decided as he lay trembling within his den of stones, had not been a serious breach of the rule of silence. He lay hugging the metal box and praying for the days of Lent to pass swiftly, while the sound of padded feet scratched about the enclosure.

Each night the wolves prowled about his camp, and the darkness was full of their howling. The days were glaring nightmares of hunger, heat, and scorching sun. He spent them at prayer and wood-gathering, trying to suppress his impatience for the coming of Holy Saturday's high noon, the end of Lent and of his vigil.

But when at last it came, Brother Francis found

himself too famished for jubilation. Wearily he packed his pouch, pulled up his cowl against the sun, and tucked his precious box beneath one arm. Thirty pounds lighter and several degrees weaker than he had been on Ash Wednesday, he staggered the six mile stretch to the abbey where he fell exhausted before its gates. The brothers who carried him in and bathed him and shaved him and anointed his desiccated tissues reported that he babbled incessantly in his delirium about an apparition in a burlap loincloth, addressing it at times as an angel and again as a saint, frequently invoking the name of Leibowitz and thanking him for a revelation of sacred relics and a racing form.

Such reports filtered through the monastic congregation and soon reached the ears of the abbot, whose eyes immediately narrowed to slits and whose jaw went rigid with the rock of policy.

"Bring him," growled that worthy priest in a tone that sent a recorder scurrying.

The abbot paced and gathered his ire. It was not that he objected to miracles, as such, if duly investigated, certified, and sealed; for miracles—even though always incompatible with administrative efficiency, and the abbot was administrator as well as priest—were the bedrock stuff on which his faith was founded. But last year there had been Brother Noyen with his miraculous hangman's noose, and the year before that, Brother Smirnov who had been mysteriously cured of the gout upon handling a probable relic of the Blessed Leibowitz, and the year before that . . . *Faugh!* The incidents had been too frequent and outrageous to tolerate. Ever since Leibowitz' beatification, the young fools had been sniffing around after shreds of the miraculous like a pack of good-natured hounds scratching eagerly at the back gate of Heaven for scraps.

It was quite understandable, but also quite unbearable. Every monastic order is eager for the canonization of its founder, and delighted to produce any bit of evidence to serve the cause in advocacy. But the abbot's flock was getting out of hand, and their zeal for miracles was making the Albertian Order of Leibowitz a laughing stock at New Vatican. He had determined to make any new bearers of miracles suffer the consequences, either as a punishment for impetuous and impertinent credulity, or as payment in penance for a gift of grace in case of later verification.

By the time the young novice knocked at his door, the abbot had projected himself into the desired state of carnivorous expectancy beneath a bland exterior.

"Come in, my son," he breathed softly.

"You sent for . . ." The novice paused, smiling happily as he noticed the familiar metal box on the abbot's table. ". . . for me, Father Juan?" he finished.

"Yes . . ." The abbot hesitated. His voice smiled with a withering acid, adding: "Or perhaps you would prefer that I come *to you*, hereafter, since you've become such a famous personage."

"Oh, no, Father!" Brother Francis reddened and gulped.

"You are seventeen, and plainly an idiot."

"That is undoubtedly true, Father."

"What improbable excuse can you propose for your outrageous vanity in believing yourself fit for Holy Orders?"

"I can offer none, my ruler and teacher. My sinful pride is unpardonable."

"To imagine that it is so great as to be unpardonable is even a vaster vanity," the priest roared.

"Yes, Father. I am indeed a worm."

The abbot smiled icily and resumed his watchful calm. "And you are now ready to deny your feverish ravings about an angel appearing to reveal to you this . . ." He gestured contemptuously at the box. ". . . this assortment of junk?"

Brother Francis gulped and closed his eyes. "I—I fear I cannot deny it, my master."

"What?"

"I cannot deny what I have seen, Father."

"Do you know what is going to happen to you now?"

"Yes, Father."

"Then prepare to take it!"

With a patient sigh, the novice gathered up his robes about his waist and bent over the table. The good abbot produced his stout hickory ruler from the drawer and whacked him soundly ten times across the bare buttocks. After each whack, the novice dutifully responded with a *"Deo Gratias!"* for this lesson in the virtue of humility.

"Do you *now* retract it?" the abbot demanded as he rolled down his sleeve.

"Father, I cannot."

The priest turned his back and was silent for a moment. "Very well," he said tersely. "Go. But do not expect to profess your solemn vows this season with the others."

Brother Francis returned to his cell in tears. His fellow novices would join the ranks of the professed monks of the order, while he must wait another year—

and spend another Lenten season among the wolves in the desert, seeking a vocation which he felt had already been granted to him quite emphatically. As the weeks passed, however, he found some satisfaction in noticing that Father Juan had not been entirely serious in referring to his find as "an assortment of junk." The archeological relics aroused considerable interest among the brothers, and much time was spent at cleaning the tools, classifying them, restoring the documents to a pliable condition, and attempting to ascertain their meaning. It was even whispered among the novices that Brother Francis had discovered true relics of the Blessed Leibowitz—especially in the form of the blueprint bearing the legend OP COBBLESTONE, REQ LEIBOWITZ & HARDIN, which was stained with several brown splotches which might have been his blood—or equally likely, as the abbot pointed out, might be stains from a decayed apple core. But the print was dated in the Year of Grace 1956, which was—as nearly as could be determined—during that venerable man's lifetime, a lifetime now obscured by legend and myth, so that it was hard to determine any but a few facts about the man.

It was said that God, in order to test mankind, had commanded wise men of that age, among them the Blessed Leibowitz, to perfect diabolic weapons and give them into the hands of latter-day Pharaohs. And with such weapons Man had, within the span of a few weeks, destroyed most of his civilization and wiped out a large part of the population. After the Deluge of Flame came the plagues, the madness, and the bloody inception of the Age of Simplification when the furious remnants of humanity had torn politicians, technicians, and men of learning limb from limb, and burned all records that might contain information that could once more lead into paths of destruction. Nothing had been so fiercely hated as the written word, the learned man. It was during this time that the word *simpleton* came to mean *honest, upright, virtuous citizen*, a concept once denoted by the term *common man*.

To escape the righteous wrath of the surviving simpletons, many scientists and learned men fled to the only sanctuary which would try to offer them protection. Holy Mother Church received them, vested them in monks' robes, tried to conceal them from the mobs. Sometimes the sanctuary was effective; more often it was not. Monasteries were invaded, records and sacred books were burned, refugees seized and hanged. Leibowitz had fled to the Cistercians, professed their vows, become a priest, and after twelve years had won permission from the Holy See to found a new monastic order to be called "the Albertians," after St. Albert the Great, teacher of Aquinas and patron saint of scientists. The new order was to be dedicated to the preservation of knowledge, secular and sacred, and the duty of the brothers was to memorize such books and papers as could be smuggled to them from all parts of the world. Leibowitz was at last identified by simpletons as a former scientist, and was martyred by hanging; but the order continued, and when it became safe again to possess written documents, many books were transcribed from memory. Precedence, however, had been given to sacred writings, to history, the humanities, and social sciences—since the memories of the memorizers were limited, and few of the brothers were trained to understand the physical sciences. From the vast store of human knowledge, only a pitiful collection of hand-written books remained.

Now, after six centuries of darkness, the monks still preserved it, studied it, re-copied it, and waited. It mattered not in the least to them that the knowledge they saved was useless—and some of it even incomprehensible. The knowledge was there, and it was their duty to save it, and it would still be with them if the darkness in the world lasted ten thousand years.

Brother Francis Gerard of Utah returned to the desert the following year and fasted again in solitude. Once more he returned, weak and emaciated, to be confronted by the abbot, who demanded to know if he claimed further conferences with members of the Heavenly Host, or was prepared to renounce his story of the previous year.

"I cannot help what I have seen, my teacher," the lad repeated.

Once more did the abbot chastise him in Christ, and once more did he postpone his profession. The document, however, had been forwarded to a seminary for study, after a copy had been made. Brother Francis remained a novice, and continued to dream wistfully of the shrine which might someday be built upon the site of his find.

"Stubborn boy!" fumed the abbot. "Why didn't somebody else see his silly pilgrim, if the slovenly fellow was heading for the abbey as he said? One more escapade for the Devil's Advocate to cry hoax about. Burlap loincloth indeed!"

The burlap had been troubling the abbot, for tradition related that Leibowitz had been hanged with a burlap bag for a hood.

Brother Francis spent seven years in the novitiate, seven Lenten vigils in the desert, and became highly proficient in the imitation of wolf-calls. For the amusement of his brethren, he would summon the pack to the vicinity of the abbey by howling from the walls after dark. By day, he served in the kitchen, scrubbed the stone floors, and continued his studies of the ancients.

Then one day a messenger from the seminary came riding to the abbey on an ass, bearing tidings of great joy. "It is known," said the messenger, "that the documents found near here are authentic as to date of origin, and that the blueprint was somehow connected with your founder's work. It's being sent to New Vatican for further study."

"Possibly a true relic of Leibowitz, then?" the abbot asked calmly.

But the messenger could not commit himself to that extent, and only raised a shrug of one eyebrow. "It is said that Leibowitz was a widower at the time of his ordination. If the name of his deceased wife could be discovered . . ."

The abbot recalled the note in the box concerning certain articles of food for a woman, and he too shrugged an eyebrow.

Soon afterwards, he summoned Brother Francis into his presence. "My boy," said the priest, actually beaming, "I believe the time has come for you to profess your solemn vows. And may I commend you for your patience and persistence. We shall speak no more of your, ah . . . encounter with the, ah, desert wanderer.

You are a good simpleton. You may kneel for my blessing, if you wish."

Brother Francis sighed and fell forward in a dead faint. The abbot blessed him and revived him, and he was permitted to profess the solemn vows of the Albertian Brothers of Leibowitz, swearing himself to perpetual poverty, chastity, obedience, and observance of the rule.

Soon afterwards, he was assigned to the copying room, apprentice under an aged monk named Horner, where he would undoubtedly spend the rest of his days illuminating the pages of algebra texts with patterns of olive leaves and cheerful cherubim.

"You have five hours a week," croaked his aged overseer, "which you may devote to an approved project of your own choosing, if you wish. If not, the time will be assigned to copying the *Summa Theologica* and such fragmentary copies of the Britannica as exist."

The young monk thought it over, then asked: "May I have the time for elaborating a beautiful copy of the Leibowitz blueprint?"

Brother Horner frowned doubtfully. "I don't know, son—our good abbot is rather sensitive on this subject. I'm afraid . . ."

Brother Francis begged him earnestly.

"Well, perhaps," the old man said reluctantly. "It seems like a rather brief project, so—I'll permit it."

The young monk selected the finest lambskin available and spent many weeks curing it and stretching it and stoning it to a perfect surface, bleached to a snowy whiteness. He spent more weeks at studying copies of his precious document in every detail, so that he knew each tiny line and marking in the complicated web of geometric markings and mystifying symbols. He pored over it until he could see the whole amazing complexity with his eyes closed. Additional weeks were spent searching painstakingly through the monastery's library for any information at all that might lead to some glimmer of understanding of the design.

Brother Jeris, a young monk who worked with him in the copy room and who frequently teased him about miraculous encounters in the desert, came to squint at it over his shoulder and asked: "What, pray, is the meaning of *Transistorized Control System for Unit Six-B?*"

"Clearly, it is the name of the thing which this diagram represents," said Francis, a trifle crossly since Jeris had merely read the title of the document aloud.

"Surely," said Jeris. "But what is the thing the diagram represents?"

"The transistorized control system for unit six-B, obviously."

Jeris laughed mockingly.

Brother Francis reddened. "I should imagine," said he, "that it represents an abstract concept, rather than a concrete *thing*. It's clearly not a recognizable picture of an object, unless the form is so stylized as to require special training to see it. In my opinion, *Transistorized Control System* is some high abstraction of transcendental value."

"Pertaining to what field of learning?" asked Jeris, still smiling smugly.

"Why . . ." Brother Francis paused. "Since our Beatus Leibowitz was an electronicist prior to his profession and ordination, I suppose the concept applies to the lost art called *electronics.*"

"So it is written. But what was the subject matter of that art, Brother?"

"That too is written. The subject matter of electronics was the Electron, which one fragmentary source defines as a Negative Twist of Nothingness."

"I am impressed by your astuteness," said Jeris. "Now perhaps you can tell me how to negate nothingness?"

Brother Francis reddened slightly and squirmed for a reply.

"A negation of nothingness should yield somethingness, I suppose," Jeris continued. "So the Electron must have been a twist of *something.* Unless the negation applies to the 'twist,' and then we would be 'Untwisting Nothing,' eh?" He chuckled. "How clever they must have been, these ancients. I suppose if you keep at it, Francis, you will learn how to untwist a nothing, and then we shall have the Electron in our midst. Where would we put it? On the high altar, perhaps?"

"I couldn't say," Francis answered stiffly. "But I have a certain faith that the Electron must have existed at one time, even though I can't say how it was constructed or what it might have been used for."

The iconoclast laughed mockingly and returned to his work. The incident saddened Francis, but did not turn him from his devotion to his project.

As soon as he had exhausted the library's meager supply of information concerning the lost art of the Albertians' founder, he began preparing preliminary sketches of the designs he meant to use on the lamb-skin. The diagram itself, since its meaning was obscure, would be redrawn precisely as it was in the blueprint, and penned in coal-black lines. The lettering and numbering, however, he would translate into a more decorative and colorful script than the plain block letters used by the ancients. And the text contained in a square block marked SPECIFICATIONS would be distributed pleasingly around the borders of the document, upon scrolls and shields supported by doves and cherubim. He would make the black lines of the diagram less stark and austere by imagining the geometric tracery to be a trellis, and decorate it with green vines and golden fruit, birds and perhaps a wily serpent. At the very top would be a representation of the Triune God, and at the bottom the coat of arms of the Albertian Order. Thus was the Transistorized Control System of the Blessed Leibowitz to be glorified and rendered appealing to the eye as well as to the intellect.

When he had finished the preliminary sketch, he showed it shyly to Brother Horner for suggestions or approval. "I can see," said the old man a bit remorsefully, "that your project is not to be as brief as I had hoped. But . . . continue with it anyhow. The design is beautiful, beautiful indeed."

"Thank you, Brother."

The old man leaned close to wink confidentially. "I've heard the case for Blessed Leibowitz' canonization has been speeded up, so possibly our dear abbot is less troubled by you-know-what than he previously was."

The news of the speed-up was, of course, happily received by all monastics of the order. Leibowitz' beatification had long since been effected, but the final step in declaring him to be a saint might require many more years, even though the case was under way; and indeed there was the possibility that the Devil's Advocate might uncover evidence to prevent the canonization from occurring at all.

Many months after he had first conceived the project, Brother Francis began actual work on the lamb-skin. The intricacies of scrollwork, the excruciatingly delicate work of inlaying the gold leaf, the hair-fine detail, made it a labor of years; and when his eyes began to trouble him, there were long weeks when he dared not touch it at all for fear of spoiling it with one little mistake. But slowly, painfully, the ancient diagram was becoming a blaze of beauty. The brothers of the abbey gathered to watch and murmur over it, and some even said that the inspiration of it was proof enough of his alleged encounter with the pilgrim who might have been Blessed Leibowitz.

"I can't see why you don't spend your time on a *useful* project," was Brother Jeris' comment, however. The skeptical monk had been using his own free-project time to make and decorate sheepskin shades for the oil lamps in the chapel.

Brother Horner, the old master copyist, had fallen ill. Within weeks, it became apparent that the well-loved monk was on his deathbed. In the midst of the monastery's grief, the abbot quietly appointed Brother Jeris as master of the copy room.

A Mass of Burial was chanted early in Advent, and the remains of the holy old man were committed to the earth of their origin. On the following day, Brother Jeris informed Brother Francis that he considered it about time for him to put away the things of a child and start doing a man's work. Obediently, the monk wrapped his precious project in parchment, protected it with heavy board, shelved it, and began producing sheepskin lampshades. He made no murmur of protest, and contented himself with realizing that someday the soul of Brother Jeris would depart by the same road as that of Brother Horner, to begin the life for which this copy room was but the staging ground; and afterwards, please God, he might be allowed to complete his beloved document.

Providence, however, took an earlier hand in the matter. During the following summer, a monsignor with several clerks and a donkey train came riding into the abbey and announced that he had come from New Vatican, as Leibowitz' advocate in the canonization proceedings, to investigate such evidence as the abbey could produce that might have bearing on the case, including an alleged apparition of the beatified which had come to one Francis Gerard of Utah.

The gentleman was warmly greeted, quartered in the suite reserved for visiting prelates, lavishly served by six young monks responsive to his every whim, of which he had very few. The finest wines were opened, the huntsman snared the plumpest quail and chaparral cocks, and the advocate was entertained each evening by fiddlers and a troupe of clowns, although the visitor persisted in insisting that life go on as usual at the abbey.

On the third day of his visit, the abbot sent for Brother Francis. "Monsignor di Simone wishes to see you," he said. "If you let your imagination run away with you, boy, we'll use your gut to string a fiddle, feed

your carcass to the wolves, and bury the bones in un-
hallowed ground. Now get along and see the good
gentleman."

Brother Francis needed no such warning. Since he
had awakened from his feverish babblings after his first
Lenten fast in the desert, he had never mentioned the
encounter with the pilgrim except when asked about it,
nor had he allowed himself to speculate any further
concerning the pilgrim's identity. That the pilgrim
might be a matter for high ecclesiastical concern frightened him a little, and his knock was timid at the monsignor's door.

His fright proved unfounded. The monsignor was a
suave and diplomatic elder who seemed keenly interested in the small monk's career.

"Now about your encounter with our blessed founder," he said after some minutes of preliminary amenities.

"Oh, but I never said he was our Blessed Leibo—"

"Of course you didn't, my son. Now I have here an
account of it, as gathered from other sources, and I
would like you to read it, and either confirm it or correct it." He paused to draw a scroll from his case and
handed it to Francis. "The sources for this version, of
course, had it on hearsay only," he added, "and only
you can describe it first hand, so I want you to edit it
most scrupulously."

"Of course. What happened was really very simple,
Father."

But it was apparent from the fatness of the scroll
that the hearsay account was not so simple. Brother
Francis read with mounting apprehension which soon
grew to the proportions of pure horror.

"You look white, my son. Is something wrong?" asked the distinguished priest.

"This . . . this . . . it wasn't like this *at all!*" gasped Francis. "He didn't say more than a few words to me. I only saw him once. He just asked me the way to the abbey and tapped the rock where I found the relics."

"No heavenly choir?"

"Oh, no!"

"And it's not true about the nimbus and the carpet of roses that grew up along the road where he walked?"

"As God is my judge, nothing like that happened at all!"

"Ah, well," sighed the advocate. "Travelers' stories are always exaggerated."

He seemed saddened, and Francis hastened to apologize, but the advocate dismissed it as of no great importance to the case. "There are other miracles, carefully documented," he explained, "and anyway—there is one bit of good news about the documents you discovered. We've unearthed the name of the wife who died before our founder came to the order."

"Yes?"

"Yes. It was Emily."

Despite his disappointment with Brother Francis' account of the pilgrim, Monsignor di Simone spent five days at the site of the find. He was accompanied by an eager crew of novices from the abbey, all armed with picks and shovels. After extensive digging, the advocate returned with a small assortment of additional artifacts, and one bloated tin can that contained a desiccated mess which might once have been sauerkraut.

Before his departure, he visited the copy room and

asked to see Brother Francis' copy of the famous blue-print. The monk protested that it was really nothing, and produced it with such eagerness his hands trembled.

"Zounds!" said the monsignor, or an oath to such effect. "Finish it, man, finish it!"

The monk looked smilingly at Brother Jeris. Brother Jeris swiftly turned away; the back of his neck gathered color. The following morning, Francis resumed his labors over the illuminated blueprint, with gold leaf, quills, brushes, and dyes.

And then came another donkey train from New Vatican, with a full complement of clerks and armed guards for defense against highwaymen, this time headed by a monsignor with small horns and pointed fangs (or so several novices would later have testified), who announced that he was the *Advocatus Diaboli*, opposing Leibowitz' canonization, and he was here to investigate—and perhaps fix responsibility, he hinted —for a number of incredible and hysterical rumors filtering out of the abbey and reaching even high officials at New Vatican. He made it clear that he would tolerate no romantic nonsense.

The abbot greeted him politely and offered him an iron cot in a cell with a south exposure, after apologizing for the fact that the guest suite had been recently exposed to smallpox. The monsignor was attended by his own staff, and ate mush and herbs with the monks in refectory.

"I understand you are susceptible to fainting spells," he told Brother Francis when the dread time came. "How many members of your family have suffered from epilepsy or madness?"

"None, Excellency."

"I'm not an 'Excellency,'" snapped the priest. "Now we're going to get the truth out of you." His tone implied that he considered it to be a simple straightforward surgical operation which should have been performed years ago.

"Are you aware that documents can be aged artificially?" he demanded.

Francis was not so aware.

"Did you know that Leibowitz' wife was named Emily, and that Emma is *not* a diminutive for Emily?"

Francis had not known it, but recalled from childhood that his own parents had been rather careless about what they called each other. "And if Blessed Leibowitz chose to call her Emma, then I'm sure . . ."

The monsignor exploded, and tore into Francis with semantic tooth and nail, and left the bewildered monk wondering whether he had ever really seen a pilgrim at all.

Before the advocate's departure, he too asked to see the illuminated copy of the print, and this time the monk's hands trembled with fear as he produced it, for he might again be forced to quit the project. The monsignor only stood gazing at it, however, swallowed slightly, and forced himself to nod. "Your imagery is vivid," he admitted, "but then, of course, we all knew that, didn't we?"

The monsignor's horns immediately grew shorter by an inch, and he departed the same evening for New Vatican.

The years flowed smoothly by, seaming the faces of the once young and adding gray to the temples. The perpetual labors of the monastery continued, supplying a slow trickle of copied and re-copied manuscript to the outside world. Brother Jeris developed ambitions of building a printing press, but when the abbot demanded his reasons, he could only reply, "So we can mass-produce."

"Oh? And in a world that's smug in its illiteracy, what do you intend to do with the stuff? Sell it as kindling paper to the peasants?"

Brother Jeris shrugged unhappily, and the copy room continued with pot and quill.

Then one spring, shortly before Lent, a messenger arrived with glad tidings for the order. The case for Leibowitz was complete. The College of Cardinals would soon convene, and the founder of the Albertian Order would be enrolled in the Calendar of Saints. During the time of rejoicing that followed the announcement, the abbot—now withered and in his dotage—summoned Brother Francis into his presence, and wheezed:

"His Holiness commands your presence during the canonization of Isaac Edward Leibowitz. Prepare to leave.

"Now don't faint on me again," he added querulously.

The trip to New Vatican would take at least three months, perhaps longer, the time depending on how far Brother Francis could get before the inevitable robber band relieved him of his ass, since he would be going unarmed and alone. He carried with him only a begging bowl and the illuminated copy of the Leibowitz print, praying that ignorant robbers would have no use for the latter. As a precaution, however, he wore a black patch over his right eye, for the peasants, being a superstitious lot, could often be put to flight by even a hint of the evil eye. Thus armed and equipped, he set out to obey the summons of his high priest.

Two months and some odd days later he met his robber on a mountain trail that was heavily wooded and far from any settlement. His robber was a short man, but heavy as a bull, with a glazed knob of a pate and a jaw like a block of granite. He stood in the trail with his legs spread wide and his massive arms folded across his chest, watching the approach of the little figure on the ass. The robber seemed alone, and armed only with a knife which he did not bother to remove from his belt thong. His appearance was a disappointment, since Francis had been secretly hoping for another encounter with the pilgrim of long ago.

"Get off," said the robber.

The ass stopped in the path. Brother Francis tossed back his cowl to reveal the eye-patch, and raised a trembling finger to touch it. He began to lift the patch slowly as if to reveal something hideous that might be hidden beneath it. The robber threw back his head and laughed a laugh that might have sprung from the throat of Satan himself. Francis muttered an exorcism, but the robber seemed untouched.

"You black-sacked jeebers wore that one out years ago," he said. "Get off."

Francis smiled, shrugged, and dismounted without protest.

"A good day to you, sir," he said pleasantly. "You may take the ass. Walking will improve my health, I think." He smiled again and started away.

"Hold it," said the robber. "Strip to the buff. And let's see what's in that package."

Brother Francis touched his begging bowl and made a helpless gesture, but this brought only another scornful laugh from the robber.

"I've seen that alms-pot trick before too," he said. "The last man with a begging bowl had half a heklo of gold in his boot. Now strip."

Brother Francis displayed his sandals, but began to strip. The robber searched his clothing, found nothing, and tossed it back to him.

"Now let's see inside the package."

"It is only a document, sir," the monk protested. "Of value to no one but its owner."

"Open it."

Silently Brother Francis obeyed. The gold leaf and the colorful design flashed brilliantly in the sunlight that filtered through the foliage. The robber's craggy jaw dropped an inch. He whistled softly.

"What a pretty! Now wouldn't me woman like it to hang on the shanty wall!"

He continued to stare while the monk went slowly sick inside. *If Thou hast sent him to test me, O Lord,* he pleaded inwardly, *then help me to die like a man, for he'll get it over the dead body of Thy servant, if take it he must.*

"Wrap it up for me," the robber commanded, clamping his jaw in sudden decision.

The monk whimpered softly. "Please, sir, you would not take the work of a man's lifetime. I spent fifteen years illuminating this manuscript, and . . ."

"Well! Did it yourself, did you?" The robber threw back his head and howled again.

Francis reddened. "I fail to see the humor, sir . . ."

The robber pointed at it between guffaws. "You! Fifteen years to make a paper bauble. So that's what you do. Tell me why. Give me one good reason. For fifteen years. Ha!"

Francis stared at him in stunned silence and could think of no reply that would appease his contempt.

Gingerly, the monk handed it over. The robber took it in both hands and made as if to rip it down the center.

"*Jesus, Mary, Joseph!*" the monk screamed, and went to his knees in the trail. "For the love of God, sir!"

Softening slightly, the robber tossed it on the ground with a snicker. "Wrestle you for it."

"Anything, sir, anything!"

They squared off. The monk crossed himself and recalled that wrestling had once been a divinely sanctioned sport—and with grim faith, he marched into battle.

Three seconds later, he lay groaning on the flat of his back under a short mountain of muscle. A sharp rock seemed to be severing his spine.

"Heh, heh," said the robber, and arose to claim his document.

Hands folded as if in prayer, Brother Francis scurried after him on his knees, begging at the top of his lungs.

The robber turned to snicker. "I believe you'd kiss a boot to get it back."

Francis caught up with him and fervently kissed his boot.

This proved too much for even such a firm fellow as

the robber. He flung the manuscript down again with a curse and climbed aboard the monk's donkey. The monk snatched up the precious document and trotted along beside the robber, thanking him profusely and blessing him repeatedly while the robber rode away on the ass. Francis sent a glowing cross of benediction after the departing figure and praised God for the existence of such selfless robbers.

And yet when the man had vanished among the trees, he felt an aftermath of sadness. Fifteen years to make a paper bauble . . . The taunting voice still rang in his ears. Why? Tell one good reason for fifteen years.

He was unaccustomed to the blunt ways of the outside world, to its harsh habits and curt attitudes. He found his heart deeply troubled by the mocking words, and his head hung low in the cowl as he plodded along. At one time he considered tossing the document in the brush and leaving it for the rains—but Father Juan had approved his taking it as a gift, and he could not come with empty hands. Chastened, he traveled on.

The hour had come. The ceremony surged about him as a magnificent spectacle of sound and stately movement and vivid color in the majestic basilica. And when the perfectly infallible Spirit had finally been invoked, a monsignor—it was di Simone, Francis noticed, the advocate for the saint—arose and called upon Peter to speak, through the person of Leo XXII, commanding the assemblage to hearken.

Whereupon, the Pope quietly proclaimed that Isaac Edward Leibowitz was a saint, and it was finished. The ancient and obscure technician was of the heavenly hagiarchy, and Brother Francis breathed a dutiful prayer to his new patron as the choir burst into the *Te Deum.*

The Pontiff strode quickly into the audience room where the little monk was waiting, taking Brother Francis by surprise and rendering him briefly speechless. He knelt quickly to kiss the Fisherman's ring and receive the blessing. As he arose, he found himself clutching the beautiful document behind him as if ashamed of it. The Pope's eyes caught the motion, and he smiled.

"You have brought us a gift, our son?" he asked.

The monk gulped, nodded stupidly, and brought it out. Christ's Vicar stared at it for a long time without apparent expression. Brother Francis' heart went sinking deeper as the seconds drifted by.

"It is a nothing," he blurted, "a miserable gift. I am ashamed to have wasted so much time at . . ." He choked off.

The Pope seemed not to hear him. "Do you understand the meaning of Saint Isaac's symbology?" he asked, peering curiously at the abstract design of the circuit.

"Whatever it means . . ." the Pope began, but broke off. He smiled and spoke of other things. Francis had been so honored not because of any official judgment concerning his pilgrim. He had been honored for his role in bringing to light such important documents and relics of the saint, for such they had been judged, regardless of the manner in which they had been found.

Francis stammered his thanks. The Pontiff gazed again at the colorful blaze of his illuminated diagram. "Whatever it means," he breathed once more, "this bit of learning, though dead, will live again." He smiled up at the monk and winked. "And we shall guard it till that day."

For the first time, the little monk noticed that the Pope had a hole in his robe. His clothing, in fact, was threadbare. The carpet in the audience room was worn through in spots, and plaster was falling from the ceiling.

But there were books on the shelves along the walls. Books of painted beauty, speaking of incomprehensible things, copied by men whose business was not to understand but to save. And the books were waiting.

"Goodby, beloved son."

And the small keeper of the flame of knowledge trudged back toward his abbey on foot. His heart was singing as he approached the robber's outpost. And if the robber happened to be taking the day off, the monk meant to sit down and wait for his return. This time he had an answer.

4

RELIGIOUS INSTITUTIONS—
FUTURE

Good News from the Vatican
ROBERT SILVERBERG

"Good News from the Vatican" is a lighthearted story about the Catholic Church in the future. But in its humor it raises some serious points about the future of religious institutions. In the Church's long history of survival, it has never been faced with the accelerating social changes it is asked to cope with today.

A religious institution has both strengths and weaknesses. It has the advantage of assuring permanence and a continuity with the past. It is the preserver of patterns and customs that create a sense of tradition with which the individual believer can unite. This enlarged sense of unity not only roots the individual in the past, but also gives him a sense of belonging and fellowship with all other individuals in the present who participate in the religious institution. Out of this sense of oneness can come a larger harmony and sense of community.

The disadvantage is that an institution tends to maintain the status quo, and do things the way they have been done before. So it is resistant to change. It also requires a degree of conformity from its members. They must fit into the established system and accept the same patterns. Individuality is discouraged. As a result substantial numbers of people—who do not fit the conventional mold—will be unhappy with the system. This is particularly true of a time like the present when individual expression is permitted and encouraged in society.

Two rituals, or repeated patterns of expression in religious institutions, are mentioned in the story, and they illustrate both the strengths and weaknesses of such rituals. They are both rites of passage—the passing from one state to another. One is the Bar Mitzvah, the celebration of the passage from childhood to manhood of the Jewish male at age thirteen. He formally joins the community in this ceremony. The rabbi in the story refuses to perform the ritual because he claims it has become so lavish as to be vulgar and meaningless. Its original intent has been lost.

The second rite of passage is the transference of leadership from one Pope to the next. The problem of succession is always a difficult one, whether the institution is political or religious. In the Catholic Church an elaborate ritual has evolved for the choosing of a new Pope, and the details of this ceremony are accurately portrayed in the story. The narrator of the story, watching the ritual and experiencing the satisfaction of sharing in a tradition that has been carried on for centuries, says, "The system has agreeable resonances. I like it."

The story incorporates a sense of ecumenism—the worldwide sharing of religious experience. A Jewish rabbi and a Catholic bishop sit with the narrator and his friends in an outdoor cafe near St. Peter's Square in Rome. They talk about the new Pope, who—if elected —plans a computer-sharing program with the head programmer of the Greek Orthodox Church and the Dalai Lama of the Buddhist faith in Tibet. Such ecumenism seems a certain religious trend of the future.

Another trend in the future that is discussed in the story is the increasing use of the computer. It was first developed during World War II, and its increasing use in many areas of our society in less than thirty years has been phenomenal. As the computer has developed in the direction of artificial intelligence, man has been pushed to define the ways in which he is like and unlike a machine. Isaac Asimov in *I, Robot* presents one of the most perceptive explorations of artificial intelligence and its potential in science fiction literature.[1]

"Good News from the Vatican" also points up the increasing difficulty of functioning as the head of a large institution. The task of being Pope is overwhelming. The amount of knowledge now required to make intelligent decisions—as the head of the Church must —begins to exceed human capacity. While the Pope in the future will not be a computer, he will need to utilize a computer for storing and processing information, which will lead to better decision-making. The computer can do some things that man cannot do; it has a more extensive memory capacity, and it can rapidly solve differential equations. But it is only a tool for man to use, not a replacement for man. It can only do what man tells it to do.

Finally, "Good News from the Vatican" assumes that a highly organized and bureaucratic religious institution can survive in the future. This is an assumption open to question when the crisis of the Catholic Church in the sixties and seventies is viewed. It has not so far been responsive to the threat of world overpopulation, nor to altering concepts of marriage and the equality of women. The ability of the Church, or any large institution, to respond to rapid social change is being tested today.

The struggle to select a new Pope portrayed in this story is a political act. Such political struggles have produced all kinds of winners, some deserving, some not, but never one quite like this winner.

[1] Isaac Asimov, *I, Robot* (New York: Doubleday, 1967).

Good News from the Vatican
ROBERT SILVERBERG

This is the morning everyone has waited for, when at last the robot cardinal is to be elected Pope. There can no longer be any doubt of the outcome. The conclave has been deadlocked for many days between the obstinate advocates of Cardinal Asciuga of Milan and Cardinal Carciofo of Genoa, and word has gone out that a compromise is in the making. All factions now are agreed on the selection of the robot. This morning I read in *Osservatore Romano* that the Vatican computer itself has taken a hand in the deliberations. The computer has been strongly urging the candidacy of the robot. I suppose we should not be surprised by this loyalty among machines. Nor should we let it distress us. We *absolutely must not* let it distress us.

"Every era gets the Pope it deserves," Bishop Fitz-Patrick observed somewhat gloomily today at breakfast. "The proper Pope for our times is a robot, certainly. At some future date it may be desirable for the Pope to be a whale, an automobile, a cat, a mountain." Bishop FitzPatrick stands well over two meters in height and his normal facial expression is a morbid, mournful one. Thus it is impossible for us to determine whether any particular pronouncement of his reflects existential despair or placid acceptance. Many years ago he was a star player for the Holy Cross championship basketball team. He has come to Rome to do research for a biography of St. Marcellus the Righteous.

We have been watching the unfolding drama of the papal election from an outdoor cafe several blocks from the Square of St. Peter's. For all of us, this has been an unexpected dividend of our holiday in Rome; the previous Pope was reputed to be in good health and there was no reason to suspect that a successor would have to be chosen for him this summer.

Each morning we drive across by taxi from our hotel near the Via Veneto and take up our regular positions around "our" table. From where we sit, we all have a clear view of the Vatican chimney through which the smoke of the burning ballots rises: black smoke if no Pope has been elected, white if the conclave has been

successful. Luigi, the owner and head waiter, automatically brings us our preferred beverages: fernet
branca for Bishop FitzPatrick, campari and soda for
Rabbi Mueller, Turkish coffee for Miss Harshaw,
lemon squash for Kenneth and Beverly, and pernod on
the rocks for me. We take turns paying the check,
although Kenneth has not paid it even once since our
vigil began. Yesterday, when Miss Harshaw paid, she
emptied her purse and found herself 350 lire short; she
had nothing else except hundred-dollar travelers'
checks. The rest of us looked pointedly at Kenneth but
he went on calmly sipping his lemon squash. After a
brief period of tension Rabbi Mueller produced a 500-
lire coin and rather irascibly slapped the heavy silver
piece against the table. The rabbi is known for his
short temper and vehement style. He is 28 years old,
customarily dresses in a fashionable plaid cassock and
silvered sunglasses, and frequently boasts that he has
never performed a bar mitzvah ceremony for his congregation, which is in Wicomico County, Maryland. He
believes that the rite is vulgar and obsolete, and invariably farms out all his bar mitzvahs to a franchised
organization of itinerant clergymen who handle such
affairs on a commission basis. Rabbi Mueller is an
authority on angels.

Our group is divided over the merits of electing a
robot as the new Pope. Bishop FitzPatrick, Rabbi
Mueller and I are in favor of the idea. Miss Harshaw,
Kenneth and Beverly are opposed. It is interesting to
note that both of our gentlemen of the cloth, one quite
elderly and one fairly young, support this remarkable
departure from tradition. Yet the three "swingers"
among us do not.

I am not sure why I align myself with the progressives. I am a man of mature years and fairly sedate ways. Nor have I ever concerned myself with the doings of the Church of Rome. I am unfamiliar with Catholic dogma and unaware of recent currents of thought within the Church. Still, I have been hoping for the election of the robot since the start of the conclave.

Why, I wonder? Is it because the image of a metal creature upon the Throne of St. Peter's stimulates my imagination and tickles my sense of the incongruous? That is, is my support of the robot purely an esthetic matter? Or is it, rather, a function of my moral cowardice? Do I secretly think that this gesture will buy the robots off? Am I privately saying, Give them the papacy and maybe they won't want other things for a while? No. I can't believe anything so unworthy of myself. Possibly I am for the robot because I am a person of unusual sensitivity to the needs of others.

"If he's elected," says Rabbi Mueller, "he plans an immediate time-sharing agreement with the Dalai Lama and a reciprocal plug-in with the head programmer of the Greek Orthodox Church, just for starters. I'm told he'll make ecumenical overtures to the Rabbinate as well, which is certainly something for all of us to look forward to."

"I don't doubt that there'll be many corrections in the customs and practices of the hierarchy," Bishop FitzPatrick declares. "For example we can look forward to superior information-gathering techniques as the Vatican computer is given a greater role in the operations of the Curia. Let me illustrate by—"

"What an utterly ghastly notion," Kenneth says. He is a gaudy young man with white hair and pink eyes. Beverly is either his wife or his sister. She rarely speaks. Kenneth makes the sign of the Cross with offensive brusqueness and murmurs, "In the name of the Father, the Son, and the Holy Automaton." Miss Harshaw giggles but chokes the giggle off when she sees my disapproving face.

Dejectedly, but not responding at all to the interruption, Bishop FitzPatrick continues, "Let me illustrate by giving you some figures I obtained yesterday afternoon. I read in the newspaper *Oggi* that during the last five years, according to a spokesman for the *Missiones Catholicae*, the Church has increased its membership in Yugoslavia from 19,381,403 to 23,501,062. But the government census taken last year gives the total population of Yugoslavia at 23,575,194. That leaves only 74,132 for the other religious and irreligious bodies. Aware of the large Moslem population of Yugoslavia, I suspected an inaccuracy in the published statistics and consulted the computer in St. Peter's, which informed me"—the bishop, pausing, produces a lengthy printout and unfolds it across much of the table—"that the last count of the Faithful in Yugoslavia, made a year and a half ago, places our numbers at 14,206,198. Therefore an overstatement of 9,294,864 has been made. Which is absurd. And perpetuated. Which is damnable."

"What does he look like?" Miss Harshaw asks. "Does anyone have any idea?"

"He's like all the rest," says Kenneth. "A shiny metal box with wheels below and eyes on top."

"You haven't seen him," Bishop FitzPatrick interjects. "I don't think it's proper for you to assume that—"

"They're all alike," Kenneth says. "Once you've seen one, you've seen all of them. Shiny boxes. Wheels. Eyes. And voices coming out of their bellies like mechanized belches. Inside, they're all too much for me to accept. Let's have another round of drinks, shall we?"

Rabbi Mueller says, "It so happens that I've seen him with my own eyes."

"You *have?*" Beverly exclaims.

Kenneth scowls at her. Luigi, approaching, brings a tray of new drinks for everyone. I hand him a 5000-lire note. Rabbi Mueller removes his sunglasses and breathes on their brilliantly reflective surfaces. He has small, watery gray eyes and a bad squint. He says, "The cardinal was the keynote speaker at the Congress of World Jewry that was held last fall in Beirut. His theme was 'Cybernetic Ecumenicism for Contemporary Man.' I was there. I can tell you that His Eminence is tall and distinguished, with a fine voice and a gentle smile. There's something inherently melancholy about his manner that reminds me greatly of our friend the bishop, here. His movements are graceful and his wit is keen."

"But he's mounted on wheels, isn't he?" Kenneth persists.

"On treads," replies the rabbi, giving Kenneth a fiery, devastating look and resuming his sunglasses. "Treads, like a tractor has. But I don't think that treads are spiritually inferior to feet, or, for that matter, to wheels. If I were a Catholic I'd be proud to have a man like that as my Pope."

"Not a man," Miss Harshaw puts in. A giddy edge enters her voice whenever she addresses Rabbi Mueller. "A robot," she says. "He's not a man, remember?"

"A *robot* like that as my Pope, then," Rabbi Mueller says, shrugging at the correction. He raises his glass. "To the new Pope!"

"To the new Pope!" cries Bishop FitzPatrick.

Luigi comes rushing from his cafe. Kenneth waves him away. "Wait a second," Kenneth says. "The election isn't over yet. How can you be so sure?"

"The *Osservatore Romano*," I say, "indicates in this morning's edition that everything will be decided today. Cardinal Carciofo has agreed to withdraw in his favor, in return for a larger real-time allotment when the new computer hours are decreed at next year's consistory."

"In other words, the fix is in," Kenneth says.

Bishop FitzPatrick sadly shakes his head. "You state things much too harshly, my son. For three weeks now we have been without a Holy Father. It is God's Will that we shall have a Pope; the conclave, unable to choose between the candidacies of Cardinal Carciofo and Cardinal Asciuga, thwarts that Will; if necessary, therefore, we must make certain accommodations with the realities of the times so that His Will shall not be further frustrated. Prolonged politicking within the conclave now becomes sinful. Cardinal Carciofo's sacrifice of his personal ambitions is not as self-seeking an act as you would claim."

Kenneth continues to attack poor Carciofo's motives for withdrawing. Beverly occasionally applauds his cruel sallies. Miss Harshaw several times declares her unwillingness to remain a communicant of a Church

whose leader is a machine. I find this dispute distasteful and swing my chair away from the table to have a
better view of the Vatican. At this moment the cardinals are meeting in the Sistine Chapel. How I wish I
were there! What splendid mysteries are being enacted
in that gloomy, magnificent room! Each prince of the
Church now sits on a small throne surmounted by a
violet-hued canopy. Fat wax tapers glimmer on the
desk before each throne. Masters-of-ceremonies move
solemnly through the vast chamber, carrying the silver
basins in which the blank ballots repose. These basins
are placed on the table before the altar. One by one the
cardinals advance to the table, take ballots, return to
their desks. Now, lifting their quill pens, they begin to
write. "I, Cardinal——, elect to the Supreme Pontifi-
cate the Most Reverend Lord my Lord Cardinal——."
What name do they fill in? Is it Carciofo? Is it
Asciuga? Is it the name of some obscure and shriveled
prelate from Madrid or Heidelberg, some last-minute
choice of the anti-robot faction in its desperation? Or
are they writing *his* name? The sound of scratching
pens is loud in the chapel. The cardinals are completing their ballots, sealing them at the ends, folding them,
folding them again and again, carrying them to the
altar, dropping them into the great gold chalice. So
have they done every morning and every afternoon for
days, as the deadlock has prevailed.

"I read in the *Herald Tribune* a couple of days ago,"
says Miss Harshaw, "that a delegation of 250 young
Catholic robots from Iowa is waiting at the Des
Moines airport for news of the election. If their man
gets in, they've got a chartered flight ready to leave,

and they intend to request that they be granted the Holy Father's first public audience."

"There can be no doubt," Bishop FitzPatrick agrees, "that his election will bring a great many people of synthetic origin into the fold of the Church."

"While driving out plenty of flesh-and-blood people!" Miss Harshaw says shrilly.

"I doubt that," says the bishop. "Certainly there will be some feelings of shock, of dismay, of injury, of loss, for some of us at first. But these will pass. The inherent goodness of the new Pope, to which Rabbi Mueller alluded, will prevail. Also I believe that technologically-minded young folk everywhere will be encouraged to join the Church. Irresistible religious impulses will be awakened throughout the world."

"Can you imagine 250 robots clanking into St. Peter's?" Miss Harshaw demands.

I contemplate the distant Vatican. The morning sunlight is brilliant and dazzling, but the assembled cardinals, walled away from the world, cannot enjoy its gay sparkle. They all have voted, now. The three cardinals who were chosen by lot as this morning's scrutators of the vote have risen. One of them lifts the chalice and shakes it, mixing the ballots. Then he places it on the table before the altar; a second scrutator removes the ballots and counts them. He ascertains that the number of ballots is identical to the number of cardinals present. The ballots now have been transferred to a ciborium, which is a goblet ordinarily used to hold the conse-crated bread of the Mass. The first scrutator withdraws a ballot, unfolds it, reads its inscription; passes it to the second scrutator, who reads it also; then it is given to

the third scrutator, who reads the name aloud. Asciuga? Carciofo? Some other? *His?*

Rabbi Mueller is discussing angels. "Then we have
the Angels of the Throne, known in Hebrew as *arelim*
or *ophanim*. There are 70 of them, noted primarily for
their steadfastness. Among them are the angels Orifiel,
Ophaniel, Zabkiel, Jophiel, Ambriel, Tychagar, Barael,
Quelamia, Paschar, Boel, and Raum. Some of these
are no longer found in Heaven and are numbered
among the fallen angels in Hell."

"So much for their steadfastness," says Kenneth.

"Then, too," the rabbi goes on, "there are the
Angels of the Presence, who apparently were circum-
cised at the moment of their creation. These are
Michael, Metatron, Suriel, Sandalphon, Uriel, Sara-
qael, Astanphaeus, Phanuel, Jehoel, Zagzagael,
Yefefiah, and Akatriel. But I think my favorite of the
whole group is the Angel of Lust, who is mentioned in
Talmud *Bereshith Rabba* 85 as follows, that when
Judah was about to pass by—"

They have finished counting the votes by this time,
surely. An immense throng has assembled in the
Square of St. Peter's. The sunlight gleams off hundreds
if not thousands of steel-jacketed crania. This must be
a wonderful day for the robot population of Rome. But
most of those in the piazza are creatures of flesh and
blood: old women in black, gaunt young pickpockets,
boys with puppies, plump vendors of sausages, and an
assortment of poets, philosophers, generals, legislators,
tourists and fishermen. How has the tally gone? We
will have our answer shortly. If no candidate has had a
majority, they will mix the ballots with wet straws before casting them into the chapel stove, and black

smoke will billow from the chimney. But if a Pope has been elected, the straw will be dry, the smoke will be white.

The system has agreeable resonances. I like it. It gives me the satisfaction one normally derives from a flawless work of art: the *Tristan* chord, let us say, or the teeth of the frog in Bosch's *Temptation of St. Anthony.* I await the outcome with fierce concentration. I am certain of the result; I can already feel the irresistible religious impulses awakening in me. Although I feel, also, an odd nostalgia for the days of flesh-and-blood popes. Tomorrow's newspapers will have no interviews with the Holy Father's aged mother in Sicily, nor with his proud younger brother in San Francisco. And will this grand ceremony of election ever be held again? Will we need another Pope, when this one whom we will soon have can be repaired so easily?

Ah. The white smoke! The moment of revelation comes!

A figure emerges on the central balcony of the facade of St. Peter's, spreads a web of cloth-of-gold, and disappears. The blaze of light against that fabric stuns the eye. It reminds me perhaps of moonlight coldly kissing the sea at Castellamare, or, perhaps even more, of the noonday glare rebounding from the breast of the Caribbean off the coast of St. John. A second figure, clad in ermine and vermilion, has appeared on the balcony. "The cardinal-archdeacon," Bishop Fitz-Patrick whispers. People have started to faint. Luigi stands beside me, listening to the proceedings on a tiny radio. Kenneth says, "It's all been fixed." Rabbi Mueller hisses at him to be still. Miss Harshaw begins to sob. Beverly softly recites the Pledge of Allegiance, crossing herself throughout. This is a wonderful moment for me. I think it is the most truly contemporary moment I have ever experienced.

The amplified voice of the cardinal-archdeacon cries, "I announce to you great joy. We have a Pope."

Cheering commences, and grows in intensity as the cardinal-archdeacon tells the world that the newly chosen Pontiff is indeed *that* cardinal, that noble and distinguished person, that melancholy and austere individual, whose elevation to the Holy See we have all awaited so intensely for so long. "He has imposed upon himself," says the cardinal-archdeacon, "the name of—"

Lost in the cheering. I turn to Luigi. "Who? What name?"

"Sisto Settimo," Luigi tells me.

Yes, and there he is, Pope Sixtus the Seventh, as we now must call him. A tiny figure clad in the silver and gold papal robes, arms outstretched to the multitude, and, yes! the sunlight glints on his cheeks, his lofty forehead, there is the brightness of polished steel. Luigi is already on his knees. I kneel beside him. Miss Harshaw, Beverly, Kenneth, even the rabbi all kneel, for beyond doubt this is a miraculous event. The Pope comes forward on his balcony. Now he will deliver the traditional apostolic benediction to the city and to the world. "Our help is in the Name of the Lord," he declares gravely. He activates the levitator-jets beneath his arms; even at this distance I can see the two small puffs of smoke. White smoke, again. He begins to rise into the air. "Who hath made heaven and earth," he says. "May Almighty God, Father, Son, and Holy Ghost, bless you." His voice rolls majestically toward us. His shadow extends across the whole piazza. Higher and higher he goes, until he is lost to sight. Kenneth taps Luigi. "Another round of drinks," he says, and presses a bill of high denomination into the innkeeper's fleshy palm. Bishop FitzPatrick weeps. Rabbi Mueller embraces Miss Harshaw. The new Pontiff, I think, has begun his reign in an auspicious way.

5

THE FALL FROM INNOCENCE

The Streets of Ashkelon
HARRY HARRISON

C hristianity, after its birth in Palestine in the first century, spread first around the Mediterranean, and then into many parts of the world. Typically, commerce or trade and religion traveled hand in hand. As traders went into foreign lands, religious ideas followed along with them. "The Streets of Ashkelon" is a story of trade and religion traveling into an alien land, but this time it is another planet, Wesker's World.

The natives on Wesker live in a state of innocence, purity, and harmony. They are an example of the Golden Age that is a common myth in many cultures. This myth says there was some better time in the past when the ills of the present world did not exist, when all was as it should be. For Christian mythology, the Golden Age is embodied in the story of the Garden of

174

Eden, a place where man lived in a state of bliss—in harmony with Nature, plant and animal. It was a time before man's lapse or fall, when he was in a state of innocence. After he ate of the tree of knowledge of good and evil, man fell from his state of bliss and was cast out of Eden. Life now became filled with suffering because he recognized that he had the free will to choose good or evil and the wrong choice could be painful.

Psychoanalyst Erich Fromm suggests that the Garden of Eden story poetically expresses the fact of man's new self-awareness that he could determine his own life. He "fell out of Nature," where—animal-like—he had "lived" by his instincts. He became conscious of himself as a separate and unique individual, became conscious that he was mortal and would die. This was the knowledge that ended his state of innocence.

Trader John Garth in "The Streets of Ashkelon" finds the animal-like natives of Wesker living in a Garden of Eden. He has no wish to disturb their innocence and believes he can accomplish the preservation of this innocence by teaching them scientific facts, but not religion. Since they hear only his view, they have no reason to doubt it. When there is only one view, there is no conflict and no need to choose. But when Father Mark arrives from Earth one day to bring Christianity to the Weskerians, he gives them a different kind of knowledge than Garth had provided. Disagreement and conflict appear for the first time on Wesker. How did the universe begin? What is the First Cause that produced everything else? Is there a God? The natives find only riddles as they struggle to penetrate the mists concealing the past.

Father Mark argues, "Have faith." He knows the existence of God can never be proved. He knows, like the Danish theologian Sören Kierkegaard (1813–55), often called the father of modern existentialism, that man must finally—to find God—make a leap to faith, which lies beyond logic. Although man exists in time, he must learn to live in timelessness; he must transcend this life to one that is beyond the limits of experience and the limitations of human knowledge.

The Weskers are confused. They have not had to cope before with complexity and with conflicting answers. When they go to Garth for guidance, he suggests they use the scientific method "which can examine all things—including itself—and give you answers that can prove the truth or falsity of any statement." Garth's faith in science is a close parallel to Father Mark's faith in religion. He is almost simplistic in his confidence in science and his belief that scientific knowledge is without conflict. He forgets that the physics of Einstein replaced the earlier physics of Newton; that newer psychological models of human personality now begin to replace the model that Freud created. Knowledge for him is clear and without conflict; it is free of ambiguity or opposed interpretations.

The natives decide to follow Garth's method. They long for the clear-cut either/or answer. They are not able to consider the possibility that man is a complex life form that must deal in complex answers. Either Father Mark's religious statements are literally true, or they are not true. In their innocence the Weskers devise a monstrous test to provide final proof. In their childlike desire for simple answers, they are unaware that new knowledge leads inescapably to complexity.

Truth, if indeed it can be known, seems to lie in the direction of a huge synthesis incorporating lesser truths that are apparently in contradiction. They demand final certainty, and in their attempt to grasp it, they commit the terrible act that drives them forever from the innocence of their Edenic life. They become aware of evil.

The Streets of Ashkelon
HARRY HARRISON

Somewhere above, hidden by the eternal clouds of Wesker's World, a thunder rumbled and grew. Trader John Garth stopped when he heard it, his boots sinking slowly into the muck, and cupped his good ear to catch the sound. It swelled and waned in the thick atmosphere, growing louder.

'That noise is the same as the noise of your sky-ship,' Itin said, with stolid Wesker logicality, slowly pulverizing the idea in his mind and turning over the bits one by one for closer examination. 'But your ship is still sitting where you landed it. It must be, even though we cannot see it, because you are the only one who can operate it. And even if anyone else could operate it we would have heard it rising into the sky. Since we did not, and if this sound is a sky-ship sound, then it must mean ...'

'Yes, another ship,' Garth said, too absorbed in his own thoughts to wait for the laborious Weskerian chains of logic to clank their way through to the end. Of course it was another spacer, it had been only a matter of time before one appeared, and undoubtedly this one was homing on the S.S. radar reflector as he had done. His own ship would show up clearly on the newcomer's screen and they would probably set down as close to it as they could.

'You better go ahead, Itin,' he said. 'Use the water so you can get to the village quickly. Tell everyone to get back into the swamps, well clear of the hard ground. That ship is landing on instruments and anyone underneath at touchdown is going to be cooked.'

This immediate threat was clear enough to the little Wesker amphibian. Before Garth finished speaking Itin's ribbed ears had folded like a bat's wing and he slipped silently into the nearby canal. Garth squelched on through the mud, making as good time as he could over the clinging surface. He had just reached the fringes of the village clearing when the rumbling grew to a head-splitting roar and the spacer broke through the low-hanging layer of clouds above. Garth shielded his eyes from the down-reaching tongue of flame and examined the growing form of the grey-black ship with mixed feelings.

After almost a standard year on Wesker's World he had to fight down a longing for human companionship of any kind. While this buried fragment of herd-spirit chattered for the rest of the monkey tribe, his trader's mind was busily drawing a line under a column of figures and adding up the total. This could very well be another trader's ship, and if it were his monopoly of the Wesker trade was at an end. Then again, this might not be a trader at all, which was the reason he stayed in the shelter of the giant fern and loosened his gun in its holster.

The ship baked dry a hundred square metres of mud, the roaring blast died, and the landing feet crunched down through the crackling crust. Metal creaked and settled into place while the cloud of smoke and steam slowly drifted lower in the humid air.

'Garth—you native-cheating extortionist—where are you?' the ship's speaker boomed. The lines of the spacer had looked only slightly familiar, but there was no mistaking the rasping tones of that voice. Garth wore a smile when he stepped out into the open and whistled shrilly through two fingers. A directional microphone ground out of its casing on the ship's fin and turned in his direction.

'What are you doing here, Singh?' he shouted towards the mike. 'Too crooked to find a planet of your own and have to come here to steal an honest trader's profits?'

'Honest!' the amplified voice roared. 'This from the man who has been in more jails than cathouses—and that a goodly number in itself, I do declare. Sorry, friend of my youth, but I cannot join you in exploiting this aboriginal pesthole. I am on course to a more fairly atmosphered world where a fortune is waiting to be made. I only stopped here since an opportunity presented to turn an honest credit by running a taxi service. I bring you friendship, the perfect companionship, a man in a different line of business who might help you in yours. I'd come out and say hello myself, except I would have to decon for biologicals. I'm cycling the passenger through the lock so I hope you won't mind helping with his luggage.'

At least there would be no other trader on the planet now, that worry was gone. But Garth still wondered what sort of passenger would be taking one-way passage to an uninhabited world. And what was behind that concealed hint of merriment in Singh's voice? He walked around to the far side of the spacer where the ramp had dropped, and looked up at the man in the cargo lock who was wrestling ineffectually with a large crate. The man turned towards him and Garth saw the clerical dog-collar and knew just what it was Singh had been chuckling about.

'What are you doing here?' Garth asked; in spite of his attempt at self-control he snapped the words. If the man noticed this he ignored it, because he was still smiling and putting out his hand as he came down the ramp.

'Father Mark,' he said, 'of the Missionary Society of Brothers. I'm very pleased to . . .'

'I said what are you doing here.' Garth's voice was under control now, quiet and cold. He knew what had to be done, and it must be done quickly or not at all.

'That should be obvious,' Father Mark said, his good nature still unruffled. 'Our missionary society has raised funds to send spiritual emissaries to alien worlds for the first time. I was lucky enough . . .'

'Take your luggage and get back into the ship. You're not wanted here and have no permission to land. You'll be a liability and there is no one on Wesker to take care of you. Get back into the ship.'

'I don't know who you are, sir, or why you are lying to me,' the priest said. He was still calm but the smile was gone. 'But I have studied galactic law and the history of this planet very well. There are no diseases or beasts here that I should have any particular fear of.

It is also an open planet, and until the Space Survey changes that status I have as much right to be here as you do.'

The man was of course right, but Garth couldn't let him know that. He had been bluffing, hoping the priest didn't know his rights. But he did. There was only one distasteful course left for him, and he had better do it while there was still time.

'Get back in that ship,' he shouted, not hiding his anger now. With a smooth motion his gun was out of the holster and the pitted black muzzle only inches from the priest's stomach. The man's face turned white, but he did not move.

'What the hell are you doing, Garth!' Singh's shocked voice grated from the speaker. 'The guy paid his fare and you have no rights at all to throw him off the planet.'

'I have this right,' Garth said, raising his gun and sighting between the priest's eyes. 'I give him thirty seconds to get back aboard the ship or I pull the trigger.'

'Well I think you are either off your head or playing a joke,' Singh's exasperated voice rasped down at them. 'If a joke, it is in bad taste, and either way you're not getting away with it. Two can play at that game, only I can play it better.'

There was the rumble of heavy bearings and the remote-controlled four-gun turret on the ship's side rotated and pointed at Garth. 'Now—down gun and give Father Mark a hand with the luggage,' the speaker commanded, a trace of humour back in the voice now. 'As much as I would like to help, Old Friend, I cannot. I feel it is time you had a chance to talk to the father;

after all, I have had the opportunity of speaking with him all the way from Earth.'

Garth jammed the gun back into the holster with an acute feeling of loss. Father Mark stepped forward, the winning smile back now and a bible taken from a pocket of his robe, in his raised hand. 'My son,' he said.

'I'm not your son,' was all Garth could choke out as defeat welled up in him. His fist drew back as the anger rose, and the best he could do was open the fist so he struck only with the flat of his hand. Still the blow sent the priest crashing to the ground and fluttered the pages of the book splattering into the thick mud.

Itin and the other Weskers had watched everything with seemingly emotionless interest, and Garth made no attempt to answer their unspoken questions. He started towards his house, but turned back when he saw they were still unmoving.

'A new man has come,' he told them. 'He will need help with the things he has brought. If he doesn't have any place for them, you can put them in the big warehouse until he has a place of his own.'

He watched them waddle across the clearing towards the ship, then went inside and gained a certain satisfaction from slamming the door hard enough to crack one of the panes. There was an equal amount of painful pleasure in breaking out one of the remaining bottles of Irish whisky that he had been saving for a special occasion. Well this was special enough, though not really what he had had in mind. The whisky was good and burned away some of the bad taste in his mouth, but not all of it. If his tactics had worked, success would have justified everything. But he had failed and in addition to the pain of failure there was the acute feeling that he had made a horse's ass out of himself. Singh had blasted off without any good-byes. There was no telling what sense he had made of the whole matter, though he would surely carry some strange stories back to the traders' lodge. Well, that could be worried about the next time Garth signed in. Right now he had to go about setting things right with the missionary. Squinting out through the rain he saw the man struggling to erect a collapsible tent while the entire population of the village stood in ordered ranks and watched. Naturally none of them offered to help.

By the time the tent was up and the crates and boxes stowed inside it the rain had stopped. The level of fluid in the bottle was a good bit lower and Garth felt more like facing up to the unavoidable meeting. In truth, he was looking forward to talking to the man. This whole nasty business aside, after an entire solitary year any human companionship looked good. *Will you join me now for dinner. John Garth,* he wrote on the back of an old invoice. But maybe the guy was too frightened to come? Which was no way to start any kind of relationship. Rummaging under the bunk, he found a box that was big enough and put his pistol inside. Itin was of course waiting outside the door when he opened it, since this was his tour as Knowledge Collector. He handed him the note and box.

'Would you take these to the new man,' he said.

'Is the new man's name New Man?' Itin asked.

'No, it's not!' Garth snapped. 'His name is Mark. But I'm only asking you to deliver this, not get involved in conversation.'

As always when he lost his temper, the literal minded Weskers won the round. 'You are not asking for conversation,' Itin said slowly, 'but Mark may ask for conversation. And others will ask me his name, if I do not know his na . . .' The voice cut off as Garth slammed the door. This didn't work in the long run either because next time he saw Itin—a day, a week, or even a month later—the monologue would be picked up on the very word it had ended and the thought rambled out to its last frayed end. Garth cursed under his breath and poured water over a pair of the tastier concentrates that he had left.

'Come in,' he said when there was a quiet knock on the door. The priest entered and held out the box with the gun.

'Thank you for the loan, Mr Garth, I appreciate the spirit that made you send it. I have no idea of what caused the unhappy affair when I landed, but I think it would be best forgotten if we are going to be on this planet together for any length of time.'

'Drink?' Garth asked, taking the box and pointing to the bottle on the table. He poured two glasses full and handed one to the priest. 'That's about what I had in mind, but I still owe you an explanation of what happened out there.' He scowled into his glass for a second, then raised it to the other man. 'It's a big universe and I guess we have to make out as best we can. Here's to Sanity.'

'God be with you,' Father Mark said, and raised his glass as well.

'Not with me or with this planet,' Garth said firmly. 'And that's the crux of the matter.' He half-drained the glass and sighed.

'Do you say that to shock me?' the priest asked with a smile. 'I assure you it doesn't.'

'Not intended to shock. I meant it quite literally. I suppose I'm what you would call an atheist, so revealed religion is no concern of mine. While these natives, simple and unlettered stone-age types that they are, have managed to come this far with no superstitions or traces of deism whatsoever. I had hoped that they might continue that way.'

'What are you saying?' the priest frowned. 'Do you mean they have no gods, no belief in the hereafter? They must die . . . ?'

'Die they do, and to dust returneth like the rest of the animals. They have thunder, trees, and water without having thunder-gods, tree sprites, or water nymphs. They have no ugly little gods, taboos, or spells to hagride and limit their lives. They are the only primitive people I have ever encountered that are completely free of superstition and appear to be much happier and sane because of it. I just wanted to keep them that way.'

'You wanted to keep them from God—from salvation?' The priest's eyes widened and he recoiled slightly.

'No,' Garth said. 'I wanted to keep them from superstition until they knew more and could think about it realistically without being absorbed and perhaps destroyed by it.'

'You're being insulting to the Church, sir, to equate it with superstition . . .'

'Please,' Garth said, raising his hand. 'No theological arguments. I don't think your society footed the bill for this trip just to attempt a conversion on me. Just accept the fact that my beliefs have been arrived at through careful thought over a period of years, and no amount of undergraduate metaphysics will change them. I'll promise not to try and convert you—if you will do the same for me.'

'Agreed, Mr Garth. As you have reminded me, my mission here is to save these souls, and that is what I must do. But why should my work disturb you so much that you try and keep me from landing? Even threaten me with your gun, and . . .' the priest broke off and looked into his glass.

'And even slug you?' Garth asked, suddenly frowning. 'There was no excuse for that, and I would like to say that I'm sorry. Plain bad manners and an even worse temper. Live alone long enough and you find yourself doing that kind of thing.' He brooded down at his big hands where they lay on the table, reading memories into the scars and calluses patterned there. 'Let's just call it frustration, for lack of a better word. In your business you must have had a lot of chance to peep into the darker places in men's minds and you should know a bit about motives and happiness. I have had too busy a life to ever consider settling down and raising a family, and right up until recently I never missed it. Maybe leakage radiation is softening up my brain, but I had begun to think of these furry and fishy Weskers as being a little like my own children, that I was somehow responsible to them.'

'We are all His children,' Father Mark said quietly.

'Well, here are some of His children that can't even imagine His existence,' Garth said, suddenly angry at himself for allowing gentler emotions to show through. Yet he forgot himself at once, leaning forward with the intensity of his feelings. 'Can't you realize the importance of this? Live with these Weskers awhile and you will discover a simple and happy life that matches the state of grace you people are always talking about. They get *pleasure* from their lives—and cause no one pain. By circumstance they have evolved on an almost barren world, so have never had a chance to grow out of a physical stone age culture. But mentally they are our match—or perhaps better. They have all learned my language so I can easily explain the many things they want to know. Knowledge and the gaining of knowledge gives them real satisfaction. They tend to be exasperating at times because every new fact must be related to the structure of all other things, but the more they learn the faster this process becomes. Someday they are going to be man's equal in every way, perhaps surpass us. If—would you do me a favour?'

'Whatever I can.'

'Leave them alone. Or teach them if you must— history and science, philosophy, law, anything that will help them face the realities of the greater universe they never even knew existed before. But don't confuse them with your hatreds and pain, guilt, sin, and punishment. Who knows the harm . . .'

'You are being insulting, sir!' the priest said, jumping to his feet. The top of his grey head barely came to the massive spaceman's chin, yet he showed no fear in defending what he believed. Garth, standing now himself, was no longer the penitent. They faced each other in anger, as men have always stood, unbending in the defence of that which they think right.

'Yours is the insult,' Garth shouted. 'The incredible egotism to feel that your derivative little mythology, differing only slightly from the thousands of others

that still burden men, can do anything but confuse
their still fresh minds! Don't you realize that they believe in truth—and have never heard of such a thing as
a lie. They have not been trained yet to understand that
other kinds of minds can think differently from theirs.
Will you spare them this . . . ?' .

'I will do my duty which is His will, Mr Garth.
These are God's creatures here, and they have souls. I
cannot shirk my duty, which is to bring them His
word, so that they may be saved and enter into the
kingdom of heaven.'

When the priest opened the door the wind caught it
and blew it wide. He vanished into the stormswept
darkness and the door swung back and forth and a
splatter of raindrops blew in. Garth's boots left muddy
footprints when he closed the door, shutting out the
sight of Itin sitting patiently and uncomplaining in the
storm, hoping only that Garth might stop for a moment
and leave with him some of the wonderful knowledge
of which he had so much.

By unspoken consent that first night was never mentioned again. After a few days of loneliness, made
worse because each knew of the other's proximity, they
found themselves talking on carefully neutral grounds.
Garth slowly packed and stowed away his stock and
never admitted that his work was finished and he could
leave at any time. He had a fair amount of interesting
drugs and botanicals that would fetch a good price.
And the Wesker Artefacts were sure to create a sensation in the sophisticated galactic market. Crafts on the
planet here had been limited before his arrival, mostly
pieces of carving painfully chipped into the hard wood

with fragments of stone. He had supplied tools and a stock of raw metal from his own supplies, nothing more than that. In a few months the Weskers had not only learned to work with the new materials, but had translated their own designs and forms into the most alien—but most beautiful—artefacts that he had ever seen. All he had to do was release these on the market to create a primary demand, then return for a new supply. The Weskers wanted only books and tools and knowledge in return, and through their own efforts he knew they would pull themselves into the galactic union.

This is what Garth had hoped. But a wind of change was blowing through the settlement that had grown up around his ship. No longer was he the centre of attention and focal point of the village life. He had to grin when he thought of his fall from power; yet there was very little humour in the smile. Serious and attentive Weskers still took turns of duty as Knowledge Collectors, but their recording of dry facts was in sharp contrast to the intellectual hurricane that surrounded the priest.

Where Garth had made them work for each book and machine, the priest gave freely. Garth had tried to be progressive in his supply of knowledge, treating them as bright but unlettered children. He had wanted them to walk before they could run, to master one step before going on to the next.

Father Mark simply brought them the benefits of Christianity. The only physical work he required was the construction of a church, a place of worship and learning. More Weskers had appeared out of the limitless planetary swamps and within days the roof was up, supported on a framework of poles. Each morning the congregation worked a little while on the walls, then hurried inside to learn the all-promising, all-encompassing, all-important facts about the universe.

Garth never told the Weskers what he thought about their new interest, and this was mainly because they had never asked him. Pride or honour stood in the way of his grabbing a willing listener and pouring out his grievances. Perhaps it would have been different if Itin was on Collecting duty; he was the brightest of the lot; but Itin had been rotated the day after the priest had arrived and Garth had not talked to him since.

It was a surprise then when after seventeen of the trebly-long Wesker days he found a delegation at his doorstep when he emerged after breakfast. Itin was their spokesman, and his mouth was open slightly. Many of the other Weskers had their mouths open as well, one even appearing to be yawning, clearly revealing the double row of sharp teeth and the purple-black throat. The mouths impressed Garth as to the seriousness of the meeting: this was the one Wesker expression he had learned to recognize. An open mouth indicated some strong emotion; happiness, sadness, anger, he could never be really sure which. The Weskers were normally placid and he had never seen enough open mouths to tell what was causing them. But he was surrounded by them now.

'Will you help us, John Garth,' Itin said. 'We have a question.'

'I'll answer any question you ask,' Garth said, with more than a hint of misgiving. 'What is it?'

'Is there a God?'

'What do you mean by "God"?' Garth asked in turn. What should he tell them?

'God is our Father in Heaven, who made us all and protects us. Whom we pray to for aid, and if we are Saved will find a place...'

'That's enough,' Garth said. 'There is no God.'

All of them had their mouths open now, even Itin, as they looked at Garth and thought about his answer. The rows of pink teeth would have been frightening if he hadn't known these creatures so well. For one instant he wondered if perhaps they had been already indoctrinated and looked upon him as a heretic, but he brushed the thought away.

'Thank you,' Itin said, and they turned and left.

Though the morning was still cool, Garth noticed that he was sweating and wondered why.

The reaction was not long in coming. Itin returned that same afternoon. 'Will you come to the church?' he asked. 'Many of the things that we study are difficult to learn, but none as difficult as this. We need your help because we must hear you and Father Mark talk together. This is because he says one thing is true and you say another is true and both cannot be true at the same time. We must find out what is true.'

'I'll come, of course,' Garth said, trying to hide the sudden feeling of elation. He had done nothing, but the Weskers had come to him anyway. There could still be grounds for hope that they might yet be free.

It was hot inside the church, and Garth was surprised at the number of Weskers who were there, more than he had seen gathered at any one time before. There were many open mouths. Father Mark sat at a table covered with books. He looked unhappy but didn't say anything when Garth came in. Garth spoke first.

'I hope you realize this is their idea—that they came to me of their own free will and asked me to come here?'

'I know that,' the priest said resignedly. 'At times they can be very difficult. But they are learning and want to believe, and that is what is important.'

'Father Mark, Trader Garth, we need your help,' Itin said. 'You both know many things that we do not know. You must help us come to religion which is not an easy thing to do.' Garth started to say something, then changed his mind. Itin went on. 'We have read the bibles and all the books that Father Mark gave us, and one thing is clear. We have discussed this and we are all agreed. These books are very different from the ones that Trader Garth gave us. In Trader Garth's books there is the universe which we have not seen, and it goes on without God, for he is mentioned nowhere; we have searched very carefully. In Father Mark's books He is everywhere and nothing can go without Him. One of these must be right and the other must be wrong. We do not know how this can be, but after we find out which is right then perhaps we will know. If God does not exist . . .'

'Of course He exists, my children,' Father Mark said in a voice of heartfelt intensity. 'He is our Father in Heaven who has created us all . . .'

'Who created God?' Itin asked and the murmur ceased and every one of the Weskers watched Father Mark intensely. He recoiled a bit under the impact of their eyes, then smiled.

'Nothing created God, since He is the Creator. He always was . . .'

'If He always was in existence—why cannot the universe have always been in existence? Without having had a creator?' Itin broke in with a rush of words. The importance of the question was obvious. The priest answered slowly, with infinite patience.

'Would that the answers were that simple, my children. But even the scientists do not agree about the creation of the universe. While they doubt—we who have seen the light *know*. We can see the miracle of creation all about us. And how can there be a creation without a Creator? That is He, our Father, our God in Heaven. I know you have doubts; that is because you have souls and free will. Still, the answer is so simple. Have faith, that is all you need. Just believe.'

'How can we believe without proof?'

'If you cannot see that this world itself is proof of His existence, then I say to you that belief needs no proof—if you have faith!'

A babble of voices arose in the room and more of the Wesker mouths were open now as they tried to force their thoughts through the tangled skein of words and separate the thread of truth.

'Can you tell us, Garth?' Itin asked, and the sound of his voice quieted the hubbub.

'I can tell you to use the scientific method which can examine all things—including itself—and give you answers that can prove the truth or falsity of any statement.'

'That is what we must do,' Itin said, 'we had reached the same conclusion.' He held a thick book before him and a ripple of nods ran across the watchers. 'We have been studying the bible as Father Mark told us to do, and we have found the answer. God will make a miracle for us, thereby proving that He is watching us. And by this sign we will know Him and go to Him.'

'That is the sin of false pride,' Father Mark said. 'God needs no miracles to prove His existence.'

'But *we* need a miracle!' Itin shouted, and though he wasn't human there was need in his voice. 'We have read here of many smaller miracles, loaves, fishes, wine, snakes—many of them, for much smaller reasons. Now all He need do is make a miracle and He will bring us all to Him—the wonder of an entire new world worshipping at His throne, as you have told us, Father Mark. And you have told us how important this is. We have discussed this and find that there is only one miracle that is best for this kind of thing.'

His boredom at the theological wrangling drained from Garth in an instant. He had not been really thinking or he would have realized where all this was leading. He could see the illustration in the bible where Itin held it open, and knew in advance what picture it was. He rose slowly from his chair, as if stretching, and turned to the priest behind him.

'Get ready!' he whispered. 'Get out the back and get to the ship; I'll keep them busy here. I don't think they'll harm me.'

'What do you mean . . . ?' Father Mark asked, blinking in surprise.

'Get out, you fool!' Garth hissed. 'What miracle do you think they mean? What miracle is supposed to have converted the world to Christianity?'

'No!' Father Mark said. 'It cannot be. It just cannot be . . . !'

'GET MOVING!' Garth shouted, dragging the priest from the chair and hurling him towards the rear wall. Father Mark stumbled to a halt, turned back. Garth leaped for him, but it was already too late. The amphibians were small, but there were so many of them. Garth lashed out and his fist struck Itin, hurling him back into the crowd. The others came on as he fought his way towards the priest. He beat at them but it was like struggling against waves. The furry, musky bodies washed over and engulfed him. He fought until they tied him, and he still struggled until they beat on his head until he stopped. Then they pulled him outside where he could only lie in the rain and curse and watch.

Of course the Weskers were marvelous craftsmen, and everything had been constructed down to the last detail, following the illustration in the bible. There was the cross, planted firmly on the top of a small hill, the gleaming metal spikes, the hammer. Father Mark was stripped and draped in a carefully pleated loincloth. They led him out of the church.

At the sight of the cross he almost fainted. After that he held his head high and determined to die as he had lived, with faith.

Yet this was hard. It was unbearable even for Garth, who only watched. It is one thing to talk of crucifixion and look at the gently carved bodies in the dim light of prayer. It is another to see a man naked, ropes cutting into his skin where he hangs from a bar of wood. And to see the needle-tipped spike raised and placed against the soft flesh of his palm, to see the hammer come back with the calm deliberation of an artisan's measured stroke. To hear the thick sound of metal penetrating flesh.

Then to hear the screams.

Few are born to be martyrs; Father Mark was not one of them. With the first blows, the blood ran from his lips where his clenched teeth met. Then his mouth was wide and his head strained back and the guttural horror of his screams sliced through the susurration of the falling rain. It resounded as a silent echo from the masses of watching Weskers, for whatever emotion opened their mouths was now tearing at their bodies with all its force, and row after row of gaping jaws reflected the crucified priest's agony.

Mercifully he fainted as the last nail was driven home. Blood ran from the raw wounds, mixing with the rain to drip faintly pink from his feet as the life ran out of him. At this time, somewhere at this time, sobbing and tearing at his own bonds, numbed from the blows on the head, Garth lost consciousness.

He awoke in his own warehouse and it was dark. Someone was cutting away the woven ropes they had bound him with. The rain still dripped and splashed outside.

'Itin,' he said. It could be no one else.

'Yes,' the alien voice whispered back. 'The others are all talking in the church. Lin died after you struck his head, and Inon is very sick. There are some that say you should be crucified too, and I think that is what will happen. Or perhaps killed by stoning on the head. They have found in the bible where it says . . .'

'I know.' With infinite weariness. 'An eye for an eye. You'll find lots of things like that once you start looking. It's a wonderful book.' His head ached terribly.

'You must go, you can get to your ship without anyone seeing you. There has been enough killing.' Itin, as
well, spoke with a new-found weariness.

Garth experimented, pulling himself to his feet. He
pressed his head to the rough wood of the wall until the
nausea stopped. 'He's dead.' He said it as a statement,
not a question.

'Yes, some time ago. Or I could not have come away
to see you.'

'And buried of course, or they wouldn't be thinking
about starting on me next.'

'And buried!' There was almost a ring of emotion in
the alien's voice, an echo of the dead priest's. 'He is
buried and he will rise on High. It is written and that is
the way it will happen. Father Mark will be so happy
that it has happened like this.' The voice ended in a
sound like a human sob.

Garth painfully worked his way towards the door,
leaning against the wall so he wouldn't fall.

'We did the right thing, didn't we?' Itin asked. There
was no answer. 'He will rise up, Garth, won't he rise?'

Garth was at the door and enough light came from
the brightly lit church to show his torn and bloody
hands clutching at the frame. Itin's face swam into
sight close to his, and Garth felt the delicate, many
fingered hands with the sharp nails catch at his clothes.

'He will rise, won't he, Garth?'

'No,' Garth said, 'he is going to stay buried right
where you put him. Nothing is going to happen because
he is dead and he is going to stay dead.'

The rain runnelled through Itin's fur and his mouth
was opened so wide that he seemed to be screaming

into the night. Only with effort could he talk, squeezing out the alien thoughts in an alien language.

'Then we will not be saved? We will not become pure?'

'You were pure,' Garth said, in a voice somewhere between a sob and a laugh. 'That's the horrible ugly dirty part of it. You were pure. Now you are . . .'

'Murderers,' Itin said, and the water ran down from his lowered head and streamed away into the darkness.

6

THE NEED TO BELIEVE

Ask and It May Be Given
WESLEY FORD DAVIS

Man is first a physical creature. Because material things can be seen and touched and measured, the fact of man's physical nature is not questioned. But he may be more; he may have a nonmaterial or spiritual nature. In the same way, the universe in which man lives is obviously material, but may also be spirit. Religion holds to the existence of the nonmaterial, even though it cannot be proved (or disproved) by science.

Some people seem more content than others to live only in the material world—eating, drinking, working, seeking pleasurable sensations. The possibility of the spiritual does not particularly concern them. But there are other individuals who have a strong spiritual nature—who are driven to find something beyond the material world. They want to transcend or climb above the physical world to discover something more. If the drive is extreme, they are called fanatics. "Ask and It May Be Given" is the story of one such modern religious fanatic named Jake. He yearns for the spiritual, while his wife is willing to settle for a mere material existence.

Because our modern world is influenced so much in its perceptions by science, which deals with the material, it has little sympathy with the person who needs to believe in something else. It is much more difficult to be a believer in the modern world than it was in the Middle Ages when the Holy Catholic Church provided a commonly shared world view. Even Jake's wife, in this story, cannot understand or accept his need, and it is her lack of faith in the spiritual that leads to tragedy.

What exactly drives a man like Jake to become a fanatic? Is it simply faith, or a revelation? Is it the psychological need to believe strongly in something, or is it the rational belief that what he does in his act of faith is just and good? Eric Hoffer explores these questions in his book *The True Believer*.[1] He points out that there is a strong correlation between adherence to political ideologies like Communism and the religious need to believe in something. The twentieth century has questioned the acceptability of religion and in its place many people have substituted political ideologies to satisfy their need to believe in something. The major ideologies of the twentieth century—Marxism, socialism, nationalism—have, according to some observers, largely replaced religion in its traditional role of supplying a meaning to the individual and giving him a sense of purpose and structure in his life. In recent years, however, particularly among the young, there has been a seeming disillusionment with ideologies, and with it a resultant revival of interest in religion. The violence and destruction associated with ideologies may be a factor in this change.

Jake in "Ask and It May Be Given" is a man who meditates, who contemplates the starry heavens in his attempt to reach beyond the Earth, to transcend the physical and reach the spiritual. The ladder or tower has always symbolized this human need; there was the biblical ladder of Jacob by which he communicated with Heaven. Jake reads C. S. Lewis's famous science fiction novel *Out of the Silent Planet*, which portrays a highly evolved religious society on Mars. And like the biblical Jacob, this modern Jake decides to build his own tower to reach the spiritual. But before he begins construction the divine light comes to him. He has a beautiful instant of revelation.

Prophets and saints have always had revelations, moments of insight into the Godhead. They are one-time, one-person moments; they cannot be reproduced experimentally by another person as the insights of science can. And so the person who has had the revelation has a hard time convincing others, and often the most skeptical are those closest to him.

One who has experienced such a revelation often has a missionary zeal to share his insight with others. Most evangelists and persons deeply committed to religion feel they have a "call," were chosen to spread the Word of God. They feel their mission is divine in origin.

Evangelists like Oral Roberts and Billy Graham have found an enthusiastic following in society today. Their zeal and convictions strike a responsive note in large numbers of people. Individuals who are baffled and uncertain in their attempts to cope with change respond to this kind of evangelical preaching. They are looking for some kind of authority figure to give them guidance in what they should do.

Jake had been advised to "expect a miracle," and he took the advice seriously. He had faith that it could happen. This faith set in motion some kind of self-fulfilling prophecy. Because he believed it would happen, it did happen. His prayer worked. His vision was of the stars, the heavens, the spiritual universe. And it was from there his miracle came. His wife, uncertain and baffled by his activities, decided to try praying for a miracle too. But her vision was of dollars, daily bread, the material world. She could not believe in Jake's spiritual world. So the answer to her prayer was a different kind of miracle.

[1] Eric Hoffer, *The True Believer* (New York: Harper and Row, 1951).

Ask and It May Be Given
WESLEY FORD DAVIS

Her nose against the window, the room lights behind her, she could see him plainly. The sky beyond the slight rise of his own self-constructed observation mound was perfectly clear, almost brilliant with a healthy new quarter moon which loomed surprisingly close, just above his head. And Venus almost cradled by the moon. Quite a sight, she had to admit. One of

the more spectacular conjunctions of the heavenly
bodies such as he waited for. Maybe this would be the
night. The night for what? she had asked. His answer
as always was irrefutable: Who knows? You never can
tell.

It was no good saying again, as she had so often,
that it happens every year, at least once a year, Venus
and the new moon nestling close to one another, setting
in the western sky, and a lot of other unusual
phenomena—maybe not every year but often enough
and predictably. And is a thing unusual if it happens
repeatedly—no matter how long the interval—and
predictably? Eclipses, comets, meteor showers. And
how often had such things heralded the birth of the
Messiah, or the end of the world, or even the end or
the beginning of a great war or an earthquake, tidal
wave, volcanic eruption, etc.?

You don't know, he would say, these things are not
reported. They're covered up. You think that a scientific, technological, materialistic, secularistic, consumer-
oriented, military-industrial-international complex of a
Western Culture could afford to acknowledge even the
possibility of anything extranatural or suprarational?
No, it couldn't, she admitted. But what did that matter? Wouldn't such a power—if such existed beyond
what is or might be rationally and naturally explicable
—assert itself in spite of what anybody or anything
merely natural and/or political might think it could or
could not afford?

Of course, of course, it would, and will, and has.
People forget and they have no imagination. What's
two thousand years? A long time in human history, but
probably not even a moment in God's mind. Besides,

you overlook one little logical ingredient. By its very
nature, the extranatural event is unexpected. See what
I mean?

Well, how the hell could you argue against that sort
of logic? Or with somebody who was studying every
day and practicing every night—at least every moonlight night—to be literally a lunatic? Down here in the
southern sky, he said, the heavenly bodies loom close.
Stare straight into the full moon and you can sense the
immensity of space beyond the moon—the unimagin-
able immensity of His universe—and after a while the
moon seems to rush right at you. No good to tell him
that if you stare straight at anything long enough, it
will seem to rush right at you.

The telephone rang. On the third ring she pulled her
nose away from the window glass and crossed the
room, wearily and a bit apprehensively, to pick up the
receiver. It was Doris, her husband's immediate sub-
ordinate's wife. Doris' husband was her husband's general sales manager. Yes, Doris. Yes, she understood.
Yes, Doris didn't mean to meddle. Yes, Doris' husband
Don didn't presume to tell Jake how to run the business. Of course not, she didn't take offense. Yes, Jake
had told her about the latest reports. Sales were lagging
behind last year's, but wasn't the whole country in a
mild recession—with the administration taking meas-
ures to cool off the economy to slow inflation? Yes, she
was a bit worried, and she'd talk with Jake. He was in
the study now going over the new advertising cam-
paign. Of course she didn't mind, she appreciated her
and Don's concern.

She poured herself a stiff martini and moved back to
the window, drink in hand. On the window seat, after

taking a long, slow sip, she turned her face close to the glass. The new moon had dropped and slid northward away from Venus. The happy conjunction of the night-time's brightest luminaries was done with again, but her husband still sat motionless, his eyes riveted on the moon. In a full lotus position, hands resting lightly on his thighs, palms upturned, spine straight, breathing easily and deeply, he sat on his observation mound.

Jeee-sus, she sighed, turning from the glass and sip-ping a long, long sip from her drink. If he was going to be a nut, why couldn't he also have had the Ford or Chevrolet agency instead of American Motors? Or even Volkswagen? If you were selling Fords or Chevies, you could afford to be a queer duck part of the time. But not if you were selling Ambassadors and Ramblers, or even Javelins and Hornets. Of course, he said, we are making and selling the most economical, safest, best engineered, most sensible cars on the road today. Every-body knows we have the best product for the money on the market today. Yes, everybody except the people who went on buying Fords and Chevrolets by the hun-dreds of thousands year after year. Even the old Mor-mon wizard George Romney had known when to get out and get into a less hazardous business. Not even the Kennedys yet had a monopoly on high-level politi-cal office to match the hold of General Motors and Ford on the car business.

Drink in hand she drifted from the living room and down a dimly lit hallway and into the den—his study. She stirred the litter on the big desk: brochures show-ing the new models at rakish angles, with slender, long-haired blondes draped on hoods that seemed a half-mile long. The latest entry—the Hornet—American

Motors' answer to Ford's new Maverick, caressed coolly but firmly by a tall, thin young man with gray streaks in his luxuriant dark hair, wearing heavy dark glasses, dressed and groomed to look as rich as Hugh Hefner and as chic as George Hamilton. That was the line taken by the national office in advertising the new *economy* car. DON'T be fooled by the price tag, mister. The base price on this little honey is just $1970, but you can go as high as $4000 on this little bomb if you can afford it.

Her husband was a bit dubious of the effectiveness of such subtleties of advertising technique. After all, this is still the South, he argued, and the old Protestant ethic of buy cheap and sell dear still has some force in these parts. He and Don had been considering a modification of the central office approach, more suitable to the damn dumb rednecks around here who had never heard of Hugh Hefner and George Hamilton.

But the desk was cluttered mostly with books, not stacked but piled with corners jutting forth at various angles for better balance and stability. From the top ends of many of them slips of paper used for markers spread like ragged bouquets. The titles were some of the things she wasn't embarrassed to mention at the Garden Club or even at the League of Women Voters. C. S. Lewis' *Miracle, Out of the Silent Planet*; Evelyn Underhill's *Practical Mysticism*; James' *Varieties of Religious Experience*; *The Diary of a Country Priest*; *The Seven-Story Mountain*; *The Power and the Glory*. Such as these were referred to even at the Great Books Discussion. But toward the tops of the stacks or turned down on the desk or lying open—more recent acquisitions: *Out of Body Travel, They Speak with Other*

Tongues, Authenticated Accounts of Psychic Phenomena, The Abundant Life, The Power Within. A whole corner of the desk was covered with books on Edgar Cayce, The Sleeping Prophet.

She drained her glass and set it down and pressed the tips of her fingers against her eyelids. This somewhat eased the dull pain behind her eyes. The sinus headaches were frequent lately. But of course, as her husband said, it was the season for them. The goddamned punk trees along the back of the house were in full bloom, and the ragweed on the empty lots, and the goldenrod. And he refused to lay his healing hands on her head. He hadn't that much control yet; he wasn't that strong a channel yet. She was his wife. How could a wife place that much faith in her own husband and his only recently felt motions of the Spirit? A prophet always has a rough time in his own home. Hadn't Our Lord himself said as much?

Her nose close to the study window, she saw her husband now in profile; his posture and attitude were the same, only now his head was cast farther back, his gaze lifted higher. The moon and Venus had dropped behind the tree line beyond the two intervening streets and the eleventh fairway of the Tierra Verde golf course. Damn it all, why had not God vouchsafed to her even *one* iota of the kind of conviction that kept her husband poised on his little prayer mound for several hours several nights a week when the weather permitted? If the weather had permitted or he had been a thoroughgoing Eastern mystic, he probably would by now have established permanent residence on the mound, with a cult of followers camped in the yard. But he was no Eastern mystic; he was a dynamic, proselytizing, apocalyptic, ex-Jewish, Christian eschatologist. He waited for the heavens to divide and split asunder and the King of the Universe to return in all His glory. Even the politicians, he said, are forever quoting from Yeats' poem, "The Second Coming." It was a fact. The Secretary of Defense and one of the Kennedys—she couldn't recall which one—had in recent speeches quoted the lines: "Things fall apart/The center cannot hold/Mere anarchy is loosed upon the world." She had pointed out to her husband that none of the politicians had quoted from the second part of the poem wherein the poet pronounced the imminence of the second coming and his vision of the New Messiah: "Somewhere in sands of the desert/A shape with lion body and the head of a man./A gaze blank and pitiless as the sun . . ." Scant comfort for the faithful. Hardly the usual conception of the Blessed Lord returning in all His glory. That's all right, her husband responded, what would you expect from a non-Christian poet, even a great one like Yeats?

One thing she had to admit, though. Since the unhappy day when, as he put it, the light was turned on and he had felt the first faint stirrings of the Spirit— that day when by accident while he was waiting for the Sunday pro-football program, he had turned on the wrong channel and was practically stabbed in the groin by the outthrust finger of The Reverend Mister Oral Roberts looming like God Almighty on the twenty-one-inch full-color screen and who said to him: Expect a miracle. Expect a miracle! Since that fateful day her husband had gone a long way toward becoming an educated man. And, too, she had to admit that so far at least his business had not gone completely to rack and ruin. It had suffered some, but there was his tremendous capacity for work. He had always been a person of tremendous energy and stamina, but now—Spirit-filled as he claimed to be—he had, as he said, the strength of ten. He could work all day, sit on his goddamned observation mound half the night, read much of the rest of the night, and still come to bed, wake her, and perform his marital duties like a long-distance runner.

Gazing through the glass, slantwise toward his silhouetted figure on the mound, she breathed a question: What is my complaint? It was difficult to specify: a vague sense of dread, an uneasy apprehensiveness, a nameless fear.

At the desk again she aimlessly pulled out drawers, stirring their contents: papers, filing cards, pencils, clippings from magazines and newspapers. He was not orderly in his own study. As your thoughts become neater, he had said, you're less bothered by certain externals. She had no great quarrel with that. They had always had maid service twice weekly. The carpets were clean, the furniture dusted. As she pulled open the long middle drawer, she felt a twinge of guilt and wondered why she did so; they had always trusted each other and respected each other's privacy. Still, as her gaze fell on the big blue sheet of heavy drawing paper, she took it from the drawer and laid it on the desk. The drawing was captioned at the bottom: PRAYER TOWER, 250 Feet.

My God, she breathed. This was no eccentricity. It was simple insanity. And his drawing of the tower was simple too. What was to be its principal support—faith? She half expected to see guy wires strung from the stars to the four corners of the platform. In the lower right-hand corner of the sheet were the essential data. A simple twelve-by-twelve wooden platform with guard rail. No roof. Three-by-three cupola in center, mounted on slender twelve-foot pole—to support and screen aviation warning light. Platform support: single central column, equipped with vertical steel ladder— approx. 250 rungs. (250 Ft. nightly vertical ascent and descent good for body as well as soul. Will this put me discernibly nearer to the heavenly bodies? No. But who knows whether or when it may bring them closer to me?) Check with State Forestry Service on Approx. cost of rangers' fire tower. Call Cone Bros. Cst. Co. on feasibility of single column support. Also city zoning authority. May be necessary to buy telescope and en-roll in astronomy classes at University to justify. *Note:* Meanwhile, also re-read C. S. Lewis' *Out of the Silent Planet* and sequels; also do research on Old Testament story of Jacob's Ladder and similar related stories in Greek and other mythologies. *Note 2:* Consult further with Aaronson on subject of early retirement.

Her hands shook as she closed the drawer on the "blueprint." Her head ached terribly, and as she rose from the desk, she realized that the aching had moved into her back and arms and shoulders. Another virus going around probably. Moving toward the kitchen for another drink, she thought of calling her mother and immediately began to laugh out loud. Five years ago when her father died, her mother had moved to California. For the past four years or so, most of her mother's time and income had been given to the practice of spiritualism in an effort to communicate with her dead husband.

Fresh drink in hand, she moved to the ringing telephone. Thank goodness for the world we live in, she thought. When you've just about reached the limit of what you can tolerate inside your own head, the telephone rings. Steadying her voice she said, "Hello." It was Alan Aaronson, who aside from being their insurance agent, was also a close friend. Hence he did not ask for her husband but simply asked her to convey a message. His out-of-town trip had ended a day sooner than he had expected, and he would be able to see Jake first thing in the morning after all, if it were convenient for Jake. She assured him that she was certain it would be and then inquired about Charlotte and her new job. The job was fine, just what Charlotte had needed for a long time—good pay, stimulating associations. He laughed. Charlotte claimed you could feel the building vibrating with importance: Building a New Florida and Helping to House a Nation. She would probably call in a day or two to tell all about it. "You know, as soon as she gets her feet on the ground." He laughed again. "You know, when you're on the nineteenth floor of the biggest office building in town, it takes a little time to feel like you've got your feet on the ground. She'll make it, though. You know she's personal secretary to the company's seventh vice-president. You know what she calls him? You know, I mean behind his back? Mr. Peter Principle." They both laughed and said good-by.

For a few moments she sat and sipped her martini. She decided to call Don and Doris. She couldn't think what else to do. When Doris answered, she apologized for the lateness of the call. But she just had to talk to somebody. "It's all right, honey," Doris said, "we were just starting to watch Johnny Carson." She asked Doris if Don would mind getting on the extension, she wanted to talk to both of them. She described as exactly as she could the sketch she had found in her husband's desk. Before she had finished, Don started to giggle. Doris broke in and scolded him, "Don, you cut that out. Can't you see that this poor child is serious and upset?" He apologized. "I'm sorry, Marian, honey. Please forgive me. It's just that for a minute there it did seem awfully funny. A two hundred and fifty foot tower in his own backyard—in Temple Heights? My God, he must be out of . . . I mean, you don't mean you take him seriously. It's probably just one of these dreams like everybody has about going off into the woods or to some island and living like Robin . . ."

She interrupted him. "You don't know, Don. My God, I live with him. I tell you it's more serious than you can imagine. I've tried to put a good face on things and . . ."

"All right, honey, I know. I didn't mean to make light of the problem. I've felt it coming on pretty strong myself. I didn't want to butt in, but I'm glad you've called us. I've been afraid now for some time that things were going to get worse before they get better. But it's best to get it out into the open. Once you know about something, you have a chance to deal with it. You agree with me?"

She agreed. She knew now that it was too much for her to cope with alone. "Now," he said, "about this particular project of his, I don't think you have to worry. There's not a chance in the world that they'd let him do it. My God, a two hundred and fifty foot tower in Temple Heights, by the golf course. Just two fairways from the club. Honey, you know it's all rambling ranch-house building in your neighborhood. Christ, honey, he might as well think of adding a two hundred and fifty foot Gothic spire to the house. Now, honey, why don't you just mix yourself a good drink and go to bed. I'll talk to Jake tomorrow. I think it's better than fifty-fifty that you won't ever hear a word from him about any observation tower."

She thanked Doris and Don for their kindness and sympathy, and quickly said good-by. The front door had slammed loudly and her husband was calling loudly, "Hey, baby. Baby. Baby, where are you?" as he moved through the living room and into the hallway. She rose to meet him and he came like a gazelle. A hundred and eighty pounds and six feet tall and in his forty-ninth year, he leapt and bounded to take her in his arms. Tears streamed down his cheeks and wetted her cheek and neck, and feeling the warmth of his tears and of his arms and body, she felt herself wholly his and him hers. Had they rejected him, she wondered, the far-off indifferent stars? She thought of a poem she had memorized in college, its key line—how did it go: Ah, love, let us then be true to one another, for the world something something something something hath neither love nor joy nor certitude nor something something . . .

His voice was husky when he finally spoke. "Baby, it's all true. Only more so. The Light of the world. Absolutely literally true. Nothing figurative or symbolical or allegorical or anagogical about it. My God, my . . ."

Rigid she drew back and pushed against his chest. Her vision blurred as the tears came, and her voice threatened to rise and become shrill, but she managed to speak evenly and cuttingly. "And what is it the heavenly bodies have revealed to the great prophet this goddamned evening?"

Releasing her, he raised his hands to swipe away the tears. His dark-blue eyes blazed in the dimly lit hallway, and his moistened cheeks shone. For a crazy moment she had the impression that he might burst into flame right before her eyes. Ignoring her sarcasm, he spoke with the assurance and conviction of Moses or Martin Luther King come down from the mountain.

"Not heavenly *bodies*, baby. *Body*. You see—*Body*. One body. All of it. Everything. You and me, the stars, this old Earth. The whole universe. He's It. It's He. Understand, baby! I saw It. I saw Him. My God. My God. I saw You."

He had turned from her and was pacing the floor. She followed him along the hallway and into the living room. As he moved toward the picture window, she could hear his heavy breathing, and as he raised his hands and leaned against the glass, she suddenly felt that the house was too small for him. She half expected the window glass to shatter and the walls to give way. She also felt what she imagined to be utter despair.

As she turned to go for a drink, she spoke listlessly over her shoulder. "Alan called. He said he could see you in the morning after all." He did not answer, but while she mixed a new batch of martinis, he joined her in the kitchen.

"I must go see Don," he said.

"At this hour?"

"Yes. Every minute now is precious." He grasped

her shoulders and stared hard into her eyes. "You're with me in this, aren't you, baby?"

"In what?"

"My ministry, honey. You see, I've had the call. More than that—not just another one that's had the call. But *the* call. I have seen Him. Not as the disciples saw Him—incarnate in the flesh. But whole. The whole God. Remember what Our Lord said to His disciples, when He raised the dead? Greater things than this shall ye do in my name. Greater things. You understand? Greater things than *raising the dead*."

Shrugging, she turned her head away. Tears welled in her eyes and coursed down her cheeks. And he moved about in the kitchen and then out into the dining room, pacing and turning like some newly caged great beast, again seeming too big for the house, and slamming his right fist into his left palm. "Of course, my darling baby," he went on, "this may seem very shocking to you at first, but you will see. This vision of mine will work through me to reach you. And millions upon millions of others. I tell you, honey, in this age of mass media *one person can turn the world around*."

He stopped his pacing and turned to her, laughing softly. "You know what, sweetheart? You won't believe this. But last week I was drawing up plans to build a two hundred and fifty foot prayer tower out there in the backyard. Dear God, how foolish is the wisdom of men. Remember the Tower of Babel?" He hesitated in thought, the back of his hand pressed against his brow. "But wait a minute. Who knows? Maybe it was the necessary gesture—the intention, I mean. But wait. That won't do. God forgive me for trying to psych You out. God forgive us for our theology."

Moving close to her, he took the martini from her hand and downed it quickly. He sat at the table—for a moment lost in thought. And she felt simply lost. She could think of nothing to say, nothing to do. When at last he looked up, she had the impression again that he might start to smolder and burst into flame. His eyes blazed and his dark-tanned cheeks shone like new gold.

"It was all so simple, baby. After all the waiting and the struggle, so very, very simple. Sitting out there on my little mound, watching the magnificent conjunction of Venus and the moon, I suddenly recalled His words in the Gospel according to John: 'Whatsoever ye shall ask in my name, that will I do.' And so I did. I simply asked: 'In Christ's name, show Yourself.' And he did, baby. You see, He did. He did indeed—which means *in fact*. At once, quicker than light, He took me—or should I say I was taken—on a trip. Beyond the universe. Beyond. Clean beyond. And I saw it all. His body. That's all there is—His body. My God, baby, do you see the implications? All the world's ills—merely a disease in the Body of God. That's just one of—"

She interrupted his harangue, resorting in her despair to her only weapon, sarcasm. "And the great Milky Way? I suppose that's God's long white beard."

With a loud whoop of laughter, he rose and clapped his hands. "How did you know, baby? How in the world did you know? But there isn't time to talk about it now. I must go see Don, baby. Starting tomorrow, he'll be taking over the agency. And I—God willing—will start making preparations to go on the air and on television. Lord, Lord, tomorrow will be some busy day. I'll have to talk to Alan about borrowing against the insurance, et cetera, and I'll try to see Fleischmann down at WFOG. We may have to trim and cut back on some things, honey. You be thinking about the whole thing while I'm gone."

Squeezing her tight, he kissed her and was gone. In a moment she heard the pleasantly modulated whining of the little Hornet as he accelerated around the long curve of the 10th fairway. And she, making her slow way to the bedroom, her head splitting and martini in hand, wondered if she could invite sleep, this night or ever again. Stopping at the bathroom for a couple of tranquilizers, she tried to remember how much she had drunk. Probably five martinis at least—maybe six. She decided against the pills.

In the bedroom she slipped into a sheer sleeping gown, turned off the table lamp, and pulled the window drapes. She stared through the glass at a distant street lamp and listened to the sudden rise and gradual diminishing of the late-night traffic. Occasionally there came the squeal of tires as some teen-ager gunned his high-powered Mustang or Firebird or Chevy Super-Sport. And then as a big Diesel semi pulled into the new interstate highway a mile or so away, she was certain she could feel the tremor of the window glass on her fingertips. In one of his saner moments her husband had spoken of the time soon when the size of both trucks and cars would be limited by law. She felt the tears on her cheeks and heard herself saying aloud: "Oh, God, what am I to do?" At last her gaze moved to the spreading canopy of the Cuban myrtle in the front yard and just beyond to the little prayer mound. Again she breathed the words aloud: "Why not? Fight fire with fire."

She closed her eyes and prayed: Dear God, for my sake, undo what you have done. Set him free of this thing you have done to him. She could think of nothing more to say. Opening her eyes, she started to turn from the window, and as she freed her hands from the glass, she was aware of a tingling sensation in her left palm matched by a tingling sensation in her forehead. Her left hand felt drawn to her forehead; it moved first slowly and then rapidly and came to rest with a slight smacking sound, cupped above her brow.

Lowering her hand gently, she moved to the bed and lay on her back. She had never felt so relaxed. Or maybe hardly ever. Sometimes after an especially satisfactory lovemaking session with Jake she had felt sleep come upon her almost without consciousness. And so it came upon her now, a delicious and complete drowsiness, and she was only vaguely aware that her headache was gone.

When she woke, she stared for a moment at the ceiling, made just visible by the light from down the hallway, wondering how long she had slept. It must have been hours, for she felt wide awake and completely rested; but rising and turning on her right elbow, she saw that it was still quite dark outside. For the moment she heard no traffic noise; then somewhere close-by a mockingbird began to sing. Of course her husband was not in bed, but that was not strange. He might be still at Don's, or he might have come and slept and gone again, to his study or to the office or God knew where. She turned the other way to look at the clock. The luminous hands showed one-fifteen. Was it possible she had slept for only a few minutes? Then down the hallway the telephone rang; she reached for the bedroom extension and lifted the receiver before the second ring. For the next few moments she had the experience, for the first time since she was a child, of reliving exactly some past event. How, she wondered, could it seem so familiar when it was all so shockingly new?

To Doris' initial inquiry, she answered, "Why, no, he isn't. Isn't he there? He left for your house about twenty-five minutes ago. He should have got . . ."

"Listen, honey, I think we had better come over. You just . . ."

"Doris, what is it? Just tell me now. Is something wrong?"

"All right, honey, now don't get upset. It may not be anything at all. But just now on the late news—after Johnny Carson—there was a report of an accident. And . . ."

The rest she listened to with half her mind, all of it so seemingly familiar. A small compact car—not a foreign make—had been struck almost broadside by a big truck and semitrailer as it had entered the freeway from Florida Avenue. The small car had been hurtled down the embankment, had exploded and burned. No immediate identification of either the car or its driver had been established. No charges were filed against the driver of the truck, since the small car had failed to yield.

"Yes, Doris, all right. Of course, I'll wait right here."

She moved down the hallway and to the kitchen. She

sat at the table waiting for Don and Doris. She drank and thought, and thought and drank. A disease in God's body, he had said. Had He felt pain? she wondered. When the tiny Hornet exploded, and car and man had burst into flame, had it been like the bursting of a wee pimple on His great cheek or the plucking of a tiny errant hair from His great white beard?

7

MORAL BEHAVIOR

The Cold Equations
TOM GODWIN

"The Cold Equations" is a story about death. Death is one of the conditions of being human, a condition that every individual—once he breaks through the innocence and unawareness of childhood—must face. He recognizes that death is not separate from life, that it is part of the biological process; that each organism grown old must give the gift of his death to a new organism. Otherwise the planet would become too crowded for life to continue. He may also recognize that the fact of death gives significance and meaning to each moment of life. Because all things move and are transient, because they do not endure forever, they must be treasured while they exist. Beauty and transience are one. The beauty of the rose lies in the knowledge that it must be enjoyed now because tomorrow it will be gone. Life is richer because of death.

221

But even so, death is not easy for the individual to accept. The young girl, Marilyn, in "The Cold Equations" represents the condition man finds himself in. She must face death all alone. She appears to be in a universe controlled by the immutable laws of Nature—a kind of blind and mindless force that is totally indifferent to man's existence. It seems to be a universe without meaning. Writers of the modern world view known as existentialism suggest it is this condition that drives man to despair.

But the theistic existentialists suggest that man—despite the fact there is no rational evidence for the existence of God—can take a "leap to faith" and find God. This is one of the functions that religious systems throughout the past seem to have served. They help sustain man in the face of death. Many religions offer the hope of an existence after death. They prescribe a burial ritual in which the community joins together to sustain each other in the face of death. As we see in "The Cold Equations," a world in which there is no sustaining religion is a grim world.

Religions have responded in a variety of ways to the possibility of this grim material universe controlled by the immutable laws of Nature, where the individual's life is brief, without significance, and ended by death. All the responses help man grapple with his fear of death. Almost all religions suggest that man is both material and nonmaterial, or spiritual. The spiritual part of man's nature (and in some primitive religions the physical part) survives his death in some form of immortality.

How can one be successful in facing death? How can one survive? There are many answers. The elaborate burial ritual of the Egyptians, documented by the pyramids, records their response to death, which they saw as the gateway to another life. The Jewish religion emphasizes life on Earth, suggesting man's concern should be to live well here, instead of worrying about the future life, although its existence is not denied. The burial for an Orthodox Jew would be a simple ritual, using a plain pine box. The Christian religion has as its major emphasis the promise to each individual of resurrection and life after death. Its central symbol, the cross, represents Christ's actual death, which assures eternal life to those who believe in him.

Many of the Oriental religions reflect a less individualistic view of immortality than does Christianity. Hinduism claims reincarnation after death—being born again into this life but in another body. Whether the individual will be born into a higher or lower level depends on his actions in this life. Eventually he can escape from this Wheel of Life through Enlightenment and reach Nirvana, where he becomes one with Brahma. Like the drop of water that finally falls into the ocean, he at last overcomes his separateness and individuality, and knows the bliss of uniting with the World Soul.

The Chinese religion Taoism does not propose any kind of life after death because death does not exist as a separate entity. Taoism sees the unity of all things; contraries are not really opposites because, constantly turning and interchanging places, the opposites are but phases of a revolving wheel. So life and death are relative phases of the Tao's embracing continuum. In the end both are resolved in an all-encompassing circle, symbol of the final unity of Tao.

Mahayana Buddhism proposes a happy land where one goes to live after death. Islam teaches that man's deeds in this world will be judged, and he will be rewarded or punished in an afterlife of Heaven or Hell.

All religions celebrate life as being sacred and of the highest value. There are patterns of behavior that will both sustain life in this world and make the individual acceptable for passage into a future life. So a standard of acceptable behavior—or moral code—is developed: the Law, the Ten Commandments, the Way, the Straight Path. Out of man's fear of death, then, grows a moral code aimed at preserving life.

"The Cold Equations" is a very powerful story. When we read it, we are reminded that man is very different from inanimate matter, whose behavior is predictable in mathematical equations. He is different, too, from animals, and one of the major ways he is different is that he has emotions. He responds with feelings to the situations he encounters. He responds emotionally to his awareness of death—his own and the deaths of those he loves. It is hard to describe what emotions are, because, although they are felt, they cannot be seen. But even if there are not words to easily describe them, you know what emotions are; you easily identify an emotional response. You know when you are having one, and you will probably recognize the feeling when you read "The Cold Equations." It is very hard to finish the story without a lump in your throat.

The Cold Equations
TOM GODWIN

He was not alone.

There was nothing to indicate the fact but the white hand of the tiny gauge on the board before him. The control room was empty but for himself; there was no sound other than the murmur of the drives—but the white hand had moved. It had been on zero when the little ship was launched from the *Stardust*; now, an hour later, it had crept up. There was something in the supplies closet across the room, it was saying, some kind of a body that radiated heat.

It could be but one kind of a body—a living, human body.

He leaned back in the pilot's chair and drew a deep, slow breath, considering what he would have to do. He was an EDS pilot, inured to the sight of death, long since accustomed to it and to viewing the dying of another man with an objective lack of emotion, and he had no choice in what he must do. There could be no alternative—but it required a few moments of conditioning for even an EDS pilot to prepare himself to walk across the room and coldly, deliberately, take the life of a man he had yet to meet.

He would, of course, do it. It was the law, stated very bluntly and definitely in grim Paragraph L, Section 8, of Interstellar Regulations: *Any stowaway discovered in an EDS shall be jettisoned immediately following discovery.*

It was the law, and there could be no appeal.

It was a law not of men's choosing but made imperative by the circumstances of the space frontier. Galactic expansion had followed the development of the hyperspace drive and as men scattered wide across the frontier there had come the problem of contact with the isolated first-colonies and exploration parties. The huge hyperspace cruisers were the product of the combined genius and effort of Earth and were long and expensive in the building. They were not available in such numbers that small colonies could possess them. The cruisers carried the colonists to their new worlds and made periodic visits, running on tight schedules, but they could not stop and turn aside to visit colonies scheduled to be visited at another time; such a delay would destroy their schedule and produce a confusion and uncertainty that would wreck the complex interdependence between old Earth and the new worlds of the frontier.

Some method of delivering supplies or assistance when an emergency occurred on a world not scheduled for a visit had been needed and the Emergency Dispatch Ships had been the answer. Small and collapsible, they occupied little room in the hold of the cruiser; made of light metal and plastics, they were driven by a small rocket drive that consumed relatively little fuel. Each cruiser carried four EDS's and when a call for aid was received the nearest cruiser would drop into normal space long enough to launch an EDS with the needed supplies or personnel, then vanish again as it continued on its course.

The cruisers, powered by nuclear converters, did not use the liquid rocket fuel but nuclear converters were far too large and complex to permit their installation in the EDS's. The cruisers were forced by necessity to carry a limited amount of the bulky rocket fuel and the fuel was rationed with care; the cruiser's computers determining the exact amount of fuel each EDS would require for its mission. The computers considered the course coördinates, the mass of the EDS, the mass of pilot and cargo; they were very precise and accurate and omitted nothing from their calculations. They could not, however, foresee, and allow for, the added mass of a stowaway.

The *Stardust* had received the request from one of the exploration parties stationed on Woden; the six men of the party already being stricken with the fever carried by the green *kala* midges and their own supply of serum destroyed by the tornado that had torn through their camp. The *Stardust* had gone through the usual procedure; dropping into normal space to launch the EDS with the fever serum, then vanishing again in hyperspace. Now, an hour later, the gauge was saying there was something more than the small carton of serum in the supplies closet.

He let his eyes rest on the narrow white door of the closet. There, just inside, another man lived and breathed and was beginning to feel assured that discovery of his presence would now be too late for the pilot to alter the situation. It *was* too late—for the man behind the door it was far later than he thought and in a way he would find terrible to believe.

There could be no alternative. Additional fuel would be used during the hours of deceleration to compensate for the added mass of the stowaway; infinitesimal increments of fuel that would not be missed until the ship had almost reached its destination. Then, at some distance above the ground that might be as near as a thousand feet or as far as tens of thousands of feet, depending upon the mass of ship and cargo and the preceding period of deceleration, the unmissed increments of fuel would make their absence known; the EDS would expend its last drops of fuel with a sputter and go into whistling free fall. Ship and pilot and stowaway would merge together upon impact as a wreckage of metal and plastic, flesh and blood, driven deep into the soil. The stowaway had signed his own death warrant when he concealed himself on the ship; he could not be permitted to take seven others with him.

He looked again at the telltale white hand, then rose to his feet. What he must do would be unpleasant for both of them; the sooner it was over, the better. He stepped across the control room, to stand by the white door.

"Come out!" His command was harsh and abrupt above the murmur of the drive.

It seemed he could hear the whisper of a furtive movement inside the closet, then nothing. He visualized the stowaway cowering closer into one corner, suddenly worried by the possible consequences of his act and his self-assurance evaporating.

"I said *out!*"

He heard the stowaway move to obey and he waited with his eyes alert on the door and his hand near the blaster at his side.

The door opened and the stowaway stepped through it, smiling. "All right—I give up. Now what?"

It was a girl.

He stared without speaking, his hand dropping away from the blaster and acceptance of what he saw coming like a heavy and unexpected physical blow. The stowaway was not a man—she was a girl in her teens, standing before him in little white gypsy sandals with the top of her brown, curly head hardly higher than his shoulder, with a faint, sweet scent of perfume coming from her and her smiling face tilted up so her eyes could look unknowing and unafraid into his as she waited for his answer.

Now what? Had it been asked in the deep, defiant voice of a man he would have answered it with action, quick and efficient. He would have taken the stowaway's identification disk and ordered him into the air lock. Had the stowaway refused to obey, he would have used the blaster. It would not have taken long; within a minute the body would have been ejected into space—had the stowaway been a man.

He returned to the pilot's chair and motioned her to seat herself on the boxlike bulk of the drive-control units that sat against the wall beside him. She obeyed, his silence making the smile fade into the meek and guilty expression of a pup that has been caught in mischief and knows it must be punished.

"You still haven't told me," she said. "I'm guilty, so what happens to me now? Do I pay a fine, or what?"

"What are you doing here?" he asked. "Why did you stow away on this EDS?"

"I wanted to see my brother. He's with the government survey crew on Woden and I haven't seen him for ten years, not since he left Earth to go into government survey work."

"What was your destination on the *Stardust*?"

"Mimir. I have a position waiting for me there. My brother has been sending money home all the time to us—my father and mother and I—and he paid for a special course in linguistics I was taking. I graduated sooner than expected and I was offered this job on Mimir. I knew it would be almost a year before Gerry's job was done on Woden so he could come on to Mimir and that's why I hid in the closet, there. There was plenty of room for me and I was willing to pay the fine. There were only the two of us kids—Gerry and I—and I haven't seen him for so long, and I didn't want to wait another year when I could see him now, even though I knew I would be breaking some kind of a regulation when I did it."

I knew I would be breaking some kind of a regulation— In a way, she could not be blamed for her ignorance of the law; she was of Earth and had not realized that the laws of the space frontier must, of necessity, be as hard and relentless as the environment that gave them birth. Yet, to protect such as her from the results of their own ignorance of the frontier, there had been a sign over the door that led to the section of the *Stardust* that housed the EDS's; a sign that was plain for all to see and heed:

UNAUTHORIZED PERSONNEL
KEEP OUT!

"Does your brother know that you took passage on the *Stardust* for Mimir?"

"Oh, yes. I sent him a spacegram telling him about my graduation and about going to Mimir on the *Stardust* a month before I left Earth. I already knew Mimir was where he would be stationed in a little over a year. He gets a promotion then, and he'll be based on Mimir and not have to stay out a year at a time on field trips, like he does now."

There were two different survey groups on Woden, and he asked, "What is his name?"

"Cross—Gerry Cross. He's in Group Two—that was the way his address read. Do you know him?"

Group One had requested the serum; Group Two was eight thousand miles away, across the Western Sea.

"No, I've never met him," he said, then turned to the control board and cut the deceleration to a fraction of a gravity; knowing as he did so that it could not avert the ultimate end, yet doing the only thing he could do to prolong that ultimate end. The sensation was like that of the ship suddenly dropping and the girl's involuntary movement of surprise half lifted her from the seat.

"We're going faster now, aren't we?" she asked. "Why are we doing that?"

He told her the truth. "To save fuel for a little while."

"You mean, we don't have very much?"

He delayed the answer he must give her so soon to ask: "How did you manage to stow away?"

"I just sort of walked in when no one was looking my way," she said. "I was practicing my Gelanese on the native girl who does the cleaning in the Ship's Supply office when someone came in with an order for supplies for the survey crew on Woden. I slipped into the closet there after the ship was ready to go and just before you came in. It was an impulse of the moment to stow away, so I could get to see Gerry—and from the way you keep looking at me so grim, I'm not sure it was a very wise impulse.

"But I'll be a model criminal—or do I mean prisoner?" She smiled at him again. "I intended to pay for my keep on top of paying the fine. I can cook and I can patch clothes for everyone and I know how to do all kinds of useful things, even a little bit about nursing."

There was one more question to ask:

"Did you know what the supplies were that the survey crew ordered?"

"Why, no. Equipment they needed in their work, I supposed."

Why couldn't she have been a man with some ulterior motive? A fugitive from justice, hoping to lose himself on a raw new world; an opportunist, seeking transportation to the new colonies where he might find golden fleece for the taking; a crackpot, with a mission—

Perhaps once in his lifetime an EDS pilot would find such a stowaway on his ship; warped men, mean and selfish men, brutal and dangerous men—but never, before, a smiling, blue-eyed girl who was willing to pay her fine and work for her keep that she might see her brother.

He turned to the board and turned the switch that would signal the *Stardust*. The call would be futile but he could not, until he had exhausted that one vain hope, seize her and thrust her into the air lock as he would an animal—or a man. The delay, in the meantime, would not be dangerous with the EDS deceleration at fractional gravity.

A voice spoke from the communicator. "*Stardust*. Identify yourself and proceed."

"Barton, EDS 34G11. Emergency. Give me Commander Delhart."

There was a faint confusion of noises as the request

went through the proper channels. The girl was watching him, no longer smiling.

"Are you going to order them to come back after me?" she asked.

The communicator clicked and there was the sound of a distant voice saying, "Commander, the EDS requests—"

"Are they coming back after me?" she asked again. "Won't I get to see my brother, after all?"

"Barton?" The blunt, gruff voice of Commander Delhart came from the communicator. "What's this about an emergency?"

"A stowaway," he answered.

"A stowaway?" There was a slight surprise to the question. "That's rather unusual—but why the 'emergency' call? You discovered him in time so there should be no appreciable danger and I presume you've informed Ship's Records so his nearest relatives can be notified."

"That's why I had to call you, first. The stowaway is still aboard and the circumstances are so different—"

"Different?" the commander interrupted, impatience in his voice. "How can they be different? You know you have a limited supply of fuel; you also know the law, as well as I do: 'Any stowaway discovered in an EDS shall be jettisoned immediately following discovery.'"

There was the sound of a sharply indrawn breath from the girl. "*What does he mean?*"

"The stowaway is a girl."

"*What?*"

"She wanted to see her brother. She's only a kid and she didn't know what she was really doing."

"I see." All the curtness was gone from the commander's voice. "So you called me in the hope I could do something?" Without waiting for an answer he went on, "I'm sorry—I can do nothing. This cruiser must maintain its schedule; the life of not one person but the lives of many depend on it. I know how you feel but I'm powerless to help you. You'll have to go through with it. I'll have you connected with Ship's Records."

The communicator faded to a faint rustle of sound and he turned back to the girl. She was leaning forward on the bench, almost rigid, her eyes fixed wide and frightened.

"What did he mean, to go through with it? To jettison me . . . to go through with it—what did he mean? Not the way it sounded . . . he couldn't have. What did he mean . . . what did he really mean?"

Her time was too short for the comfort of a lie to be more than a cruelly fleeting delusion.

"He meant it the way it sounded."

"*No!*" She recoiled from him as though he had struck her, one hand half upraised as though to fend him off and stark unwillingness to believe in her eyes.

"It will have to be."

"No! You're joking—you're insane! You can't mean it!"

"I'm sorry." He spoke slowly to her, gently. "I should have told you before—I should have, but I had to do what I could first; I had to call the *Stardust*. You heard what the commander said."

"But you can't—if you make me leave the ship, I'll *die*."

"I know."

She searched his face and the unwillingness to believe left her eyes, giving way slowly to a look of dazed horror.

"You know?" She spoke the words far apart, numb and wonderingly.

"I know. It has to be like that."

"You mean it—you really mean it." She sagged back against the wall, small and limp like a little rag doll and all the protesting and disbelief gone. "You're going to do it—you're going to make me die?"

"I'm sorry," he said again. "You'll never know how sorry I am. It has to be that way and no human in the universe can change it."

"You're going to make me die and I didn't do anything to die for—I didn't *do* anything—"

He sighed, deep and weary. "I know you didn't, child. I know you didn't—"

"EDS." The communicator rapped brisk and metallic. "This is Ship's Records. Give us all information on subject's identification disk."

He got out of his chair to stand over her. She clutched the edge of the seat, her upturned face white under the brown hair and the lipstick standing out like a blood-red cupid's bow.

"*Now?*"

"I want your identification disk," he said—

She released the edge of the seat and fumbled at the chain that suspended the plastic disk from her neck with fingers that were trembling and awkward. He reached down and unfastened the clasp for her, then returned with the disk to his chair.

"Here's your data, Records: Identification Number T837—"

"One moment," Records interrupted. "This is to be filed on the gray card, of course?"

"Yes."

"And the time of the execution?"

"I'll tell you later."

"Later? This is highly irregular; the time of the subject's death is required before—"

He kept the thickness out of his voice with an effort. "Then we'll do it in a highly irregular manner—you'll hear the disk read, first. The subject is a girl and she's listening to everything that's said. Are you capable of understanding that?"

There was a brief, almost shocked, silence, then Records said meekly: "Sorry. Go ahead."

He began to read the disk, reading it slowly to delay the inevitable for as long as possible, trying to help her by giving her what little time he could to recover from her first horror and let it resolve into the calm of acceptance and resignation.

"Number T8374 dash Y54. Name: Marilyn Lee Cross. Sex: Female. Born: July 7, 2160. *She was only eighteen.* Height: 5–3. Weight: 110. *Such a slight weight, yet enough to add fatally to the mass of the shell-thin bubble that was an EDS.* Hair: Brown. Eyes: Blue. Complexion: Light. Blood Type: O. *Irrelevant data.* Destination: Port City, Mimir. *Invalid data—*"

He finished and said, "I'll call you later," then turned once again to the girl. She was huddled back against the wall, watching him with a look of numb and wondering fascination.

"They're waiting for you to kill me, aren't they? They want me dead, don't they? You and everybody on the cruiser want me dead, don't you?" Then the numbness broke and her voice was that of a frightened and bewildered child. "Everybody wants me dead and I didn't *do* anything. I didn't hurt anyone—I only wanted to see my brother."

"It's not the way you think—it isn't that way, at all," he said. "Nobody wants it this way; nobody would ever let it be this way if it was humanly possible to change it."

"Then why is it? I don't understand. Why is it?"

"This ship is carrying *kala* fever serum to Group One on Woden. Their own supply was destroyed by a tornado. Group Two—the crew your brother is in—is eight thousand miles away across the Western Sea and their helicopters can't cross it to help Group One. The fever is invariably fatal unless the serum can be had in time, and the six men in Group One will die unless this ship reaches them on schedule. These little ships are always given barely enough fuel to reach their destination and if you stay aboard your added weight will cause it to use up all its fuel before it reaches the ground. It will crash, then, and you and I will die and so will the six men waiting for the fever serum."

It was a full minute before she spoke, and as she considered his words the expression of numbness left her eyes.

"Is that it?" she asked at last. "Just that the ship doesn't have enough fuel?"

"Yes."

"I can go alone or I can take seven others with me—is that the way it is?"

"That's the way it is."

"And nobody wants me to have to die?"

"Nobody."

"Then maybe— Are you sure nothing can be done about it? Wouldn't people help me if they could?"

"Everyone would like to help you but there is nothing anyone can do. I did the only thing I could do when I called the *Stardust*."

"And it won't come back—but there might be other cruisers, mightn't there? Isn't there any hope at all that there might be someone, somewhere, who could do something to help me?"

She was leaning forward a little in her eagerness as she waited for his answer.

"No."

The word was like the drop of a cold stone and she again leaned back against the wall, the hope and eagerness leaving her face. "You're sure—you *know* you're sure?"

"I'm sure. There are no other cruisers within forty light years; there is nothing and no one to change things."

She dropped her gaze to her lap and began twisting a pleat of her skirt between her fingers, saying no more as her mind began to adapt itself to the grim knowledge.

It was better so; with the going of all hope would go the fear; with the going of all hope would come resignation. She needed time and she could have so little of it. How much?

The EDS's were not equipped with hull-cooling units; their speed had to be reduced to a moderate level before entering the atmosphere. They were decelerating at .10 gravity; approaching their destination at a far higher speed than the computers had calculated on. The *Stardust* had been quite near Woden when she launched the EDS; their present velocity was putting them nearer by the second. There would be a critical point, soon to be reached, when he would have to resume deceleration. When he did so the girl's weight would be multiplied by the gravities of deceleration, would become, suddenly, a factor of paramount importance; the factor the computers had been ignorant of when they determined the amount of fuel the EDS should have. She would have to go when deceleration began; it could be no other way. When would that be—how long could he let her stay?

"How long can I stay?"

He winced involuntarily from the words that were so like an echo of his own thoughts. How long? He didn't know; he would have to ask the ship's computers. Each EDS was given a meager surplus of fuel to compensate for unfavorable conditions within the atmosphere and relatively little fuel was being consumed for the time being. The memory banks of the computers would still contain all data pertaining to the course set for the EDS; such data would not be erased until the EDS reached its destination. He had only to give the computers the new data; the girl's weight and the exact time at which he had reduced the deceleration to .10.

"Barton." Commander Delhart's voice came abruptly from the communicator, as he opened his mouth to call the *Stardust*. "A check with Records shows me you haven't completed your report. Did you reduce the deceleration?"

So the commander knew what he was trying to do.

"I'm decelerating at point ten," he answered. "I cut the deceleration at seventeen fifty and the weight is a hundred and ten. I would like to stay at point ten as long as the computers say I can. Will you give them the question?"

It was contrary to regulations for an EDS pilot to make any changes in the course or degree of deceleration the computers had set for him but the commander made no mention of the violation, neither did he ask the reason for it. It was not necessary for him to ask; he had not become commander of an interstellar cruiser without both intelligence and an understanding of human nature. He said only: "I'll have that given the computers."

The communicator fell silent and he and the girl waited, neither of them speaking. They would not have to wait long; the computers would give the answer within moments of the asking. The new factors would be fed into the steel maw of the first bank and the electrical impulses would go through the complex circuits. Here and there a relay might click, a tiny cog turn over, but it would be essentially the electrical impulses that found the answer; formless, mindless, invisible, determining with utter precision how long the pale girl beside him might live. Then five little segments of metal in the second bank would trip in rapid succession against an inked ribbon and a second steel maw would spit out the slip of paper that bore the answer.

The chronometer on the instrument board read 18:10 when the commander spoke again.

"You will resume deceleration at nineteen ten."

She looked toward the chronometer, then quickly away from it. "Is that when . . . when I go?" she asked. He nodded and she dropped her eyes to her lap again.

"I'll have the course corrections given you," the

commander said. "Ordinarily I would never permit anything like this but I understand your position. There is nothing I can do, other than what I've just done, and you will not deviate from these new instructions. You will complete your report at nineteen ten. Now—here are the course corrections."

The voice of some unknown technician read them to him and he wrote them down on the pad clipped to the edge of the control board. There would, he saw, be periods of deceleration when he neared the atmosphere when the deceleration would be five gravities—and at five gravities, one hundred ten pounds would become five hundred fifty pounds.

The technician finished and he terminated the contact with a brief acknowledgment. Then, hesitating a moment, he reached out and shut off the communicator. It was 18:13 and he would have nothing to report until 19:10. In the meantime, it somehow seemed indecent to permit others to hear what she might say in her last hour.

He began to check the instrument readings, going over them with unnecessary slowness. She would have to accept the circumstances and there was nothing he could do to help her into acceptance; words of sympathy would only delay it.

It was 18:20 when she stirred from her motionlessness and spoke.

"So that's the way it has to be with me?"

He swung around to face her. "You understand now, don't you? No one would ever let it be like this if it could be changed."

"I understand," she said. Some of the color had returned to her face and the lipstick no longer stood out so vividly red. "There isn't enough fuel for me to stay; when I hid on this ship I got into something I didn't know anything about and now I have to pay for it."

She had violated a man-made law that said KEEP OUT but the penalty was not for men's making or desire and it was a penalty men could not revoke. A physical law had decreed: *h amount of fuel will power an EDS with a mass of m safely to its destination*; and a second physical law had decreed: *h amount of fuel will not power an EDS with a mass of m plus x safely to its destination.*

EDS's obeyed only physical laws and no amount of human sympathy for her could alter the second law.

"But I'm afraid. I don't want to die—not now. I want to live and nobody is doing anything to help me; everybody is letting me go ahead and acting just like nothing was going to happen to me. I'm going to die and nobody *cares*."

"We all do," he said. "I do and the commander does and the clerk in Ship's Records; we all care and each of us did what little he could to help you. It wasn't enough—it was almost nothing—but it was all we could do."

"Not enough fuel—I can understand that," she said, as though she had not heard his own words. "But to have to die for it. *Me*, alone—"

How hard it must be for her to accept the fact. She had never known danger of death; had never known the environments where the lives of men could be as fragile and fleeting as sea foam tossed against a rocky shore. She belonged on gentle Earth, in that secure and peaceful society where she could be young and gay and laughing with the others of her kind; where life was precious and well-guarded and there was always the assurance that tomorrow would come. She belonged in that world of soft winds and a warm sun, music and moonlight and gracious manners and not on the hard, bleak frontier.

"How did it happen to me so terribly quickly? An hour ago I was on the *Stardust*, going to Mimir. Now the *Stardust* is going on without me and I'm going to die and I'll never see Gerry and Mama and Daddy again—I'll never see anything again."

He hesitated, wondering how he could explain it to her so she would really understand and not feel she had, somehow, been the victim of a reasonlessly cruel injustice. She did not know what the frontier was like; she thought in terms of safe-secure Earth. Pretty girls were not jettisoned on Earth; there was a law against it. On Earth her plight would have filled the newscasts and a fast black Patrol ship would have been racing to her rescue. Everyone, everywhere, would have known of Marilyn Lee Cross and no effort would have been spared to save her life. But this was not Earth and there were no Patrol ships; only the *Stardust*, leaving them behind at many times the speed of light. There was no one to help her, there would be no Marilyn Lee Cross smiling from the newscasts tomorrow. Marilyn Lee Cross would be but a poignant memory for an EDS pilot and a name on a gray card in Ship's Records.

"It's different here; it's not like back on Earth," he said. "It isn't that no one cares; it's that no one can do anything to help. The frontier is big and here along its rim the colonies and exploration parties are scattered so thin and far between. On Woden, for example, there are only sixteen men—sixteen men on an entire world. The exploration parties, the survey crews, the little first-colonies—they're all fighting alien environments, trying to make a way for those who will follow after. The environments fight back and those who go first usually make mistakes only once. There is no margin of safety along the rim of the frontier; there can't be until the way is made for the others who will come later, until the new worlds are tamed and settled. Until then men will have to pay the penalty for making mistakes with no one to help them because there is no one *to* help them."

"I was going to Mimir," she said. "I didn't know about the frontier; I was only going to Mimir and *it's* safe."

"Mimir is safe but you left the cruiser that was taking you there."

She was silent for a little while. "It was all so wonderful at first; there was plenty of room for me on this ship and I would be seeing Gerry so soon . . . I didn't know about the fuel, didn't know what would happen to me—"

Her words trailed away and he turned his attention to the viewscreen, not wanting to stare at her as she fought her way through the black horror of fear toward the calm gray of acceptance.

Woden was a ball, enshrouded in the blue haze of its atmosphere, swimming in space against the background of star-sprinkled dead blackness. The great mass of Manning's Continent sprawled like a gigantic hourglass in the Eastern Sea with the western half of the Eastern Continent still visible. There was a thin line of shadow along the right-hand edge of the globe and the Eastern Continent was disappearing into it as the planet turned on its axis. An hour before the entire continent had been in view, now a thousand miles of it had gone into the thin edge of shadow and around to the night that lay on the other side of the world. The dark blue spot that was Lotus Lake was approaching the shadow. It was somewhere near the southern edge of the lake that Group Two had their camp. It would be night there, soon, and quick behind the coming of night the rotation of Woden on its axis would put Group Two beyond the reach of the ship's radio.

He would have to tell her before it was too late for her to talk to her brother. In a way, it would be better for both of them should they not do so but it was not for him to decide. To each of them the last words would be something to hold and cherish, something that would cut like the blade of a knife yet would be infinitely precious to remember, she for her own brief moments to live and he for the rest of his life.

He held down the button that would flash the grid lines on the viewscreen and used the known diameter of the planet to estimate the distance the southern tip of Lotus Lake had yet to go until it passed beyond radio range. It was approximately five hundred miles. Five hundred miles; thirty minutes—and the chronometer read 18:30. Allowing for error in estimating, it could not be later than 19:05 that the turning of Woden would cut off her brother's voice.

The first border of the Western Continent was already in sight along the left side of the world. Four thousand miles across it lay the shore of the Western Sea and the Camp of Group One. It had been in the

Western Sea that the tornado had originated, to strike with such fury at the camp and destroy half their pre-fabricated buildings, including the one that housed the medical supplies. Two days before the tornado had not existed; it had been no more than great gentle masses of air out over the calm Western Sea. Group One had gone about their routine survey work, unaware of the meeting of air masses out at sea, unaware of the force the union was spawning. It had struck their camp without warning; a thundering, roaring destruction that sought to annihilate all that lay before it. It had passed on, leaving the wreckage in its wake. It had destroyed the labor of months and had doomed six men to die and then, as though its task was accomplished, it once more began to resolve into gentle masses of air. But for all its deadliness, it had destroyed with neither malice nor intent. It had been a blind and mindless force, obeying the laws of nature, and it would have followed the same course with the same fury had men never existed.

Existence required Order and there was order; the laws of nature, irrevocable and immutable. Men could learn to use them but men could not change them. The circumference of a circle was always pi times the diameter and no science of Man would ever make it otherwise. The combination of chemical A with chemical B under condition C invariably produced reaction D. The law of gravitation was a rigid equation and it made no distinction between the fall of a leaf and the ponderous circling of a binary star system. The nuclear conversion process powered the cruisers that carried men to the stars; the same process in the form of a nova would destroy a world with equal efficiency. The laws *were*, and the universe moved in obedience to them. Along the frontier were arrayed all the forces of nature and sometimes they destroyed those who were fighting their way outward from Earth. The men of the frontier had long ago learned the bitter futility of cursing the forces that would destroy them, for the forces were blind and deaf; the futility of looking to the heavens for mercy, for the stars of the galaxy swung in their long, long sweep of two hundred million years, as inexorably controlled as they by the laws that knew neither hatred nor compassion. The men of the frontier knew—but how was a girl from Earth to fully understand? *H amount of fuel will not power an EDS with a mass of m plus x safely to its destination.* To himself and her brother and parents she was a sweet-faced girl in her teens; to the laws of nature she was *x*, the unwanted factor in a cold equation.

She stirred again on the seat. "Could I write a letter? I want to write to Mama and Daddy and I'd like to talk to Gerry. Could you let me talk to him over your radio there?"

"I'll try to get him," he said.

He switched on the normal-space transmitter and pressed the signal button. Someone answered the buzzer almost immediately.

"Hello. How's it going with you fellows now—is the EDS on its way?"

"This isn't Group One; this is the EDS," he said. "Is Gerry Cross there?"

"Gerry? He and two others went out in the helicopter this morning and aren't back yet. It's almost sundown, though, and he ought to be back right away —in less than an hour at the most."

"Can you connect me through to the radio in his 'copter?"

"Huh-uh. It's been out of commission for two months—some printed circuits went haywire and we can't get any more until the next cruiser stops by. Is it something important—bad news for him, or something?"

"Yes—it's very important. When he comes in get him to the transmitter as soon as you possibly can."

"I'll do that; I'll have one of the boys waiting at the field with a truck. Is there anything else I can do?"

"No, I guess that's all. Get him there as soon as you can and signal me."

He turned the volume to an inaudible minimum, an act that would not affect the functioning of the signal buzzer, and unclipped the pad of paper from the control board. He tore off the sheet containing his flight instructions and handed the pad to her, together with pencil.

"I'd better write to Gerry, too," she said as she took them. "He might not get back to camp in time."

She began to write, her fingers still clumsy and uncertain in the way they handled the pencil and the top of it trembling a little as she poised it between words. He turned back to the viewscreen, to stare at it without seeing it.

She was a lonely little child, trying to say her last good-by, and she would lay out her heart to them. She would tell them how much she loved them and she would tell them to not feel badly about it, that it was only something that must happen eventually to everyone and she was not afraid. The last would be a lie and it would be there to read between the sprawling uneven lines; a valiant little lie that would make the hurt all the greater for them.

Her brother was of the frontier and he would understand. He would not hate the EDS pilot for doing nothing to prevent her going; he would know there had been nothing the pilot could do. He would understand, though the understanding would not soften the shock and pain when he learned his sister was gone. But the others, her father and mother—they would not understand. They were of Earth and they would think in the manner of those who had never lived where the safety margin of life was a thin, thin line—and sometimes not at all. What would they think of the faceless, unknown pilot who had sent her to her death?

They would hate him with cold and terrible intensity but it really didn't matter. He would never see them, never know them. He would have only the memories to remind him; only the nights to fear, when a blue-eyed girl in gypsy sandals would come in his dreams to die again—

He scowled at the viewscreen and tried to force his thoughts into less emotional channels. There was nothing he could do to help her. She had unknowingly subjected herself to the penalty of a law that recognized neither innocence nor youth nor beauty, that was incapable of sympathy or leniency. Regret was illogical—and yet, could knowing it to be illogical ever keep it away?

She stopped occasionally, as though trying to find the right words to tell them what she wanted them to know, then the pencil would resume its whispering to the paper. It was 18:37 when she folded the letter in a square and wrote a name on it. She began writing another, twice looking up at the chronometer as though she feared the black hand might reach its rendezvous before she had finished. It was 18:45 when she folded it as she had done the first letter and wrote a name and address on it.

She held the letters out to him. "Will you take care of these and see that they're enveloped and mailed?"

"Of course." He took them from her hand and placed them in a pocket of his gray uniform shirt.

"These can't be sent off until the next cruiser stops by and the *Stardust* will have long since told them about me, won't it?" she asked. He nodded and she went on. "That makes the letters not important in one way but in another way they're very important—to me, and to them."

"I know. I understand, and I'll take care of them."

She glanced at the chronometer, then back to him. "It seems to move faster all the time, doesn't it?"

He said nothing, unable to think of anything to say, and she asked, "Do you think Gerry will come back to camp in time?"

"I think so. They said he should be in right away."

She began to roll the pencil back and forth between her palms. "I hope he does. I feel sick and scared and I want to hear his voice again and maybe I won't feel so alone. I'm a coward and I can't help it."

"No," he said, "you're not a coward. You're afraid, but you're not a coward."

"Is there a difference?"

He nodded. "A lot of difference."

"I feel so alone. I never did feel like this before; like I was all by myself and there was nobody to care what happened to me. Always, before, there was Mama and Daddy there and my friends around me. I had lots of friends, and they had a going-away party for me the night before I left."

Friends and music and laughter for her to remember —and on the viewscreen Lotus Lake was going into the shadow.

"Is it the same with Gerry?" she asked. "I mean, if he should make a mistake, would he have to die for it, all alone and with no one to help him?"

"It's the same with all along the frontier; it will always be like that so long as there is a frontier."

"Gerry didn't tell us. He said the pay was good and he sent money home all the time because Daddy's little shop just brought in a bare living but he didn't tell us it was like this."

"He didn't tell you his work was dangerous?"

"Well—yes. He mentioned that, but we didn't understand. I always thought danger along the frontier was something that was a lot of fun; an exciting adventure, like in the three-D shows." A wan smile touched her face for a moment. "Only it's not, is it? It's not the same at all, because when it's real you can't go home after the show is over."

"No," he said. "No, you can't."

Her glance flicked from the chronometer to the door of the air lock then down to the pad and pencil she still held. She shifted her position slightly to lay them on the bench beside her, moving one foot out a little. For the first time he saw that she was not wearing Vegan gypsy sandals but only cheap imitations; the expensive

Vegan leather was some kind of grained plastic, the silver buckle was gilded iron, the jewels were colored glass. *Daddy's little shop just brought in a bare living* —She must have left college in her second year, to take the course in linguistics that would enable her to make her own way and help her brother provide for her parents, earning what she could by part-time work after classes were over. Her personal possessions on the *Stardust* would be taken back to her parents—they would neither be of much value nor occupy much storage space on the return voyage.

"Isn't it—" She stopped, and he looked at her questioningly. "Isn't it cold in here?" she asked, almost apologetically. "Doesn't it seem cold to you?"

"Why, yes," he said. He saw by the main temperature gauge that the room was at precisely normal temperature. "Yes, it's colder than it should be."

"I wish Gerry would get back before it's too late. Do you really think he will, and you didn't just say so to make me feel better?"

"I think he will—they said he would be in pretty soon." On the viewscreen Lotus Lake had gone into the shadow but for the thin blue line of its western edge and it was apparent he had overestimated the time she would have in which to talk to her brother. Reluctantly, he said to her, "His camp will be out of radio range in a few minutes; he's on that part of Woden that's in the shadow"—he indicated the viewscreen—"and the turning of Woden will put him beyond contact. There may not be much time left when he comes in—not much time to talk to him before he fades out. I wish I could do something about it—I would call him right now if I could."

"Not even as much time as I will have to stay?"

"I'm afraid not."

"Then—" She straightened and looked toward the air lock with pale resolution. "Then I'll go when Gerry passes beyond range. I won't wait any longer after that —I won't have anything to wait for."

Again there was nothing he could say.

"Maybe I shouldn't wait at all. Maybe I'm selfish— maybe it would be better for Gerry if you just told him about it afterward."

There was an unconscious pleading for denial in the way she spoke and he said, "He wouldn't want you to do that, to not wait for him."

"It's already coming dark where he is, isn't it? There will be all the long night before him, and Mama and Daddy don't know yet that I won't ever be coming back like I promised them I would. I've caused everyone I love to be hurt, haven't I? I didn't want to—I didn't intend to."

"It wasn't your fault," he said. "It wasn't your fault at all. They'll know that. They'll understand."

"At first I was so afraid to die that I was a coward and thought only of myself. Now, I see how selfish I was. The terrible thing about dying like this is not that I'll be gone but that I'll never see them again; never be able to tell them that I didn't take them for granted; never be able to tell them I knew of the sacrifices they made to make my life happier, that I knew all the things they did for me and that I loved them so much more than I ever told them. I've never told them any of those things. You don't tell them such things when you're young and your life is all before you—you're so very afraid of sounding sentimental and silly.

"But it's so different when you have to die—you wish you had told them while you could and you wish you could tell them you're sorry for all the little mean things you ever did or said to them. You wish you could tell them that you didn't really mean to ever hurt their feelings and for them to only remember that you always loved them far more than you ever let them know."

"You don't have to tell them that," he said. "They will know—they've always known it."

"Are you sure?" she asked. "How can you be sure? My people are strangers to you."

"Wherever you go, human nature and human hearts are the same."

"And they will know what I want them to know—that I love them?"

"They've always known it, in a way far better than you could ever put in words for them."

"I keep remembering the things they did for me, and it's the little things they did that seem to be the most important to me, now. Like Gerry—he sent me a bracelet of fire-rubies on my sixteenth birthday. It was beautiful—it must have cost him a month's pay. Yet, I remember him more for what he did the night my kitten got run over in the street. I was only six years old and he held me in his arms and wiped away my tears and told me not to cry, that Flossy was gone for just a little while, for just long enough to get herself a new fur coat and she would be on the foot of my bed the very next morning. I believed him and quit crying and went to sleep dreaming about my kitten coming back. When I woke up the next morning, there was

Flossy on the foot of my bed in a brand-new white fur coat, just like he had said she would be.

"It wasn't until a long time later that Mama told me Gerry had got the pet-shop owner out of bed at four in the morning and, when the man got mad about it, Gerry told him he was either going to go down and sell him the white kitten right then or he'd break his neck."

"It's always the little things you remember people by; all the little things they did because they wanted to do them for you. You've done the same for Gerry and your father and mother; all kinds of things that you've forgotten about but that they will never forget."

"I hope I have. I would like for them to remember me like that."

"They will."

"I wish—" She swallowed. "The way I'll die—I wish they wouldn't ever think of that. I've read how people look who die in space—their insides all ruptured and exploded and their lungs out between their teeth and then, a few seconds later, they're all dry and shapeless and horribly ugly. I don't want them to ever think of me as something dead and horrible, like that."

"You're their own, their child and their sister. They could never think of you other than the way you would want them to; the way you looked the last time they saw you."

"I'm still afraid," she said. "I can't help it, but I don't want Gerry to know it. If he gets back in time, I'm going to act like I'm not afraid at all and—"

The signal buzzer interrupted her, quick and imperative.

"Gerry!" She came to her feet. "It's Gerry, now!"

He spun the volume control knob and asked: "Gerry Cross?"

"Yes," her brother answered, an undertone of tenseness to his reply. "The bad news—what is it?"

She answered for him, standing close behind him and leaning down a little toward the communicator, her hand resting small and cold on his shoulder.

"Hello, Gerry." There was only a faint quaver to betray the careful casualness of her voice. "I wanted to see you—"

"Marilyn!" There was sudden and terrible apprehension in the way he spoke her name. "What are you doing on that EDS?"

"I wanted to see you," she said again. "I wanted to see you, so I hid on this ship—"

"You *hid* on it?"

"I'm a stowaway . . . I didn't know what it would mean—"

"*Marilyn!*" It was the cry of a man who calls hopeless and desperate to someone already and forever gone from him. "What have you done?"

"I . . . it's not—" Then her own composure broke and the cold little hand gripped his shoulder convulsively. "Don't, Gerry—I only wanted to see you; I didn't intend to hurt you. Please, Gerry, don't feel like that —"

Something warm and wet splashed on his wrist and he slid out of the chair, to help her into it and swing the microphone down to her own level.

"Don't feel like that—Don't let me go knowing you feel like that—"

The sob she had tried to hold back choked in her throat and her brother spoke to her. "Don't cry, Marilyn." His voice was suddenly deep and infinitely gentle, with all the pain held out of it. "Don't cry, Sis—you mustn't do that. It's all right, Honey—everything is all right."

"I—" Her lower lip quivered and she bit into it. "I didn't want you to feel that way—I just wanted us to say good-by because I have to go in a minute."

"Sure—sure. That's the way it'll be, Sis. I didn't mean to sound the way I did." Then his voice changed to a tone of quick and urgent demand. "EDS—have you called the *Stardust?* Did you check with the computers?"

"I called the *Stardust* almost an hour ago. It can't turn back, there are no other cruisers within forty light-years, and there isn't enough fuel."

"Are you sure that the computers had the correct data—sure of everything?"

"Yes—do you think I could ever let it happen if I wasn't sure? I did everything I could do. If there was anything at all I could do now, I would do it."

"He tried to help me, Gerry." Her lower lip was no longer trembling and the short sleeves of her blouse were wet where she had dried her tears. "No one can help me and I'm not going to cry any more and everything will be all right with you and Daddy and Mama, won't it?"

"Sure—sure it will. We'll make out fine."

Her brother's words were beginning to come in more faintly and he turned the volume control to maximum. "He's going out of range," he said to her. "He'll be gone within another minute."

"You're fading out, Gerry," she said. "You're going out of range. I wanted to tell you—but I can't now. We must say good-by so soon—but maybe I'll see you again. Maybe I'll come to you in your dreams with my hair in braids and crying because the kitten in my arms is dead; maybe I'll be the touch of a breeze that whispers to you as it goes by; maybe I'll be one of those gold-winged larks you told me about, singing my silly head off to you; maybe, at times, I'll be nothing you can see but you will know I'm there beside you. Think of me like that, Gerry; always like that and not—the other way."

Dimmed to a whisper by the turning of Woden, the answer came back:

"Always like that, Marilyn—always like that and never any other way."

"Our time is up, Gerry—I have to go, now. Good—" Her voice broke in mid-word and her mouth tried to twist into crying. She pressed her hand hard against it and when she spoke again the words came clear and true:

"Good-by, Gerry."

Faint and ineffably poignant and tender, the last words came from the cold metal of the communicator:

"Good-by, little sister—"

She sat motionless in the hush that followed, as though listening to the shadow-echoes of the words as they died away, then she turned away from the communicator, toward the air lock, and he pulled down the black lever beside him. The inner door of the air lock slid swiftly open, to reveal the bare little cell that was waiting for her, and she walked to it.

She walked with her head up and the brown curls brushing her shoulders, with the white sandals stepping as sure and steady as the fractional gravity would permit and the gilded buckles twinkling with little lights of blue and red and crystal. He let her walk alone and made no move to help her, knowing she would not want it that way. She stepped into the air lock and turned to face him, only the pulse in her throat to betray the wild beating of her heart.

"I'm ready," she said.

He pushed the lever up and the door slid its quick barrier between them, enclosing her in black and utter darkness for her last moments of life. It clicked as it locked in place and he jerked down the red lever. There was a slight waver to the ship as the air gushed from the lock, a vibration to the wall as though something had bumped the outer door in passing, then there was nothing and the ship was dropping true and steady again. He shoved the red lever back to close the door on the empty air lock and turned away, to walk to the pilot's chair with the slow steps of a man old and weary.

Back in the pilot's chair he pressed the signal button of the normal-space transmitter. There was no response; he had expected none. Her brother would have to wait through the night until the turning of Woden permitted contact through Group One.

It was not yet time to resume deceleration and he waited while the ship dropped endlessly downward with him and the drives purred softly. He saw that the white hand of the supplies closet temperature gauge was on zero. A cold equation had been balanced and he was alone on the ship. Something shapeless and ugly was hurrying ahead of him, going to Woden where its brother was waiting through the night, but the empty ship still lived for a little while with the presence of the girl who had not known about the forces that killed with neither hatred nor malice. It seemed, almost, that she still sat small and bewildered and frightened on the metal box beside him, her words echoing hauntingly clear in the void she had left behind her:

I didn't do anything to die for—I didn't do anything—

8

THE PROBLEM OF GOOD AND EVIL—A TAOISTIC VIEW

Dazed
THEODORE STURGEON

"Dazed" is a story that explores the problem of evil. Evil is not a common word in our vocabulary today, but it has been in the past—for example, it was a major concern of the New England Puritans. All religions have had to deal with the matter of evil—that which seems opposed to man's good, that which brings him sorrow, suffering, and misfortune. Man would like to protect himself from evil, so he must ask: What causes it? How can it be controlled? Does it exist in the heart of man or is it an outside cosmic force?

If the religion of a people has multiple gods, the matter of evil can be more easily understood. Some gods are evil, some good. Zoroastrianism, a religion of ancient Persia, had a Prince of Light and a Prince of Darkness struggling against each other in a dualistic system. But the Judeo-Christian tradition practices

monotheism, the belief in one God, and so the explanation of evil becomes more difficult. God is described as
omniscient (all-knowing), omnipotent (all-powerful),
and omnipresent (ever-present). How, then, is the existence of evil to be understood? Why does God allow
it to exist if he is a benevolent God who loves man?

This problem is one theologians have struggled with
throughout the long existence of Christianity. Evil does
exist, they almost all agree. It is there, along with good,
and God has left man free to choose one or the other.
The wise use of his free will to make choices is man's
major responsibility.

If evil exists, where is it to be found? In man's nature? Here the opinion is split, and a violent disagreement has long existed. One group says man is fallen
(as symbolized by Adam's fall in the Garden) and
man has evil in his heart. He is innately evil. The other
group as loudly insists that man is innately good. Evil
exists outside man—perhaps in his social institutions.
The little child is born pure and only becomes affected
by evil as he lives in society.

Theodore Sturgeon in "Dazed" asks again: How are
we to understand evil? To explore the question he
creates a protagonist who, in 1950, looks at the world
around him and is dazed by the amount of suffering,
pain, and evil he sees. Most distressing to him are all
the senseless wars. And yet, as he looks at people, they
seem to be brighter and better educated than ever before in the world's history. "Why," he asks, do "smart
people do dumb things?" Why do they worry only
about security instead of trying to solve problems?
Why aren't they concerned with the far more important

matter of the relationship of man to his planet? Why, from the actions of these apparently good people, does evil result? Something is wrong. What?

For his answer, Sturgeon turns to China and the very old religion of Taoism. Based on the teachings of Lao-tzu, who lived over twenty-five hundred years ago, Taoism defines "the Way" man must live on this earth to achieve harmony. Heaven, Earth, and man are a single, indivisible unity controlled by cosmic law—Tao. All parts must be balanced; if man lives so that he disturbs the balance, the cosmos breaks down. The universe possesses two interacting forces—yin and yang. Yang is the positive, masculine force—active, dry, bright, warm, sunlight and fire. Yin is the negative, female principle—passive, wet, dark, cold, mysterious, shadow and water. These two principles are not in conflict, but in harmony. By following the Tao, the "road" or "proper way to go," man can act so as to make sure that yin and yang are in balance. Taoism's bible, the *Tao Te Ching*, explains this way and how man should order his life to achieve it.

The world that Sturgeon describes in "Dazed" is unbalanced because yin and yang have become disturbed and their equilibrium lost. But as Sturgeon continues his discussion of the apparent existence of evil in the world, he yokes Taoism with the Christian terminology of the Devil. The problem in the world is too much good; *the Devil is dead.* But Sturgeon reminds us that the Devil is called Lucifer, the bringer of light. Lucifer and Christ are not in opposition; they are—like yin and yang—both good and both necessary. They are parts of the same whole. Man's problems come from their imbalance—from the absence, not the presence, of Lucifer! The problem, then, can only be solved by bringing Lucifer back into the world!

The view of man's nature expressed in this story is very positive. The problems of the world are not the fault merely of human beings, but rather of too much likeness. Man has reduced his possibilities to either/or, and selected one, forcing all to follow the same choice. The totalitarian world of *Nineteen Eighty-four* begins to appear. This produces the imbalance that disrupts society. Instead, man must learn to let opposites exist together, for without this, the natural balance of life is disrupted and there are unforeseen and negative consequences. As the ecological view suggests, all things are interrelated, and the delicate balance of the whole must be preserved if life on this planet is to survive.

The way in which the protagonist of "Dazed" receives his understanding of the apparent evil in a world of good people is interesting. He does not reason it out—according to Western intellectual patterns—but rather receives the insight in the intuitive flash of Oriental religions. In a mystical moment of illumination by the divine (which Zen Buddhism calls "satori") he is given a gift of understanding and enlightenment.

Dazed
THEODORE STURGEON

I

I work for a stockbroker on the twenty-first floor. Things have not been good for stockbrokers recently, what with tight money and hysterical reaction to the news and all that. When business gets really bad for a brokerage it often doesn't fail—it merges. This has something to do with the public image. The company I work for is going through the agony. For the lower echelons—me—that means detail you wouldn't believe, with a reduced staff. In other words, night work. Last night I worked without looking up until my whole body was the shape of the chair and there was a blue haze around the edges of everything I could see. I finished a stack and peered at the row of stacks still to be done and tried to get up. It took three tries before my hips and knees would straighten enough to let me totter into the hall and down to the men's room. It never occurred to me to close the office door and I guess the confusion, all the strange faces coming and going for the past few days, extended to the security man downstairs. However it happened, there was a dazed man in my office when I came back a moment later.

He was well dressed—I guess that, too, helped him pass the guards—in a brown sharkskin suit with funny lapels, what you might call up-to-the-minute camp. He wore an orange knitted tie the like of which you only see in a new boutique or an old movie. I'd say he was in his twenties—not yet twenty-five. And dazed.

When I walked in and stopped dead he gave me a lost look and said, "This is my office."

I said the only thing I could think of. "Oh?"

He pivoted slowly all the way around, looking at the desk, the shelves, the files.

When he came around to face me again he said, "This isn't my office."

He had to be with the big five-name brokerage house that was gobbling up my company in its time of need. I asked him.

"No," he said, "I work for *Fortune*."

"Look," I said, "you're not only in the wrong office, you're in the wrong building. Time-Life is on Sixth Avenue—been there since nineteen fifty-two."

"Fifty-*two*—" He looked around the room again. "But I—but it's—"

He sat down on the settle. I had the idea he'd have collapsed on the floor if the settle hadn't been there. He asked me what day it was. I think I misunderstood.

"Thursday," I said. I looked at my watch. "Well, it's now Friday."

"I mean, what's the date?"

I pointed to the desk calendar right beside him. He looked at it twice, each one a long careful look. I never saw a man turn the color he turned. He covered his eyes. Even his lips went white.

"Oh, my God."

"You all right?" I asked—a very stupid question.

"Tell me something," he said after a while. "Has there been a war?"

"You have to be kidding."

He took his hand down and looked at me, so lost, so frightened. Not frightened. There has to be a word.

Anguished. He needed answers—needed them. Not questions, not now.

I said, "It's been going on a long time."

"A lot of young guys killed?"

"Upwards of fifty thousand." Something made me add: "Americans. The other side, five, six times that."

"Oh, my God," he said again. Then: "It's my fault."

Now I have to tell you up front that it never occurred to me for one second that this guy was on any kind of a drug trip. Not that I'm an expert, but there are times when you just know. Whatever was bothering him was genuine—at least genuine to him. Besides, there was something about him I had to like. Not the clothes, not the face, just the guy, the kind of guy he was.

I said, "Hey, you look like hell and I'm sick and tired of what I'm doing. Let's take a break and go to the Automat for coffee."

He gave me that lost look again. "Is the lid off on sex? I mean, young kids—"

"Like rabbits," I said. "Also your friendly neighborhood movie—I don't know what they're going to do for an encore." I had to ask him, "Where've you been?"

He shook his head and said candidly, "I don't know where it was. Are people leaving their jobs—and school—going off to live on the land?"

"Some," I said. "Come on."

I switched off the overhead light, leaving my desk lamp lit. He got to his feet as if he were wired to the switch, but then just stood looking at the calendar.

"Are there bombings?"

"Three yesterday, in Newark. Come on."

"Oh, my God," he said and came. I locked the door and we went down the corridor to the elevators. Air wheezed in the shaft as the elevator rose. "It always whistles like that late at night," he said. I had never noticed that but knew he was right as soon as he said it. He also said weakly, "You don't feel like walking down?"

"Twenty-one flights?"

The doors slid open. The guy didn't want to get in. But I mean, he *really* didn't. I stood on the crack while he screwed up his courage. It didn't take long but I could see it was a mighty battle. He won it and came in, turned around and leaned against the back wall. I pushed the button and we started down. He looked pretty bad. I said something to him but he put up a hand, waved my words away before they were out. He didn't move again until the doors opened and then he looked into the lobby as if he didn't know what to expect. But it was just the lobby, with the oval information desk we called the fishbowl and the shiny floor and the portable wooden desk, like a lectern, where you signed in and out after hours and where the guard was supposed to be. We breezed by it and out into Rockefeller Center. He took a deep breath and immediately coughed.

"What's that smell?"

I'd been about to say something trivial about the one good thing about working late—you could breathe the air, but I didn't say it.

"The smog, I guess."

"Smog. Oh yes, smoke and fog. I remember." Then he seemed to remember something else, something that brought his predicament, whatever it was, back with a hammer blow. "Well of course," he said as if to himself. "Has to be."

On Sixth Avenue (New Yorkers still won't call it Avenue of the Americas) we passed two laughing couples. One of the girls was wearing a see-through top made of plastic chainmail. The other had on a very maxi coat swinging open over hotpants. My companion was appreciative but not astonished. I think what he said was, "That, too—" nodding his head. He watched every automobile that passed and his eyes flicked over the places where they used to sell books and back-date periodicals, every single one of them now given over to peepshows and beaver magazines. He had the same nod of his head for this.

We reached the Automat and it occurred to me that an uncharacteristic touch of genius had made me suggest it. I had first seen the Automat when I had ridden in on my mother's hip more years ago than I'll mention —and many times since—and very little has changed —except, of course, the numbers on the little off-white cards that tell you how many nickels you have to put in the slot to claim your food. After a few years' absence one tends to yelp at the sight of them. I always do and the strange young man with me did, too. Aside from that, there is a timeless quality about the place, especially in the small hours of the morning. The overage, overpainted woman furtively eating catsup is there as she, or someone just like her, has been for fifty years; and the young couple, homely to you but beautiful to each other, full of sleepiness and discovery; and the working stiff in the case-hardened slideway of his life, grabbing a bite on the way from bed to work and not yet awake—no need to be—and his counterpart headed in the other direction; no need for him to be awake either. And all around: the same marble change counter with the deep worn pits in it from countless millions of coins dropped and scooped; behind it the same weary automaton; and around you the same nickel (not chrome) framing for the hundreds of little glass-fronted doors through which the food always looks so much better than it is. All in all, it's a fine place for the reorientation of time-travelers.

"Are you a time-traveler?" I asked, following my own whimsy and hoping to make him smile.

He didn't smile. "No," he said. "Yes, I—well—" flickering panic showed in his eyes—"I don't really know."

We bought our coffee straight out of the lion's mouth and carried it to a corner table. I think that when we were settled there he really looked at me for the first time.

He said, "You've been very kind."

"Well," I said, "I was glad of the break."

"Look, I'm going to tell you what happened. I guess I don't expect you to believe me. I wouldn't in your place."

"Try me," I offered. "And anyway—what difference does it make whether I believe you?"

" 'Belief or nonbelief has no power over objective truth.' " I could tell by his voice he was quoting somebody. The smile I had been looking for almost came and he said, "You're right. I'll tell you what happened because—well, because I want to. Have to."

I said fine and told him to shoot. He shot.

* * *

I work in Circulation Promotion [he began]. Or maybe I should say I *worked*—I guess I should. You'll have to pardon me, I'm a little confused. There's so much—

Maybe I should start over. It didn't begin in Rockefeller Center. It started, oh, I don't know how long ago, with me wondering about things. Not that I'm anything special—I'm not saying I am—but it seems nobody else wonders about the same things I do. I mean, people are so close to what happens that they don't seem to know what's going on.

Wait, I don't want to confuse you, too. One of us is enough. Let me give you an example.

World War II was starting up when I was a kid and one day a bunch of us sat around, trying to figure out who would be fighting who. Us and the British and French on one side, sure—the Germans and Austrians and Italians on the other—that was clear enough. And the Japanese. But beyond that?

It's all history and hindsight now and there's no special reason to think about it, but at the time it was totally impossible for anyone to predict the lineup that actually came about. Go back in the files of newspaper editorials—*Harper's* or *Reader's Digest* or any other— and you'll see what I mean. Nobody predicted that up to the very end of the war our best and strongest friend would be at peace with our worst and deadliest enemy. I mean, if you put it on personal terms—if you and I are friends and there's somebody out to kill me and I find out that you and he are buddies—could we even so much as speak to each other again? Yet here was the Soviet Union, fighting shoulder to shoulder with us against the Nazis, while for nearly five years they were at peace with Japan!

And about Japan: there were hundreds of thousands of Chinese who had been fighting a life-and-death war against the Japanese for ten years—ten years, man!—and along with them, Koreans. So we spent billions getting ourselves together to mount air strikes against Japan from thousands of miles away—New Guinea, the Solomons, Saipan, Tinian. Do you know how far it is from the Chinese mainland to Tokyo, across the Sea of Japan? Six hundred miles. Do you know how far it is from Pusan, Korea, to Hiroshima? A hundred and thirty!

I'm sorry. I get excited like that to this day when I think of it. But damn it—why didn't we negotiate to move in and set up airstrips on the mainland and Korea? Do you think the natives would have turned us down? Or is it that we just don't like chop suey? Oh, sure—there are a lot of arguments like backing up Chiang against the Communists and I even read somewhere that it was not our policy to interfere in Southeast Asia. (Did I say something funny?) But you know Chiang and the Communists had a truce—and kept it too—to fight the common enemy.

Well—all right. All that seems a long way from what happened to me, I suppose, but it's the kind of thing I've spent my life wondering about. It's not just wars that bring out the thing I'm talking about, though God knows they make it plainer to see. Italy and Germany sharpening their newest weapons and strategies in the Spanish civil war, for example, or Mussolini's invasion of Ethiopia—hell, the more sophisticated people got the less they could see what was in front of them. Any kid in a kindergarten knows a bully when he sees one and has sense enough at least to be afraid. Any sixth-grader knows how to organize a pressure group against a bad guy. Wars, you see, are really life-and-death situations, where what's possible, practical —logical—has a right to emerge. When it doesn't— you have to wonder. French peasants taxed till they bled to build the Maginot Line all through the thirties, carefully preparing against the kind of war they fought in nineteen fourteen.

But let's look some place else. Gonorrhea could be absolutely stamped out in six months, syphilis maybe in a year. I picked up a pamphlet last month—hey, I have to watch that "last month," "nowadays," things like that—anyway, the pamphlet drew a correlation between smoking cigarettes and a rising curve of lung cancer, said scientific tests prove that something in cigarettes can cause cancer in mice. Now I bet if the government came out with an official statement about that, people would read it and get scared—and go on smoking cigarettes. You're smiling again. That's funny?

"It isn't funny," I told the dazed man. "Here—let me bring some more coffee."

"On me this time." He spilled coins on the table. "But you were smiling, all the same."

"It wasn't that kind of a smile, like for a funny," I told him. "The Surgeon General came out with a report years ago. Cigarette advertising is finally banned from TV, but how much difference does it make? Look around you."

While he was looking around him I was looking at his coins. Silver quarters. Silver dimes. Nickels: 1948,

1950, 1945. I began to feel very strange about this dude. Correction: my feel-strange went up another notch.

He said, "A lot of the people who aren't smoking are coughing, too."

We sat there together, looking around. Again he had shown me something I had always seen, never known. How many people cough.

I went for more coffee.

II

He went on:

Every four weeks I get—got?—got a makeready. A makeready is a copy of a magazine with all the proofing done and the type set, your last look before the presses roll. I have to admit it gives me—used to give me—a sense of importance to get it free (it's an expensive magazine) even before the "men high in government, industry, commerce and the professions" (as it says in the circulation promotion letters I write) had a chance to read it and move and shake, for they are the movers and shakers.

Anyway, there's this article in the new—not current; *really* new—issue called *The Silent Generation*. It's all about this year's graduating class, the young men who in June would go into the world and begin to fit their hands to the reins. This is nineteen fifty I'm talking about, you understand, in the spring. And it was frightening. I mean, it spooked me while I read it and it spooked me more and more as I thought about it—the stupidity of it, the unbelievable blindness of people—not necessarily people as a whole, but these people in the article—*The Class of 1950*—young and bright and informed. They had their formal education behind them and you assumed it was fresh in their minds—not only what they had learned, but the other thing college is really for: learning how to learn.

And yet what do you suppose they were concerned about? What was it they talked about until three o'clock in the morning? What kind of plans were they making for themselves—and for all the rest of us (for they were going to be the ones who run things)? Democracy? Ultimate purpose? The relationship of man to his planet—or of modern man to history? Hell, no.

According to this article, they worried about fringe benefits. Retirement income, for God's sake! Speed of promotion in specialized versus diversified industry! Did they spend their last few collegiate weeks in sharpening their new tools or in beering it up—or even in one last panty raid? Uh-uh. They spent them moving from office to office of the campus recruiters for big electronic and chemical and finance companies, working out the deal that would get them the steadiest, surest income and the biggest scam on the side and the softest place to lie down at the end of it.

The Silent Generation, the guy who wrote the article called them. He himself graduated in the late 'thirties and he had a lot to say about *his* generation. There was a lot wrong about them and they did some pretty crazy things. They argued a lot with each other and with their elders and betters and they joined things like the Young Socialist League—not so much because they were really lefties, but because those groups seemed the only ones around that gave a damn about the state the world was in. Most of all, you knew they were there. They were a noisy generation. They had that mixture of curiosity and rebellion that let you know they were alive.

The writer looked at the Class of '50 with a kind of despair—and something like terror, too. Because if they came to run things, experience wouldn't merely modify them and steady them. It would harden them like an old man's arteries. It would mean more-of-the-same until they'd be living in a completely unreal world of their own with no real way of communicating with the rest of us. Growing and changing and trying new ways would only frighten them. They'd have the power, and what they'd use it for would be to suppress growth and change, not knowing that societies need growth and change to live, just like trees or babies or art or science. So all he could see ahead was a solid, silent, prosperous standstill—and then some sudden and total collapse, like a tree gone to dry rot.

Well I don't know what you think of all this—or if you understand how hard it hit me. But I've tried to explain to you how all my life I've been plagued by these—well, I call them wonderments—how, when something makes no sense, it kind of hurts. When I was a toddler I couldn't sleep for wanting someone to tell me why a wet towel is darker than a dry one when water has no color. In grade school nobody could tell me why the sound of a falling bomb gets lower and lower in pitch as it approaches the ground, when by all the laws of physics it ought to rise. And in high school I wouldn't buy the idea about a limitation on the velocity of light. (And I still don't.) About things like these I've never lost faith that somebody, some day, would come up with an answer that would satisfy me—and sure enough, from time to time somebody does. But when I was old enough to wonder why smart people do dumb things that kind of faith could only last so long. And I began to feel that there was some other factor, or force, at work.

Do you remember *Gulliver's Travels?* When he was in Lilliput there was a war between the Lilliputians and another nation of little people—I forget what they called themselves—and Gulliver intervened and ended the war. Anyway, he researched the two countries and found they had once been one. And he tried to find out what caused so many years of bitter enmity between them after they split. He found that there had been two factions in that original kingdom—the Big Endians and the Little Endians. And do you know where that started? Far back in their history, at breakfast one morning, one of the king's courtiers opened his boiled egg at the big end and another told him that was wrong, it should be opened at the small end! The point Dean Swift was making is that from such insignificant causes grow conflicts that can last centuries and kill thousands. Well, he was near the thing that's plagued me all my life, but he was content to say it happened that way. What blowtorches me is—*why. Why* are human beings capable of hating each other over such trifles? Why, when an ancient triviality is proved to be the cause of trouble, don't people just stop fighting?

But I'm off on wars again—I guess because when you're talking about stupidity, wars give you too many good examples. So tell me—why, when someone's sure to die of an incurable disease and needs something for pain—why don't they give him heroin instead of morphine? Is it because heroin's habit-forming? What difference could that possibly make? And besides, morphine is, too. I'll tell you why—it's because heroin makes you feel wonderful and morphine makes you feel numb and gray. In other words, heroin's fun (mind you, I'm talking about terminal cases, dying in agony, not normally healthy people) and morphine is not— and if it's fun, there must be something evil or wrong about it. A dying man is not supposed to be made to feel good. And laws that keep venereal disease from being recognized and treated; and laws against abortion; and all the obscenity statutes—right down at the root these are all anti-pleasure laws. Would you like the job of explaining that to a man from Mars, who hadn't been brought up with them? He couldn't follow reasoning like that any more than he could understand why we have never designed a heat engine—which is essentially what an internal combustion engine is—that can run without a cooling system—a system designed to dissipate heat!

And lots more.

So maybe you see what happened to me when I read the article about the Class of 'fifty. The article peaked a tall pyramid inside me, brought everything to a sharp point.

"Have you a pencil?" said the young man. All this time and he hadn't yet lost the dazed look. I guess it was hard to blame him. "Pens are no good on paper napkins," he said.

I handed him my felt-tip. "Try this."

He tried it. "Hey, this is great. This is really keen." A felt-tip does fine on paper napkins. He studied it as if

he had never seen such a thing before. "Really keen,"
he said again. Then he drew this:

"Yin-yang," I said. "Right?"

He nodded. "One of the oldest symbols on Earth.
Then you know what it means."

"Well, some anyway. All opposites—life and death,
light and dark, male and female, heavy and light—
anything that has an opposite."

"That's it," he said. "Well, let me show you something." Using another napkin, folded into two, as a
straightedge, he lay it across the symbol.

"You see, if you were to travel in a straight line
across a diameter—any diameter—you'd have to go on
both black and white somewhere along the way. You
can't go all the way on just one color without bending
the line or going a short way, less than the diameter.

"Now let's say this circle is the board on which the
game of human affairs is played. The straight line can
be any human course—a life, a marriage, a philosophy,
a business. The optimum course is a full diameter, and
that's what most people naturally strive for; a few
might travel short chords or bent ones—sick ones.
Most people can and do travel the diameter. For each
person, life, marriage, whatever, there's a different starting point and a different arrival point, but if they travel
the one straight line that goes through the center, they
will travel black country exactly as much as white, yin
as much as yang. The balance is perfect, no matter
where you start or which way you go. Got it?"

"I see what you mean," I said. "Your coffee's cold."

"So's yours. Now look: suppose some force came along and shifted one of these colors away from the center point, like this—" And he drew again.

We studied his drawing. He drew well and quickly.

He said, "You see, if the shift were gradual, then from the very second it began there would be some people—some lives, philosophies—who would no longer have that perfect balance between black and white, between yin and yang. Nothing wrong with the course they traveled—they still aim for the very center and pass on through.

"And if the shift continued to where I've drawn it, you can see that some people might travel all the way on the white only.

"And *that's* what has happened to us. *That's* the answer to what seems to be human stupidity. There's nothing wrong with people! Far and away most of them want to travel that one straight line, and they do. It isn't their fault that the rules have been changed and that the only way to the old balance for anyone is to travel a course that is sick or twisted or short.

"The coffee *is* cold. Oh, God, I've been running off at the mouth. You'll want to get back to the office."

"No, I won't," I said. "The hell with it. You go on." For somewhere along the line he had filled me with a deep, strange excitement. The things that he said had plagued him all his life—or things like them—had plagued me, too. How often had I stood in a voting booth, trying to decide between Tweedle-Dee and Tweedle-Dum, the Big Endians versus the Little Endians? Why can't you tell someone, "Honesty is the best policy—" or "Do as you would be done by—" and straighten his whole life out, even when it might make the difference between life and death? Why do people go on smoking cigarettes? Why is a woman's breast—which for thousands of artists has been a source of beauty and for millions of children the source of life—regarded as obscene? Why do we manipulate to increase the cost of this road or that school so we can "bring in Federal money" as if the Federal money weren't coming from our own pockets? And since most people try to be decent and honest and kind—why do they do the stupid things they do?

What in the name of God put us into Viet Nam? What are ghettoes all about? Why can't the honest sincere liberals just shut up and quietly move into the ghettoes any time they can guarantee that someone from the ghetto can take their place in the old neighborhood—and keep right on doing it until there are no more ghettoes? Why can't they establish a country called Suez out of territory on both sides of the canal—and populate it from Israel and all the Arab countries and all the refugees and finance it with canal tolls and put in atomic power plants to de-salt seawater and make the desert bloom, and forbid weapons and this-or-that "quarters" and hatred? In other words, why are simple solutions always impossible? Why is any solution that does not involve killing people unacceptable? What makes us undercopulate and overbreed when the perfect balance is available to everybody?

And at this weary time of a quiet morning in the Automat, I was pinioned by the slender bright shard of hope that my dazed friend had answers.

Go back to the office? Really, the hell with it.

"You go ahead," I said, and he did.

III

Well, okay [he went on], I read that article about the class of '50—the Silent Generation—and I began to get mad-scared, and it grew and grew until I felt I had to do something about it. If the class of '50 ever got to run things, they'd have the money, they'd have the power. In a very real sense they'd have the guns. It would be the beginning of a long period—maybe forever—of more-of-the-same-ness. There didn't seem any way to stop it.

Now I'd worked out this yin-yang theory when I was a college sophomore, because it was the only theory that would fit all the facts. Given that some force had shifted the center, good people, traveling straight the way they should, had to do bad things because they could never, never achieve that balance. There was only one thing I didn't know.

What force had moved the center?

I sat in the office, dithering and ignoring my work, and tried to put myself together. *Courage, mon camarade, le diable est mort,* is what I said to myself. That mean anything to you?

No?

Okay—when I was a kid I read a book called *The Cloister and the Hearth,* by Charles Reade. It was about a kid raised in a monastery who went into the world—an eighteenth-century kind of world, or earlier, I forget now. Anyway, one of the people he meets is a crazy Frenchman, always kicking up his heels and cheering people up and at the worst of times that's what he'd say: *Courage, buddy—the devil is dead.* It stuck with me and I used to say it when everything fell apart and there seemed nowhere to turn and nothing to grab hold of. I said it now, and you know, it was like a flash bulb going off between my ears.

Mind you, it was real things I was fretting about, not myths or fantasies or religious principles. It was over-population and laws against fun and the Dust Bowl (remember that? Well, look it up some time) and no-where to put the garbage, and greed and killing and cruelty and apathy.

I took a pad of paper and drew these same diagrams and sat looking at them. I was very excited, I felt I was very near an answer.

Yin and Yang. Good and evil—sure—but nobody who understands it would ever assign good to one color and bad to the other. The whole point is, they both have to be there and in perfect balance. Light and dark, male and female, closed and open, life and death, that-which-is-outgoing and that-which-comes-together —all of it, everything—opposition, balance.

Well now, for a long time the devil has had a bad name. Say a bad press. And why not? Just for the sake of argument, say it is the yang country he used to rule and that is the one that was forced aside. Anyone living and thinking in a straight line could spend his whole life and career and all his thinking in yin country. He'd have to know that yang was there, but he'd never en-counter it, never experience it. More than likely he'd be afraid of it because that's what ignorance does to people, even good people.

And the ones who did have some experience of yang, the devil's country, would find much more of the other as they went along, because the balance would be gone. And the more the shift went on, the more innocent, well-meaning, thoughtful people ran the course of their lives and thoughts, the worse they would think of the devil's country and the worse they would talk about it and him. It would get so you couldn't trust the books; they'd all been written from the one point of view, the majority side of imbalance. It would begin to look as if the yang part of the universe were a blot which had to be stamped out to make a nice clean all-yin universe—and you have your John Knox types and your Cotton Mathers: just good people traveling straight and strong and acting from evidence that was all wrong by reason that couldn't be rational.

And I thought, *That's it!*

The devil is dead!

I have to do something about it.

But what?

Tell somebody, that's what. Tell everybody, but let's be practical. There must be somebody, somewhere, who knows what to do about it—or at least how to explain about the yin-yang and how it's gone wrong, so that everybody could rethink what we've done, what we've been.

Then I remembered the *Saturday Review*. The *Saturday Review* has a personals column in it that's read by all sorts of people—judging by the messages. But I mean *all* kinds of people. If I could write the right ad, word it just the right way . . .

I felt like a damn fool, Year of Our Lord 1950, turning all my skills as a professional copywriter to telling the world that the devil was dead, but it was an obsession, you see, and I had to do something, even something insane. I had to start somewhere.

So I wrote the ad.

> THE TROUBLE IS the light-bearer's torch is out and we're all on the same end of the seesaw. Help or we'll die of it. Whoever knows the answer call DU6-1212 Extension 2103.

I'm not going to tell you how many drafts I wrote or all the reasons why, copywise, that was best, mixed metaphors and all. I knew that whoever could help would know what I was asking.

Now comes the hard part. For you, I mean, not me. Me, I did what I had to. You're going to have to believe it.

Well, maybe you don't have to. Just—well, just suspend disbelief until you hear me out, okay?

All right. I wrote up the copy and addressed an envelope. I put on a stamp and a special delivery. I put in the copy and a check. I sealed it and crossed the hall—you know where the mail chute is—right across from my door. Your door. It was late by then, everyone had gone home and my footsteps echoed and I could hear that funny whistle under the elevator doors. I slid the envelope into the slot and let go, and my phone rang.

I'd never heard it ring quite like that before. I can say that, yet I can't tell you how it was different.

I sprinted into the office and sat down and picked up the phone. I'm glad I sat down first.

There was this Voice . . .

I have a hell of an ear, you know that? I've thought a lot about that Voice and recalled it to myself and I can tell you what it was made of—a tone, its octave and the fifth harmonic. I mean if you can imagine a voice made of three notes, two an octave apart and the third reinforcing, but not really three notes at all, because they sounded absolutely together like one. Then, they weren't pure notes, but voice-tones, with all the overtones that means. And none of that tells you anything either, any more than if I described the physical characteristics of a vibrating string and the sound it produced—when the string happened to be on a cello played by Pablo Casals. You know how it is in a room full of people when you suddenly become aware of a single voice that commands attention because of what it is, not what it says. When a voice like that has, in addition, something to say—well, you listen.

I listened. The first thing I heard—I didn't even have a chance to say hello—was: "You're right. You're absolutely right."

I said, "Who is this?" and the Voice sighed a little and waited.

Then it said, "Let's not go into that. It would be best if you figured it out by yourself."

As things turned out, that was a hundred percent on target. I think if the Voice hadn't taken that tack I'd have hung up, or anyway wasted a lot of time in being convinced.

The Voice said, "What matters is your ad in the *Saturday Review*."

"I just mailed it!"

"I just read it," the Voice said, then explained: "Time isn't quite the same here." At least I think that's what it said. It said, "How far are you willing to go to make everything right again?"

I didn't know what to say. I remember holding the phone away from my face and looking at it as if it could tell me something. Then I listened again. The Voice told me everything I was going through, carefully, not bored exactly but the way you explain to a child that you know what's bothering him.

The Voice said, "You know who I am but you won't think the words. You don't want to believe any part of this but you have to and you know you will. You're so pleased with yourself for being right that you cannot think straight—which is only one of the reasons you can't think straight. Now pull yourself together and answer my question."

I couldn't remember the question, so I had to be asked once more—how far was I willing to go to make everything right again?

You have to understand that this Voice meant what it said. If you'd heard it, you'd have believed it—anybody would. I knew I was being asked to make a commitment and that was pretty scary, but over and above that I knew I was being told that everything could be made right again—that the crazy tilt that had been plaguing mankind for hundreds, maybe thousands of years could be fixed. And I might be the guy to do it—me, for God's sake.

If I had any doubts, any this-can't-be kind of feelings—they disappeared. How far would I go?

I said, "All the way."

The Voice said, "Good. If this works you can take the credit. If it doesn't you take the blame—and you'll have to live with the idea that you might have done it and you failed. I won't be able to help you with that."

I said, anyway I'd know I'd tried.

The Voice said, "Even if you succeed you may not like what has to be done."

I said, "Suppose I don't do it—what will happen?"

The Voice said, "You ever read 1984?"

I said I had.

The Voice said, "Like that, only more so and sooner. There isn't any other way it can go now."

That's what I'd been thinking—that's what had upset me when I read the article.

"I'll do it," is all I said.

The Voice said that was fine.

It said, "I'm going to send you to see somebody. You have to persuade him. He won't talk to me and he's the only one who can do anything."

I began to have cold feet. "But who is he? Where? What do I say?"

"You know what to say. Or I wouldn't be talking to you."

I asked, "What do I have to do?"

And all I was told was to take the elevator. Then the line went dead.

So I turned out the lights and went to the door—and then I remembered and went back for my drawings of the yin-yang, one as it ought to be and the other showing it out of balance. I held them like you'd hold an airline ticket on a first flight. I went to the elevators.

How am I going to make you believe this?

Well, you're right—it doesn't matter if you do or not. Okay, here's what happened.

I pushed the call button and the door opened instantly, the way it does once in a while. I stepped into the elevator and turned around—and there I was.

The door hadn't closed, the car hadn't moved. It all happened when I was turning around. The door was open, but not in the hallway on the twenty-first floor. The scene was gray. Hard gray outdoor ground and gray mist. I stood a while looking out and my heart was thumping like someone was pounding me on the back with fists. But nothing happened, so I stepped out.

I was scared.

Nothing happened. The gray fog was neither still nor blowing. Sometimes there seemed to be shapes out there somewhere—trees, rocks, buildings—but then there was nothing and maybe it was all a vast plain. It had an outdoors feel to it—that's all I can say for sure.

The elevator door was solidly behind me, which was reassuring. I took one step away from it—a little one, I'll have you know—and called out. It took three tries before my voice would work.

"Lucifer!"

A voice answered me. Somehow it wasn't as—well, as grand as the one I'd heard over the phone, but in other ways it was bigger.

It said, "Who is that? What do you want?"

It was cranky. It was the voice of someone interrupted, someone who felt damn capable of handling the interruption, too. And this time there really was something looming closer through the fog.

I clapped my hands over my face. I felt my knees hit the gray dirt. I didn't kneel down, you understand. The knees just buckled as if they didn't belong to me any more. But hell, the wings. Bat's wings, leathery, and a tail with a point on it like a big arrowhead. That face, eyes. And thirty feet tall, man!

He touched my shoulder and I would have screamed like a schoolgirl if I'd had the breath for it.

"Come on now." It was a different voice altogether —he'd changed it—but it was his all the same. He said, "I don't look like that. That came out of your head. Here—look at me."

I looked. I guess it was funny, me kind of peeping up quickly so in case it was more than I could take I could hide my face again—as if that would do any good. But I'd had more than I could handle.

What I saw was a middle-aged guy in a buff corduroy jacket and brown slacks. He had graying hair and a smooth suntanned forehead and the brightest blue eyes I have ever seen. He helped me to my feet.

He said, "I don't look like this either, but—" he shrugged and smiled.

I said, "Well, thanks anyway—" and felt stupid. I looked around at the fog. "Where is this?"

He kind of waved his hand. "I can't really say. Where would you want it to be?"

How do you answer a question like that? I couldn't.

He could. He put the back of his hand against my cheek and gently turned my face toward him and bent close. He did something I can only describe as what you do when you pick up a magazine and run your thumb across the edge of the pages and flip it open

somewhere. Only he did it inside my head somehow.
Anyway there was a blaze of golden light that made me
blink.

When I got my eyes adjusted to it the gray was gone.
When I was a kid I worked one year on a farm in
Vermont. I used to go for the cows in the late afternoon. The day pasture was huge, with a stand of pine
at the upper end and the whole thing was steep as a
roof, with granite outcroppings all over, gray, and
white limestone. That's where we were, the very smell
of it, the little lake with the dirt road around the end of
it far down at the bottom and the wind hissing through
the pine trees up there and a woodchuck ducking out
of sight on the skyline. I could even see three of the
Holsteins, standing level on the sidehill in that miraculous way they have as if they had two short legs and
two long ones. I never did figure out how they do
it.

And I got a flash of panic, too, because my elevator
door was gone—but he seemed to know and just
waved his hand casually over to my left. And there it
was, a Rockefeller Center elevator door in the middle
of a Vermont pasture. Funny. When I was fourteen
that door in the pasture would have scared the hell out
of me. Now I was scared without it. I looked around
me and smelled the late August early evening and
marveled.

"It's so real," is what I said.

"Seems real."

"But I was here—right here—when I was a kid."

"Seemed real then, too, didn't it?"

I think he was trying to make me rethink all along the line—not so much to doubt things, but to wipe everything clean and start over.

"Belief or nonbelief has no power over objective truth," is what he told me. He said that if two people believe the same thing from the same evidence, it means that they believe the same thing, nothing more.

While I was chewing on that he took the sketches out of my hand—the same ones I just did for you. I had quite forgotten I was holding them. He looked at them and grunted. "It's like that, is it?"

I took back the sketches and began to make my speech.

I said, "You see, it's like this. Here the balance is—" and he kind of laughed a little and said wait, wait, we don't have to go through all that.

I think he meant, words. I mean he touched the side of my face again and made me face him and did that thing with his eyes inside my head. Only this time it was like taking both your thumbs and pulling open the pages of a book that are sort of stuck together. I wouldn't say it hurt but I wouldn't want much more of it either. I remember a single flash of shame that things I'd read, studied, things I'd thought out, I'd been careless with or had forgotten. And all the while—a very short while—he was digging in my head he was curing the shame, too. I began to understand that what he could get from me wasn't just what I'd learned and understood—it was everything, *everything* that had ever passed through my pipeline. And all in a moment.

Then he stepped back and said, "Bastard!"

I thought, what have I done?

He laughed at me. "Not you. *Him.*"

I thought, oh. The Voice on the phone. The one who sent me.

He looked at me with those sixty-thousand candle-power eyes and laughed again and wagged his head.

"I swore I'd have nothing to do with him any more," he said, "and now look—he's thrown me a hook."

I guess I looked mixed-up, because I was. He began to talk to me kindly, trying to make me feel better.

He said, "It's not easy to explain. You've learned so much that just ain't so and you've learned it from people who also didn't understand. Couldn't. It goes back a long time. I mean, for you it does. For me—well, time is different here."

He thought a bit and said, "Calling me Lucifer was real bright of you, you know that? Lucifer means 'bringer of light.' If you're going to stick with the yin-yang symbol—and it's a good one—you'll see that there's a center for the dark part and a center for the light—sometimes they're drawn in, a little dot on each part right where a pollywog's eye would be. I am that dot and the Voice you heard is the other one. Lucifer I may be, but I'm not the devil. I'm just the other. It takes two of us to make the whole. What I just might have overlooked is that it takes two of us to keep the whole. Really, I had no idea—" and he leaned forward and got another quick look inside my head—"no idea at all that things would get into such a mess so quickly. Maybe I shouldn't have left."

I had to ask him. "Why did you?"

He said, "I got mad. I had a crazy notion one day and wanted to try something and he didn't want me to do it. But I did it anyway and then when it got me into trouble he wouldn't pull me out of it. I had to play it all the way through. It hurt." He laughed a funny laugh. I understood that 'it hurt' was a gigantic understatement. "So I got mad and cut out and came here. He's been yelling and sending messages and all, ever since, but I paid him no mind until you."

"Why me?"

"Yes," he said, "why you?" He thought it over. "Tell me something—have you got anything to keep you where you are? I mean a wife or a career or kids or something that would get hurt if you suddenly disappeared?"

"Nothing like that, no. Some friends—but no wife, no folks. And my job's just a job."

"Thought so," he said. Talking to himself, he said, "Bastard. Built this one from the ground up, he did. Knew damn well I'd get a jolt when I saw what a rotten mess this was." Then he said very warmly. "Don't take that personally. You can't help it."

I couldn't help it. I couldn't help taking it a little personally either.

Maybe I was a little sharp when I said, "Well—are you going to come back or not?"

He gave it right back to me.

"I really don't know," he said. "Why don't I leave it to you? You decide."

"Me?"

"Why not? You got yourself into this."

"Did I?"

"No matter how carefully he set you up for it, friend, he had to get your permission first. Right?"

I remembered that Voice: *How far are you willing to go?*

The one I had called Lucifer fixed me with the blazing eyes. "I am going to lay it right on you. I will do what you say. If you tell me to stay here, to stay out of it, it's going to be like Orwell said: 'To visualize the future you must visualize a boot stamping eternally on a human face.' But if I come back it's going to be almost as bad. Things are really out of hand, so much that it can't be straightened out overnight. It would take years. People aren't made to take the truth on sight and act on it. They have to be prodded and pushed—usually by being made so miserable in so many ways that they get mad. When enough of them get mad enough they'll find the way."

"Well, good, then."

He mimicked me. I think he was a little sore and just maybe he didn't want to go back to work.

" 'Well, good, then,' " he mocked me. "We'll have to shovel stupidity on them. We'll have to get them into long meaningless wars. We'll make them live under laws that absolutely make no sense and keep passing more of them. We'll lay taxes on them until they can't have luxuries and comforts without getting into trouble and we'll lay on more until it hurts to buy enough just to live."

I said, "That's the same thing as the boot!"

He said, "No it isn't. Let the class of '50 take over and you'll have that. Orwell said *eternally* and he was right. No conflict, no dissent, no division, no balance. If I come back, there'll be plenty of all that. People will die—lots of them. And hurt—plenty."

"There's no other way?"

"Look," he said, "you can't give people what they want. They have to earn it or take it. When they start

doing that there'll be bombings and riots and people—
especially young people—will do what they want to and
what works for them, not what they're told. They'll
find their own ways—and it won't be anything like
what grandpa said."

I thought about all that and then about the class of
'50 and the stamping boot.

"Come back," I said.

He sighed and said, "Oh, God."

I don't know what he meant. But I think he was
glad.

Suddenly—well, it seemed sudden—there was more
light outside the Automat than inside. I felt as dazed as
my friend looked.

I said, "And what have you been doing since nineteen fifty?"

He said, "Don't you understand? All this happened
last night! Last night was nineteen fifty! I got back into
the elevator and walked into my—your—the office and
there you were!"

"And the dev—Lucif—whoever it was, he's back,
too?"

"Time is different for him. He came back right
away. You've already told me enough about what's
been happening since then. He's back. He's been back.
Things are moving toward the center again. It's hard to
do, but it's happening."

I stuck my spoon into my cold old coffee and swirled
it around and thought of the purposeless crime and the
useless deaths and the really decent people who didn't
know they were greedy, and a deep joy began to kindle
inside me.

"Then maybe it's not all useless."

"Oh, God, it better not be," he whispered. "Because all of it is my fault."

"No, it isn't. Things are going to be all right." As I said that I was sure of it. I looked at him, so lost and dazed—and I thought, *I am going to help this guy. I am going to help him help me to understand better, to work out how we can bring it all into balance again.* I wondered if he knew he was a messiah, that he had saved the world. I don't think he did.

Sudden thought: "Hey," I said, "did he tell you why he dropped out mad like that? What was it—he did something the other one didn't want him to do?"

"Didn't I mention that? Sorry," said the dazed man. "He got tired of being a—a force. Whatever you call it. Spirit. He wanted to be a man for a while, to see what it was like. He could do it—but he couldn't get out of it again without the other's help. So he walked around for a while as a man—"

"And?"

"And got crucified."

9

BIRTH AND DEATH—MYTHS
OF BEGINNING AND ENDING

Eyes of Onyx
EDWARD BRYANT

"Eyes of Onyx" is a story of birth and death. These are the two most significant events that each individual experiences in his life, and two of the most fascinating for him to ponder. Because he possesses self-consciousness, he can escape beyond himself enough to observe himself. He realizes the world existed before he was born, and will exist after he dies. Then, reasoning from analogy, he wonders if the world also had a birth or creation, and will experience an end or death. His mind is boggled at the dimensions of the questions he has raised. They are beyond Earth, cosmic in scope, from the black void of beginning to the black void of ending, with only the momentary illumination of his consciousness to shed light on the mystery. He is unable to collect data to provide answers because

298

he is limited by time and space, and the answers he is searching for transcend these limitations.

But man is a creator who delights in organizing chaos into meaningful patterns. In a brilliant, intuitive flash of imagination, he creates an image that represents or stands for his awareness that the universe has dimensions beyond those he can experience in his limited condition. He makes a myth of the creation of the world, and another of its ending. There are many different myths of beginning and ending. To ask whether they are true—indeed how they all can be true if they are different—is to miss the point. Myths are not intended to be literally true or factual. They are complex symbols that stand for an awareness man cannot talk about any other way. Because humans are alike but also uniquely individual, different cultures create birth and death myths that are similar in their purpose but imaginatively different in their individual details.

The Christian story of the birth or creation of the cosmos and of man is told in the Book of Genesis. The story of the birth of Christ, God's revelation of himself to man, is told in the Gospels of the New Testament. "Eyes of Onyx" is another telling of the myth, the Godhead's revelation to man of supernatural forces that lie beyond his limited physical world. But this is not an account full of hope and love, as is the New Testament account of Christ's birth. It is ominous, dark, and threatening. One immediately thinks of the great twentieth-century Irish poet, William Butler Yeats, who expressed the same sense of foreboding about the future in his famous poem, "The Second Coming." Commenting on the violence and destructive wars of our time, he once said, "The best lack all conviction, while the worst are full of passionate intensity." He saw an ending of two thousand years of Christian history, wondering, "And what rough beast, its hour come round at last,/Slouches toward Bethlehem to be born?"

The apocalypse, or vision of the end of the world, is a common one in different religions. This impulse to conceive of an end to the world seems as universal as the impulse to symbolize the beginning. The apocalyptic vision can take many forms. The myth may suggest a final end to the world, or merely an ending of one cycle of man's history, as in "Eyes of Onyx." The Revelation of St. John in the New Testament predicts that God, who is beyond time, will intercede in man's time, and in one great final battle, purge the world of evil and bring about the Kingdom of Heaven on earth.

"Eyes of Onyx," an apocalyptic story, but a less optimistic one, does not suggest a final end, but merely the ending of one cycle of man's history, and the beginning of a new one. It is a myth set in the twentieth century, and seems a comment on technological man's vision of himself. As science and technology began to flower in the nineteenth century, man—caught up in a faith that the change they were producing was progress —held a vision that the world of poverty and suffering might be transformed. A millennial kingdom of peace and abundance seemed to be possible.

But our twentieth-century vision of technology's power for good is changing. We realize—through pollution, overpopulation, and destructive weapons of war—technology can transform the world for the worse rather than only for the better. The underdeveloped nations, and indeed the poor in the United States, realize—through radio, film, and television—how little they have compared to those who live in economic plenty. Frustrated in their hopes for improvement, they are filled with disappointment, rage, and hate. A new spirit stirs, demanding fulfillment. It is of this birth that Edward Bryant writes in "Eyes of Onyx."

Eyes of Onyx
EDWARD BRYANT

It happened last December. It was just a regular night, with me and Pop working late in the grease pit. Our *morada* isn't much, just a combination house and filling station. We bought it back when Mom was alive. It doesn't make us rich—that's for sure—but we manage to scratch a living off the local trade and the tourists that break down every once in a while. The government would give us better if we begged for it, but Pop's always been kind of touchy about things like that. We still go to a legit cash-or-get-out medic when we get sick, too.

I had to drop out of upper-level before graduation, so I don't have a great education as far as educations go these days. What with every other brain getting three degrees, or at least the card to try it, I don't seem too smart. But with me it was either slice out or starve. So there I was.

It was getting close to Christmas, and we were working late. We had an old '79 Starliner with a pitted gyro up on the rack. It was owned by some anglo from up the strip in Berdoo who hadn't had the sense to trade it in on a newer model when he had the chance. About eleven o'clock Pop sent me out to get another set of metric wrenches from the storage shack across the road.

We didn't really need those wrenches, but I went anyway. Once I came right out and told Pop that he didn't have to send me away when he needed a drink. He just said soft and slow that he had a little pride left. Since then I haven't crossed him about it.

So I left. I suppose I should mention that our place is located on one of the lower-level approaches to the big Inter-Cont Expressway. Since we're just a small trinkets business, we couldn't get a decent frontline franchise like the big chains. Those outfits like Enerco keep coming around trying to buy Pop out, but he won't sell. Too damn stubborn, he says. He had to sell out once and he won't do it again. The company men, they don't know what Pop's talking about. They figure he's just a nutball case, so they throw up their hands, slice out and try again in a few more months. Same thing happens every time.

It was good to get out of the stink of kerosene and oil and into some open air. I like being a mechanic okay, but my nose must be extra sensitive. Those fumes still get to me even though I've worked with cars for the last ten years—since I was six.

There was just a skiff of snow on the pavement, and I could see more of those big flakes floating down real slow in the glare from our neons. The air was calm and chilly, and you could just barely hear the advertising from downcity. Overhead, the clouds had cut out most of the big floating glitter-signs. There was only one I could read. It was lower than the rest and spelled out first DO XMAS RIGHT in red and then BUY GEMCO in green. Back when I was a kid I used to like watching the stars at night, before they started putting up the glitter-signs.

So I got the wrench-set Pop wanted and had started back across the road when a hassle down at MacLain's caught my ear. Old man MacLain owns a motel—if you want to call it that. Picture a big fat decaying egg carton with little rotten egg cartons crumbling in a line along side; that's MacLain's motel. It's never been repaired since it was built and probably won't be fixed before Renewal Authority razes it.

Old man MacLain is definitely a *mierda*. That's the way I've felt ever since he got so pissed at me for keeping his sweet little daughter out all week once. I don't see what kick he had coming; what we were doing was our own business. After all, just like any other smart parent, he'd put her on the six-month shots when she started to bleed. I mean, what did he expect her to do? Pop doesn't like old MacLain either—says he's a *hijo de puta*. Which is strong for Pop.

My ears told me that MacLain was upset; I can tell that whine any day of the week. He had a face to go along with it; little eyes, mean; oily nose; fat mouth buried in about six chins. If a voice can be completely ugly, old MacLain looked just like he sounded. I was curious, so I walked down to the motel. If I thought the Starliner in the shop was old and crusty, I changed my mind when I saw the heap parked in front of Mac-

Lain's Quality Western Motel. It must have dated back to the sixties at least, and it didn't look like it could even make the minimum speed on the I-C strip.

Midway between the wreck and MacLain's place was MacLain himself and this man and woman. The man was one of those thin, intense-looking people, the kind on holovision that have ideals and never get anywhere. The woman—I supposed she was his wife—stood a little ways behind as if he was protecting her. She wasn't any Miss North America, but she was kind of quiet-beautiful, if you know what I mean. Not spectacular like·Monica Marlo or one of the other sexy vidstars, but kind of good looking anyway—real dark skin with black eyes and black hair pulled back on top of her head. You could also see plain that she was going to have a kid soon.

Old man MacLain sounded pretty mad, even worse than usual. He was raving about how he wasn't running no Soc/Welfare establishment and that they—the man and woman—would have to card it up or else they wouldn't be staying in his motel.

The man kept explaining quietly and patiently, like for about the fourteenth time, that he and his wife had made a long trip from back east and didn't have any credit left. Then he said that his wife thought she was going to have the baby a little early and they couldn't find a doctor or a place to stay. That started that freak MacLain off to yelling again about him not wanting anything like this in his rooms, and how they ought to leave and keep looking for a doctor. This was even though he knew as well as me that the local government med was on vacation over the holidays.

Finally, while I held back and just watched, the man

and woman gave up. The man's thin shoulders sort of slumped like he'd lost out on something important as he took the woman's arm and helped her back across the lot toward their car. MacLain just stood there with a righteous look on his fat face.

Now I don't go out and dig up good deeds. I look out for just Pop and me, and that's the way to do it these days. If you stick out your neck you're liable to get a blade through it. Even so, I looked at those two eastern straights—they should have known better than to head across country with no credit—and knew I'd feel like hell if I didn't do something.

So that's why I walked up to the guy just as he was opening the car door and touched his arm. I told him I figured that Pop and me could put them up for the night over at our place if they wanted to come. The guy looked at me like he couldn't quite believe it. Then he decided I was spinning straight so he spent about a minute shaking my hand and thanking me. The woman didn't say anything but just smiled into my eyes. I started feeling good all over for some reason. It was like a double jag of coke. It was starting to shake me up. But I felt even better when we turned to walk to the station and I saw the look on MacLain's face.

I took them into the garage and lined out the situation to Pop. He looked at me a little odd and squeezed my shoulder. Then he got busy taking care of the man and the prospective mother, and all of a sudden he was the way he used to be before Mom died. He even put the woman in Mom's room. Not only that, he had her lie down in Mom's old bed after I'd changed the sheets. No one had slept there for eight or nine years. The woman didn't seem to feel so good now, and I got a hunch that the nine months bit was about to run out. I was right.

Pop was an old hand at this sort of thing even if I was his only kid; he'd delivered me back on our old place when there wasn't a medic around for forty miles. He saw that the husband was close to stepping off the deep end, so he sent the guy out into the living room and put him to work tearing clean sheets into nice neat strips. It kept him busy.

I helped Pop as best I could until it looked like the baby was going to come okay. Then Pop told me I was getting on his nerves and would I please slice out. He really meant it, so I left.

I went outside into the cold air again. It helped. It seemed to me that I was almost as jittery as that husband. For no reason at all I wondered if praying for that woman would help. We haven't had much to do with religion since the Church got sucked up into the Universalist bit in the late seventies. That was even before Mom died. I remember Pop saying something at supper about how he was fed up with the hypocrites. It was about this time he finally knew we weren't going to be able to keep on living out in the Valley so he let some big management company buy up our farm for about half what it was worth. That's when we moved in here closer to the city and bought the station. A little later Mom died, and Pop's strength just sort of went out of him. He wasn't himself anymore—not the way he'd been. I can remember the time when Pop was like one of the big rocks in the hills around our place in the Valley. I was pretty small then, but I can still see in my mind how tall and strong Pop was. Then we had to sell out, and it was like the water seeping into cracks in a rock. The water freezes and expands and the stone begins to split. When Mom died it was that much more ice. Pop sort of broke apart and drifted along. I don't think you can really blame him.

I'd just got to thinking about how Pop had seemed more like his old self tonight when I heard this God-awful bawling from inside, so I went back in. The door to Mom's room was open again, and Pop was in the doorway wearing the strangest look I'd ever seen. He walked past like he didn't even see me and went into the little room we use as an office. He closed the door, but I could see through the glassed-in pass-through that Pop was using the phone. He was only on the air for a few seconds. Then he cut off and came back to the room where the baby was crying.

It wasn't ten minutes before a chopper from Salk Memorial set down on the pavement in front of the station and three white-coated medics hopped down from the cabin. The med team didn't say much when I let them in—just asked in a kind of bored way where the baby was. Naturally, they closed that door to Mom's room behind them.

I went outside again. The clouds were beginning to clear away. The big glitter-signs were all back in view now, but there was something brighter up there. Between CONSOLIDATED TRAVELAIRE and CHEVCO CENTER was a white glow that looked like a big star. I remembered from the morning vidcast that it was a comet, Yamamura 1990b or something like that—one of those things that only comes around every 2000 years or so.

I didn't expect the medics to be there long. I figured they'd check to make sure the woman and her baby weren't bleeding to death, record the birth, and head back to the holiday traffic victims filling up the hospitals.

When I was just a kid, I'd wanted to be part of a med team. Of course I zapped that idea when I dropped out. But I still admire them. Med men always seem cool and calm and act like they never find a case they can't handle. This team was different. When they came out of the house they looked bad. One of them was talking. Most of the time he was talking to himself because the other two weren't listening. The shortest of the medics sort of looked grimly ahead and didn't pay any mind to the one with the mouth. The third med walked like he was in the middle of a dream. They ignored me. They all walked past, climbed into the chopper and lofted out. A couple seconds and they were just another green star over downcity.

I wasn't exactly sure what I should do now, so I went back inside. This time Pop at least said something to me.

"Juan, you can see her now."

By this time I was curious, so I went into that room. The woman was lying back in the bed with her dark hair all undone and falling around her neck and with the baby snuggled up against her. I've seen babies before, but there was something different about this one —not a physical thing, but a feeling that sang and shouted inside my mind. There was a power inside that room. I could feel it. It was like being inside the guts of a reactor plant, only a thousand times as powerful. I was scared, like that reactor was going to blow. Then the power started to calm me down. All I can say is that this was the first time I ever looked at a baby from on my knees.

Well, that's the story. Like I said, it all happened last December, and it's summer now. That guy, his wife, and their daughter all left in a couple days, just as soon as the woman could travel. Pop lent them a transfer chit and gave them some fuel for that antique they drove. That should have been the end of it, but it wasn't.

The Fed police showed up a week later and caused some real trouble. They kept asking questions we couldn't answer, so finally they left.

Lately I've been paying attention to the vidcasts and tabloids like I never used to. People are getting edgy, just like they're expecting something big to happen. So far there are just little hints and stirrings in the background, and something's going on. I can feel it. It's got me on the hook. That's right—interested. Maybe a little scared too.

Yeah, right, I know what this all sounds like.

But there's a catch.

I remember that tiny black girl-child opening her eyes and looking at me there on my knees. I can't get those eyes out of my mind. They were two pieces of onyx—just as dark and hard, and just as cold shining. And they were full of hate and anger, before they shut again.

Pop, he talks about mutations and telepathy. Me, I got another idea about this whole bit, and it's strange because I'm not any church-freak. I think about two thousand years ago there was a God of Love and he gave us a chance and we screwed it good. But now the old God's dead. There's a new man on top and we're getting a new deal. And this time, man, the chance is going to be something else.

Really something else.

10

THE APOCALYPTIC VISION
OF THE END

The Nine Billion Names of God
ARTHUR C. CLARKE

Arthur C. Clarke is one of science fiction's major writers, probably best known for his *Space Odyssey 2001*. In this famous little story, "The Nine Billion Names of God," we encounter another apocalyptic vision of the end of the world. But it is not a threatening, fearful vision. It is gentle and quiet. The vision suggests that all is well in the world, that the harmonious whole moves in a cosmic dance, and man has carried out his rhythmic part of the universal mystery.

The setting of the story is high in the Himalayan Mountains of Tibet, and the title suggests the universality of the divine. As the lama explains, "All the many names of the Supreme Being—God, Jehovah, Allah, and so on—they are only man-made labels." They are different words invented by different cultures, but they all stand for the same divine ground or Godhead. The lama, in his vision, sees very clearly the task of man—through continuous study to acquire knowledge of God. The monks in his lamasery are not unwilling to partake of physical pleasures, but such pleasures have limited value. They are part of the physical or natural world, and the monks see man's primary purpose as understanding the supernatural or spiritual world.

The story portrays a meeting of the Western and the Eastern minds. The high lama and his monks in the Tibetan lamasery embrace the Buddhist religion. The Eastern mind (as suggested by the Swiss psychologist Carl Jung) turns inward to the spirit, finding meaning in a nonmaterial reality within—in an introverted view. The Western mind turns outward to find meaning in the world outside itself—in an extroverted view. One of the major religious events of the twentieth century is the meeting of the Western mind, shaped by the Judeo-Christian world view, with the Eastern mind, shaped by Hinduism and Buddhism. This encounter grows out of the improved travel and communications systems that technology brings us. The result of the encounter seems to promise a creative shaping of new religious concepts. Such a result is found, for example, in the thinking of Aldous Huxley (author of the novel *Brave New World*), who in "The *Bhagavad Gita* and the Perennial Philosophy" writes about his response to this sacred scripture of Hinduism.

The Western mind, concerned with understanding the material world, has produced technology, and in "The Nine Billion Names of God," the most sophisticated fruit of the technology—the computer—comes to the East. The world where clock time is all-important comes to a time of eternity. It is a strange encounter. Imagine a computer in a lamasery. George, the technician who accompanies the computer, displays the typical ethnocentrism of a limited mind. The Buddhist monks do things differently and hold different values, so he is sure they must be crazy; they are "poor suckers." He cannot imagine that a point of view different from his own might provide him with a new awareness.

He fails to note the wisdom of the high lama, who accepts technology as a useful tool but refuses to let it master and destroy the life of the lamasery. The purpose of the lamasery is to acquire knowledge of God, and he uses technology only to serve that purpose. Electric power is used to drive the prayer wheels; the computer aids the work of assembling all the names of God. But as the story ends, George is instructed. He finds a new awareness in the high mountains of Tibet.

The Nine Billion Names of God
ARTHUR C. CLARKE

"This is a slightly unusual request," said Dr. Wagner, with what he hoped was commendable restraint. "As far as I know, it's the first time anyone's been asked to supply a Tibetan monastery with an Automatic Sequence Computer. I don't wish to be inquisitive, but I should hardly have thought that your—ah—establishment had much use for such a machine. Could you explain just what you intend to do with it?"

"Gladly," replied the lama, readjusting his silk robes

and carefully putting away the slide rule he had been using for currency conversions. "Your Mark V Computer can carry out any routine mathematical operation involving up to ten digits. However, for our work we are interested in *letters*, not numbers. As we wish you to modify the output circuits, the machine will be printing words, not columns of figures."

"I don't quite understand. . . ."

"This is a project on which we have been working for the last three centuries—since the lamasery was founded, in fact. It is somewhat alien to your way of thought, so I hope you will listen with an open mind while I explain it."

"Naturally."

"It is really quite simple. We have been compiling a list which shall contain all the possible names of God."

"I beg your pardon?"

"We have reason to believe," continued the lama imperturbably, "that all such names can be written with not more than nine letters in an alphabet we have devised."

"And you have been doing this for three centuries?"

"Yes: we expected it would take us about fifteen thousand years to complete the task."

"Oh," Dr. Wagner looked a little dazed. "Now I see why you wanted to hire one of our machines. But exactly what is the *purpose* of this project?"

The lama hesitated for a fraction of a second, and Wagner wondered if he had offended him. If so, there was no trace of annoyance in the reply.

"Call it ritual, if you like, but it's a fundamental part of our belief. All the many names of the Supreme Being—God, Jehovah, Allah, and so on—they are only man-made labels. There is a philosophical problem of some difficulty here, which I do not propose to discuss, but somewhere among all the possible combinations of letters that can occur are what one may call the *real* names of God. By systematic permutation of letters, we have been trying to list them all."

"I see. You've been starting at AAAAAAA . . . and working up to ZZZZZZZ. . . ."

"Exactly—though we use a special alphabet of our own. Modifying the electromatic typewriters to deal with this is, of course, trivial. A rather more interesting problem is that of devising suitable circuits to eliminate ridiculous combinations. For example, no letter must occur more than three times in succession."

"Three? Surely you mean two."

"Three is correct: I am afraid it would take too long to explain why, even if you understood our language."

"I'm sure it would," said Wagner hastily. "Go on."

"Luckily, it will be a simple matter to adapt your Automatic Sequence Computer for this work, since once it has been programed properly it will permute each letter in turn and print the result. What would have taken us fifteen thousand years it will be able to do in a hundred days."

Dr. Wagner was scarcely conscious of the faint sounds from the Manhattan streets far below. He was in a different world, a world of natural, not man-made, mountains. High up in their remote aeries these monks had been patiently at work, generation after generation, compiling their lists of meaningless words. Was there any limit to the follies of mankind? Still, he must give no hint of his inner thoughts. The customer was always right. . . .

"There's no doubt," replied the doctor, "that we can modify the Mark V to print lists of this nature. I'm much more worried about the problem of installation and maintenance. Getting out to Tibet, in these days, is not going to be easy."

"We can arrange that. The components are small enough to travel by air—that is one reason why we chose your machine. If you can get them to India, we will provide transport from there."

"And you want to hire two of our engineers?"

"Yes, for the three months that the project should occupy."

"I've no doubt that Personnel can manage that." Dr. Wagner scribbled a note on his desk pad. "There are just two other points—"

Before he could finish the sentence the lama had produced a small slip of paper.

"This is my certified credit balance at the Asiatic Bank."

"Thank you. It appears to be—ah—adequate. The second matter is so trivial that I hesitate to mention it—but it's surprising how often the obvious gets overlooked. What source of electrical energy have you?"

"A diesel generator providing fifty kilowatts at a hundred and ten volts. It was installed about five years ago and is quite reliable. It's made life at the lamasery much more comfortable, but of course it was really installed to provide power for the motors driving the prayer wheels."

"Of course," echoed Dr. Wagner. "I should have thought of that."

* * *

The view from the parapet was vertiginous, but in time one gets used to anything. After three months, George Hanley was not impressed by the two-thousand-foot swoop into the abyss or the remote checkerboard of fields in the valley below. He was leaning against the wind-smoothed stones and staring morosely at the distant mountains whose names he had never bothered to discover.

This, thought George, was the craziest thing that had ever happened to him. "Project Shangri-La," some wit back at the labs had christened it. For weeks now the Mark V had been churning out acres of sheets covered with gibberish. Patiently, inexorably, the computer had been rearranging letters in all their possible combinations, exhausting each class before going on to the next. As the sheets had emerged from the electromatic typewriters, the monks had carefully cut them up and pasted them into enormous books. In another week, heaven be praised, they would have finished. Just what obscure calculations had convinced the monks that they needn't bother to go on to words of ten, twenty, or a hundred letters, George didn't know. One of his recurring nightmares was that there would be some change of plan, and that the high lama (whom they'd naturally called Sam Jaffe, though he didn't look a bit like him) would suddenly announce that the project would be extended to approximately A.D. 2060. They were quite capable of it.

George heard the heavy wooden door slam in the wind as Chuck came out onto the parapet beside him. As usual, Chuck was smoking one of the cigars that made him so popular with the monks—who, it seemed, were quite willing to embrace all the minor and most of the major pleasures of life. That was one thing in their favor: they might be crazy, but they weren't bluenoses. Those frequent trips they took down to the village, for instance . . .

"Listen, George," said Chuck urgently. "I've learned something that means trouble."

"What's wrong? Isn't the machine behaving?" That was the worst contingency George could imagine. It might delay his return, and nothing could be more horrible. The way he felt now, even the sight of a TV commercial would seem like manna from heaven. At least it would be some link with home.

"No—it's nothing like that." Chuck settled himself on the parapet, which was unusual because normally he was scared of the drop. "I've just found what all this is about."

"What d'ya mean? I thought we knew."

"Sure—we know what the monks are trying to do. But we didn't know *why.* It's the craziest thing—"

"Tell me something new," growled George.

"—but old Sam's just come clean with me. You know the way he drops in every afternoon to watch the sheets roll out. Well, this time he seemed rather excited, or at least as near as he'll ever get to it. When I told him that we were on the last cycle he asked me, in that cute English accent of his, if I'd ever wondered what they were trying to do. I said, 'Sure'—and he told me."

"Go on: I'll buy it."

"Well, they believe that when they have listed all His names—and they reckon that there are about nine billion of them—God's purpose will be achieved. The human race will have finished what it was created to do, and there won't be any point in carrying on. Indeed, the very idea is something like blasphemy."

"Then what do they expect us to do? Commit suicide?"

"There's no need for that. When the list's completed, God steps in and simply winds things up ... bingo!"

"Oh, I get it. When we finish our job, it will be the end of the world."

Chuck gave a nervous little laugh.

"That's just what I said to Sam. And do you know what happened? He looked at me in a very queer way, like I'd been stupid in class, and said, 'It's nothing as trivial as *that.*' "

George thought this over for a moment.

"That's what I call taking the Wide View," he said presently. "But what d'you suppose we should do about it? I don't see that it makes the slightest difference to us. After all, we already knew that they were crazy."

"Yes—but don't you see what may happen? When the list's complete and the Last Trump doesn't blow— or whatever it is they expect—*we* may get the blame. It's our machine they've been using. I don't like the situation one little bit."

"I see," said George slowly. "You've got a point there. But this sort of thing's happened before, you know. When I was a kid down in Louisiana we had a crackpot preacher who once said the world was going to end next Sunday. Hundreds of people believed him —even sold their homes. Yet when nothing happened, they didn't turn nasty, as you'd expect. They just decided that he'd made a mistake in his calculations and went right on believing. I guess some of them still do."

"Well, this isn't Louisiana, in case you hadn't noticed. There are just two of us and hundreds of these monks. I like them, and I'll be sorry for old Sam when his lifework backfires on him. But all the same, I wish I was somewhere else."

"I've been wishing that for weeks. But there's nothing we can do until the contract's finished and the transport arrives to fly us out."

"Of course," said Chuck thoughtfully, "we could always try a bit of sabotage."

"Like hell we could! That would make things worse."

"Not the way I meant. Look at it like this. The machine will finish its run four days from now, on the present twenty-hours-a-day basis. The transport calls in a week. O.K.—then all we need to do is to find something that needs replacing during one of the overhaul periods—something that will hold up the works for a couple of days. We'll fix it, of course, but not too quickly. If we time matters properly, we can be down at the airfield when the last name pops out of the register. They won't be able to catch us then."

"I don't like it," said George. "It will be the first time I ever walked out on a job. Besides, it would make them suspicious. No, I'll sit tight and take what comes."

"I *still* don't like it," he said, seven days later, as the tough little mountain ponies carried them down the winding road. "And don't you think I'm running away because I'm afraid. I'm just sorry for those poor old guys up there, and I don't want to be around when they find what suckers they've been. Wonder how Sam will take it?"

"It's funny," replied Chuck, "but when I said good-by I got the idea he knew we were walking out on him—and that he didn't care because he knew the machine was running smoothly and that the job would soon be finished. After that—well, of course, for him there just isn't any After That. . . ."

George turned in his saddle and stared back up the mountain road. This was the last place from which one could get a clear view of the lamasery. The squat, angular buildings were silhouetted against the afterglow of the sunset: here and there, lights gleamed like portholes in the side of an ocean liner. Electric lights, of course, sharing the same circuit as the Mark V. How much longer would they share it? wondered George. Would the monks smash up the computer in their rage and disappointment? Or would they just sit down quietly and begin their calculations all over again?

He knew exactly what was happening up on the mountain at this very moment. The high lama and his assistants would be sitting in their silk robes, inspecting the sheets as the junior monks carried them away from the typewriters and pasted them into the great volumes. No one would be saying anything. The only sound would be the incessant patter, the never-ending rainstorm of the keys hitting the paper, for the Mark V itself was utterly silent as it flashed through its thousands of calculations a second. Three months of this, thought George, was enough to start anyone climbing up the wall.

"There she is!" called Chuck, pointing down into the valley. "Ain't she beautiful!"

She certainly was, thought George. The battered old DC3 lay at the end of the runway like a tiny silver cross. In two hours she would be bearing them away to freedom and sanity. It was a thought worth savoring like a fine liqueur. George let it roll round his mind as the pony trudged patiently down the slope.

The swift night of the high Himalayas was now almost upon them. Fortunately, the road was very good, as roads went in that region, and they were both carrying torches. There was not the slightest danger, only a certain discomfort from the bitter cold. The sky overhead was perfectly clear, and ablaze with the familiar, friendly stars. At least there would be no risk, thought George, of the pilot being unable to take off because of weather conditions. That had been his only remaining worry.

He began to sing, but gave it up after a while. This vast arena of mountains, gleaming like whitely hooded ghosts on every side, did not encourage such ebullience. Presently George glanced at his watch.

"Should be there in an hour," he called back over his shoulder to Chuck. Then he added, in an afterthought: "Wonder if the computer's finished its run. It was due about now."

Chuck didn't reply, so George swung round in his saddle. He could just see Chuck's face, a white oval turned toward the sky.

"Look," whispered Chuck, and George lifted his eyes to heaven. (There is always a last time for everything.)

Overhead, without any fuss, the stars were going out.

11

REGENERATION AND
NEW BEGINNINGS

A Rose for Ecclesiastes
ROGER ZELAZNY

"A Rose for Ecclesiastes" is a story about death and rebirth or resurrection. This death is not of a single man, but of an entire, highly sophisticated civilization on Mars. Ecclesiastes, of course, is a book of the Old Testament, which, although beautifully poetic, is also powerfully pessimistic. Ecclesiastes, the Preacher, asks, "Who knows what is good for man while he lives the few days of his vain life, which he passes like a shadow?" After a lifetime of searching for an answer, the Preacher notes, ". . . the fate of the sons of man and the fate of beasts is the same; as one dies, so dies the other." He concludes, "Behold, all was vanity and a striving after wind, and there was nothing to be gained under the sun." It is a song of futility.

The twentieth century finds itself in a like state of

futility, and so Ecclesiastes has been a favorite source of ideas and images for modern writers. T. S. Eliot recreates the dust, dry wind, and despair of Ecclesiastes in the major poetic statement of this century, "The Waste Land." The poem closes with a hope for water and regeneration in the desert. Ernest Hemingway, in his novel *The Sun Also Rises*, takes a line from the Book of Ecclesiastes for his title. Ours is an age of anxiety and despair when many have given up hope. The Martians in "A Rose for Ecclesiastes" are as hopeless. In resignation they say, "We have seen all things, we have heard and felt all things. The dance was good. Now let it end."

Religion offers hope, and many religions possess myths of resurrection or renewal. The yearly cycling of the seasons suggests that rebirth is fundamental in Nature. The plant sprouts, blooms, and withers. But it leaves a seed, dormant through the winter, which sprouts in the spring. Day sinks into night, and renews itself with the sunrise. The moon wanes to a slender crescent, and then waxes full again. T. S. Eliot in "The Waste Land" suggests that modern man, living in large cities, has so isolated himself from Nature, and the rebirth myths of religion, that he has forgotten his need to continually renew his life. He leads a sterile, meaningless existence. "April is the cruellest month" because it reminds him that he cannot flower with new life as the lilacs can. Unless rains fall in the desert of his life to bring regeneration, he will perish.

"A Rose for Ecclesiastes" is the story of a poet from Earth, Gallinger, who brings life and a hope of rebirth to the dying Martians. The rose, the "fire of life," symbolizes this new beginning. Like life itself, the rose is fleetingly beautiful and must be enjoyed in each moment of its brief existence.

Poetry and the dance are very old forms of expression that have always been closely associated with religious rituals and ceremonies, as they are in this story. The dance symbolizes the rhythmic harmony of the universe in motion. The dancer becomes one with that cosmic harmony as he dances. The poet is the seer, the man who is gifted with clearer vision and insight than his fellowmen. He, therefore, becomes the prophet who, by divine intuition, can predict the nature and direction of the future. It is he who is most skilled at handling the Word. The Word, or language, is man's most sacred possession because it makes him unique and sets him apart from the animals. Religion has always recognized this almost mystical or magical quality of the Word and regarded with reverence the sayer of the Word—the poet-prophet—for the Word has power to transform.

In the story, Gallinger, the poet, brings about a transformation in the life of the Martians. But he himself is also transformed. As the story opens, he is arrogant and full of vanity. He is not liked by the other members of his expedition, one of whom describes him as "proud as Lucifer." Gallinger is guilty of hubris, or excessive pride, a flaw that the ancient Greeks regarded as the greatest weakness in man's nature.

By the story's end, Gallinger has been transformed by love and born into a new awareness. But this is not a conventional story with a typically happy ending. It is a very rich and complex story full of paradoxes, those apparent contradictions that turn out to be true. Gallinger accomplishes a miracle in which he does not believe. He is transformed by a girl's love that never existed. Pride, man's greatest sin, is also his greatest virtue. There is nothing new under the sun, but every birth is a new thing. "A Rose for Ecclesiastes" is not simple, but like all complex literature, it is rewarding when mastered.

A Rose for Ecclesiastes
ROGER ZELAZNY

I

I was busy translating one of my *Madrigals Macabre* into Martian on the morning I was found acceptable. The intercom had buzzed briefly, and I dropped my pencil and flipped on the toggle in a single motion.

"Mister G," piped Morton's youthful contralto, "the old man says I should 'get hold of that damned conceited rhymer' right away, and send him to his cabin. —Since there's only one damned conceited rhymer . . ."

"Let not ambition mock thy useful toil." I cut him off.

So, the Martians had finally made up their minds! I knocked an inch and a half of ash from a smouldering butt, and took my first drag since I had lit it. The entire month's anticipation tried hard to crowd itself into the moment, but could not quite make it. I was frightened to walk those forty feet and hear Emory say the words I already knew he would say; and that feeling elbowed the other one into the background.

So I finished the stanza I was translating before I got up.

It took only a moment to reach Emory's door. I knocked twice and opened it, just as he growled, "Come in."

"You wanted to see me?" I sat down quickly to save him the trouble of offering me a seat.

"That was fast. What did you do, run?"

I regarded his paternal discontent:

Little fatty flecks beneath pale eyes, thinning hair, and an Irish nose; a voice a decibel louder than anyone else's . . .

Hamlet to Claudius: "I was working."

"Hah!" he snorted. "Come off it. No one's ever seen you do any of that stuff."

I shrugged my shoulders and started to rise.

"If that's what you called me down here—"

"Sit down!"

He stood up. He walked around his desk. He hovered above me and glared down. (A hard trick, even when I'm in a low chair.)

"You are undoubtedly the most antagonistic bastard I've ever had to work with!" he bellowed, like a belly-stung buffalo. "Why the hell don't you act like a human being sometime and surprise everybody? I'm willing to admit you're smart, maybe even a genius, but—oh, Hell!" He made a heaving gesture with both hands and walked back to his chair.

"Betty has finally talked them into letting you go in." His voice was normal again. "They'll receive you this afternoon. Draw one of the jeepsters after lunch, and get down there."

"Okay," I said.

"That's all, then."

I nodded, got to my feet. My hand was on the doorknob when he said:

"I don't have to tell you how important this is. Don't treat them the way you treat us."

I closed the door behind me.

I don't remember what I had for lunch. I was nervous, but I knew instinctively that I wouldn't muff it. My Boston publishers expected a Martian Idyll, or at least a Saint-Exupéry job on space flight. The National Science Association wanted a complete report on the Rise and Fall of the Martian Empire.

They would both be pleased. I knew.

That's the reason everyone is jealous—why they hate me. I always come through, and I can come through better than anyone else.

I shoveled in a final anthill of slop, and made my way to our car barn. I drew one jeepster and headed it toward Tirellian.

Flames of sand, lousy with iron oxide, set fire to the buggy. They swarmed over the open top and bit through my scarf; they set to work pitting my goggles.

The jeepster, swaying and panting like a little donkey I once rode through the Himalayas, kept kicking me in the seat of the pants. The Mountains of Tirellian shuffled their feet and moved toward me at a cockeyed angle.

Suddenly I was heading uphill, and I shifted gears to accommodate the engine's braying. Not like Gobi, not like the Great Southwestern Desert, I mused. Just red, just dead . . . without even a cactus.

I reached the crest of the hill, but I had raised too much dust to see what was ahead. It didn't matter, though, I have a head full of maps. I bore to the left and downhill, adjusting the throttle. A cross-wind and solid ground beat down the fires. I felt like Ulysses in Malebolge—with a terza-rima speech in one hand and an eye out for Dante.

I sounded a rock pagoda and arrived.

Betty waved as I crunched to a halt, then jumped down.

"Hi," I choked, unwinding my scarf and shaking out a pound and a half of grit. "Like, where do I go and who do I see?"

She permitted herself a brief Germanic giggle—more at my starting a sentence with "like" than at my discomfort—then she started talking. (She is a top linguist, so a word from the Village Idiom still tickles her!)

I appreciated her precise, furry talk; informational, and all that. I had enough in the way of social pleasantries before me to last at least the rest of my life. I looked at her chocolate-bar eyes and perfect teeth, at her sun-bleached hair, close-cropped to the head (I hate blondes!), and decided that she was in love with me.

"Mr. Gallinger, the Matriarch is waiting inside to be introduced. She has consented to open the Temple records for your study." She paused here to pat her hair and squirm a little. Did my gaze make her nervous?

"They are religious documents, as well as their only history," she continued, "sort of like the Mahabharata. She expects you to observe certain rituals in handling them, like repeating the sacred words when you turn pages—she will teach you the system."

I nodded quickly, several times.

"Fine, let's go in."

"Uh—" she paused. "Do not forget their Eleven Forms of Politeness and Degree. They take matters of form quite seriously—and do not get into any discussions over the equality of the sexes—"

"I know all about their taboos," I broke in. "Don't worry. I've lived in the Orient, remember?"

She dropped her eyes and seized my hand. I almost jerked it away.

"It will look better if I enter leading you."

I swallowed my comments and followed her, like Samson in Gaza.

Inside, my last thought met with a strange correspondence. The Matriarch's quarters were a rather abstract version of what I imagine the tents of the tribes of Israel to have been like. Abstract, I say, because it was all frescoed brick, peaked like a huge tent, with animal-skin representations, like gray-blue scars, that looked as if they had been laid on the walls with a palette knife.

The Matriarch, M'Cwyie, was short, white-haired, fiftyish, and dressed like a Gypsy queen. With her rainbow of voluminous skirts she looked like an inverted punch bowl set atop a cushion.

Accepting my obeisances, she regarded me as an owl might a rabbit. The lids of those black, black eyes jumped upwards as she discovered my perfect accent. —The tape recorder Betty had carried on her interviews had done its part, and I knew the language reports from the first two expeditions, verbatim. I'm all hell when it comes to picking up accents.

"You are the poet?"

"Yes," I replied.

"Recite one of your poems, please."

"I'm sorry, but nothing short of a thorough translating job would do justice to your language and my poetry, and I don't know enough of your language yet."

"Oh?"

"But I've been making such translations for my own amusement, as an exercise in grammar," I continued. "I'd be honored to bring a few of them along one of the times that I come here."

"Yes. Do so."

Score one for me!

She turned to Betty.

"You may go now."

Betty muttered the parting formalities, gave me a strange sidewise look, and was gone. She apparently had expected to stay and "assist" me. She wanted a piece of the glory, like everyone else. But I was the Schliemann at this Troy, and there would be only one name on the Association report!

M'Cwyie rose, and I noticed that she gained very little height by standing. But then I'm six-six and look like a poplar in October: thin, bright red on top, and towering above everyone else.

"Our records are very, very old," she began. "Betty says that your word for their age is 'millennia'."

I nodded appreciatively.

"I'm very eager to see them."

"They are not here. We will have to go into the Temple—they may not be removed."

I was suddenly wary.

"You have no objections to my copying them, do you?"

"No. I see that you respect them, or your desire would not be so great."

"Excellent."

She seemed amused. I asked her what was funny.

"The High Tongue may not be so easy for a foreigner to learn."

It came through fast.

No one on the first expedition had gotten this close. I had no way of knowing that this was a double-language deal—a classical as well as a vulgar. I knew some of their Prakrit, now I had to learn all their Sanskrit.

"Ouch! and damn!"

"Pardon, please?"

"It's nontranslatable, M'Cwyie. But imagine yourself having to learn the High Tongue in a hurry, and you can guess at the sentiment."

She seemed amused again, and told me to remove my shoes.

She guided me through an alcove . . .

. . . and into a burst of Byzantine brilliance!

No Earthman had ever been in this room before, or I would have heard about it. Carter, the first expedition's linguist, with the help of one Mary Allen, M.D., had learned all the grammar and vocabulary that I knew while sitting cross-legged in the antechamber.

We had had no idea this existed. Greedily, I cast my eyes about. A highly sophisticated system of esthetics lay behind the décor. We would have to revise our entire estimation of Martian culture.

For one thing, the ceiling was vaulted and corbeled; for another, there were side columns with reverse flutings; for another—oh hell! The place was big. Posh. You could never have guessed it from the shaggy outsides.

I bent forward to study the gilt filigree on a ceremonial table. M'Cwyie seemed a bit smug at my intentness, but I'd still have hated to play poker with her.

The table was loaded with books.

With my toe, I traced a mosaic on the floor.

"Is your entire city within this one building?"

"Yes, it goes far back into the mountain."

"I see," I said, seeing nothing.

I couldn't ask her for a conducted tour, yet.

She moved to a small stool by the table.

"Shall we begin your friendship with the High Tongue?"

I was trying to photograph the hall with my eyes, knowing I would have to get a camera in here, somehow, sooner or later. I tore my gaze from a statuette and nodded, hard.

"Yes, introduce me."

I sat down.

For the next three weeks alphabet-bugs chased each other behind my eyelids whenever I tried to sleep. The sky was an unclouded pool of turquoise that rippled calligraphies whenever I swept my eyes across it. I drank quarts of coffee while I worked and mixed cocktails of Benzedrine and champagne for my coffee breaks.

M'Cwyie tutored me two hours every morning, and

occasionally for another two in the evening. I spent an additional fourteen hours a day on my own, once I had gotten up sufficient momentum to go ahead alone.

And at night the elevator of time dropped me to its bottom floors . . .

I was six again, learning my Hebrew, Greek, Latin, and Aramaic. I was ten, sneaking peeks at the *Iliad*. When Daddy wasn't spreading hellfire, brimstone, and brotherly love, he was teaching me to dig the Word, like in the original.

Lord! There are so many originals and so *many* words! When I was twelve I started pointing out the little differences between what he was preaching and what I was reading.

The fundamentalist vigor of his reply brooked no debate. It was worse than any beating. I kept my mouth shut after that and learned to appreciate Old Testament poetry.

—Lord, I am sorry! Daddy—Sir—I am sorry!—It couldn't be! It couldn't be . . .

On the day the boy graduated from high school, with the French, German, Spanish, and Latin awards, Dad Gallinger had told his fourteen-year-old, six-foot scarecrow of a son that he wanted him to enter the ministry. I remember how his son was evasive:

"Sir," he had said, "I'd sort of like to study on my own for a year or so, and then take pre-theology courses at some liberal-arts university. I feel I'm still sort of young to try a seminary, straight off."

The Voice of God: "But you have the gift of tongues, my son. You can preach the Gospel in all the lands of Babel. You were born to be a missionary. You say you are young, but time is rushing by you like a whirlwind. Start early, and you will enjoy added years of service."

The added years of service were so many added tails to the cat repeatedly laid on my back. I can't see his face now, I never can. Maybe it is because I was always afraid to look at it then.

And years later, when he was dead, and laid out, in black, amidst bouquets, amidst weeping congregationalists, amidst prayers, red faces, handkerchiefs, hands patting your shoulders, solemn-faced comforters . . . I looked at him and did not recognize him.

We had met nine months before my birth, this stranger and I. He had never been cruel—stern, demanding, with contempt for everyone's shortcomings—but never cruel. He was also all that I had had of a mother. And brothers. And sisters. He had tolerated my three years at St. John's, possibly because of its name, never knowing how liberal and delightful a place it really was.

But I never knew him, and the man atop the catafalque demanded nothing now; I was free not to preach the Word.

But now I wanted to, in a different way. I wanted to preach a word that I could never have voiced while he lived.

I did not return for my Senior year in the fall. I had a small inheritance coming, and a bit of trouble getting control of it since I was still under eighteen. But I managed.

It was Greenwich Village I finally settled upon.

Not telling any well-meaning parishioners my new address, I entered into a daily routine of writing poetry and teaching myself Japanese and Hindustani. I grew a fiery beard, drank espresso, and learned to play chess. I wanted to try a couple of the other paths to salvation.

After that, it was two years in India with the Old Peace Corps—which broke me of my Buddhism, and gave me my *Pipes of Krishna* lyrics and the Pulitzer they deserved.

Then back to the States for my degree, grad work in linguistics, and more prizes.

Then one day a ship went to Mars. The vessel settling in its New Mexico nest of fires contained a new language.—It was fantastic, exotic, and esthetically overpowering. After I had learned all there was to know about it, and written my book, I was famous in new circles:

"Go, Gallinger. Dip your bucket in the well, and bring us a drink of Mars. Go, learn another world—but remain aloof, rail at it gently like Auden—and hand us its soul in iambics."

And I came to the land where the sun is a tarnished penny, where the wind is a whip, where two moons play at hot-rod games, and a hell of sand gives you the incendiary itches whenever you look at it.

I rose from my twistings on the bunk and crossed the darkened cabin to a port. The desert was a carpet of endless orange, bulging from the sweepings of centuries beneath it.

"I a stranger, unafraid—This is the land—I've got it made!"

I laughed.

I had the High Tongue by the tail already—or the roots, if you want your puns anatomical, as well as correct.

The High and Low Tongues were not so dissimilar as they had first seemed. I had enough of the one to get me through the murkier parts of the other. I had the grammar and all the commoner irregular verbs down cold; the dictionary I was constructing grew by the day, like a tulip, and would bloom shortly. Every time I played the tapes, the stem lengthened.

Now was the time to tax my ingenuity, to really drive the lessons home. I had purposely refrained from plunging into the major texts until I could do justice to them. I had been reading minor commentaries, bits of verse, fragments of history. And one thing had impressed me strongly in all that I read.

They wrote about concrete things: rocks, sand, water, winds; and the tenor couched within these elemental symbols was fiercely pessimistic. It reminded me of some Buddhist texts, but even more so, I realized from my recent *recherches*, it was like parts of the Old Testament. Specifically it reminded me of the Book of Ecclesiastes.

That, then, would be it. The sentiment, as well as the vocabulary, was so similar that it would be a perfect exercise. Like putting Poe into French. I would never be a convert to the Way of Malann, but I would show them that an Earthman had once thought the same thoughts, felt similarly.

I switched on my desk lamp and sought King James amidst my books.

Vanity of vanities, saith the Preacher, vanity of vanities; all is vanity. What profit hath a man . . .

My progress seemed to startle M'Cwyie. She peered at me, like Sartre's Other, across the tabletop. I ran through a chapter in the Book of Locar. I didn't look up, but I could feel the tight net her eyes were working about my head, shoulders, and rapid hands. I turned another page.

Was she weighing the net, judging the size of the catch? And what for? The books said nothing of fishers on Mars. Especially of men. They said that some god named Malann had spat, or had done something disgusting (depending on the version you read), and that life had gotten underway as a disease in inorganic matter. They said that movement was its first law, and that the dance was the only legitimate reply to the inorganic . . . the dance's quality its justification,—fication . . . and love is a disease in organic matter—Inorganic matter?

I shook my head. I had almost been asleep.

"M'narra."

I stood and stretched. Her eyes outlined me greedily now. So I met them, and they dropped.

"I grow tired. I want to rest awhile. I didn't sleep much last night."

She nodded, Earth's shorthand for "yes," as she had learned from me.

"You wish to relax, and see the explicitness of the doctrine of Locar in its fullness?"

"Pardon me?"

"You wish to see a Dance of Locar?"

"Oh." Their damned circuits of form and periphrasis here ran worse than the Koreans! "Yes. Surely. Any time it's going to be done, I'd be happy to watch."

I continued, "In the meantime, I've been meaning to ask you whether I might take some pictures—"

"Now is the time. Sit down. Rest. I will call the musicians."

She bustled out through a door I had never been past.

Well now, the dance was the highest art, according to Locar, not to mention Havelock Ellis, and I was about to see how their centuries-dead philosopher felt it should be conducted. I rubbed my eyes and snapped over, touching my toes a few times.

The blood began pounding in my head, and I sucked in a couple deep breaths. I bent again and there was a flurry of motion at the door.

To the trio who entered with M'Cwyie I must have looked as if I were searching for the marbles I had just lost, bent over like that.

I grinned weakly and straightened up, my face red from more than exertion. I hadn't expected them *that* quickly.

Suddenly I thought of Havelock Ellis again in his area of greatest popularity.

The little redheaded doll, wearing, sari-like, a diaphanous piece of the Martian sky, looked up in wonder— as a child at some colorful flag on a high pole.

"Hello," I said, or its equivalent.

She bowed before replying. Evidently I had been promoted in status.

"I shall dance," said the red wound in that pale, pale cameo, her face. Eyes, the color of dream and her dress, pulled away from mine.

She drifted to the center of the room.

Standing there, like a figure in an Etruscan frieze, she was either meditating or regarding the design on the floor.

Was the mosaic symbolic of something? I studied it. If it was, it eluded me; it would make an attractive bathroom floor or patio, but I couldn't see much in it beyond that.

The other two were paint-spattered sparrows like M'Cwyie, in their middle years. One settled to the floor with a triple-stringed instrument faintly resembling a *samisen*. The other held a simple woodblock and two drumsticks.

M'Cwyie disdained her stool and was seated upon the floor before I realized it. I followed suit.

The *samisen* player was still tuning up, so I leaned toward M'Cwyie.

"What is the dancer's name?"

"Braxa," she replied, without looking at me, and raised her left hand, slowly, which meant yes, and go ahead, and let it begin.

The stringed thing throbbed like a toothache, and a tick-tocking, like ghosts of all the clocks they had never invented, sprang from the block.

Braxa was a statue, both hands raised to her face, elbows high and outspread.

The music became a metaphor for fire.

Crackle, purr, snap . . .

She did not move.

The hissing altered to splashes. The cadence slowed. It was water now, the most precious thing in the world, gurgling clear then green over mossy rocks.

Still she did not move.

Glissandos. A pause.

Then, so faint I could hardly be sure at first, the tremble of the winds began. Softly, gently, sighing and halting, uncertain. A pause, a sob, then a repetition of the first statement, only louder.

Were my eyes completely bugged from my reading, or was Braxa actually trembling, all over, head to foot.

She was.

She began a microscopic swaying. A fraction of an inch right, then left. Her fingers opened like the petals of a flower, and I could see that her eyes were closed.

Her eyes opened. They were distant, glassy, looking through me and the walls. Her swaying became more pronounced, merged with the beat.

The wind was sweeping in from the desert now, falling against Tirellian like waves on a dike. Her fingers moved, they were the gusts. Her arms, slow pendulums, descended, began a countermovement.

The gale was coming now. She began an axial movement and her hands caught up with the rest of her body, only now her shoulders commenced to writhe out a figure eight.

The wind! The wind, I say. O wild, enigmatic! O muse of St.-John Perse!

The cyclone was twisting round those eyes, its still center. Her head was thrown back, but I knew there was no ceiling between her gaze, passive as Buddha's, and the unchanging skies. Only the two moons, perhaps, interrupted their slumber in that elemental Nirvana of uninhabited turquoise.

Years ago, I had seen the Devadasis in India, the street dancers, spinning their colorful webs, drawing in the male insect. But Braxa was more than this: she was a Ramadjany, like those votaries of Rama, incarnation of Vishnu, who had given the dance to man: the sacred dancers.

The clicking was monotonously steady now; the whine of the strings made me think of the stinging rays of the sun, their heat stolen by the wind's halations; the blue was Sarasvati and Mary, and a girl named Laura. I heard a sitar from somewhere, watched this statue come to life, and inhaled a divine afflatus.

I was again Rimbaud with his hashish, Baudelaire with his laudanum, Poe, De Quincey, Wilde, Mallarmé, and Aleister Crowley. I was, for a fleeting second, my father in his dark pulpit and darker suit, the hymns and the organ's wheeze transmuted to bright wind.

She was a spun weather vane, a feathered crucifix hovering in the air, a clothesline holding one bright garment lashed parallel to the ground. Her shoulder was bare now, and her right breast moved up and down like a moon in the sky, its red nipple appearing momentarily above a fold and vanishing again. The music was as formal as Job's argument with God. Her dance was God's reply.

The music slowed, settled; it had been met, matched, answered. Her garment, as if alive, crept back into the more sedate folds it originally held.

She dropped low, lower, to the floor. Her head fell upon her raised knees. She did not move.

There was silence.

I realized, from the ache across my shoulders, how tensely I had been sitting. My armpits were wet. Rivulets had been running down my sides. What did one do now? Applaud?

I sought M'Cwyie from the corner of my eye. She raised her right hand.

As if by telepathy the girl shuddered all over and stood. The musicians also rose. So did M'Cwyie.

I got to my feet, with a charley horse in my left leg, and said, "It was beautiful," inane as that sounds.

I received three different High Forms of "thank you."

There was a flurry of color and I was alone again with M'Cwyie.

"That is the one hundred seventeenth of the two thousand two hundred twenty-four dances of Locar."

I looked down at her.

"Whether Locar was right or wrong, he worked out a fine reply to the inorganic."

She smiled.

"Are the dances of your world like this?"

"Some of them are similar. I was reminded of them as I watched Braxa—but I've never seen anything exactly like hers."

"She is good," M'Cwyie said. "She knows all the dances."

A hint of her earlier expression which had troubled me . . .

It was gone in an instant.

"I must tend to my duties now." She moved to the table and closed the books. "M'narra."

"Good-bye." I slipped into my boots.

"Good-bye, Gallinger."

I walked out the door, mounted the jeepster, and roared across the evening into night, my wings of risen desert flapping slowly behind me.

II

I had just closed the door behind Betty, after a brief grammar session, when I heard the voices in the hall.

My vent was opened a fraction, so I stood there and eavesdropped:

Morton's fruity treble: "Guess what? He said 'hello' to me a while ago."

"Hmmph!" Emory's elephant lungs exploded. "Either he's slipping, or you were standing in his way and he wanted you to move."

"Probably didn't recognize me. I don't think he sleeps any more, now he has that language to play with. I had night watch last week, and every night I passed his door at 0300—I always heard that recorder going. At 0500, when I got off, he was still at it."

"The guy *is* working hard," Emory admitted, grudgingly. "In fact, I think he's taking some kind of dope to keep awake. He looks sort of glassy-eyed these days. Maybe that's natural for a poet, though."

Betty had been standing there, because she broke in then:

"Regardless of what you think of him, it's going to take me at least a year to learn what he's picked up in three weeks. And I'm just a linguist, not a poet."

Morton must have been nursing a crush on her bovine charms. It's the only reason I can think of for his dropping his guns to say what he did.

"I took a course in modern poetry when I was back at the university," he began. "We read six authors—Yeats, Pound, Eliot, Crane, Stevens, and Gallinger—and on the last day of the semester, when the prof was feeling a little rhetorical, he said, 'These six names are written on the century, and all the gates of criticism and Hell shall not prevail against them.'

"Myself," he continued, "I thought his *Pipes of*

Krishna and his *Madrigals* were great. I was honored to be chosen for an expedition he was going on.

"I think he's spoken two dozen words to me since I met him," he finished.

The Defence: "Did it ever occur to you," Betty said, "that he might be tremendously self-conscious about his appearance? He was also a precocious child, and probably never even had school friends. He's sensitive and very introverted."

"Sensitive? Self-conscious?" Emory choked and gagged. "The man is as proud as Lucifer, and he's a walking insult machine. You press a button like 'Hello' or 'Nice day' and he thumbs his nose at you. He's got it down to a reflex."

They muttered a few other pleasantries and drifted away.

Well, bless you, Morton boy. You little pimple-faced, Ivy-bred connoisseur! I've never taken a course in my poetry, but I'm glad someone said that. The Gates of Hell. Well, now! Maybe Daddy's prayers got heard somewhere, and I am a missionary, after all!

Only...

... Only a missionary needs something to convert people *to*. I have my private system of esthetics, and I suppose it oozes an ethical by-product somewhere. But if I ever had anything to preach, really, even in my poems, I wouldn't care to preach it to such lowlifes as you. If you think I'm a slob, I'm also a snob, and there's no room for you in Heaven—it's a private place, where Swift, Shaw, and Petronius Arbiter come to dinner.

And oh, the feasts we have! The Trimalchio's, the Emory's we dissect!

We finish you with the soup, Morton!

I turned and settled at my desk. I wanted to write something. Ecclesiastes could take a night off. I wanted to write a poem, a poem about the one hundred seventeenth dance of Locar; about a rose following the light, traced by the wind, sick, like Blake's rose, dying . . .

I found a pencil and began.

When I had finished I was pleased. It wasn't great— at least, it was no greater than it needed to be—High Martian not being my strongest tongue. I groped, and put it into English, with partial rhymes. Maybe I'd stick it in my next book. I called it *Braxa*:

> In a land of wind and red,
> where the icy evening of Time
> freezes milk in the breasts of Life,
> as two moons overhead—
> cat and dog in alleyways of dream—
> scratch and scramble agelessly my
>   flight . . .
> This final flower turns a burning
>   head.

I put it away and found some phenobarbital. I was suddenly tired.

When I showed my poem to M'Cwyie the next day, she read it through several times, very slowly.

"It is lovely," she said. "But you used three words from your own language. 'Cat' and 'dog,' I assume, are two small animals with a hereditary hatred for one another. But what is 'flower'?"

"Oh," I said. "I've never come across your word for

'flower,' but I was actually thinking of an Earth flower, the rose."

"What is it like?"

"Well, its petals are generally bright red. That's what I meant, on one level, by 'burning head.' I also wanted it to imply fever, though, and red hair, and the fire of life. The rose, itself, has a thorny stem, green leaves, and a distinct, pleasant aroma."

"I wish I could see one."

"I suppose it could be arranged. I'll check."

"Do it, please. You are a—" She used the word for "prophet," or religious poet, like Isaiah or Locar. "—and your poem is inspired. I shall tell Braxa of it."

I declined the nomination, but felt flattered.

This, then, I decided, was the strategic day, the day on which to ask whether I might bring in the microfilm machine and the camera. I wanted to copy all their texts, I explained, and I couldn't write fast enough to do it.

She surprised me by agreeing immediately. But she bowled me over with her invitation.

"Would you like to come and stay here while you do this thing? Then you can work night and day, any time you want—except when the Temple is being used, of course."

I bowed.

"I should be honored."

"Good. Bring your machines when you want, and I will show you a room."

"Will this afternoon be all right?"

"Certainly."

"Then I will go now and get things ready. Until this afternoon . . ."

"Good-bye."

I anticipated a little trouble from Emory, but not much. Everyone back at the ship was anxious to see the Martians, talk with the Martians, poke needles in the Martians, ask them about Martian climate, diseases, soil chemistry, politics, and mushrooms (our botanist was a fungus nut, but a reasonably good guy) —and only four or five had actually gotten to see them. The crew had been spending most of its time excavating dead cities and their acropolises. We played the game by strict rules, and the natives were as fiercely insular as the nineteenth-century Japanese. I figured I would meet with little resistance, and I figured right.

In fact, I got the distinct impression that everyone was happy to see me move out.

I stopped in the hydroponics room to speak with our mushroom master.

"Hi, Kane. Grow any toadstools in the sand yet?"

He sniffed. He always sniffs. Maybe he's allergic to plants.

"Hello, Gallinger. No, I haven't had any success with toadstools, but look behind the car barn next time you're out there. I've got a few cacti going."

"Great," I observed. Doc Kane was about my only friend aboard, not counting Betty.

"Say, I came down to ask you a favor."

"Name it."

"I want a rose."

"A what?"

"A rose. You know, a nice red American Beauty job—thorns, pretty smelling—"

"I don't think it will take in this soil. *Sniff, sniff.*"

"No, you don't understand. I don't want to plant it, I just want the flowers."

"I'd have to use the tanks." He scratched his hairless dome. "It would take at least three months to get your flowers, even under forced growth."

"Will you do it?"

"Sure, if you don't mind the wait."

"Not at all. In fact, three months will just make it before we leave." I looked about at the pools of crawling slime, at the trays of shoots. "—I'm moving up to Tirellian today, but I'll be in and out all the time. I'll be here when it blooms."

"Moving up there, eh? Moore said they're an in-group."

"I guess I'm 'in' then."

"Looks that way—I still don't see how you learned their language, though. Of course, I had trouble with French and German for my PhD., but last week I heard Betty demonstrate it at lunch. It just sounds like a lot of weird noises. She says speaking it is like working a *Times* crossword and trying to imitate birdcalls at the same time."

I laughed, and took the cigarette he offered me.

"It's complicated," I acknowledged. "But, well, it's as if you suddenly came across a whole new class of mycetae here—you'd dream about it at night."

His eyes were gleaming.

"Wouldn't that be something! I might, yet, you know."

"Maybe you will."

He chuckled as we walked to the door.

"I'll start your roses tonight. Take it easy down there."

"You bet. Thanks."

Like I said, a fungus nut, but a fairly good guy.

My quarters in the Citadel of Tirellian were directly adjacent to the Temple, on the inward side and slightly to the left. They were a considerable improvement over my cramped cabin, and I was pleased that Martian culture had progressed sufficiently to discover the desirability of the mattress over the pallet. Also, the bed was long enough to accommodate me, which *was* surprising.

So I unpacked and took 16 35 mm. shots of the Temple, before starting on the books.

I took 'stats until I was sick of turning pages without knowing what they said. So I started translating a work of history.

"Lo. In the thirty-seventh year of the Process of Cillen the rains came, which gave rise to rejoicing, for it was a rare and untoward occurrence, and commonly construed a blessing.

"But it was not the life-giving semen of Malann which fell from the heavens. It was the blood of the universe, spurting from an artery. And the last days were upon us. The final dance was to begin.

"The rains brought the plague that does not kill, and the last passes of Locar began with their drumming . . ."

I asked myself what the hell Tamur meant, for he was an historian and supposedly committed to fact. This was not their Apocalypse.

Unless they could be one and the same . . . ?

Why not? I mused. Tirellian's handful of people were the remnant of what had obviously once been a highly developed culture. They had had wars, but no holocausts; science, but little technology. A plague, a plague that did not kill . . . ? Could that have done it? How, if it wasn't fatal?

I read on, but the nature of the plague was not discussed. I turned pages, skipped ahead, and drew a blank.

M'Cwyie! M'Cwyie! When I want to question you most, you are not around!

Would it be a *faux pas* to go looking for her? Yes, I decided. I was restricted to the rooms I had been shown, that had been an implicit understanding. I would have to wait to find out.

So I cursed long and loud, in many languages, doubtless burning Malann's sacred ears, there in his Temple.

He did not see fit to strike me dead, so I decided to call it a day and hit the sack.

I must have been asleep for several hours when Braxa entered my room with a tiny lamp. She dragged me awake by tugging at my pajama sleeve.

I said hello. Thinking back, there is not much else I could have said.

"Hello."

"I have come," she said, "to hear the poem."

"What poem?"

"Yours."

"Oh."

I yawned, sat up, and did things people usually do when awakened in the middle of the night to read poetry.

"That is very kind of you, but isn't the hour a trifle awkward?"

"I don't mind," she said.

Someday I am going to write an article for the *Journal of Semantics*, called "Tone of Voice: An Insufficient Vehicle for Irony."

However, I was awake, so I grabbed my robe.

"What sort of animal is that?" she asked, pointing at the silk dragon on my lapel.

"Mythical," I replied. "Now look, it's late. I am tired. I have much to do in the morning. And M'Cwyie just might get the wrong idea if she learns you were here."

"Wrong idea?"

"You know damned well what I mean!" It was the first time I had had an opportunity to use Martian profanity, and it failed.

"No," she said, "I do not know."

She seemed frightened, like a puppy being scolded without knowing what it has done wrong.

I softened. Her red cloak matched her hair and lips so perfectly, and those lips were trembling.

"Here now, I didn't mean to upset you. On my world there are certain, uh, mores, concerning people of different sex alone together in bedrooms, and not allied by marriage . . . Um, I mean, you see what I mean?"

"No."

They were jade, her eyes.

"Well, it's sort of . . . Well, it's sex, that's what it is."

A light was switched on in those jade lamps.

"Oh, you mean having children!"

"Yes. That's it! Exactly."

She laughed. It was the first time I had heard laughter in Tirellian. It sounded like a violinist striking his high strings with the bow, in short little chops. It was not an altogether pleasant thing to hear, especially because she laughed too long.

When she had finished she moved closer.

"I remember, now," she said. "We used to have such rules. Half a Process ago, when I was a child, we had such rules. But," she looked as if she were ready to laugh again, "there is no need for them now."

My mind moved like a tape recorder played at triple speed.

Half a Process! HalfaProcessaProcessaProcess! No! Yes!

Half a Process was two hundred forty-three years, roughly speaking!

—Time enough to learn the 2,224 dances of Locar.

—Time enough to grow old, if you were human.

—Earth-style human, I mean.

I looked at her again, pale as the white queen in an ivory chess set.

She was human, I'd stake my soul—alive, normal, healthy, I'd stake my life—woman, my body . . .

But she was two and a half centuries old, which made M'Cwyie Methuselah's grandma. It flattered me to think of their repeated complimenting of my skills, as linguist, as poet. These superior beings!

But what did she mean 'there is no such need for them now'? Why the near-hysteria? Why all those funny looks I'd been getting from M'Cwyie?

I suddenly knew I was close to something important, besides a beautiful girl.

"Tell me," I said, in my Casual Voice, "did it have anything to do with 'the plague that does not kill,' of which Tamur wrote?"

"Yes," she replied, "the children born after the Rains could have no children of their own, and—"

"And what?" I was leaning forward, memory set at "record."

"—and the men had no desire to get any."

I sagged backward against the bedpost. Racial sterility, masculine impotence, following phenomenal weather. Had some vagabond cloud of radioactive junk from God knows where penetrated their weak atmosphere one day? One day long before Schiaparelli saw the canals, mythical as my dragon, before those "canals" had given rise to some correct guesses for all the wrong reasons, had Braxa been alive, dancing, here —damned in the womb since blind Milton had written of another paradise, equally lost?

I found a cigarette. Good thing I had thought to bring ashtrays. Mars had never been a tobacco industry either. Or booze. The ascetics I had met in India had been Dionysiac compared to this.

"What is that tube of fire?"

"A cigarette. Want one?"

"Yes, please."

She sat beside me, and I lighted it for her.

"It irritates the nose."

"Yes. Draw some into your lungs, hold it there, and exhale."

A moment passed.

"Ooh," she said.

A pause, then, "Is it sacred?"

"No, it's nicotine," I answered, "a very *ersatz* form of divinity."

Another pause.

"Please don't ask me to translate 'ersatz'."

"I won't. I get this feeling sometimes when I dance."

"It will pass in a moment."

"Tell me your poem now."

An idea hit me.

"Wait a minute," I said, "I may have something better."

I got up and rummaged through my notebooks, then I returned and sat beside her.

"These are the first three chapters of the Book of Ecclesiastes," I explained. "It is very similar to your own sacred books."

I started reading.

I got through eleven verses before she cried out, "Please don't read that! Tell me one of yours!"

I stopped and tossed the notebook onto a nearby table. She was shaking, not as she had quivered that day she danced as the wind, but with the jitter of unshed tears. She held her cigarette awkwardly, like a pencil. Clumsily, I put my arm about her shoulders.

"He is so sad," she said, "like all the others."

So I twisted my mind like a bright ribbon, folded it, and tied the crazy Christmas knots I love so well. From German to Martian, with love, I did an impromptu paraphrasal of a poem about a Spanish dancer. I thought it would please her. I was right.

"Ooh," she said again. "Did you write that?"

"No, it's by a better man than I."

"I don't believe you. You wrote it."

"No, a man named Rilke did."

"But you brought it across to my language.—Light another match, so I can see how she danced."

I did.

" 'The fires of forever,' " she mused, "and she stamped them out, 'with small, firm feet.' I wish I could dance like that."

"You're better than any Gipsy," I laughed, blowing it out.

"No, I'm not. I couldn't do that."

Her cigarette was burning down, so I removed it from her fingers and put it out, along with my own.

"Do you want me to dance for you?"

"No," I said. "Go to bed."

She smiled, and before I realized it, had unclasped the fold of red at her shoulder.

And everything fell away.

And I swallowed, with some difficulty.

"All right," she said.

So I kissed her, as the breath of fallen cloth extinguished the lamp.

III

The days were like Shelley's leaves: yellow, red, brown, whipped in bright gusts by the west wind. They swirled past me with the rattle of microfilm. Almost all the books were recorded now. It would take scholars years to get through them, to properly assess their value. Mars was locked in my desk.

Ecclesiastes, abandoned and returned to a dozen times, was almost ready to speak in the High Tongue.

I whistled when I wasn't in the Temple. I wrote reams of poetry I would have been ashamed of before. Evenings I would walk with Braxa, across the dunes or up into the mountains. Sometimes she would dance for me; and I would read something long, and in dactylic hexameter. She still thought I was Rilke, and I almost kidded myself into believing it. Here I was, staying at the Castle Duino, writing his *Elegies*.

> ... It is strange to inhabit the Earth no more
> to use no longer customs scarce acquired,
> nor interpret roses ...

No! Never interpret roses! Don't. Smell them (sniff, Kane!), pick them, enjoy them. Live in the moment. Hold to it tightly. But charge not the gods to explain. So fast the leaves go by, are blown ...

And no one ever noticed us. Or cared.

Laura. Laura and Braxa. They rhyme, you know, with a bit of a clash. Tall, cool, and blonde was she (I hate blondes!), and Daddy had turned me inside out, like a pocket, and I thought she could fill me again. But the big, beat word-slinger, with Judas-beard and dog-trust in his eyes, oh, he had been a fine decoration at her parties. And that was all.

How the machine cursed me in the Temple! It blasphemed Malann and Gallinger. And the wild west wind went by and something was not far behind.

The last days were upon us.

A day went by and I did not see Braxa, and a night. And a second. A third.

I was half-mad. I hadn't realized how close we had

become, how important she had been. With the dumb assurance of presence, I had fought against questioning roses.

I had to ask. I didn't want to, but I had no choice.

"Where is she, M'Cwyie? Where is Braxa?"

"She is gone," she said.

"Where?"

"I do not know."

I looked at those devil-bird eyes. Anathema maranatha rose to my lips.

"I must know."

She looked through me.

"She has left us. She is gone. Up into the hills, I suppose. Or the desert. It does not matter. What does anything matter? The dance draws to a close. The Temple will soon be empty."

"Why? Why did she leave?"

"I do not know."

"I must see her again. We lift off in a matter of days."

"I am sorry, Gallinger."

"So am I," I said, and slammed shut a book without saying "M'narra."

I stood up.

"I will find her."

I left the Temple. M'Cwyie was a seated statue. My boots were still where I had left them.

All day I roared up and down the dunes, going nowhere. To the crew of the *Aspic* I must have looked like a sandstorm, all by myself. Finally, I had to return for more fuel.

Emory came stalking out.

"Okay, make it good. You look like the abominable dust man. Why the rodeo?"

"Why, I, uh, lost something."

"In the middle of the desert? Was it one of your sonnets? They're the only thing I can think of that you'd make such a fuss over."

"No, dammit! It was something personal."

George had finished filling the tank. I started to mount the jeepster again.

"Hold on there!" He grabbed my arm.

"You're not going back until you tell me what this is all about."

I could have broken his grip, but then he could order me dragged back by the heels, and quite a few people would enjoy doing the dragging. So I forced myself to speak slowly, softly:

"It's simply that I lost my watch. My mother gave it to me and it's a family heirloom. I want to find it before we leave."

"You sure it's not in your cabin, or down in Tirellian?"

"I've already checked."

"Maybe somebody hid it to irritate you. You know you're not the most popular guy around."

I shook my head.

"I thought of that. But I always carry it in my right pocket. I think it might have bounced out going over the dunes."

He narrowed his eyes.

"I remember reading on a book jacket that your mother died when you were born."

"That's right," I said, biting my tongue. "The watch

belonged to her father and she wanted me to have it. My father kept it for me."

"Hmph!" he snorted. "That's a pretty strange way to look for a watch, riding up and down in a jeepster."

"I could see the light shining off it that way," I offered, lamely.

"Well, it's starting to get dark," he observed. "No sense looking any more today.

"Throw a dust sheet over the jeepster," he directed a mechanic.

He patted my arm.

"Come on in and get a shower, and something to eat. You look as if you could use both."

Little fatty flecks beneath pale eyes, thinning hair, and an Irish nose; a voice a decibel louder than anyone else's ...

His only qualifications for leadership!

I stood there, hating him. Claudius! If only this were the fifth act!

But suddenly the idea of a shower, and food, came through to me. I could use both badly. If I insisted on hurrying back immediately, I might arouse more suspicion.

So I brushed some sand from my sleeve.

"You're right. That sounds like a good idea."

"Come on, we'll eat in my cabin."

The shower was a blessing, clean khakis were the grace of God, and the food smelled like Heaven.

"Smells pretty good," I said.

We hacked up our steaks in silence. When we got to the dessert and coffee, he suggested:

"Why don't you take the night off? Stay here and get some sleep."

I shook my head.

"I'm pretty busy. Finishing up. There's not much time left."

"A couple days ago you said you were almost finished."

"Almost, but not quite."

"You also said they'll be holding a service in the Temple tonight."

"That's right. I'm going to work in my room."

He shrugged his shoulders.

Finally, he said, "Gallinger," and I looked up because my name means trouble.

"It shouldn't be any of my business," he said, "but it is. Betty says you have a girl down there."

There was no question mark. It was a statement hanging in the air. Waiting.

—*Betty, you're a bitch. You're a cow and a bitch. And a jealous one, at that. Why didn't you keep your nose where it belonged, shut your eyes? Your mouth?*

"So?" I said, a statement with a question mark.

"So," he answered it, "it is my duty, as head of this expedition, to see that relations with the natives are carried on in a friendly, and diplomatic, manner."

"You speak of them," I said, "as though they are aborigines. Nothing could be further from the truth."

I rose.

"When my papers are published, everyone on Earth will know that truth. I'll tell them things Doctor Moore never even guessed at. I'll tell the tragedy of a doomed race, waiting for death, resigned and disinterested. I'll tell why, and it will break hard, scholarly hearts. I'll write about it, and they will give me more prizes, and this time I won't want them.

"My God!" I exclaimed. "They had a culture when our ancestors were clubbing the sabre-tooth and finding out how fire works!"

"*Do* you have a girl down there?"

"Yes!" I said. *Yes, Claudius! Yes, Daddy! Yes, Emory!* "I do. But I'm going to let you in on a scholarly scoop now. They're already dead. They're sterile. In one more generation there won't be any Martians."

I paused, then added, "Except in my papers, except on a few pieces of microfilm and tape. And in some poems, about a girl who did give a damn and could only bitch about the unfairness of it all by dancing."

"Oh," he said.

After awhile:

"You *have* been behaving differently these past couple months. You've even been downright civil on occasion, you know. I couldn't help wondering what was happening. I didn't know anything mattered that strongly to you."

I bowed my head.

"Is she the reason you were racing around the desert?"

I nodded.

"Why?"

I looked up.

"Because she's out there, somewhere. I don't know where, or why. And I've got to find her before we go."

"Oh," he said again.

Then he leaned back, opened a drawer, and took out something wrapped in a towel. He unwound it. A framed photo of a woman lay on the table.

"My wife," he said.

It was an attractive face, with big, almond eyes.

"I'm a Navy man, you know," he began. "Young officer once. Met her in Japan.

"Where I come from it wasn't considered right to marry into another race, so we never did. But she was my wife. When she died I was on the other side of the world. They took my children, and I've never seen them since. I couldn't learn what orphanage, what home, they were put into. That was long ago. Very few people know about it."

"I'm sorry," I said.

"Don't be. Forget it. But," he shifted in his chair and looked at me, "if you do want to take her back with you—do it. It'll mean my neck, but I'm too old to ever head another expedition like this one. So go ahead."

He gulped his cold coffee.

"Get your jeepster."

He swiveled the chair around.

I tried to say "thank you" twice, but I couldn't. So I got up and walked out.

"Sayonara, and all that," he muttered behind me.

"Here it is, Gallinger!" I heard a shout.

I turned on my heel and looked back up the ramp.

"Kane!"

He was limned in the port, shadow against light, but I had heard him sniff.

I returned the few steps.

"Here what is?"

"Your rose."

He produced a plastic container, divided internally. The lower half was filled with liquid. The stem ran down into it. The other half, a glass of claret in this horrible night, was a large, newly opened rose.

"Thank you," I said, tucking it into my jacket.

"Going back to Tirellian, eh?"

"Yes."

"I saw you come aboard, so I got it ready. Just missed you at the Captain's cabin. He was busy. Hollered out that I could catch you at the barns."

"Thanks again."

"It's chemically treated. It will stay in bloom for weeks."

I nodded. I was gone.

Up into the mountains now. Far. Far. The sky was a bucket of ice in which no moons floated. The going became steeper, and the little donkey protested. I whipped him with the throttle and went on. Up. Up. I spotted a green, unwinking star, and felt a lump in my throat. The encased rose beat against my chest like an extra heart. The donkey brayed, long and loudly, then began to cough. I lashed him some more and he died.

I threw the emergency brake on and got out. I began to walk.

So cold, so cold it grows. Up here. At night? Why? Why did she do it? Why flee the campfire when night comes on?

And I was up, down, around, and through every chasm, gorge, and pass, with my long-legged strides and an ease of movement never known on Earth.

Barely two days remain, my love, and thou hast forsaken me. Why?

I crawled under overhangs. I leapt over ridges. I scraped my knees, and elbow. I heard my jacket tear.

No answer, Malann? Do you really hate your people

this much? Then I'll try someone else. Vishnu, you're
the Preserver. Preserve her, please! Let me find her.

Jehovah?

Adonis? Osiris? Thammuz? Manitou? Legba? Where
is she?

I ranged far and high, and I slipped.

Stones ground underfoot and I dangled over an edge.
My fingers so cold. It was hard to grip the rock.

I looked down.

Twelve feet or so. I let go and dropped, landed rolling.

Then I heard her scream.

I lay there, not moving, looking up. Against the
night, above, she called.

"Gallinger!"

I lay still.

"Gallinger!"

And she was gone.

I heard stones rattle and knew she was coming down
some path to the right of me.

I jumped up and ducked into the shadow of a
boulder.

She rounded a cut-off, and picked her way, uncertainly, through the stones.

"Gallinger?"

I stepped out and seized her shoulders.

"Braxa."

She screamed again, then began to cry, crowding
against me. It was the first time I had ever heard her
cry.

"Why?" I asked. "Why?"

But she only clung to me and sobbed.

Finally, "I thought you had killed yourself."

"Maybe I would have," I said. "Why did you leave Tirellian? And me?"

"Didn't M'Cwyie tell you? Didn't you guess?"

"I didn't guess, and M'Cwyie said she didn't know."

"Then she lied. She knows."

"What? What is it she knows?"

She shook all over, then was silent for a long time. I realized suddenly that she was wearing only her flimsy dancer's costume. I pushed her from me, took off my jacket, and put it about her shoulders.

"Great Malann!" I cried. "You'll freeze to death!"

"No," she said, "I won't."

I was transferring the rose case to my pocket.

"What is that?" she asked.

"A rose," I answered. "You can't make it out much in the dark. I once compared you to one. Remember?"

"Yu-Yes. May I carry it?"

"Sure." I stuck it in the jacket pocket.

"Well? I'm still waiting for an explanation."

"You really do not know?" she asked.

"No!"

"When the Rains came," she said, "apparently only our men were affected, which was enough. . . . Because I—wasn't—affected—apparently—"

"Oh," I said. "Oh."

We stood there, and I thought.

"Well, why did you run? What's wrong with being pregnant on Mars? Tamur was mistaken. Your people can live again."

She laughed, again that wild violin played by a Paganini gone mad. I stopped her before it went too far.

"How?" she finally asked, rubbing her cheek.

"Your people live longer than ours. If our child is normal it will mean our races can intermarry. There must still be other fertile women of your race. Why not?"

"You have read the Book of Locar," she said, "and yet you ask me that? Death was decided, voted upon, and passed, shortly after it appeared in this form. But long before, the followers of Locar knew. They decided it long ago. 'We have done all things,' they said, 'we have seen all things, we have heard and felt all things. The dance was good. Now let it end.'"

"You can't believe that."

"What I believe does not matter," she replied. "M'Cwyie and the Mothers have decided we must die. Their very title is now a mockery, but their decisions will be upheld. There is only one prophecy left, and it is mistaken. We will die."

"No," I said.

"What, then?"

"Come back with me, to Earth."

"No."

"All right, then. Come with me now."

"Where?"

"Back to Tirellian. I'm going to talk to the Mothers."

"You can't! There is a Ceremony tonight!"

I laughed.

"A ceremony for a god who knocks you down, and then kicks you in the teeth?"

"He is still Malann," she answered. "We are still his people."

"You and my father would have gotten along fine," I

snarled. "But I am going, and you are coming with me, even if I have to carry you—and I'm bigger than you are."

"But you are not bigger than Ontro."

"Who the hell is Ontro?"

"He will stop you, Gallinger. He is the Fist of Malann."

IV

I scudded the jeepster to a halt in front of the only entrance I knew, M'Cwyie's. Braxa, who had seen the rose in a headlamp, now cradled it in her lap, like our child, and said nothing. There was a passive, lovely look on her face.

"Are they in the Temple now?" I wanted to know.

The Madonna expression did not change. I repeated the question. She stirred.

"Yes," she said, from a distance, "but you cannot go in."

"We'll see."

I circled and helped her down.

I led her by the hand, and she moved as if in a trance. In the light of the new-risen moon, her eyes looked as they had the day I met her, when she had danced. I snapped my fingers. Nothing happened.

So I pushed the door open and led her in. The room was half-lighted.

And she screamed for the third time that evening:

"Do not harm him, Ontro! It is Gallinger!"

I had never seen a Martian man before, only

women. So I had no way of knowing whether he was a freak, though I suspected it strongly.

I looked up at him.

His half-naked body was covered with moles and swellings. Gland trouble, I guessed.

I had thought I was the tallest man on the planet, but he was seven feet tall and overweight. Now I knew where my giant bed had come from!

"Go back," he said. "She may enter. You may not."

"I must get my books and things."

He raised a huge left arm. I followed it. All my belongings lay neatly stacked in the corner.

"I must go in. I must talk with M'Cwyie and the Mothers."

"You may not."

"The lives of your people depend on it."

"Go back," he boomed. "Go home to *your* people, Gallinger. Leave *us!*"

My name sounded so different on his lips, like someone else's. How old was he? I wondered. Three hundred? Four? Had he been a Temple guardian all his life? Why? Who was there to guard against? I didn't like the way he moved. I had seen men who moved like that before.

"Go back," he repeated.

If they had refined their martial arts as far as they had their dances, or, worse yet, if their fighting arts were a part of the dance, I was in for trouble.

"Go on in," I said to Braxa. "Give the rose to M'Cwyie. Tell her that I sent it. Tell her I'll be there shortly."

"I will do as you ask. Remember me on Earth, Gallinger. Good-bye."

I did not answer her, and she walked past Ontro and into the next room, bearing her rose.

"Now will you leave?" he asked. "If you like, I will tell her that we fought and you almost beat me, but I knocked you unconscious and carried you back to your ship."

"No," I said, "either I go around you or go over you, but I am going through."

He dropped into a crouch, arms extended.

"It is a sin to lay hands on a holy man," he rumbled, "but I will stop you, Gallinger."

My memory was a fogged window, suddenly exposed to fresh air. Things cleared. I looked back six years.

I was a student of Oriental Languages at the University of Tokyo. It was my twice-weekly night of recreation. I stood in a 30-foot circle in the Kodokan, the *judogi* lashed about my high hips by a brown belt. I was *Ikkyu*, one notch below the lowest degree of expert. A brown diamond above my right breast said "Jiu-Jitsu" in Japanese, and it meant *atemiwaza*, really, because of the one striking technique I had worked out, found unbelievably suitable to my size, and won matches with.

But I had never used it on a man, and it was five years since I had practiced. I was out of shape, I knew, but I tried hard to force my mind *tsuki no kokoro*, like the moon, reflecting the all of Ontro.

Somewhere, out of the past, a voice said, "*Hajime*, let it begin."

I snapped into my *neko-ashi-dachi* cat stance, and his eyes burned strangely. He hurried to correct his own position—and I threw it at him!

My one trick!

My long left leg lashed up like a broken spring. Seven feet off the ground my foot connected with his jaw as he tried to leap backward.

His head snapped back and he fell. A soft moan escaped his lips. *That's all there is to it,* I thought. *Sorry, old fellow.*

And as I stepped over him, somehow, groggily, he tripped me, and I fell across his body. I couldn't believe he had strength enough to remain conscious after that blow, let alone move. I hated to punish him any more.

But he found my throat and slipped a forearm across it before I realized there was a purpose to his action.

No! Don't let it end like this!

It was a bar of steel across my windpipe, my carotids. Then I realized that he was still unconscious, and that this was a reflex instilled by countless years of training. I had seen it happen once, in *shiai*. The man had died because he had been choked unconscious and still fought on, and his opponent thought he had not been applying the choke properly. He tried harder.

But it was rare, so very rare!

I jammed my elbows into his ribs and threw my head back in his face. The grip eased, but not enough. I hated to do it, but I reached up and broke his little finger.

The arm went loose and I twisted free.

He lay there panting, face contorted. My heart went out to the fallen giant, defending his people, his religion, following his orders. I cursed myself as I had never cursed before, for walking over him, instead of around.

I staggered across the room to my little heap of possessions. I sat on the projector case and lit a cigarette.

I couldn't go into the Temple until I got my breath back, until I thought of something to say.

How do you talk a race out of killing itself?

Suddenly—

—Could it happen? Would it work that way? If I read them the Book of Ecclesiastes—if I read them a greater piece of literature than any Locar ever wrote— and as somber—and as pessimistic—and showed them that our race had gone on despite one man's condemning all of life in the highest poetry—showed them that the vanity he had mocked had borne us to the Heavens —would they believe it?—would they change their minds?

I ground out my cigarette on the beautiful floor, and found my notebook. A strange fury rose within me as I stood.

And I walked into the Temple to preach the Black Gospel according to Gallinger, from the Book of Life.

There was silence all about me.

M'Cwyie had been reading Locar, the rose set at her right hand, target of all eyes.

Until I entered.

Hundreds of people were seated on the floor, barefoot. The few men were as small as the women, I noted.

I had my boots on.

Go all the way, I figured. *You either lose or you win—everything!*

A dozen crones sat in a semicircle behind M'Cwyie. The Mothers.

The barren earth, the dry wombs, the fire-touched. I moved to the table.

"Dying yourselves, you would condemn your people," I addressed them, "that they may not know the life you have known—the joys, the sorrows, the fullness.—But it is not true that you all must die." I addressed the multitude now. "Those who say this lie. Braxa knows, for she will bear a child—"

They sat there, like rows of Buddhas. M'Cwyie drew back into the semicircle.

"—my child!" I continued, wondering what my father would have thought of this sermon.

". . . And all the women young enough may bear children. It is only your men who are sterile.—And if you permit the doctors of the next expedition to examine you, perhaps even the men may be helped. But if they cannot, you can mate with the men of Earth.

"And ours is not an insignificant people, an insignificant place," I went on. "Thousands of years ago, the Locar of our world wrote a book saying that it was. He spoke as Locar did, but we did not lie down, despite plagues, wars, and famines. We did not die. One by one we beat down the diseases, we fed the hungry, we fought the wars, and, recently, have gone a long time without them. We may finally have conquered them. I do not know.

"But we have crossed millions of miles of nothingness. We have visited another world. And our Locar had said, 'Why bother? What is the worth of it? It is all vanity, anyhow.'

"And the secret is," I lowered my voice, as at a poetry reading, "he was right! It *is* vanity, it *is* pride! It is the *hubris* of rationalism to always attack the prophet, the mystic, the god. It is our blasphemy which has made us great, and will sustain us, and which the gods secretly admire in us.—All the truly sacred names of God are blasphemous things to speak!"

I was working up a sweat. I paused dizzily.

"Here is the Book of Ecclesiastes," I announced, and began:

" 'Vanity of vanities, saith the Preacher, vanity of vanities; all is vanity. What profit hath a man . . .' "

I spotted Braxa in the back, mute, rapt.

I wondered what she was thinking.

And I wound the hours of night about me, like black thread on a spool.

Oh, it was late! I had spoken till day came, and still I spoke. I finished Ecclesiastes and continued Gallinger.

And when I finished, there was still only a silence.

The Buddhas, all in a row, had not stirred through the night. And after a long while M'Cwyie raised her right hand. One by one the Mothers did the same.

And I knew what that meant.

It meant no, do not, cease, and stop.

It meant that I had failed.

I walked slowly from the room and slumped beside my baggage.

Ontro was gone. Good that I had not killed him . . .

After a thousand years M'Cwyie entered.

She said, "Your job is finished."

I did not move.

"The prophecy is fulfilled," she said. "My people are rejoicing. You have won, holy man. Now leave us quickly."

My mind was a deflated balloon. I pumped a little air back into it.

"I'm not a holy man," I said, "just a second-rate poet with a bad case of *hubris*."

I lit my last cigarette.

Finally, "All right, what prophecy?"

"The Promise of Locar," she replied, as though the explaining were unnecessary, "that a holy man would come from the heavens to save us in our last hours, if all the dances of Locar were completed. He would defeat the Fist of Malann and bring us life."

"How?"

"As with Braxa, and as the example in the Temple."

"Example?"

"You read us his words, as great as Locar's. You read to us how there is 'nothing new under the sun.' And you mocked his words as you read them—showing us a new thing.

"There has never been a flower on Mars," she said, "but we will learn to grow them.

"You are the Sacred Scoffer," she finished. "He-Who-Must-Mock-in-the-Temple—you go shod on holy ground."

"But you voted 'no'," I said.

"I voted not to carry out our original plan, and to let Braxa's child live instead."

"Oh." The cigarette fell from my fingers. How close it had been! How little I had known!

"And Braxa?"

"She was chosen half a Process ago to do the dances —to wait for you."

"But she said that Ontro would stop me."

M'Cwyie stood there for a long time.

"She had never believed the prophecy herself. Things are not well with her now. She ran away, fearing it was true. When you completed it and we voted, she knew."

"Then she does not love me? Never did?"

"I am sorry, Gallinger. It was the one part of her duty she never managed."

"Duty," I said flatly. . . . Dutydutyduty! Tra-la!

"She has said good-bye, she does not wish to see you again.

". . . and we will never forget your teachings," she added.

"Don't," I said, automatically, suddenly knowing the great paradox which lies at the heart of all miracles. I did not believe a word of my own gospel, never had.

I stood, like a drunken man, and muttered "M'narra."

I went outside, into my last day on Mars.

I have conquered thee, Malann—and the victory is thine! Rest easy on thy starry bed. God damned!

I left the jeepster there and walked back to the *Aspic,* leaving the burden of life so many footsteps behind me. I went to my cabin, locked the door, and took forty-four sleeping pills.

But when I awakened, I was in the dispensary, and alive.

I felt the throb of engines as I slowly stood up and somehow made it to the port.

Blurred Mars hung like a swollen belly above me, until it dissolved, brimmed over, and streamed down my face.

12

THE PURPOSE OF MAN

Evolution's End
ROBERT ARTHUR

What is man's purpose on Earth? This is one of the most fundamental questions he asks himself. For in the answer, he senses, lies the hope of leading a rich and satisfying life. If he can discover the purpose, he can work to fulfill it; he can know the harmony of becoming what he was intended to be. This hope is a bright possibility.

But there is another way to ask the question, with the possibility of a darker answer. What is the purpose of the universe? Is man a significant part of that purpose—if indeed there is one—or is man merely an artifact, a chance appearance without significance? Religion has never seriously considered any answers except that the universe does have a purpose and man is a central part of that purpose. The task of religion is to provide meaning for man, not destroy it.

"Evolution's End" explores the story of man's creation again and asks: Is man in his present form the final end of creation? If he has evolved in the past, is it not likely that he is continuing to change, and in the distant future will become something different from what he now is? What will that form be like? This is one of the favorite themes of science fiction writers when they create visions of the far-distant future. Biologists point out two trends that seem to be at work as life forms have evolved on Earth. There is a movement from simplicity to complexity. Older life forms are simpler in their cell structure and move on to larger aggregates of cells existing in complex relationships with each other. In addition, a striving for unity seems also to be fundamental. Pierre Teilhard de Chardin, a French Jesuit priest and geologist, explores the direction of evolution in *The Future of Man.*[1] He believes that a significant direction of change in modern man, compared to primitive man, is his growing *self-knowledge*. This, in turn, leads to an evolution of the moral value of our actions. As we acquire increased self-knowledge or -awareness, we recognize that we are one part of a whole. We are discovering the fundamental law of ecology—no one can take action that affects him alone, for the ripples of its effect will reach out to all around him. As we realize this, a sense of moral responsibility begins to develop.

"Evolution's End," besides exploring the evolutionary direction of man, raises another interesting question: How much knowledge is enough? Is there a limit to how much man should know? Beyond a certain point, will additional knowledge have a destructive rather than a creative effect on man's life? The English poet John Milton, one of the most intelligent thinkers of the seventeenth century, gave his answer clearly to the question in his long epic poem, "Paradise Lost." There were limits beyond which man should not go in his drive to acquire knowledge of the universe; man was only man and should retain his humility, not strive to become all-knowing as God is. Science reversed his decision, assuming that the greatest good for man was to pursue knowledge energetically, regardless of where it led him. Only in very recent years, with some of the recent advances in the field of biology, have scientists begun to question the wisdom of the relentless pursuit of truth. The unlocking of the genetic code suggests to man that with further research he may have the tools to alter radically the physical and mental structure of man. He can begin to play God in recreating himself. Should he? Will the product he creates be an improvement over that which has resulted naturally from endless eons of evolutionary creation?

[1] Pierre Teilhard de Chardin, *The Future of Man* (New York: Harper and Row, 1969).

Evolution's End
ROBERT ARTHUR

Aydem was pushing the humming vacuum duster along the endless stone corridors of the great underground Repository of Natural Knowledge when Ayveh, coming up quietly behind him, put her hands over his eyes.

He whirled, to see Ayveh's laughing face, mischief dancing on it.

"Ayveh!" he exclaimed eagerly. "But what are you doing here? It is forbidden any woman—"

"I know." Ayveh threw back her head, her long hair, richly golden, rippling down her shoulders to contrast with the pale apple-green of the shapeless linen robe she wore—a robe identical to Aydem's, the universal garb of the human slaves of the more-than-human Masters who ruled the world. It was an underground world. Generations since, the Masters, their great, thin-skulled heads and mighty brains proving uncomfortably vulnerable to the ordinary rays of the sun, had retreated underground.

"But Dmu Dran wishes to see you, Aydem," the girl Ayveh went on, "and he sent me to fetch you. There are visitors arriving and you must convey them from the tube station to his demonstration chambers. They are very important visitors."

"But why did he not transmit the order to me by directed thinking?" Aydem asked, puzzled. "He knows that even out here, in the Exhibit Section, I would receive it."

"Perhaps he sent me because he knew I wished to see you," Ayveh suggested happily. "And because he knew you hungered for the sight of me. There are times, Aydem, when Dmu Dran actually seems to understand what feelings are."

"A Master understand feelings?" Aydem's tone was scornful. "The Masters are nothing but brains. Great machines for thought, which know nothing of joy or sorrow or hunger for another."

"Shh!" Frightened, Ayveh put her fingers to his lips.

"You must not say such things. Generous as Dmu Dran is, he is still a Master, and if his mind should chance to be listening, he would have to punish you. It might even mean the fuel chambers."

Aydem kissed the fingers that had stopped his speech. Then, seeing the mingled fear and longing in her face, he drew her close and kissed her savagely, tasting the sweetness of her lips until a pulse was beating like a hammer in his throat.

Shaken, Ayveh freed herself and looked about, fearful that someone might have seen. There was no one. The corridors of the exhibit chambers of this tremendous museum of natural history of which their Master, Dmu Dran, was curator, wound endlessly away in darkness except for the tiny lighted area that enclosed them.

"There is no one to see," Aydem reassured her. "I alone tend the exhibit chambers, and only I am permitted to leave the Master's quarters without orders. And if any did see, who would tell?"

"Ekno," the girl whispered. "He would tell. He would like to see you sent into the fuel chambers, because he knows that we—that we—"

Her voice faltered and trailed off at the look of grimness in the man's face. Aydem stared down at her, at her loveliness, before he spoke. He himself stood nearly six feet tall, and his dark hair was a shaggy mane dropping almost to his shoulders. He was beardless, for all facial hair had been removed by an unguent when he was a youth—a whim of Dmu Dran's, though many Masters were less fastidious.

His body held the sturdiness of the trunk of an oak—which he had never seen. And though his duties were light in this mechanized, sub-surface world to which man's life on Mother Earth had retreated with the evolution of the Masters, muscles corded his body and were but lightly hidden by the green robe that swathed him.

And there was a tension in those muscles now, as if they would explode into action if only they had something to seize upon and rend and tear.

"Ayveh," he said, "I have seen the mating papers. I took them from the machine to the Master a period ago. Our request to be assigned as each other's mate has been denied. On the basis of the Selector Machine rating, I have been assigned to Teema, your assistant in overseeing the Master's household, and you to Ekno, who tends to minor repairs."

"That ugly hairy one?" Horror almost robbed Ayveh of her voice. "Who smells so bad and is always looking after me when I pass? No! I—I would rather kill myself first."

"I"—there was savagery in Aydem's words—"would rather kill the Masters!"

"Oh no!" the girl whispered in terror. "You must not speak it. If you harmed Dmu Dran—if it became known even that you wished to—we should all be destroyed. Not in the fuel chambers. We should go to the example cells. And we would not die—for a long time."

"Better that," Aydem said stonily, "than to be slaves, to be mated to those we despise, to keep forever our silence and obey orders, to live and die like beasts!"

Then, at Ayveh's sudden gasp of terror, Aydem whirled.

His own features paled as he drew himself to attention. For Dmu Dran, their Master, had come silently up behind them as they spoke, the air-suspended chair which carried him making no sound.

And Dmu Dran, his great round face blank, his large popping eyes unreadable, stared at Aydem with an unusual intensity. Yet no thoughts were coming from the mind within the huge, globular, thin-walled skull over which only a little wispy hair, like dried hay, was plastered.

Had Dmu Dran heard? Had he caught the emanations of violent emotion which must have been spreading all over the vicinity from Aydem? Was he now probing into their minds for the words they had just spoken? If he knew or guessed them, their fate would be a terrible one.

But when Dmu Dran spoke—for mental communication with the undeveloped slave mind was fatiguing for a Master—his voice was mild.

"I fear," he said, in a thin piping tone, "that my servants are not happy. Perhaps they are upset by the mating orders that have arrived?"

Aydem of course was supposed to know nothing of the contents of the orders, having in theory no ability to read. But since Dmu Dran evidently knew he *could* read—he had been taught in his boyhood by a wise old slave long dead—boldness seemed the only course.

"Master," he said, "the girl Ayveh and I hoped to be mates. It is true we are not happy, because we have been assigned to others."

"Happiness." Dmu Dran spoke the word reflectively. "Unhappiness. Mmm. Those are things not given us to feel. You are aware emotion is not a desirable characteristic in a slave?"

"Aye, Master," Aydem agreed submissively.

"The selector machine," Dmu Dran went on, "shows both you and the girl Ayveh to be capable of much emotion. It also indicates in both of you a brain capacity large for a slave. It is for these reasons you have been denied each other. It is desired that slaves should be strong and healthy, intelligent, but not too intelligent, and lacking in emotion so they will not become discontented. You understand these things, do you not?"

"Aye, Master," Aydem agreed in some astonishment. Ayveh pressed close to him, frightened by the strange conduct of Dmu Dran—for no Master ever spoke so familiarly with a slave.

Dmu Dran was silent, as if thinking. While he waited, Aydem reflected that Dmu Dran was not exactly as other Masters were. To an untrained eye, all Masters looked much alike—a great, globular head set upon a small neckless body, the neck having disappeared in the course of evolution of the great head, so that the weight might be better rested on the stronger back and shoulder muscles.

But Dmu Dran was perceptibly taller than other Masters Aydem had seen. Aydem had not seen many —there were only some thousand of them, and they lived in small groups in far-flung underground Centers, if not entirely alone, as did Dmu Dran. Dmu Dran's cranium was also slightly smaller in diameter.

Now an odd expression touched the flat countenance of the Master.

"Aydem," he said, "you have seen the contents of these halls many times. But Ayveh has not. So come with me now, both of you. We have a little time, and I wish to view some specimens. It is many years since I last examined them."

He turned his chair, and Aydem, exchanging a look of puzzlement with Ayveh, followed him down the corridor between the great, glass-enclosed, hermetically sealed exhibits.

As they went, light sprang on alongside them, activated by the heat of their bodies on thermo-couples, and died away behind them. The Master led them several hundred yards, and halted at last in a section devoted to ancient animals of the Earth's youth.

There were here many beasts, huge and ferocious in appearance, reproduced in their natural environment, seen, save by Aydem, not more than half a dozen times a year. Only six or eight Masters were born each year, just enough to keep the total of a thousand from dwindling. They visited the Repository of Natural Knowledge in the course of their educational studies.

In the glass cases that lined the miles of corridors were exhibits, many of them animated so cunningly that the artificial replicas of man and animal of the past seemed endowed with life, encompassing all the natural history of the world from the mists of the unknown, millions of years before, to the present day. But since the great brains of the Masters needed to be apprised of a fact but once to make it theirs forever, there was never really occasion for a Master to come here twice.

Now Dmu Dran, Aydem and Ayveh stood before a great, orange-colored beast with black stripes, a snarl frozen upon his features, huge fangs, many inches in length, protruding from his jaws. Even though he was but a model of a beast dead many millennia, Ayveh instinctively drew closer to Aydem, as if the creature were indeed about to leap, and as if they were part of that group of men and women, much like themselves, that faced it in desperation with long, pointed sticks in their hands.

"The saber-tooth tiger," Dmu Dran said. "When it reigned on this Earth uncounted years ago, it was master of Aiden, the world above, a scourge feared and hated by all other animals. For many thousands of years it grew more and more powerful, its dominance contested by few. By its great teeth it was known— terrible weapons for rending and tearing its prey. But in the end it ceased to be. Why did a beast like that, which no natural enemy could oppose, die, think you?"

"It must indeed have been a fearful opponent that conquered it, Master," Ayveh ventured uncertainly.

What might have been a smile, had a Master known smiling, rippled over the pale moon-face.

"Nature killed it," Dmu Dran informed them. "Nature destroyed it by her very generosity. Those tusks you see that gave it its name—Nature continued to add to their length and strength. But, alas! In her enthusiasm, she made them so long in the course of time that their possessor could not close its mouth, could not eat, and so eventually starved to death. Aye, Nature evolved her great and dread child right out of existence."

"That was indeed strange." Aydem frowned. "I do not understand. Why did she do so?"

"Nature has curious ways." Dmu Dran shrugged. "And having an infinity of time, she can afford an infinity of experiments. What she is not satisfied with, though she has made it supreme, she destroys."

Dmu Dran shot his chair a few yards to the left.

"And here," he said, "is another great beast that was once master of the world when it was young."

The creature he now indicated stood far above a man's head, even a slave's. Three times, four times, five times higher than a slave did it tower.

"The great dinosaur of the Earth's infancy," Dmu Dran told them. "The hugest beast ever to shake the world with its tread. That one"—he pointed—"the largest land animal ever evolved. The enemies that could conquer it were few or none. Unmolested by the lesser denizens of the day and the night, it ruled the Earth by its very bulk. Yet it too passed. Why, think you?"

Aydem and Ayveh were silent, so Dmu Dran explained.

"Again Nature was overgenerous. To this creature whose bulk made it sovereign, it added still more bulk. Alack! In time she so increased the size of the beast that it could not get enough to eat, though it fed twenty-four hours of the day. It simply could not ingest fuel enough for its huge body. So in the end it too passed."

The man and the girl were still silent, their eyes wide with wonder. Dmu Dran abruptly shot his air car a hundred yards down the corridor and stopped again, the lights coming on automatically the moment he paused.

He was now before the section devoted to the evolution of man himself, beginning with a creature half man, half beast, and rising to a reproduction of the Masters who now ruled the world.

Uneducated though they were, Aydem and Ayveh

saw and understood the procession of figures, each more erect, each less hairy, each larger-headed than the one before it.

Near the end of the line was an upright figure which caused Ayveh to gasp, it was so like Aydem.

"Man of the Early Machine Age"

Dmu Dran read the inscription on the imperishable metal plate at the foot of the figure. "Aye, your Aydem does look like him. For it was man of that period, balanced between ignorance and knowledge, that we Masters thought it best our slaves should resemble. But here is the exhibit that I have most pondered upon."

He moved a few feet, and they stood before the last half dozen figures.

"There"—and Dmu Dran, with one short arm, indicated a figure as tall as Aydem, but differing from the one just before it in that its head was half again as large—"there is the first of the Masters. A mutant, with a brain-weight double anything ever known in man before. John Master, his name was, and it was appropriate. For in the last ten thousand years, all humankind save slaves have been his descendants—not men now, but Masters. I have often speculated upon the chance that saw him born, and wondered if, had he never been conceived and brought to issue, the human species might not have turned in quite another direction."

Dmu Dran was silent, thinking, and the two slaves did not intrude upon his thoughts. Instead they studied the figures following this John Master of the large head. Each was larger-headed than the one before it, each smaller-bodied, shorter-necked, until the last figure might have been Dmu Dran himself.

"It is an interesting point on which to wonder," Dmu Dran said after a time. "How would mankind have evolved had not my ancestor been born? The old records show that he was a cold and ruthless man, without sentiment. That by the power of his logical mind, and with the aid of his children, he seized the rule of the world and made his descendants supreme forever. Forever? Well—supreme ever since. So that now, we Masters, the highest species of animal ever to evolve, are despotic rulers of the world, and if we wished, of the Solar System—even of the Universe.

"But we do not wish. The Solar System, save for this world, is lifeless, and it has never been worth our while to consider whether the stars beyond were worth reaching. We feel nothing, we enjoy nothing, for the capacity for those things has been bred out of us—evolved away in the course of yesterday's eons. We merely think, with our almost perfect brains, here in the bowels of the Earth, served by our slaves in a world almost effortless even for them.

"We are, so far as we know—and there is little we do not know—the Masters, nature's final product, evolution's end!"

Abruptly Dmu Dran's piping voice ceased, leaving tiny echoes rustling in the corridors. Aydem and Ayveh were alarmed and uneasy. Could Dmu Dran by chance be mad? Madness did sometimes afflict a Master, though rarely one of Dmu Dran's age. Usually they were much younger or much older, when the unexplainable insanity that was the only ailment the Masters had not conquered, took them.

"I sometimes think," Dmu Dran said after a moment, in a quieter tone now, "that though we consider ourselves the last step in evolution's chain, we may be wrong. Who knows what plans Nature has for us? None of us. But we shall. I am going to put it to the test, the momentous test that may decide the whole future of the world, aye, of the Universe itself. For know, my servants, that my visitors today are the Masters of the Supreme Council, come at my invitation to examine a machine that I have made my life's work.

"It is a matter of electricity and rays that will stimulate the latent change that lies in all plants and animals. So that in one generation, an animal may progress from the form it was born with to the form its descendants a thousand generations away would have. Aye—in less than a generation, in a few periods!

"And I am going to propose to the Supreme Council that a chosen few of us Masters subject ourselves to the influence of this machine, that we may know what we are to become, in Nature's hidden scheme, in the persons of our grandchildren many times removed. I shall propose to them we raise ourselves now to the glories of the final form destined to the Masters, and I think they will agree.

"For we Masters, the favored children of Nature, will hardly be loath to rise to the final position scarcely lower than gods that our philosophers have foreseen as ultimately ours!"

Excitement shone in Dmu Dran's popping eyes. But in a moment it died. He gestured.

"Return to your quarters, my servants. I shall meet my visitors myself, Aydem. Say nothing to anyone, and worry not for the moment concerning the mating assignments. Nothing will be done about such matters until I—know."

With that cryptic remark, he shot away down the corridor in his air-chair as Aydem and Ayveh stared at each other in perplexity and mounting hope.

In the periods of waiting that followed, there was tension in the slaves' quarters. All knew of the unprecedented visit of the Supreme Council, and somehow word got about that the mating assignments had come, but had not yet been announced by Dmu Dran.

Curiosity regarding these matters, however, was not as strong as it might have been had not slaves been for so many generations bred for docility and lack of emotion. Aydem and Ayveh's fellow servants exhibited only mild curiosity about any occurrence, and when not working, for the most part contented themselves with eating, sleeping, and playing simple games.

Only Ekno, the hairy one who coveted Ayveh, had a brain that busied itself with affairs outside its immediate concern. And Ekno, hatred in his face as he watched Aydem covertly, knew that something of great import was transpiring. He could scarcely contain himself to know what, and even took the great risk, unthinkable to the others, of snooping about Dmu Dran's private quarters under the pretense of making repairs, hoping to pick up some scrap of information.

In time, after many secret sessions in Dmu Dran's demonstration chambers, the Supreme Council left, each Master boarding his private air-car and being shot away through the great maze of tunnels that honeycombed the earth to his home center. With the President of the Council, the oldest living Master, went a large, heavy package which Aydem transported to his car with great care, little dreaming that the destiny of

himself and Ayveh and countless millions of their un-
born descendants lay within those careful wrappings.

After this, for some periods more, nothing happened. The other slaves almost forgot anything unusual
had occurred. Only Ekno still watched Aydem's every
move, eager for some evidence of wrong-doing he
could present to Dmu Dran, or even to the Board of
Slave Mating, supreme authority in regard to all slaves.

But with Dmu Dran's strange words ringing in his
mind, Aydem made no move Ekno could seize upon.
Save when outside the living quarters, to which Ekno
by the nature of his duties was usually confined,
Aydem and Ayveh did not even exchange words.

But Aydem's chief duty was to keep the interminable corridors of the exhibit section free from the
natural rock dust that gathered, and only he was permitted to enter it. Ekno dared not follow him there, so
it was there he and Ayveh met.

It was a great risk Ayveh took, for no woman was
permitted to leave the living quarters at all. But Dmu
Dran's words had given them courage. And it was possible for her, since she was chief of the women, to slip
away from her duties for stolen moments from time to
time.

On these occasions they exchanged few words. Their
hearts spoke for them, and their tongues could be silent. Aydem eagerly showed the girl through the multitudinous exhibits that traced man's life on the planet.

Long years these had fascinated him. Countless periods he had spent studying them, and scanning the
engraved metal placards that explained each detail of
what he saw.

Though Ayveh could not read, he could interpret for her. And many of the exhibits spoke for themselves. Almost all were animated. A touch of a button set them in motion, and countless replicas of countless types of men who had walked the world and vanished, went through the acts of life again.

In engrossed silence, Aydem and Ayveh watched hairy men of the Earth's infancy defend themselves with fire and spear and arrow against the attacks of wild animals. They saw other men, higher in the scale of evolution, build simple dwellings, strike fire from flints or produce it from spun sticks, hunt, plant seed, weave cloth, cook, and do all the multitudinous acts that were necessary to existence.

Most of all, Aydem was fascinated not by the exhibits showing the machine world just before the coming of the Masters, but by the reproductions of man in his younger days. Haltingly he tried to explain to Ayveh that he felt within himself a kinship to those long dead men who had made bows and arrows, planted and reaped their crops with their hands, had tamed wild horses and on their backs ridden down the wild boar and the wolf, had, with spear and arrow, defended themselves against their enemies.

He stretched his arms, and his mighty muscles coiled and knotted.

"Sometimes in my sleep," he told Ayveh, his eyes burning, "I am no longer within these underground dominions of the Masters, but am free upon Aiden, the Earth's surface. I know what it must be like, for I can see it all in my dreams. I can feel the warm touch of what they call the sun, and underfoot the roughness of the growing things called grass. Animals, not artificial like these, but alive, roam the land, and in my dreams I combat them."

"It must be a wonderful place," Ayveh whispered wistfully. "So strange and different from this."

"Sometimes I feel as if I were going to burst, forever locked away within these walls of rock where the Masters choose to live!" Aydem burst out. "I wish to work, to fight, to conquer—"

Somewhere nearby there was a scraping noise. Ayveh gasped with terror, and Aydem whirled instantly. The sound of running footsteps sprang up several corridors away. Aydem dashed in that direction, caught a glimpse of a man running toward the living quarters.

He put on a burst of speed, but the other outdistanced him and ducked through a door before Aydem could get close enough to identify the spying one.

"But it was Ekno," he said, his voice grim, as he hurried back to take the frightened Ayveh to her quarters. "It was Ekno, and he was spying on us. He overheard. He will report to Dmu Dran."

"But the Master," Ayveh faltered, "he did not mind before—"

Aydem took her hand.

"There is no telling what a Master will do," he growled. "He may have been amusing himself. We must be prepared. Do not sleep this period. Wait for me behind this door that leads from the quarters to the exhibits. Come if I call. Have food with you."

"But Aydem!" Ayveh exclaimed, wide-eyed. "You would not question the decree of a Master?"

"If Dmu Dran condemns me to the fuel chamber," Aydem answered, "I will kill him and we will try to escape. See!"

From beneath his tunic he withdrew a knife with a long gleaming blade and a heavy handle.

"I have had this long," he boasted. "It is part of an exhibit that became out of order. I fixed it under Dmu Dran's direction. And stole this unnoticed. I will kill Dmu Dran with it if I must. There are many tunnels that may have been abandoned leading out from this center. I have heard it whispered, by old Temu who taught me when I was young, that one leads to the world above. We will seek it. We will seek escape. If we must, we will die. But I will not go to the fuel chambers."

He looked at her white face.

"But I can go alone—" he began.

Ayveh flung herself into his arms.

"No, Aydem, no!" she whispered. "Where you go, I will go. If you live, I will live. If you die, I will die."

He kissed her then strongly, passionately. And as he kissed her, the command came. By directed thinking. To report at once to Dmu Dran.

With unfaltering stride Aydem entered Dmu Dran's personal quarters. As he went in, he passed Ekno, and there was a smirk of triumph on the hairy one's features. Aydem did not deign to glance at the other. He closed the door behind him, and was in the presence of Dmu Dran.

The flat, pop-eyed face of the Master was as blank as ever.

"Aydem, my servant," he piped, "a charge has been placed against you. A serious charge. You merit punishment. If I do not punish you, the charge may come to the attention of the Board of Slave Mating. It will wish to know why. It will send for you, and when you are placed beneath the instruments, it will know I have been guilty of a crime too. It will know that you are far above the allowed intelligence quotient for a slave, and that I have falsified your records since childhood, as I have falsified those of the servant Ayveh."

Aydem stared at him in speechless astonishment.

"You are startled, Servant Aydem," the Master said. "But it is true I, a Master, have violated one of the most rigid rules of the few that Masters must observe. I have deliberately preserved from destruction in the fuel chambers a man and a woman of as high a physical and mental level as the world has known since the days of the first Master.

"I have done this for reasons of my own. I think we shall soon know whether I have been right to—"

He did not finish, for behind him a section of the wall grew luminous, and a figure began to appear, seemingly within it.

Dmu Dran made a gesture. Aydem withdrew quickly to one side, beyond the seeing range of the communicator panel, and the Master turned. A voice, piping but stern, spoke from the wall:

"Dmu Dran! Nalu Tah, president of the Supreme Council, speaks."

"Dmu Dran listens."

"Dmu Dran! Of the ten subjects upon whom the Supreme Council has been testing the apparatus devised by you for the precipitating of evolutionary change, the last has just gone mad. The brain capacity of all increased by fifty per cent, and the skulls enlarged during their subjection to the rays of your apparatus. Each, however, after reaching an increase of approximately fifty per cent in brain size, was afflicted by the dread madness. All have been destroyed. Dmu Dran, you are ordered to report at once to Judicial Center to make explanation, and be judged."

"Dmu Dran hears."

The glow in the wall died. The great-headed figure of the president of the Supreme Council vanished. Dmu Dran let out a little sigh.

"Mad," he whispered. "All went mad. As some are going mad already, and as in a hundred thousand years all will, the entire race of Masters. So that they will be no more. In a hundred thousand years, the supreme creation of Nature, the mightiest thinking machine she has ever produced, will be destroyed. By the irresistible forces of Nature herself, adding always to the gift she has given, until the weight of it crushes us out of existence. Yes, crushes us literally out of existence."

He turned, faced the wondering Aydem.

"Aydem, my servant," he said, "I have been right. I have feared a certain thing, and I have learned that my fears are well founded. I have concentrated the evolutionary development of a hundred thousand years in certain selected Masters, and all have gone mad. The reason I can easily guess. Their brains grew in size, until the very weight of the brain crushed many of its own cells. The very multiplicity of the cells piled layer upon top of layer destroyed the more delicate. The process can already be seen at work occasionally now. In time it will encompass all.

"The bulk of the dinosaur, which made it supreme, killed it. The teeth of the saber-tooth tiger destroyed it.

And the brain of the Masters, which had made them supreme, is foredestined to destroy them just as utterly.

"Aydem, you are a man as men were before the sudden branching that produced the Masters. A branching that I now know was but another experiment on Nature's part, leading nowhere. Hark you—the ultimate evolution of man is yet to come. Yes, yet to come.

"Yet, if the Masters live out their existence, Nature may well be foiled, or at the least, set back a thousand million years in her plans. For in a hundred thousand years, when the Masters are gone, man may well be gone too.

"Yet, if the Masters were to vanish now, while you and Ayveh lived, from *your* loins might spring the line that will yet reach upward to the stars."

Dmu Dran's voice piped off into silence. But he was not finished speaking, for after a moment he shook himself and continued.

"What man will be like in the end I do not know. He will not be a great-headed thinking machine, I am sure. He will have a mind, yes, but soul too, and body, all balanced into a whole that will far surpass us, the Masters.

"What I am going to do is hard. Yet perhaps I am but a tool of Nature's too. Perhaps she designed me for this very purpose—to put evolution back upon its proper track.

"Aydem, you may never understand. That does not matter. These are my last orders. Take Ayveh. Go to the very end of the exhibit section. There, in a section where the rooms have been crushed by falling rock, you will find one stone perfectly round and seemingly too great for a thousand men to move. Upon one side is a red spot. Push at this spot. The rock will roll aside and you will see an entrance. Descend. A passageway will lead you upward, and in time you will come out upon Aiden, the surface of the Earth above—a region into which we Masters have not chosen to venture save but fleetingly for a thousand years.

"You will have the half of one period in which to do this. Then I will press a button here beside me. The details you would not understand. But when I do, every inch of these vast tunnels that we Masters have created throughout the Earth's interior will collapse. Every Master will die at the same instant. And every slave—for there are none living save yourselves whose blood may go into the lifestream of the Man to come. It would take centuries for them to evolve again as a group to your level. So you two, Aydem and Ayveh, will be, to all historical appearance, the first man and woman. The gap between you and your ancestors will be broken when I press this button.

"You will not understand my reasons, I say. But you will survive above, for you have long studied the great exhibit chambers and know what you must do to wrest a living from Nature. In time you will forget that such things as Masters ever existed. And your kind will mount upward toward the stars, on a true course which has been sidetracked for only a little while."

Dmu Dran fell silent, as if musing, and his pale round face seemed sad. Aydem, in truth, understood but little. Yet he understood Dmu Dran's instructions, and his heart leaped within his breast.

Dmu Dran looked up.

"Go now," he ordered.

Aydem forced his way through the tangle of weeds and roots that choked the entrance of the cave, in which the long tunnel he and Ayveh had traversed for an interminable time ended. He stood upright, and drew Ayveh after him.

They had emerged upon the surface of the Earth at night. The moon, a thing of wondrous beauty to them, rode the heavens low in the east, a great orange ball. A summer night's wind breathed through the great masses of tangled vegetation that surrounded them, and the scent of flowers was carried by it.

The man and the woman breathed deep, speechless with wonder and joy. Somewhere near, a nightbird was trilling, and from farther away came the cry of an unknown animal. Both sounds alike were music to their ears.

"Free!" Aydem whispered exultingly. "Ayveh, we are free! We are slaves no more!"

Bathed by the moonlight, caressed by the night breeze, they stood close together, his arm about her, and feasted their eyes and ears on the world.

"The knife I stole," Aydem said, "I will keep. With it we will make what we need, kill what we need. Ayveh, Ayveh—"

His words broke off. Of a sudden the very earth beneath them had begun to tremble. It seemed to shudder. One long-drawn puff of air, like a hollow death-gasp, seemed forced from the cavern before which they stood, and the ground under them shook. Ayveh was thrown into Aydem's arms, and he held her close until the violent tremor had passed.

"Dmu Dran has pressed the button," he said, understanding. "The Masters are no more. Ayveh, my mate, the Masters are no more! We are free, and there is no one to come after us. We will know struggle and conflict and labor, but we are free!"

He held her close and kissed her. Then at last, hand in hand, they set out together into the world Dmu Dran had given them. Aydem—the first man. And Ayveh—the first woman.

13

ALIEN INTELLIGENCE
IN THE UNIVERSE

The Fire Balloons
RAY BRADBURY

"The Fire Balloons" is a
story that allows us to talk about what religion may
become in the future. It takes into consideration the
effects science and technology have had in reshaping
man's view of himself and his place in the universe. The
amount of new information that science has provided
for man in the last one hundred years is staggering. To
synthesize that information into a new and workable
world view for mankind is such an overwhelming task
that it has not yet successfully been completed. But the
fermenting of ideas in the religious field today—although it oftentimes appears chaotic—suggests that the
process is under way. However, because the old must
give way to make room for the new, the creative process
in its early stages may often seem more like destruction.
A delightful little story like "The Fire Balloons" gives

us a vehicle for talking about some of the new directions this creative process may take as it begins to shape itself.

What are some of these effects of science and technology requiring man to alter his world view? First, improved travel and communications are so widespread that the comparative study of cultures is inevitable. From these comparisons we learn that different cultures have different concepts of what is right and what is wrong. But although what is sinful in one culture is acceptable in another, each culture survives. This has forced organized religion to move away from its absolutist concept of sin to a more relative position. In "The Fire Balloons" Father Peregrine and Father Stone can talk about sin on Earth, but when they journey in missionary zeal to Mars to save the natives, they find their definitions of sin are meaningless in that culture. As in "The Streets of Ashkelon," the priests have little sensitivity for appreciating the values of cultural patterns different from their own. The priests in both stories are true believers who set out with single-minded zeal to convert the natives whether they need it or not.

The second effect of technology that asks man to alter his image of himself is the view of the planet Earth from the moon. Man has always been earthbound, looking up and out into the heavens. Now the moonshots have carried cameras to the moon, and man has seen himself from space. It is an incredible view! He realizes that far from dreaming about going to Heaven as he has in the past, right now at this moment he is on a heavenly body, traveling through the universe. He recognizes that races and nations on Earth are truly not alien to each other, but all fellow travelers on the spaceship Earth. He needs a universal concept of God that recognizes the powerful unity of humans of all races. As Father Peregrine keeps explaining in "The Fire Balloons," form does not matter. Content is everything. We must learn to get past the outer appearance to the universal spirit inside.

This story raises an interesting question that so far has been explored only in science fiction. How would the discovery of intelligent life elsewhere in the universe alter man's concept of himself and his God? Religion conventionally has presumed that man is the only intelligent life in the universe. Science now begins to seriously consider the possibility of life beyond our planet, and a term, *exobiology*, has already been coined for his study. Radio telescopes have been established to monitor radio waves from outer space. These telescopes may detect radio signals suggesting intelligence elsewhere in the universe. If indeed alien intelligence is discovered, religion will need to incorporate this new awareness.

The Fire Balloons
RAY BRADBURY

Fire exploded over summer night lawns. You saw sparkling faces of uncles and aunts. Skyrockets fell up in the brown shining eyes of cousins on the porch, and the cold charred sticks thumped down in dry meadows far away.

The Very Reverend Father Joseph Daniel Peregrine
opened his eyes. What a dream: he and his cousins
with their fiery play at his grandfather's ancient Ohio
home so many years ago!

He lay listening to the great hollow of the church,
the other cells where other Fathers lay. Had they, too,
on the eve of the flight of the rocket *Crucifix,* lain with
memories of the Fourth of July? Yes. This was like
those breathless Independence dawns when you waited
for the first concussion and rushed out on the dewy
sidewalks, your hands full of loud miracles.

So here they were, the Episcopal Fathers, in the
breathing dawn before they pinwheeled off to Mars,
leaving their incense through the velvet cathedral of
space.

"Should we go at all?" whispered Father Peregrine.
"Shouldn't we solve our own sins on Earth? Aren't we
running from our lives here?"

He arose, his fleshy body, with its rich look of straw-
berries, milk, and steak, moving heavily.

"Or is it sloth?" he wondered. "Do I dread the journey?"

He stepped into the needle-spray shower.

"But I shall take you to Mars, body." He addressed
himself. "Leaving old sins here. And on to Mars to find
new sins?" A delightful thought, almost. Sins no one
had ever thought of. Oh, he himself had written a little
book: *The Problem of Sin on Other Worlds,* ignored as
somehow not serious enough by his Episcopal brethren.

Only last night, over a final cigar, he and Father
Stone had talked of it.

"On Mars sin might appear as virtue. We must

guard against virtuous acts there that, later, might be found to be sins!" said Father Peregrine, beaming. "How exciting! It's been centuries since so much adventure has accompanied the prospect of being a missionary!"

"*I* will recognize sin," said Father Stone bluntly, "*even* on Mars."

"Oh, we priests pride ourselves on being litmus paper, changing color in sin's presence," retorted Father Peregrine, "but what if Martian chemistry is such we do not color *at all!* If there are new senses on Mars, you must admit the possibility of unrecognizable sin."

"If there is no malice aforethought, there is no sin or punishment for same—the Lord assures us that," Father Stone replied.

"On Earth, yes. But perhaps a Martian sin might inform the subconscious of its evil, telepathically, leaving the conscious mind of man free to act, seemingly without malice! What *then?*"

"What *could* there be in the way of new sins?"

Father Peregrine leaned heavily forward. "Adam *alone* did not sin. Add Eve and you add temptation. Add a second man and you make adultery possible. With the addition of sex or people, you add sin. If men were armless they could not strangle with their hands. You would not have that particular sin of murder. Add arms, and you add the possibility of a new violence. Amoebas cannot sin because they reproduce by fission. They do not covet wives or murder each other. Add sex to amoebas, add arms and legs, and you would have murder and adultery. Add an arm or leg or person, or take away each, and you add or subtract possible evil. On Mars, what if there are five new senses, organs, invisible limbs we can't conceive of—then mightn't there be five *new sins?*"

Father Stone gasped. "I think you *enjoy* this sort of thing!"

"I keep my mind alive, Father; just alive, is all."

"Your mind's always juggling, isn't it?—mirrors, torches, plates."

"Yes. Because sometimes the Church seems like those posed circus tableaus where the curtain lifts and men, white, zinc-oxide, talcum-powder statues, freeze to represent abstract Beauty. Very wonderful. But I hope there will always be room for me to dart about among the statues, don't you, Father Stone?"

Father Stone had moved away. "I think we'd better go to bed. In a few hours we'll be jumping up to see your *new* sins, Father Peregrine."

The rocket stood ready for the firing.

The Fathers walked from their devotions in the chilly morning, many a fine priest from New York or Chicago or Los Angeles—the Church was sending its best—walking across town to the frosty field. Walking, Father Peregrine remembered the Bishop's words:

"Father Peregrine, you will captain the missionaries, with Father Stone at your side. Having chosen you for this serious task, I find my reasons deplorably obscure, Father, but your pamphlet on planetary sin did not go unread. You are a flexible man. And Mars is like that uncleaned closet we have neglected for millenniums. Sin has collected there like bric-a-brac. Mars is twice Earth's age and has had double the number of Saturday nights, liquor baths, and eye-poppings at women as naked as white seals. When we open that closet door, things will fall on us. We need a quick, flexible man— one whose mind can dodge. Anyone a little too dog-matic might break in two. I feel you'll be resilient. Father, the job is yours."

The Bishop and the Fathers knelt.

The blessing was said and the rocket given a little shower of holy water. Arising, the Bishop addressed them:

"I know you will go with God, to prepare the Mar-tians for the reception of His Truth. I wish you all a *thoughtful* journey."

They filed past the Bishop, twenty men, robes whis-pering, to deliver their hands into his kind hands before passing into the cleansed projectile.

"I wonder," said Father Peregrine, at the last mo-ment, "if Mars is hell? Only waiting for our arrival before it bursts into brimstone and fire."

"Lord, be with us," said Father Stone.

The rocket moved.

Coming out of space was like coming out of the most beautiful cathedral they had ever seen. Touching Mars was like touching the ordinary pavement outside the church five minutes after having *really* known your love for God.

The Fathers stepped gingerly from the steaming rocket and knelt upon Martian sand while Father Peregrine gave thanks.

"Lord, we thank Thee for the journey through Thy rooms. And, Lord, we have reached a new land, so we must have new eyes. We shall hear new sounds and must needs have new ears. And there will be new sins, for which we ask the gift of better and firmer and purer hearts. Amen."

They arose.

And here was Mars like a sea under which they trudged in the guise of submarine biologists, seeking life. Here the territory of hidden sin. Oh, now carefully they must all balance, like gray feathers, in this new element, afraid that walking *itself* might be sinful; or breathing, or simple fasting!

And here was the mayor of First Town come to meet them with outstretched hand. "What can I do for you, Father Peregrine?"

"We'd like to know about the Martians. For only if we know about them can we plan our church intelligently. Are they ten feet tall? We will build large doors. Are their skins blue or red or green? We must know when we put human figures in the stained glass so we may use the right skin color. Are they heavy? We will build sturdy seats for them."

"Father," said the mayor, "I don't think you should worry about the Martians. There are two races. One of them is pretty well dead. A few are in hiding. And the second race—well, they're not quite human."

"Oh?" Father Peregrine's heart quickened.

"They're round luminous globes of light, Father, living in those hills. Man or beast, who can say? But they act intelligently, I hear." The mayor shrugged. "Of course, they're not men, so I don't think you'll care——"

"On the contrary," said Father Peregrine swiftly. "Intelligent, you say?"

"There's a story. A prospector broke his leg in those

hills and would have died there. The blue spheres of light came at him. When he woke, he was down on a highway and didn't know how he got there."

"Drunk," said Father Stone.

"That's the story," said the mayor. "Father Peregrine, with most of the Martians dead, and only these blue spheres, I frankly think you'd be better off in First City. Mars is opening up. It's a frontier now, like in the old days on Earth, out West, and in Alaska. Men are pouring up here. There's a couple thousand black Irish mechanics and miners and day laborers in First Town who need saving, because there're too many wicked women came with them, and too much ten-century-old Martian win——"

Father Peregrine was gazing into the soft blue hills.

Father Stone cleared his throat. "Well, Father?"

Father Peregrine did not hear. "Spheres of blue *fire?*"

"Yes, Father."

"Ah," Father Peregrine sighed.

"Blue balloons." Father Stone shook his head. "A circus!"

Father Peregrine felt his wrists pounding. He saw the little frontier town with raw, fresh-built sin, and he saw the hills, old with the oldest and yet perhaps an even newer (to him) sin.

"Mayor, could your black Irish laborers cook one more day in hellfire?"

"I'd turn and baste them for you, Father."

Father Peregrine nodded to the hills. "Then that's where we'll go."

There was a murmur from everyone.

"It would be so simple," explained Father Peregrine, "to go into town. I prefer to think that if the Lord walked here and people said, 'Here is the beaten path,' He would reply, 'Show me the weeds. I will *make* a path.' "

"But——"

"Father Stone, think how it would weigh upon us if we passed sinners by and did not extend our hands."

"But globes of fire!"

"I imagine man looked funny to other animals when we first appeared. Yet he has a soul, for all his homeliness. Until we prove otherwise, let us assume that these fiery spheres have souls."

"All right," agreed the mayor, "but you'll be back to town."

"We'll see. First, some breakfast. Then you and I, Father Stone, will walk alone into the hills. I don't want to frighten those fiery Martians with machines or crowds. Shall we have breakfast?"

The Fathers ate in silence.

At nightfall Father Peregrine and Father Stone were high in the hills. They stopped and sat upon a rock to enjoy a moment of relaxation and waiting. The Martians had not as yet appeared and they both felt vaguely disappointed.

"I wonder——" Father Peregrine mopped his face. "Do you think if we called 'Hello!' they might answer?"

"Father Peregrine, won't you ever be serious?"

"Not until the good Lord is. Oh, don't look so terribly shocked, please. The Lord is not serious. In fact, it is a little hard to know just what else He is except loving. And love has to do with humor, doesn't it? For you cannot love someone unless you put up with him, can you? And you cannot put up with someone constantly unless you can laugh at him. Isn't that true? And certainly we are ridiculous little animals wallowing in the fudge bowl, and God must love us all the more because we appeal to His humor."

"*I* never thought of God as humorous," said Father Stone.

"The Creator of the platypus, the camel, the ostrich, and man? Oh, come now!" Father Peregrine laughed.

But at this instant, from among the twilight hills, like a series of blue lamps lit to guide their way, came the Martians.

Father Stone saw them first. "Look!"

Father Peregrine turned and the laughter stopped in his mouth.

The round blue globes of fire hovered among the twinkling stars, distantly trembling.

"Monsters!" Father Stone leaped up. But Father Peregrine caught him. "Wait!"

"We should've gone to town!"

"No, listen, look!" pleaded Father Peregrine.

"I'm afraid!"

"Don't be. This is God's work!"

"The devil's!"

"No, now, quiet!" Father Peregrine gentled him and they crouched with the soft blue light on their upturned faces as the fiery orbs drew near.

And again, Independence Night, thought Father Peregrine, tremoring. He felt like a child back in those July Fourth evenings, the sky blowing apart, breaking into powdery stars and burning sound, the concussions jingling house windows like the ice on a thousand thin ponds. The aunts, uncles, cousins crying, "Ah!" as to some celestial physician. The summer sky colors. And the Fire Balloons, lit by an indulgent grandfather, steadied in his massively tender hands. Oh, the memory of those lovely Fire Balloons, softly lighted, warmly billowed bits of tissue, like insect wings, lying like folded wasps in boxes and, last of all, after the day of riot and fury, at long last from their boxes, delicately unfolded, blue, red, white, patriotic—the Fire Balloons! He saw the dim faces of dear relatives long dead and mantled with moss as Grandfather lit the tiny candle and let the warm air breathe up to form the balloon plumply luminous in his hands, a shining vision which they held, reluctant to let it go; for, once released, it was yet another year gone from life, another Fourth, another bit of Beauty vanished. And then up, up, still up through the warm summer night constellations, the Fire Balloons had drifted, while redwhite-and-blue eyes followed them, wordless, from family porches. Away into deep Illinois country, over night rivers and sleeping mansions the Fire Balloons dwindled, forever gone. . . .

Father Peregrine felt tears in his eyes. Above him the Martians, not one but a *thousand* whispering Fire Balloons, it seemed, hovered. Any moment he might find his long-dead and blessed grandfather at his elbow, staring up at Beauty.

But it was Father Stone.

"Let's go, please, Father!"

"I must speak to them." Father Peregrine rustled forward, not knowing what to say, for what had he ever said to the Fire Balloons of time past except with his mind: *you are beautiful, you are beautiful*, and that was not enough now. He could only lift his heavy arms and call upward, as he had often wished to call after the enchanted Fire Balloons, "Hello!"

But the fiery spheres only burned like images in a dark mirror. They seemed fixed, gaseous, miraculous, forever.

"We come with God," said Father Peregrine to the sky.

"Silly, silly, silly." Father Stone chewed the back of his hand. "In the name of God, Father Peregrine, stop!"

But now the phosphorescent spheres blew away into the hills. In a moment they were gone.

Father Peregrine called again, and the echo of his last cry shook the hills above. Turning, he saw an avalanche shake out dust, pause, and then, with a thunder of stone wheels, crash down the mountain upon them.

"Look what you've done!" cried Father Stone.

Father Peregrine was almost fascinated, then horrified. He turned, knowing they could run only a few feet before the rocks crushed them into ruins. He had time to whisper, *Oh, Lord!* and the rocks fell!

"Father!"

They were separated like chaff from wheat. There was a blue shimmering of globes, a shift of cold stars, a roar, and then they stood upon a ledge two hundred feet away watching the spot where their bodies should have been buried under tons of stone.

The blue light evaporated.

The two Fathers clutched each other. "What happened?"

"The blue fires lifted us!"

"We ran, *that* was it!"

"No, the globes saved us."

"They couldn't!"

"They *did*."

The sky was empty. There was a feel as if a great bell had just stopped tolling. Reverberations lingered in their teeth and marrows.

"Let's get away from here. You'll have us killed."

"I haven't feared death for a good many years, Father Stone."

"We've proved nothing. Those blue lights ran off at the first cry. It's useless."

"No." Father Peregrine was suffused with a stubborn wonder. "Somehow, they saved us. That proves they have souls."

"It proves only that they *might* have saved us. Everything was confused. We might have escaped, ourselves."

"They are not animals, Father Stone. Animals do not save lives, especially of strangers. There is mercy and compassion here. Perhaps, tomorrow, we may prove more."

"Prove what? How?" Father Stone was immensely tired now; the outrage to his mind and body showed on his stiff face. "Follow them in helicopters, reading chapter and verse? They're not human. They haven't eyes or ears or bodies like ours."

"But I feel something about them," replied Father Peregrine. "I know a great revelation is at hand. They saved us. They *think*. They had a choice; let us live or die. That proves free will!"

Father Stone set to work building a fire, glaring at the sticks in his hands, choking on the gray smoke. "I myself will open a convent for nursling geese, a monastery for sainted swine, and I shall build a miniature apse in a microscope so that paramecium can attend services and tell their beads with their flagella."

"Oh, Father Stone."

"I'm sorry." Father Stone blinked redly across the fire. "But this is like blessing a crocodile before he chews you up. You're risking the entire missionary expedition. We belong in First Town, washing liquor from men's throats and perfume off their hands!"

"Can't you recognize the human in the inhuman?"

"I'd much rather recognize the inhuman in the human."

"But if I prove these things sin, know sin, know a moral life, have free will and intellect, Father Stone?"

"That will take much convincing."

The night grew rapidly cold and they peered into the fire to find their wildest thoughts, while eating biscuits and berries, and soon they were bundled for sleep under the chiming stars. And just before turning over one last time Father Stone, who had been thinking for many minutes to find something to bother Father Peregrine about, stared into the soft pink charcoal bed and said, "No Adam and Eve on Mars. No Original Sin. Maybe the Martians live in a state of God's grace. Then we can go back down to town and start work on the Earthmen."

Father Peregrine reminded himself to say a little prayer for Father Stone, who got so mad and who was now being vindictive, God help him. "Yes, Father Stone, but the Martians killed some of our settlers. That's sinful. There must have been an Original Sin and a Martian Adam and Eve. We'll find them. Men are men, unfortunately, no matter what their shape, and inclined to sin."

But Father Stone was pretending sleep.

Father Peregrine did not shut his eyes.

Of course they couldn't let these Martians go to hell, could they? With a compromise to their consciences, could they go back to the new colonial towns, those towns so full of sinful gullets and women with scintilla eyes and white oyster bodies rollicking in beds with lonely laborers? Wasn't that the place for the Fathers? Wasn't this trek into the hills merely a personal whim? Was he really thinking of God's Church, or was he quenching the thirst of a spongelike curiosity? Those blue round globes of St. Anthony's fire—how they burned in his mind! What a challenge, to find the man behind the mask, the human behind the inhuman. Wouldn't he be proud if he could say, even to his secret self, that he had converted a rolling huge pool table full of fiery spheres! What a sin of pride! Worth doing penance for! But then one did many prideful things out of Love, and he loved the Lord so much and was so happy at it that he wanted everyone else to be happy too.

The last thing he saw before sleep was the return of the blue fires, like a flight of burning angels silently singing him to his worried rest.

The blue round dreams were still there in the sky when Father Peregrine awoke in the early morning.

Father Stone slept like a stiff bundle, quietly. Father

Peregrine watched the Martians floating and watching him. They were human—he *knew* it. But he must prove it or face a dry-mouthed, dry-eyed Bishop telling him kindly to step aside.

But how to prove humanity if they hid in the high vaults of the sky? How to bring them nearer and provide answers to the many questions?

"They saved us from the avalanche."

Father Peregrine arose, moved off among the rocks, and began to climb the nearest hill until he came to a place where a cliff dropped sheerly to a floor two hundred feet below. He was choking from his vigorous climb in the frosty air. He stood, getting his breath.

"If I fell from here, it would surely kill me."

He let a pebble drop. Moments later it clicked on the rocks below.

"The Lord would never forgive me."

He tossed another pebble.

"It wouldn't be suicide, would it, if I did it out of Love . . . ?"

He lifted his gaze to the blue spheres. "But first, another try." He called to them: "Hello, hello!"

The echoes tumbled upon each other, but the blue fires did not blink or move.

He talked to them for five minutes. When he stopped, he peered down and saw Father Stone, still indignantly asleep, below in the little camp.

"I must prove everything." Father Peregrine stepped to the cliff rim. "I am an old man. I am not afraid. Surely the Lord will understand that I am doing this for Him?"

He drew a deep breath. All his life swam through his eyes and he thought, In a moment shall I die? I am afraid that I love living much too much. But I love other things more.

And, thinking thus, he stepped off the cliff.

He fell.

"Fool!" he cried. He tumbled end over end. "You were wrong!" The rocks rushed up at him and he saw himself dashed on them and sent to glory. "Why did I do this thing?" But he knew the answer, and an instant later was calm as he fell. The wind roared around him and the rocks hurtled to meet him.

And then there was a shift of stars, a glimmering of blue light, and he felt himself surrounded by blueness and suspended. A moment later he was deposited, with a gentle bump, upon the rocks, where he sat a full moment, alive, and touching himself, and looking up at those blue lights that had withdrawn instantly.

"You saved me!" he whispered. "You wouldn't let me die. You knew it was wrong."

He rushed over to Father Stone, who still lay quietly asleep. "Father, Father, wake up!" He shook him and brought him round. "Father, they saved me!"

"Who saved you?" Father Stone blinked and sat up.

Father Peregrine related his experience.

"A dream, a nightmare; go back to sleep," said Father Stone irritably. "You and your circus balloons."

"But I was awake!"

"Now, now, Father, calm yourself. There now."

"You don't believe me? Have you a gun? Yes, there, let me have it."

"What are you going to do?" Father Stone handed over the small pistol they had brought along for protection against snakes or other similar and unpredictable animals.

Father Peregrine seized the pistol. "I'll prove it!"

He pointed the pistol at his own hand and fired.

"Stop!"

There was a shimmer of light, and before their eyes the bullet stood upon the air, poised an inch from his open palm. It hung for a moment, surrounded by a blue phosphorescence. Then it fell, hissing, into the dust.

Father Peregrine fired the gun three times—at his hand, at his leg, at his body. The three bullets hovered, glittering, and, like dead insects, fell at their feet.

"You see?" said Father Peregrine, letting his arm fall, and allowing the pistol to drop after the bullets. "They know. They understand. They are not animals. They think and judge and live in a moral climate. What animal would save me from myself like this? There is no animal would do that. Only another man, Father. Now, do you believe?"

Father Stone was watching the sky and the blue lights, and now, silently, he dropped to one knee and picked up the warm bullets and cupped them in his hand. He closed his hand tight.

The sun was rising behind them.

"I think we had better go down to the others and tell them of this and bring them back up here," said Father Peregrine.

By the time the sun was up, they were well on their way back to the rocket.

Father Peregrine drew the round circle in the center of the blackboard.

"This is Christ, the son of the Father."

He pretended not to hear the other Fathers' sharp intake of breath.

"This is Christ, in all his Glory," he continued.

"It looks like a geometry problem," observed Father Stone.

"A fortunate comparison, for we deal with symbols here. Christ is no less Christ, you must admit, in being represented by a circle or a square. For centuries the cross has symbolized his love and agony. So this circle will be the Martian Christ. This is how we shall bring Him to Mars."

The Fathers stirred fretfully and looked at each other.

"You, Brother Mathias, will create, in glass, a replica of this circle, a globe, filled with bright fire. It will stand upon the altar."

"A cheap magic trick," muttered Father Stone.

Father Peregrine went on patiently: "On the contrary. We are giving them God in an understandable image. If Christ had come to us on Earth as an octopus, would we have accepted him readily?" He spread his hands. "Was it then a cheap magic trick of the Lord's to bring us Christ through Jesus, in man's shape? After we bless the church we build here and sanctify its altar and this symbol, do you think Christ would refuse to inhabit the shape before us? You know in your hearts He would not refuse."

"But the body of a soulless animal!" said Brother Mathias.

"We've already gone over that, many times since we returned this morning, Brother Mathias. These creatures saved us from the avalanche. They realized that self-destruction was sinful, and prevented it, time after time. Therefore we must build a church in the hills, live with them, to find their own special ways of sinning, the alien ways, and help them to discover God."

The Fathers did not seem pleased at the prospect.

"Is it because they are so odd to the eye?" wondered Father Peregrine. "But what is a shape? Only a cup for the blazing soul that God provides us all. If tomorrow I found that sea lions suddenly possessed free will, intellect, knew when not to sin, knew what life was and tempered justice with mercy and life with love, then I would build an undersea cathedral. And if the sparrows should, miraculously, with God's will, gain everlasting souls tomorrow, I would freight a church with helium and take after them, for all souls, in any shape, if they have free will and are aware of their sins, will burn in hell unless given their rightful communions. I would not let a Martian sphere burn in hell, either, for it is a sphere only in mine eyes. When I close my eyes it stands before me, an intelligence, a love, a soul—and I must not deny it."

"But that glass globe you wish placed on the altar," protested Father Stone.

"Consider the Chinese," replied Father Peregrine imperturbably. "What sort of Christ do Christian Chinese worship? An oriental Christ, naturally. You've all seen oriental Nativity scenes. How is Christ dressed? In Eastern robes. Where does He walk? In Chinese settings of bamboo and misty mountain and crooked tree. His eyelids taper, his cheekbones rise. Each country, each race adds something to Our Lord. I am reminded of the Virgin of Guadalupe, to whom all Mexico pays its love. Her skin? Have you noticed the paintings of her? A dark skin, like that of her wor-

shipers. Is this blasphemy? Not at all. It is not logical
that men should accept a God, no matter how real, of
another color. I often wonder why our missionaries do
well in Africa, with a snow-white Christ. Perhaps because white is a sacred color, in albino, or any other
form, to the African tribes. Given time, mightn't Christ
darken there too? The form does not matter. Content
is everything. We cannot expect these Martians to
accept an alien form. We shall give them Christ in
their own image."

"There's a flaw in your reasoning, Father," said Father Stone. "Won't the Martians suspect us of hypoc-
risy? They will realize that *we* don't worship a round,
globular Christ, but a man with limbs and a head. How
do we explain the difference?"

"By showing there is none. Christ will fill any vessel
that is offered. Bodies or globes, he is there, and each
will worship the same thing in a different guise. What
is more, we must *believe* in this globe we give the Martians. We must believe in a shape which is meaningless
to us as to form. This spheroid *will* be Christ. And we
must remember that we ourselves, and the shape of our
Earth Christ, would be meaningless, ridiculous, a
squander of material to these Martians."

Father Peregrine laid aside his chalk. "Now let us go
into the hills and build our church."

The Fathers began to pack their equipment.

The church was not a church but an area cleared of
rocks, a plateau on one of the low mountains, its soil
smoothed and brushed, and an altar established
whereon Brother Mathias placed the fiery globe he had
constructed.

At the end of six days of work the "church" was ready.

"What shall we do with this?" Father Stone tapped an iron bell they had brought along. "What does a bell mean to *them?*"

"I imagine I brought it for our own comfort," admitted Father Peregrine. "We need a few familiarities. This church seems so little like a church. And we feel somewhat absurd here—even I; for it is something new, this business of converting the creatures of another world. I feel like a ridiculous play actor at times. And then I pray to God to lend me strength."

"Many of the Fathers are unhappy. Some of them joke about all this, Father Peregrine."

"I know. We'll put this bell in a small tower for their comfort, anyway."

"What about the organ?"

"We'll play it at the first service, tomorrow."

"But, the Martians——"

"I know. But again, I suppose, for our own comfort, our own music. Later we may discover theirs."

They arose very early on Sunday morning and moved through the coldness like pale phantoms, rime tinkling on their habits; covered with chimes they were, shaking down showers of silver water.

"I wonder if it *is* Sunday here on Mars?" mused Father Peregrine, but seeing Father Stone wince, he hastened on, "It might be Tuesday or Thursday—who knows? But no matter. My idle fancy. It's Sunday to *us.* Come."

The Fathers walked into the flat wide area of the "church" and knelt, shivering and blue-lipped.

Father Peregrine said a little prayer and put his cold fingers to the organ keys. The music went up like a flight of pretty birds. He touched the keys like a man moving his hands among the weeds of a wild garden, startling up great soarings of beauty into the hills.

The music calmed the air. It smelled the fresh smell of morning. The music drifted into the mountains and shook down mineral powders in a dusty rain.

The Fathers waited.

"Well, Father Peregrine." Father Stone eyed the empty sky where the sun was rising, furnace-red. "I don't see our friends."

"Let me try again." Father Peregrine was perspiring.

He built an architecture of Bach, stone by exquisite stone, raising a music cathedral so vast that its furthest chancels were in Nineveh, its furthest dome at St. Peter's left hand. The music stayed and did not crash in ruin when it was over, but partook of a series of white clouds and was carried away among other lands.

The sky was still empty.

"They'll come!" But Father Peregrine felt the panic in his chest, very small, growing. "Let us pray. Let us ask them to come. They read minds; they *know*."

The Fathers lowered themselves yet again, in rustlings and whispers. They prayed.

And to the East, out of the icy mountains of seven o'clock on Sunday morning or perhaps Thursday morning or maybe Monday morning on Mars, came the soft fiery globes.

They hovered and sank and filled the area around the shivering priests. "Thank you; oh, thank you, Lord." Father Peregrine shut his eyes tight and played the music, and when it was done he turned and gazed upon his wondrous congregation.

And a voice touched his mind, and the voice said:

"We have come for a little while."

"You may stay," said Father Peregrine.

"For a little while only," said the voice quietly. "We have come to tell you certain things. We should have spoken sooner. But we had hoped that you might go on your way if left alone."

Father Peregrine started to speak, but the voice hushed him.

"We are the Old Ones," the voice said, and it entered him like a blue gaseous flare and burned in the chambers of his head. "We are the old Martians, who left our marble cities and went into the hills, forsaking the material life we had lived. So very long ago we became these things that we now are. Once we were men, with bodies and legs and arms such as yours. The legend has it that one of us, a good man, discovered a way to free man's soul and intellect, to free him of bodily ills and melancholies, of deaths and transfigurations, of ill humors and senilities, and so we took on the look of lightning and blue fire and have lived in the winds and skies and hills forever after that, neither prideful nor arrogant, neither rich nor poor, passionate nor cold. We have lived apart from those we left behind, those other men of this world, and how we came to be has been forgotten, the process lost; but we shall never die, nor do harm. We have put away the sins of the body and live in God's grace. We covet no other property; we have no property. We do not steal, nor kill, nor lust, nor hate. We live in happiness. We cannot reproduce; we do not eat or drink or make war. All the sensualities and childishnesses and sins of the body were stripped away when our bodies were put aside. We have left sin behind, Father Peregrine, and it is burned like the leaves in the autumn, and it is gone like the soiled snow of an evil winter, and it is gone like the sexual flowers of a red-and-yellow spring, and it is gone like the panting nights of hottest summer, and our season is temperate and our clime is rich in thought."

Father Peregrine was standing now, for the voice touched him at such a pitch that it almost shook him from his senses. It was an ecstasy and a fire washing through him.

"We wish to tell you that we appreciate your building this place for us, but we have no need of it, for each of us is a temple unto himself and needs no place wherein to cleanse himself. Forgive us for not coming to you sooner, but we are separate and apart and have talked to no one for ten thousand years, nor have we interfered in any way with the life of this planet. It has come into your mind now that we are the lilies of the field; we toil not, neither do we spin. You are right. And so we suggest that you take the parts of this temple into your own new cities and there cleanse others. For, rest assured, we are happy and at peace."

The Fathers were on their knees in the vast blue light, and Father Peregrine was down, too, and they were weeping, and it did not matter that their time had been wasted; it did not matter to them at all.

The blue spheres murmured and began to rise once more, on a breath of cool air.

"May I"—cried Father Peregrine, not daring to ask,

eyes closed—"may I come again, someday, that I may learn from you?"

The blue fires blazed. The air trembled.

Yes. Someday he might come again. Someday.

And then the Fire Balloons blew away and were gone, and he was like a child, on his knees, tears streaming from his eyes, crying to himself, "Come back, come back!" And at any moment Grandfather might lift him and carry him upstairs to his bedroom in a long-gone Ohio town....

They filed down out of the hills at sunset. Looking back, Father Peregrine saw the blue fires burning. No, he thought, we couldn't build a church for the likes of you. You're Beauty itself. What church could compete with the fireworks of the pure soul?

Father Stone moved in silence beside him. And at last he spoke:

"The way I see it is there's a Truth on every planet. All parts of the Big Truth. On a certain day they'll all fit together like the pieces of jigsaw. This has been a shaking experience. I'll never doubt again, Father Peregrine. For this Truth here is as true as Earth's Truth, and they lie side by side. And we'll go on to other worlds, adding the sum of the parts of the Truth until one day the whole Total will stand before us like the light of a new day."

"That's a lot, coming from you, Father Stone."

"I'm sorry now, in a way, we're going down to the town to handle our own kind. Those blue lights now. When they settled about us, and that *voice* ..." Father Stone shivered.

Father Peregrine reached out to take the other's arm. They walked together.

"And you know," said Father Stone finally, fixing his eyes on Brother Mathias, who strode ahead with the glass sphere tenderly carried in his arms, that glass sphere with the blue phosphorous light glowing forever inside it, "you know, Father Peregrine, that globe there——"

"Yes?"

"It's Him. It *is* Him, after all."

Father Peregrine smiled, and they walked down out of the hills toward the new town.

14

THE POWER OF LOVE

The Man Who Learned Loving
THEODORE STURGEON

All religions, despite individual differences, seek like goals, and one of the most important is to develop a sense of community. "Love one another." The message is always the same. Man is a social creature who cannot fulfill himself in isolation; he needs a community of fellowmen. But even in a small community, it is not easy for him to maintain the bonds of love to ensure harmonious relations. The larger the community, the more difficult the task. Love is the uniting of that which was separate. Theologian Pierre Teilhard de Chardin says that "nothing, absolutely nothing . . . can arrest the progress of social man toward even greater interdependence and cohesion." The drive toward unity is clear.

To fulfill this principle of togetherness, or bondage in love, is the deepest concern of religious people

431

today. It is not easy to live in love, however, regardless of how strong the desire may be. Mensch, in "The Man Who Learned Loving," spends a lifetime fulfilling his vision of what love should be. The story presents a conflict between two alternate paths a person may take to love. Should he withdraw from a secular or worldly society that is not interested in love? He can live apart in a monastery or in a commune with a small group of people who share his conviction that living in love is more important than accumulating material possessions. On the other hand, is that love more responsible which participates in society and attempts to influence it to create more loving relationships? Does one escape the system or attempt to change the system? Which act is more loving?

A loving relationship is one in which each participant leaves the other free. He shares the relationship because he chooses, not because he must to survive. There is no weaker member dependent on the stronger; no slave and no master. There is no conflict of interest. "The Man Who Learned Loving" makes the assumption that this kind of freedom to love can be accomplished when power is equalized. With equality, conflict ends. To give away one's power until he has no more than anyone else is to love.

Anthropologist Margaret Mead says:

> The technological capabilities of the modern world have bound together all men, one species in one community, and this new interdependence is creating a climate of opinion in which the older dependence of the have-nots on the benevolence of the haves is being replaced by a new idea of

partnership in the use of technology. In international organizations the older societies, which at present have the greatest technical resources, and the newer societies, which need these resources, can work together as partners of equal dignity, members one of another.[1]

The man who learns loving discovers a way to actually implement the new society of partnership that Margaret Mead describes.

Psychologist Rollo May points out that in a technological age, the responsible use of power becomes more important than ever before in man's history.[2] It is no longer defensible to claim innocence of the destructive consequences of the misuse of power. The power that is increasingly available through science and technology is an agent of change. The task of the new religion must be to teach man to use technology as an instrument of love. "The Man Who Learned Loving" is the story of a man who masters this new kind of love.

[1] Ruth Nanda Anshen, ed., *Twentieth Century Faith: Hope and Survival* (New York: Harper and Row, 1972).

[2] Rollo May, *Power and Innocence: A Search for the Sources of Violence* (New York: Norton, 1972).

The Man Who Learned Loving
THEODORE STURGEON

His name was Mensch; it once was a small joke between them, and then it became a bitterness. "I wish to God I could have you now the way you were," she said, "moaning at night and jumping up and walking around in the dark and never saying why, and letting us go hungry and not caring how we lived or how we looked. I used to bitch at you for it, but I never minded, not really. I held still for it. I would've, just for always, because with it all you did your own thing, you were a free soul."

"I've always done my own thing," said Mensch, "and I did so tell you why."

She made a disgusted sound. "Who could understand all that?" It was dismissal, an old one; something she had recalled and worked over and failed to understand for years, a thing that made tiredness. "And you used to love people—really love them. Like the time that kid wiped out the fire-hydrant and the street-light in front of the house and you fought off the fuzz and the schlock lawyer and the ambulance and everybody, and got him to the hospital and wouldn't let him sign the papers because he was dazed. And turning that cheap hotel upside down to find Victor's false teeth and bring them to him after they put him in jail. And sitting all day in the waiting room the time Mrs. What's-her-name went for her first throat cancer treatment, you didn't even know her. There wasn't anything you wouldn't do for people."

"I've always done what I could. I didn't stop."

Scorn. "So did Henry Ford. Andrew Carnegie. The Krupp family. Thousands of jobs, billions in taxes for everybody. I know the stories."

"My story's not quite the same," he said mildly.

Then she said it all, without hate or passion or even much emphasis; she said in a burnt-out voice, "We loved each other and you walked out."

They loved each other. Her name was Fauna; it once was a small joke between them. Fauna the Animal and Mensch the Man, and the thing they had between them. "Sodom is a-cumen in," he misquoted Chaucer. "Lewd sing cuckold" (because she had a husband back there somewhere amongst the harpsichord lessons and the mildewed unfinished hooked rugs and the skeleton of a play and all the other abandoned projects in the attic of her life). She didn't get the reference. She wasn't bright—just loving. She was one of those people who waits for the right thing to come along and drops all others as soon as she finds out they aren't the main one. When someone like that gets the right thing, it's forever, and everyone says, my how you've changed. She hasn't changed.

But when the right thing comes along, and it doesn't work out, she'll never finish anything again. Never.

They were both very young when they met and she had a little house back in the woods near one of those resort towns that has a reputation for being touristy-artsy-craftsy and actually does have a sprinkling of real artists in and around it. Kooky people are more than tolerated in places like that providing that a) they attract, or at least do not repel, the tourists and b) they never make any important money. She was a slender pretty girl who liked to be naked under loose floor-length gowns and take care of sick things as long as they couldn't talk—broken-wing birds and philodendrons and the like—and lots of music—lots of *kinds* of music; and cleverly doing things she wouldn't finish until the real thing came along. She had a solid title to the little house and a part-time job in the local frame shop; she was picturesque and undemanding and never got involved in marches and petitions and the like. She just believed in being kind to everyone around her and thought . . . well, that's not quite right. She hadn't ever thought it out all the way, but she *felt* that if you're kind to everyone the kindness will somehow spread over the world like a healing stain, and that's what you do about wars and greed and injustice. So she was an acceptable, almost approved fixture in the town even when they paved her dirt road and put the lamp-post and fire-hydrant in front of it.

Mensch came into this with long hair and a guitar strapped to his back, a head full of good books and a lot of very serious restlessness. He knew nothing about loving and Fauna taught him better than she knew. He moved in with Fauna the day after she discovered his guitar was tuned like a lute. He had busy hands too, and a way of finishing what he started, yes, and making a dozen more like them—beautifully designed kitchen pads for shopping lists made out of hand-rubbed local woods, which used adding-machine rolls and had a hunk of hacksaw-blade down at the bottom so you could neatly tear off a little or a lot, and authentic reproductions of fireplace bellows and apple-peelers and stuff like that which could be displayed in the shoppes (not stores, they were shoppes) on the village green, and bring in his share. Also he knew about transistors and double-helical gears and eccentric linkages and things like Wankels and fuel-cells. He fiddled around a lot in the back room with magnets and axles and colored fluids of various kinds, and one day he had an idea and began fooling with scissors and cardboard and some metal parts. It was mostly frame and a rotor, but it was made of certain things in a certain way.

When he put it together the rotor began to spin, and he suddenly understood it. He made a very slight adjustment and the rotor, which was mostly cardboard, uttered a shrill rising sound and spun so fast that the axle, a ten-penny nail, chewed right through the cardboard bearings and the rotor took off and flew across the room, showering little unglued metal bits. He made no effort to collect the parts, but stood up blindly and walked into the other room. Fauna took one look at him and ran to him and held him: what is it? what's the matter? but he just stood there looking stricken until the tears began rolling down his cheeks. He didn't seem to know it.

That was when he began moaning suddenly in the middle of the night, jumping up and walking around in the dark. When she said years later that he would never tell her why, it was true, and it wasn't, because what he told her was that he had something in his head so important that certain people would kill him to get it, and certain other people would kill him to suppress it, and that he wouldn't tell her what it was because he loved her and didn't want her in danger. She cried a lot and said he didn't trust her, and he said he did, but he wanted to take care of her, not throw her to the wolves. He also said—and this is what the moaning and night-walking was all about—that the thing in his head could make the deserts bloom and could feed hungry people all over the world, but that if he let it loose it could be like a plague too, not because of what it was but because of what people would do with it; and the very first person who died because of it would die because of him, and he couldn't bear the idea of that. He really had a choice to make, but before he

could make it he had to decide whether the death of
one person was too great a price to pay for the happiness and security of millions, and then if the deaths of
a thousand would be justified if it meant the end of
poverty for all. He knew history and psychology and he
had a mathematician's head as well as those cobbler's
hands, and he knew damned well what would happen if
he took this way or that. For example, he knew where
he could unload the idea and all responsibility for it for
enough money to keep him and Fauna—and a couple
hundred close friends, if it came to that—in total
luxury for the rest of their lives; all he would have to
do would be to sign it away and see it buried forever in
a corporate vault, for there were at least three industrial giants which would urgently bid against one another for the privilege.

Or kill him.

He also thought of making blueprints and scattering
millions of copies over cities all over the world, and of
finding good ethical scientists and engineers and banding them together into a firm which would manufacture
and license the device and use it only for good things.
Well you can do that with a new kind of rat-killer or
sewing machine, but not with something so potent that
it will change the face of the earth, eliminate hunger,
smog, and the rape of raw materials—not when it will
also eliminate the petrochemical industry (except for
dyes and plastics), the electric power companies, the
internal combustion engine and everything involved in
making it and fuelling it, and even atomic energy for
most of its purposes.

Mensch tried his very best to decide not to do anything at all about it, which was the moaning and night-

walking interval and that just wouldn't work—the thing would not let him go. Then he decided what to do, and what he must do in order to do it. His first stop was at the town barbershop.

Fauna held still for this and for his getting a job at Flextronics, the town's light industry, which had Government contracts for small computer parts and which was scorned by the town's art, literary and library segment. The regular hours appalled her, and although he acted the same (he certainly didn't look the same) around the house, she became deeply troubled. She had never seen so much money as he brought in every payday, and didn't want to, and for the first time in her life had to get stubborn about patching and improvising and doing without instead of being able to blame poverty for it. The reasons she found now for living that way seemed specious even to her, which only made her stubborn about it, and more of a kook than ever. Then he bought a car, which seemed to her an immorality of sorts.

What tore it was when somebody told her he had gone to the town board meeting, which she had never done, and had proposed that the town pass ordinances against sitting on the grass on the village green, playing musical instruments on town thoroughfares, swimming at the town swimming hole after sundown, and finally, hiring more police. When she demanded an explanation he looked at her sadly for a long time, then would not deny it, would not discuss it, and moved out.

He got a clean room in a very square boarding house near the factory, worked like hell until he got his college credits straightened out, went to night school until he had another degree. He took to hanging around the

Legion post on Saturday nights and drank a little beer and bought a lot of whiskey for other people. He learned a whole portfolio of dirty jokes and dispensed them carefully, two-thirds sex, one-third bathroom. Finally he took a leave of absence from his job, which was, by this time, section manager, and moved down the river to a college town where he worked full time on a post-graduate engineering degree while going to night school to study law. The going was very tough around then because he had to pinch every nickel to be able to make it and still keep his pants creased and his brown shoes shiny, which he did. He still found time to join the local church and became a member of the vestry board and a lay preacher, taking as his text the homilies from *Poor Richard's Almanac* and delivering them (as did their author) as if he believed every word.

When it was time he redesigned his device, not with cardboard and glue, but with machined parts that were 70% monkey-puzzle—mechanical motions that cancelled each other, and wiring which energized coils which shorted themselves out. He patented parts and certain groupings of parts, and finally the whole contraption. He then took his degrees and graduate degrees, his published scholarly papers, his patents and his short hair-cut, together with a letter of introduction from his pastor, to a bank, and borrowed enough to buy into a failing company which made portable conveyor belts. His device was built into the drive segment, and he went on the road to sell the thing. It sold very well. It should. A six-volt automobile battery would load coal with that thing for a year without needing replacement or recharging, and no wonder, because the loading was being powered by that little black lump in the drive segment, which, though no bigger than a breadbox, and requiring no fuel, would silently and powerfully spin a shaft until the bearings wore out.

It wasn't too long before the competition was buying Mensch's loaders and tearing them down to see where all that obscene efficiency was coming from. The monkey-puzzle was enough to defeat most of them, but one or two bright young men, and a grizzled oldster or so were able to realize that they were looking at something no bigger than a breadbox which would turn a shaft indefinitely without fuel, and to wonder what things would be likely with this gadget under the hood of a car or in the nacelles of aircraft, or pumping water in the desert, or generating light and power 'way back in the hills and jungles without having to build roads or railways or to string powerlines. Some of these men found their way to Mensch. Either he hired them and tied them up tight with ropes of gold and fringe benefits, or had them watched and dissuaded, or discredited, or, if need be, ruined.

Inevitably someone was able to duplicate the Mensch Effect, but by that time Mensch had a whole office building full of lawyers with their pencils sharpened and their instructions ready. The shrewd operator who had duplicated the effect, and who had sunk everything he had and could borrow into retooling an engine factory for it, found himself in such a snarl of infringement, torts, ceases-and-desists, and prepaid royalty demands that he sold his plant at cost to Mensch and gratefully accepted a job managing it. And he was only the first.

The military moved in at about this point, but Mensch was ready for them and their plans to take over his patents and holdings as a national resource. He let himself be bunted higher and higher in the chain of command, while his refusals grew stronger and the threats greater and greater, until he emerged at the top in the company of the civilian who commanded them all. This meeting was brought about by a bishop, for never in all these busy years did Mensch overlook his weekly duty at the church of his choice, nor his tithes, nor his donations of time for an occasional Vacation Bible School or picnic or bazaar. And Mensch, on this pinnacle of wealth, power and respectability, was able to show the President the duplicate set of documents he had placed in a Swiss bank, which on the day his patents were pre-empted by the military, would donate them to research institutes in Albania and points north and east. That was the end of that.

The following year a Mensch-powered car won the Indy. It wasn't as fast as the Granatelli entry; it just voomed around and around the brickyard without making any stops at all. There was, of course, a certain amount of static for a while, but the inevitable end was that the automobile industry capitulated, and with it the fossil-fuel people. Electric light and power had to follow and, as the gas and steam and diesel power sources obsolesce and are replaced by Mensch prime-movers, the atomic plants await their turn.

It was right after the Indianapolis victory that Mensch donated his blueprints to Albania anyway— after all, he had never said he wouldn't—and they showed up about the same time in Hong Kong and quickly reached the mainland. There was a shrill claim from the Soviet Union that the Mensch Effect had been discovered in the 19th century by Siolkovsky, who had set it aside because he was more interested in rockets, but even the Russians couldn't keep that up for long without laughing along with the audience, and they fell to outstripping all other nations in development work. No monkey-puzzle on earth can survive this kind of effort—monkey-puzzles need jungles of patent law to live and thrive—and it was not long before the Soviets (actually, it was a Czech scientist, which is the same thing, isn't it? Well, the Soviets said it was) were able to proclaim that they had improved and refined the device to a simple frame supporting one moving part, the rotor, each made, of course, of certain simple substances which, when assembled, began to work. It was, of course, the same frame and rotor with which Mensch, in terror and tears, had begun his career, and the Czech, that is, Soviet "refinement" was, like all else, what he had predicted and aimed himself toward.

For now there wasn't a mechanics' magazine in the world, nor hardly a tinkerer's workshop anywhere, that didn't begin turning out Mensch rotors. Infringements occurred so widely that even Mensch's skyscraper-full of legal-eagles couldn't have begun to stem the flood. And indeed they did not try, because—

For the second time in modern history (the first was an extraordinary man named Kemal Ataturk) a man of true national-dictator stature set his goal, achieved it, and abdicated. It didn't matter one bit to Mensch that the wiser editorialists, with their knowledgeable index fingers placed alongside their noses, were pointing out that he had defeated himself, shattered his own empire by extending its borders, and that by releasing his patents into the public domain he was making an empty gesture to the inevitable. Mensch knew what he had done, and why, and what other people thought of it just did not matter.

"What does matter," he said to Fauna in her little house by the old fire-hydrant and the quaint street-lamp, "is that there isn't a kraal in Africa or a hamlet in Asia that can't pump water and plow land and heat and light its houses by using a power plant simple enough to be built by any competent mechanic any-where. There are little ones to rock cradles and power toys and big ones to light whole cities. They pull trains and sharpen pencils, and they need no fuel. Already desalted Mediterranean water is pouring into the northern Sahara; there'll be whole new cities there, just as there were five thousand years ago. In ten years the air all over the earth will be measurably cleaner, and already the demand for oil is down so much that off-shore drilling is almost completely stopped. 'Have' and 'have-not' no longer means what it once meant, be-cause everyone has access to cheap power. And that's why I did it, don't you see?" He really wanted very much to make her understand.

"You cut your hair," she said bitterly. "You wore those awful shoes and went to church and got college degrees and turned into a—a typhoon."

"Tycoon," he corrected absently. "Ah, but Fauna, listen: I wanted to be listened to. The way to get what I wanted was short hair, was brown shoes, was pub-lished post-graduate papers, was the banks and busi-nesses and government and all of those things that were already there for me to use."

"You didn't need all that. I think you just wanted to

move things and shake things and be in the newspapers and history books. You could've made your old motor right here in his house and showed it to people and sold it and stayed here and played the lute, and it would have been the same thing."

"No, there you're wrong," said Mensch. "Do you know what kind of a world we live in? We live in a world where, if a man came up with a sure cure for cancer, and if that man were found to be married to his sister, his neighbors would righteously burn down his house and all his notes. If a man built the most beautiful tower in the country, and that man later begins to believe that Satan should be worshipped, they'll blow up his tower. I know a great and moving book written by a woman who later went quite crazy and wrote crazy books, and nobody will read her great one any more. I can name three kinds of mental therapy that could have changed the face of the earth, and in each one the men who found it went on to insane Institutes and so-called religions and made fools of themselves— dangerous fools at that—and now no one will look at their really great early discoveries. Great politicians have been prevented from being great statesmen because they were divorced. And I wasn't going to have the Mensch machine stolen or buried or laughed at and forgotten just because I had long hair and played the lute. You know, it's easy to have long hair and play the lute and be kind to people when everyone else around is doing it. It's a much harder thing to be the one who does something first, because then you have to pay a price, you get jeered at and they shut you out."

"So you joined them," she accused.

"I used them," he said flatly. "I used every road and

path that led to where I was going, no matter who built it or what it was built for."

"And you paid your price," she all but snarled. "Millions in the banks, thousands of people ready to fall on their knees if you snap your fingers. Some price. You could have had love."

He stood up then and looked at her. Her hair was much thinner now, but still long and fine. He reached for it, lifted some. It was white. He let it go.

He thought of fat Biafran babies and clean air and un-polluted beaches, cheaper food, cheaper transportation, cheaper manufacturing and maintenance, more land to lessen the pressure and hysteria during the long slow process of population control. What had moved him to deny himself so much, to rebel, to move and shake and shatter the status quo the way he had, rather than conforming—conforming!—to long hair and a lute? *You could have had love.*

"But I did," he said; and then, knowing she would never, could never understand, he got in his silent fuel-less car and left.

15

TRANSCENDENCE: THE FUTURE OF RELIGION

And I Have Come Upon This Place by Lost Ways
JAMES TIPTREE, JR.

"And I Have Come Upon This Place by Lost Ways" is a beautiful tale to end this collection of science fiction stories about religion. It is a miniature summary—in pictures—of the ideas we have been exploring in this anthology. So it is a kind of ending; and yet out of the ending grows a new kind of beginning—a rebirth. It is like the marvelously eternal life that mankind has forever handed forward. The death of each generation is its gift of life to the next generation. Life creates life; the same life but yet different, as the infinite number of combinations in the genetic pool produces unique new individuals who need new myths of what they can become.

"And I Have Come Upon This Place by Lost Ways" gives us an image of a future world stretching from simple men living in a very primitive culture, to intel-

447

lectually advanced men who have made a kind of religion out of science, to one individual who does not fit into the sacred structures of science, who wants to go beyond and search for something more. The story is almost a symbol of our world today, which encompasses very primitive societies to which science is unknown, and very sophisticated cultures where science and technology have been made into gods.

Evan Dilwyn, the protagonist of "And I Have Come Upon This Place by Lost Ways" is a new initiate into the sanctuary of the Scientists. He only occupies a position on the fringes because his field is anthropology, which lies in the lesser social sciences and therefore does not give him as much status as a hard Scientist would have. All the imagery in the story suggests a world where Science has been institutionalized and elevated into a religion. The Research Chief is the High Scientist. Work is carried on in "the high-status Labs, the temples of Hardscience." The computer printouts are the sacred writings, and the holy of holies is the Main Computer.

The sensors and scanners and bioanalysers now make direct observations of data, freeing man of the need to use his senses. The computer, fed the data, synthesizes it and thereby frees man's brain of the need to think. A scientific utopia has been achieved. The status quo can be maintained because the perfect system is at hand.

But Evan is not so sure. He wants to experience reality directly instead of knowing it only through a machine. He knows he has replaced Foster, the previous anthropologist, because Foster was not conventional enough in his thinking and behavior. Foster would not agree that the system of machines can function better than man, that man hardly needs himself anymore.

Evans discovers that he, too, is a heretic. He discovers he is driven to climb the unknown mountain, even though it means going alone and risking everything. It is rightly called the Mountain of Leaving. Finally, he must combat the mountain unaided, with only his physical strength and his courageous spirit. There is no promise of reward, nothing to be gained, but still he must go because he is a man, that unique creature who is always inspired to climb beyond, to transcend himself, and gain a vision he has not seen before.

The mountain, which is the central image in this concluding story, has always been a symbol for man of his aspiration toward the divinity of the heavens. The gods of the Greeks inhabited Mt. Olympus. Moses went up Mt. Sinai where the Ten Commandments were revealed to him. Jesus prayed upon the mountain. Man will always—symbolically—find mountains because he needs to climb.

We must, finally, allow room for these adventurers who climb mountains to new horizons. They search out the seed of our rebirth. It is they who, filled with wonder, curiosity, and a sense of quest, will always struggle up alone, catch a new awareness of what man can become to fulfill himself, and hand the religious vision back to waiting mankind. The gift of light is eternal.

And I Have Come Upon This Place by Lost Ways
JAMES TIPTREE, JR.

It was so beautiful.

Evan's too-muscular stomach tightened as he came into the Senior Commons and saw them around the great view port. Forgetting his mountain, forgetting even his ghastly vest he stared like a layman at the white-clad Scientists in the high evening sanctum of their ship. He still could not believe.

A Star Research Ship, he marveled. A Star Science Mission and I am on it. Saved from a Technician's mean life, privileged to be a Scientist and search the stars for knowledge——

"What'll it be, Evan?"

Young Doctor Sunny Isham was at the bevbar. Evan mumbled amenities, accepted a glass. Sunny was the other junior Scientist and in theory Evan's equal. But Sunny's parents were famous Research Chiefs and the tissue of his plain white labcoat came from god knew where across the galaxy.

Evan pulled his own coarse whites across his horrible vest and wandered toward the group around the port. Why had he squandered his dress credit on Aldebaranian brocade when all these Star Scientists came from Aldebtech? Much better to have been simple Evan Dilwyn the general issue Galtech nobody —and an anthrosyke to boot.

To his relief the others ignored his approach. Evan skirted the silence around the lean tower of the Mission Chief and found a niche behind a starched ruff belong-

ing to the Deputy, Doctor Pontreve. Pontreve was
murmuring to the Astrophysics Chief. Beyond them
was a blonde dazzle—little Cyberdoctor Ava Ling. The
girl was joking with the Sirian colleague. Evan listened
to them giggle, wondering why the Sirian's scaly blue
snout seemed more at home here than his own broad
face. Then he looked out the port and his stomach
knotted in a different way.

On the far side of the bay where the ship had landed
a vast presence rose into the sunset clouds. The many-
shouldered Clivorn, playing with its unending cloud-
veils, oblivious of the alien ship at its feet. *An'druinn*,
the Mountain of Leaving, the natives called it. Why
"leaving," Evan wondered for the hundredth time, his
eyes seeking for the thing he thought he had glimpsed.
No use, the clouds streamed forever. And the routine
survey scans could not——

The Deputy had said something important.

"The ship is always on status go," rumbled the Captain's voice from the bevbar. "What does the Chief
say?"

Evan's gasp went unnoticed; their attention was on
the Research Chief. For a moment the high Scientist
was silent, smoke of his THC cheroot drifting from his
ebony nostrils. Evan gazed up at the hooded eyes, willing him to say no. Then the smoke quivered faintly:
Affirmative.

"Day after next, then." The Captain slapped the bar.

They would leave without looking! And no ship
would ever survey this sector again.

Evan's mouth opened but before he could find courage Sunny Isham was smoothly reminding the Deputy
of the enzyme his bioscan had found. "Oh, Sunny, may

I touch you?" Ava Ling teased. And then a glance
from the Chief started everyone moving toward the
refectory, leaving Evan alone by the port.

They would process Sunny's enzyme. And they
should, Evan told himself firmly. It was the only valid
finding the computers had come up with on this planet.
Whereas his mountain . . . he turned wistfully to The
Clivorn now sinking behind its golden mists across the
bay. If once he could see, could go and feel with his
hands——

He choked back the Unscientism. *The computer has
freed man's brain,* he repeated fiercely. Was he fit to be
a Scientist? His neck hot, he wheeled from the port and
hurried after his superiors.

Dinner was another magic scene. Evan's mood
softened in the glittering ambience, the graceful small
talk. The miracle of his being here. He knew what the
miracle was: his old uncle at Galcentral fighting for an
outworld nephew's chance. And the old man had won.
When this ship's anthrosyke fell sick, Evan Dilwyn's
name was topmost on the roster. And here he was
among Star Scientists, adding his mite to man's noblest
work. Where only merit counted, merit and honesty
and devotion to the Aims of Research——

Ava Ling's glance jolted him out of his dream. The
Captain was relating an anecdote of Evan's predecessor, the anthrosyke Foster.

"——hammering upon the lock with these wretched
newt-women hanging all over him," the Captain
chuckled. "Seems the Mothers thought he was buying
the girls as well as their boxes. When he wouldn't take
them in they nearly tore him apart. Clothes all torn,

covered with mud." His blue eyes flicked Evan. "What a decon job!"

Evan flushed. The Captain was bracing him for the numerous decontaminations he had required for field trips out of seal. Each decon was charged against his personal fund, of course, but it was a nuisance. And bad form. The others never went out of seal, they collected by probes and robots or—very rarely—a trip by sealed bubble-sled. But Evan couldn't seem to get his data on local cultures that way. Natives just wouldn't interact with his waldobot. He must develop the knack before he used up all his fund.

"Oh, they are beautiful!" Ava Ling was gazing at the three light-crystal caskets adorning the trophy wall. These were the "boxes" Foster had taken from the newt people. Evan frowned, trying to recall the passage in Foster's log.

"Soul boxes!" he heard himself blurt. "The boxes they kept their souls in. If they lost them the girls were dead, that's why they fought. But how could——" His voice trailed off.

"No souls in them now," said Doctor Pontreve lightly. "Well, what do we say? Does this wine have a point or does it not?"

When they finally adjourned to the gameroom it was Evan's duty to dim the lights and activate the servobots. He kept his eyes from the ports where The Clivorn brooded in its clouds, and went out to the laughter and flashes spilling from the gameroom. They were at the controls of a child's laser game called Sigma.

"Turning in?" Little Ava Ling panted brightly,

momentarily out of the game. Evan caught her excited scent.

"I don't know," he smiled. But she had already turned away.

He stalked on, hating his own primitive olfactory reflexes, and pushed through the portal of the command wing of the Laboratories. Sound cut off as it closed behind him. The corridor gleamed in austere silence. He was among the high-status Labs, the temples of Hardscience. Beside him was the ever-lighted alcove holding the sacred tape of Mission Requirements in its helium seal.

He started down the hall, his nape as always pricking faintly. Into these Laboratories flowed all the data from the sensors, the probes, the sampling robots and bioanalysers and cyberscans, to be shaped by the Scientists' skills into forms appropriate to the Mission Requirements and fit to be fed finally into the holy of holies, the Main Computer of the ship, which he was now approaching. From here the precious Data beamed automatically back across the galaxy into the Computer of Mankind at Galcentral.

By the entrance to the Master Console a sentry stood, guarding against Unauthorized Use. Evan tensed as he crossed the man's impassive gaze, tried to hold himself more like a Scientist. In his bones he felt himself an imposter here; he belonged back in Technician's gray, drudging out an anonymous life. Did the sentry know it too? With relief he turned into the staff wing and found his own little cubby.

His console was bare. His assistant had dutifully cleaned up his unprofessional mess of tapes and—embarrassing weakness—handwritten notes. Evan tried to feel grateful. It was not Scientific to mull over raw findings, they should be fed at once into the proper program. *The computer has freed man's brain,* he told himself, tugging at a spool rack.

From behind the rack fell a bulging file. That stupid business he had tried of correlating a culture's social rigidity with their interest in new information, as represented by himself and his waldobot. The results had seemed significant, but he had no suitable computer categories into which he could program. An anthrosyke had twenty-six program nouns. . . . Sunny Isham had over five hundred for his molecular biology. But that was Hardscience, Evan reminded himself. He began to feed the worthless file into his disposer, idly flicking on his local note-tapes.

"——other mountains are called Oremal, Vosnuish, and so on," he heard himself say. "Only The Clivorn has the honorific *An* or *The.* Its native name *An'druinn* or The Mountain of Leaving may refer to the practice of ritual exile or death by climbing the mountain. But this does not appear to fit the rest of the culture. The Clivorn is not a taboo area. Herdsmen's paths run all over the slopes below the glaciation line. The tribe has a taboo area on the headland around their star-sighting stones and the fish-calling shrine. Moreover, the formal third-person case of the word *Leaving* suggests that it is not the natives who leave but some others who leave or have left. But who could that be? An invading tribe? Not likely; the inland ranges are uninhabited and all travel is by coracle along the coasts. And the terrain beyond *An'druinn* seems imp——"

These were his notes made before he began to search the survey scans of The Clivorn for something to explain its name—a cave or cairn or artifact or even a pass or trail. But the clouds had been too dense until that day when he had thought he'd seen that line. *Seen!* He winced. Did he hope to do Science with his feeble human senses?

"——transistorized tar pits of the galaxy!" said a hoarse voice.

Evan whirled. He was alone with the tape.

"Computer of mankind!" sneered the voice. Evan realized it was the voice of his predecessor, the anthrosyke Foster, imperfectly erased from the old tape beyond his own notes. As he jumped to wipe it Foster's ghost-voice said loudly, "A planetary turd of redundant data on stellar processes on which no competent mind has looked for five hundred years."

Evan gasped. His hand missed the wiper, succeeded only in turning the volume down.

"Research!" Foster was cackling drunkenly. "Get their hands *dirty?*" A blur of static; Evan found himself crouching over the console. Horrified he made out the words. "Shamans! Hereditary button-pushing imbeciles!" More blur, and Foster was mumbling something about DNA. "Call that *life?*" he croaked, "the behavior of living beings? . . . In all the galaxy, the most complex, the most difficult . . . our only hope . . ." The voice faded again.

Evan saw the spool was almost finished.

"Scientific utopia!" Foster guffawed. "The perfectly engineered society. No war. We no longer need study ourselves, because we're perfect." A gurgling noise blotted out the words. Foster had been drinking alcohol in his Laboratory, Evan realized. Out of his mind.

"And I'm their court clown." There was a long belch. "Learn a few native words, bring back some trinkets . . . good old Foster. Don't rock the boat." The voice made indistinct groaning noises and then cried clearly, "On your hands and knees! Down on the stones, alone. Simmelweiss. Galois. Dirty work. The hard lonely work of——"

The spool ran out.

Through the whirling in his head Evan heard brisk heel-taps. He stood up as his door opened. It was Deputy Pontreve.

"Whatever are you up to, Evan? Did I hear voices?"

"Just my—local notes, sir."

Pontreve cocked his head.

"On that mountain, Evan?" His voice was dry.

Evan nodded. The thought of their leaving flooded back upon him.

"Doctor Pontreve, sir, it seems such a pity not to check it. This area won't be surveyed again."

"But what can we conceivably hope to find? And above all, what has this *mountain* to do with your specialty?"

"Sir, my cultural studies point to something anomalous there. Some—well, I don't exactly know what yet. But I'm sure I got a glimpse——"

"Of the mythical Time Gate, perhaps?" Pontreve's smile faded. "Evan. There is a time in every young Scientist's life which crucially tests his vocation. Is he a Scientist? Or is he merely an *over-educated Technician?* Science must not, will not betray itself back into phenomenology and impressionistic speculation. . . . You may not know this, Evan," Pontreve went on in a different tone, "but your uncle and I were at PreSci together. He has done a great deal for you. He has faith in you. I would feel it deeply if you failed him."

Evan's heart shrank. Pontreve must have helped his uncle get him here. Appalled, he heard himself saying:

"But Doctor Pontreve, if Uncle has faith in me he'd want me to have faith in myself. Isn't it true that useful discoveries have been made by men who persisted in what seemed to be only a—hunch?"

Pontreve drew back.

"To speak of idle curiosity, which is all you really suffer from, Evan, in the same breath with the inspired intuition, the serendipity of the great Scientists of history? You shock me. I lose sympathy." He eyed Evan, licked his lips. "For your uncle's sake, lad," he said tightly, "I beg of you. Your position is shaky enough now. Do you want to lose everything?"

An acrid odor was in Evan's nostrils. Fear. Pontreve was really frightened. But why?

"Come out of this now, that's an order."

In silence Evan followed the Deputy down the corridors and back into the Commons. No one was in sight except three scared-looking Recreation youngsters waiting outside the gameroom for their nightly duty. As he passed Evan could hear the grunting of the senior Scientists in final duel.

He slammed on into his quarters, for once leaving the view opaque, and tried to sort the nightmare. Pontreve's pinched face roiled with Foster's drunken heresy in his brain. Such fear. But of what? What if Evan did disgrace himself? Was there something that would be investigated, perhaps found out?

Was it possible that a Scientist could have been *bribed*?

That would account for the fear . . . and the "miracle."

Evan gritted his jaw. If so, Pontreve was a false Scientist! Even his warnings were suspect, Evan thought angrily, twisting on his airbed in vain search of something tangible to combat. The memory of Ava Ling's fragrance raked him. He slapped the port filters and was flooded with cold light.

The planet's twin moons were at zenith. Beneath them the mountain loomed unreal as foam in the perpetual racing mists. The Clivorn was not really a large mountain, perhaps a thousand meters to the old glaciation line, but it rose from sea level alone. Torch-glows winked from the village at its feet. A fish-calling dance in progress.

Suddenly Evan saw that the clouds were parting over The Clivorn's upper crags. As only once before, the turrets above the glacier's mark were coming clear. The last veils blew by.

Evan peered frantically. Nothing . . . No, wait! And there it was, a faintly-flickering dead level line around the whole top. Say two-hundred meters below the crest. What could it be?

The clouds closed back. Had he really seen anything?

Yes!

He leaned his forehead against the port. Pontreve had said, *there comes a time in every Scientist's life* . . . in a million barren planets he might never have another such chance. The knowledge of what he was about to do grew in his guts and he was scared to death.

Before he could lose courage he flung himself back and slammed his sleep-inducer to full theta.

Next morning he dressed formally, spent a few minutes with his Terms of Grant codex and marched into Pontreve's office. The appointment ritual went smoothly.

"Doctor Deputy-Administrator," Evan's throat was dry. "As accredited Anthrosyke of this Mission I hereby exercise my prerogative of ordering an all-band full sensor probe of the terrain above five hundred meters indicated by these coordinates."

Pontreve's pursed lips sagged. "An all-band probe? But the cost——"

"I certify that my autonomous funds are adequate," Evan told him. "Since this is our last on-planet day, I would like to have it done soonest, sir, if you would."

In the full daylight bustle of the Labs, before the ranked Technicians, Apprentices and Mechs, Pontreve could say no more. Evan was within his rights. The older man's face grayed and he was silent before ordering his aide to produce the authorization forms. When they were placed before Evan he stabbed his finger on the line where Evan must certify that the scan was relevant to his Requirements of Specialization.

Evan set his thumbprint down hard, feeling the eyes of the Techstaff on him. This would take the last of his fund. But he had seen the Anomaly!

"Sir, you'll be interested to know I've had more evidence since——since our meeting."

Pontreve said nothing. Evan marched back to his lab, conscious of the whispers traveling through the wing. The probe would not take long once the sensor configuration was keyed in. He told his assistant to be ready to receive it and settled to wait.

Endless heartbeats later his man came back holding the heavily-sealed official canister before him in both hands. Evan realized he had never touched an original before; all-band scans were in practice ordered only by the Chief and then rarely.

He took a deep breath and broke the seals. It would be a long decoding job.

At shiftover he was still sitting, stone-faced at his console. Noon-break had sounded, the Labs had emptied and filled. A silence grew in the staff wing, broken finally by Pontreve's footsteps down the hall. Evan stood up slowly. Pontreve did not speak.

"Nothing, sir," Evan said into the Deputy's eyes. "I'm . . . sorry."

The eyes narrowed and a pulse twitched Pontreve's lip. He nodded in a preoccupied manner and went away.

Evan continued to stand, mechanically reviewing his scan. According to every sensor and probe The Clivorn was an utterly ordinary mountain. It rose up in rounded folds to the glaciation limit and then topped off in strikingly weathered crags. The top was quite bare. There were no caves, no tunnels, no unusual minerals, no emissions, no artifacts nor traces of any sort. At the height where Evan had seen the strange line there was perhaps a faint regularity or tiny shelf, a chance coincidence of wind-eroded layers. The reflection of moonlight on this shelf must have been what he'd seen as a flickering line.

Now he was finished as a Scientist.

For an anthrosyke to waste his whole fund on scanning a bare mountain was clear grounds for personality reassessment. At least. Surely he could also be indicted for misuse of Ship's Resources. And he had defied a Deputy-Administrator.

Evan felt quite calm, but his mind strayed oddly. What would have happened, he wondered, if he had found a genuine Anomaly? A big alien artifact, say; evidence of prior contact by an advanced race. Would it have been believed? Would anyone have looked? He had always believed that Data were Data. But what if the wrong person found them in the wrong, Unscientific way?

Well, he at any rate was no longer a Scientist.

He began to wonder if he was even alive, locked into this sealed ship. He seemed to have left his cubby; he was moving down the corridors leading to the lock.

Something was undoubtedly going to happen to him very soon. Perhaps they would begin by confining him to quarters. His was an unheard-of malfeasance, they might well be looking up precedents.

Meanwhile he was still free to move. To order the Tech-crew to open the personnel lock, to sign him out a bubble-sled.

Almost without willing it he was out in the air of the planet.

Delphis Gamma Five, the charts called it. To the natives it was simply the World, *Ardhvenne*. He opened the bubble. The air of *Ardhvenne* was fresh. The planet was in fact not far from the set of abscissae Evan knew only as terranormal.

Beneath his sled the sea arm was running in long salty swells lit here and there by racing fingers of sunlight. Where the sun struck the rocks the spray was dazzling white. A flying creature plummeted past him from the low clouds into the swells below, followed by a tree of spray.

He drove on across the bay to the far shore by the village and grounded in a sandy clutter of fishnets. The sled's voder came alive.

"Doctor Dilwyn." It was Pontreve's voice. "You will return immediately."

"Acknowledged," said Evan absently. He got out of the sled and set the autopilot. The sled rose, wheeled over him and fled away over the water to the gleaming ship.

Evan turned and started up the path toward the village, where he had come on his field trip the week before. He doubted that they would send after him. It would be too costly in time and decontamination.

It felt good to walk on natural earth with the free wind at his back. He hunched his shoulders, straining the formal labcoat. He had always been ashamed of his stocky, powerful body. Not bred to the Scientist life. He drew a lungful of air, turned the corner of a rock outcrop and came face to face with a native.

The creature was his own height with a wrinkled olive head sticking out of a wool poncho. Its knobby shanks were bare, and one hand held a club set with a soft-iron spike. Evan knew it for an elderly pseudo-female. She had just climbed out of a trench in which she had been hacking peat for fuel.

"Good day, Aunt," he greeted her.

"Good three-spans-past-high-sun," she corrected him tartly. Temporal exactitude was important here. She clacked her lips and turned to stack her peat sods. Evan went on toward the village. The natives of *Ardhvenne* were one of the usual hominid variants, distinguished by rather unstable sex morphology on a marsupial base.

Peat smoke wrinkled his nose as he came into the village street. It was lined by a double file of dry-rock huts, thatched with straw and set close together for warmth. Under the summer sun it was bleak enough. In winter it must be desolate.

Signs of last night's ceremonials were visible in the form of burnt-out resin brooms and native males torpid against the sunnier walls. A number of empty gourds lay in the puddles. On the shady side were mounds of dirty wool which raised small bald heads to stare at him. The local sheep-creatures, chewing cud. The native wives, Evan remembered, would now be in the houses feeding the young. There was a desultory clucking of fowl in the eaves. A young voice rose in song and fell silent.

Evan moved down the street. The males' eyes followed him in silence. They were a taciturn race, like many who lived by rocks and sea.

It came to him that he had no idea at all what he was doing. He must be in profound shock or fugue. Why had he come here? In a moment he must turn back and submit himself to whatever was in store. He thought about that. A trial, undoubtedly. A long Reassessment mess. Then what? Prison? No, they would not waste his training. It would be CNPTS, Compulsory Non-Preferred Technicians Service. He thought about the discipline, the rituals. The brawling Tech Commons. The dorms. End of hope. And his uncle heart-broken.

He shivered. He could not grasp the reality.

What would happen if he didn't go back? What if

the ship had to leave tomorrow as programmed? It couldn't be worth sterilizing this whole area just for him. He would be recorded as escaped, lost perhaps after a mental breakdown.

He looked around the miserable village. The huts were dark and reeked inside. Could he live here? Could he teach these people anything?

Before him was the headman's house.

"Good, uh, four-spans-past-high-sun, Uncle."

The headman clicked noncommittally. He was a huge-limbed creature, sprawled upon his lounging bench. Beside him was the young male Parag from whom Evan had obtained most of his local information.

Evan found a dry stone and sat down. Above the huts streamed the unceasing mist-veils. The Clivorn was a shadow in the sky; revealed, hidden, revealed again. A naked infant wandered out, its mouth sticky with gruel. It came and stared at Evan, one foot scratching the other leg. No one spoke. These people were capable of convulsive activity, he knew. But when there was nothing urgent to be done they simply sat, as they had sat for centuries. Incurious.

With a start Evan realized that he was comparing these scraggy hominids to the Scientists at ease in their ship. He must be mad. The ship—the very symbol of man's insatiable search for knowledge! How could he be so insane, just because they had rejected his data— or rather, his non-data? He shook his head to clear the heresy.

"Friend Parag," he said thickly.

Parag's eyes came 'round.

"Next sun-day is the time of going of the sky ship. It

is possible that I-alone-without-co-family will remain here."

The chief's eyes came open and swiveled toward him too.

Parag clicked I-hear.

Evan looked up at the misty shoulders of The Clivorn. There was sunlight on one of the nearly vertical meadows cradled in its crags. It was just past *Ardhvenne*'s summer solstice, the days were very long now. In his pocket was the emergency ration from the sled.

Suddenly he knew why he was here. He stood up staring at The Clivorn. *An'druinn*, The Mountain of Leaving.

"An easy homeward path, Uncle." He had inadvertently used the formal farewell. He began to walk out of the village on the main Path. Other trails ran straight up the mountain flank behind the huts; the females used these to herd their flocks. But the main Path ran in long straight graded zigzags. On his previous trips he had gone along it as far as the cairn.

The cairn was nothing but a crumbled double-walled fire hearth, strewn with the remains of gourds and dyed fleeces. The natives did not treat it as a sacred place. It was simply the lower end of the Path of Leaving and a good place to boil dyes.

Beyond the cairn the Path narrowed to eroded gravel, a straight scratch winding over The Clivorn's shoulders to the clouds. The dead and dying were carried up this way, Evan knew, and abandoned when they died or when the bearers had had enough. Sometimes relatives returned to pile stones beside the corpse, and doubtless to retrieve the deceased's clothing. He had already passed a few small heaps of weathered rocks and bones.

Up this path also were driven those criminals or witches of whom the tribe wished to be rid. None ever returned, Parag told him. Perhaps they made it to another village. More likely, they died in the mountains. The nearest settlement was ninety kilometers along the rugged coast.

He topped the first long grade over the lowest ridge, walking easily with the wind at his back. The gravel was almost dry at this season though The Clivorn was alive with springs. Alongside ran a soppy sponge of peat moss and heather in which Evan could make out bones every few paces now.

When the Path turned back into the wind he found that the thin mists had already hidden the village below. A birdlike creature soared over him, keening and showing its hooked beak. One of the tenders of The Clivorn's dead. He watched it ride off on the gale, wondering if he were a puzzle to its small brain.

When he looked down there were three olive figures ahead of him on the Path. The native Parag with two other males. They must have climbed the sheep-trails to meet him here. Now they waited stolidly as he plodded up.

Evan groped through the friends-met-on-a-journey greeting.

Parag responded. The other two merely clicked and stood waiting, blocking the Path. What did they want? Perhaps they had come after a strayed animal.

"An easy home-going," Evan offered in farewell. When they did not stir he started uphill around them.

Parag confronted him.

"You go on the Path."

"I go on the Path," Evan confirmed. "I will return at sun-end."

"No," said Parag. "You go on the Path of Leaving."

"I will return," insisted Evan. "At sun-end we will have friendly speech."

"No." Parag's hand shot out and gripped Evan's jacket. He yanked.

Evan jumped back. The others surged forward. One of them was pointing at Evan's shoes. "Not needful."

Evan understood now. Those who went on this Path took nothing. They assumed he was going to his death and they had come for his clothing.

"No!" he protested. "I will return! I go not to Leaving!"

Scowls of olive anger closed in. Evan realized how very poor they were. He was stealing valuable garments, a hostile act.

"I go to village now! I will return with you!"

But it was too late. They were pawing at him, jerking the strange fastenings with scarred olive claws. Dirty hair-smell in his nose. Evan pushed at them and half his jacket ripped loose. He began running straight up the hillside. They started after him. To his surprise he saw that his civilized body was stronger and more agile than theirs. He was leaving them behind as he lunged up from sheep-track to track.

At the ridge he risked a look back and shouted, "Friends! I will return!" One of them was brandishing a sheep-goad.

He whirled and pounded on up the ridge. Next moment he felt a hard blow in his side and went reeling. The sheep-goad clattered by his legs. His side—they had speared him! He gulped air on a skewer of pain and made himself run on. Up. No track here but a smooth marsh tipped skyward. He ran stumbling on the tussocks, on and up. Mist-wraiths flew by.

At a rock cornice he looked back. Below him three misty figures were turning away. Not following, up The Clivorn.

His breathing steadied. The pain in his side was localized now. He wedged his torn sleeve between arm and ribs and began to climb again. He was on the great sinew that was The Clivorn's lowest shoulder. As he climbed he found he was not quite alone in the streaming wraith-world; now and then a sheep bounded up with an absurd *kek-kek-kek* and froze to stare at him down its pointed nose.

He was, he realized, a dead man as far as the village was concerned. A dead man to the ship, a dead man here. Could he make the next village, wounded as he was? Without compass, without tools? And the pocket with his ration had been torn away. His best hope was to catch one of the sheep-creatures. That was not easily done by a single man. He would have to devise some sort of trap.

Curiously uncaring of his own despair he climbed on. The first palisades were behind him now. Before him was a steep meadow moist with springs of clear peat water, sprigged with small flowers. Great boulders stood, or rather hung here, tumbled by the vanished batteries of ice. In the milky dazzle their cold black shadows were more solid than they. The sun was coming with the wind, lighting the underside of the cloud-wrack above him.

He clambered leaning sideways against the wind, his

free hand clutching at wet rocks, tufts of fern. His heart was going too fast. Even when he rested it did not slow but hammered in his chest. The wound must be deeper than he'd thought. It was burning now and it hurt increasingly to lift his feet. Presently he found that he had made no progress at all but marched in place drunkenly for a dozen steps.

He ground his teeth, gasping through them. The task was to focus on a certain rock ahead—not too far—and push himself up into the sky. One rock at a time. Rest. Pick another, push on. Rest. Push on. Finally he had to stop between rocks. Breath was a searing ache. He wiped at the slaver on his jaw.

Make ten steps, then. Stop. Ten steps. Stop. Ten steps. . . .

A vague track came underfoot. Not a sheep-track, he was above the sheep. Only the huge creatures of the clouds ranged here. The track helped, but he fell often to his knees. On ten steps. Fall. Struggle up. Ten steps. On your knees in the stones, someone had said. There was no more sunlight.

He did not at first understand why he was facing rocky walls. He looked up, stupid with pain, and saw he was against the high, the dreadful cliffs. Somewhere above him was The Clivorn's head. It was nearly dark.

He sobbed, leaning on the stone flanks. When his body quieted he heard water and staggered to it among the rocks. A spouting streamlet, very cold, acid-clear. The Water of Leaving. His teeth rattled.

While he was drinking a drumming sound started up in the cliff beside him and a big round body caromed out, smelling of fat and fur. A giant rock-coney. He drank again, shivering violently, and pulled himself to the crevice out of which the creature had come. Inside was a dry heathery nest. With enormous effort he got himself inside and into the coney's form. It was safe here, surely. Safe as death. Almost at once he was unconscious.

Pain woke him in the night. Above the pain he watched the stars racing the mists. The moons rose and cloud-shadows walked on the silver wrinkled sea below him. The Clivorn hung over him, held him fast. He was of The Clivorn now, living its life, seeing through its eyes.

Over the ridgeline, a hazy transience. Moon-glints on a forest of antlers. The beasts of Clivorn were drifting in the night. Clouds streamed in and they were gone. The wind moaned unceasing, wreathing the flying scud.

Moonlight faded to rose-whiteness. Cries of birds. Outside his den a musky thing lapped at the stream, chittered and fled. He moved. He was all pain now, he could not lie still. He crawled out into the pale rose dawn hoping for warmth, and drank again at Clivorn's water, leaning on the rock.

Slowly, with mindless caution he looked around. Above the thrumming of the wind he heard a wail. It rose louder.

An opening came in the cloud stream below. He saw the headland beyond the bay. On it was a blinding rose-gold splinter. The Ship. Thin vapor was forming at its feet.

While he watched it began to slide gently upwards, faster and faster. He made a sound as if to call out, but it was no use. Clouds came between. When they opened again the headland was empty. The wailing died, leaving only the winds of Clivorn.

They had left him.

Cold came round his heart. He was utterly lost now. A dead man. Free as death.

His head seemed light now and he felt a strange frail energy. Up on his right there seemed to be a ledge leading onto a slanting shield of rock. Could he conceivably go on? The thought that he should do something about killing a sheep troubled him briefly, died. He found he was moving upward. It was like his dreams of being able to soar. Up—easily—so long as he struck nothing, breathed without letting go of the thing in his side.

He had reached the slanting shield and was actually climbing now. Hand up and grasp, pull, foot up, push. A few steps sidling along a cleft. The Clivorn's gray lichened face was close to his. He patted it foolishly, caught himself from walking into space. Hand up, grasp. Pull. Foot up. How had he come so high? Handhold. Left hand would not grip hard. He forced it, felt warm wet start down his side. Pull.

The rocks had changed now. No longer smooth but wildly crystalloid. He had cut his cheek. Igneous extrusion weathered into fantastic shelves.

"I am above the great glaciation," he muttered to the carved chimney that rose beside him, resonating in the gale. Everything seemed acutely clear. His hand was caught overhead.

He frowned up at it, furious. Nothing there. He wrenched. Something. He was perched, he saw, on a small snug knob. Wind was a steady shrieking. Silver-gold floodlights wheeled across him; the sun was high now, somewhere above the cloud. One hand was still stuck in something above his head. Odd.

He strained at it, hauling himself upright.

As he rose, his head and shoulders jolted ringingly. Then it was gone and he was spread-eagled, hanging on The Clivorn, fighting agony. When it ebbed he saw that there was nothing here. What was it? What had happened?

He tried to think, decided painfully that it had been an hallucination. Then he saw that the rock beside his face was sterile. Lichenless. And curiously smooth, much less wind-eroded.

Something must have been shielding it slightly for a very long time. Something which had resisted him and then snapped away.

An energy-barrier.

Bewildered he turned his head into the wind-howl, peered along the cliffs. To either side of him a band of unweathered rock about a meter broad stretched away level around The Clivorn's crags. It was overhung in places by the rocks above. Invisible from a flyer, really.

This must be the faint shelf-line he had found on the scans. The effect of long shielding by an energy-barrier. But why hadn't the detectors registered this energy? He puzzled, finally saw that the barrier could not be constant. It must only spring into existence when something came near, triggered it. And it had yielded when he pushed hard. Was it set to allow passage to larger animals which could climb these rocks?

He studied the surfaces. How long? How long had it been here, intermittently protecting this band of rock? Millennia of weathering, above and below. It was above the ice-line. Placed when the ice was here? By whom?

This sourceless, passive energy was beyond all human technology and beyond that of the few advanced aliens that man had so far encountered.

There rose within him a tide of infinite joy, carrying on it like a cork his rational conviction that he was delirious. He began to climb again. Up. Up. The barrier was fifty meters below him now. He dislodged a stone, looked under his arm to see it fall. He thought he detected a tiny flash, but he could not see whether it had been deflected or not. Birds or falling stones would make such sparkles. That could have been the flickering he had glimpsed.

He climbed. Wetness ran down his side, made red ropes. The pain rode him, he carried it strongly up. Handhold. Wrench. Toehold. Push. Rest. Handhold. "I am pain's horse," he said aloud.

He had been in dense clouds for some time now, the wind-thrum loud in the rock against his body. But something was going wrong with his body and legs. They dragged, would not lift clear. After a bit he saw what it was. The rock face had leveled. He was crawling rather than climbing.

Was it possible he had reached The Clivorn's brow?

He rose to his knees, frightened in the whirling mists. Beside him was a smear of red. My blood with Clivorn's, he thought. On my knees in the stones. My hands are dirty. Sick hatred of The Clivorn washed through him, hatred of the slave for the iron, the stone that outwears his flesh. The hard lonely job. . . . Who was Simmelweiss? "Clivorn, I hate you," he mumbled weakly. There was nothing here.

He swayed forward—and suddenly felt again the gluey resistance, the jolting crackle and release. Another energy-barrier on Clivorn's top.

He fell through it into still air, scrabbled a length and collapsed, hearing the silence. The rocks were wonderfully cool to his torn cheek. But they were not unweathered here, he saw. It came to him slowly that this second barrier must have been activated by the first. It was only here when something pushed up through the one below.

Before his eyes as he lay was a very small veined flower. A strange cold pulse boomed under his ear. The Clivorn's heartbeat, harmonics of the gale outside his shield.

The changing light changed more as he lay there. Some time later, he was looking at the stones scattered beyond the little plant. Water-clear gold pebbles, with here and there between them a singular white fragment shaped like a horn. The light was very odd. Too bright. After a while he managed to raise his head.

There was a glow in the mist ahead of him.

His body felt disconnected, and inexplicable agonies whose cause he could no longer remember bit into his breath. He began to crawl clumsily. His belly would not lift. But his mind was perfectly clear now and he was quite prepared.

Quite unstartled, as the mist passed, to see the shining corridor—or path, really, for it was made of a watery stonework from which the golden pebbles had crumbled—the glowing corridor-path where no path could be, stretching up from The Clivorn's summit among the rushing clouds.

The floor of the path was not long, perhaps a hundred meters if the perspective was true. A lilac-blue color showed at the upper end. Freshness flowed down, mingled with The Clivorn's spume.

He could not possibly get up it just now. . . . But he could look.

There was machinery, too, he saw. An apparatus of gelatinous complexity at the boundary where the path merged with Clivorn rock. He made out a dialed face pulsing with lissajou figures—the mechanism which must have been activated by his passage through the barriers, and which in turn had materialized this path.

He smiled and felt his smile nudge gravel. He seemed to be lying with his cheek on the tawny pebbles at the foot of the path. The alien air helped the furnace in his throat. He looked steadily up the path. Nothing moved. Nothing appeared. The lilac-blue, was it sky? It was flawlessly smooth. No cloud, no bird.

Up there at the end of the path—what? A field perhaps? A great arena into which other such corridor-paths converged? He couldn't imagine.

No one looked down at him.

In his line of sight, above the dialed face was a device like a translucent pair of helices. One coil was full of liquid coruscations. In the other were only a few sparks of light. While he watched, one of the sparks on the empty side winked out and the filled end flickered. Then another. He wondered, watched. It was regular.

A timing device. The read-out of an energy bank perhaps. And almost at an end. When the last one goes, he thought, the gate will be finished. It has waited here, how long?

Receiving maybe a few sheep, a half-dead native. The beasts of Clivorn.

There are only a few minutes left.

With infinite effort he made his right arm move. But his left arm and leg were dead weights. He dragged himself half his length forward, almost to where the path began. Another meter . . . but his arm had no more strength.

It was no use. He was done.

If I had climbed yesterday, he thought. Instead of the scan. The scan was by flyer, of course, circling The Clivorn. But the thing here couldn't be seen by a flyer because it wasn't here then. It was only in existence when something triggered the first barrier down below, pushed up through them both. Something large, warm-blooded maybe. Willing to climb.

The computer has freed man's brain.

But computers did not go hand by bloody hand across The Clivorn's crags. Only a living man, stupid enough to wonder, to drudge for knowledge on his knees. To risk. To experience. To be lonely.

No cheap way.

The shining Ship, the sealed Star Scientists had gone. They would not be back.

He had finished struggling now. He lay quiet and watched the brilliance at the end of the alien timer wink out. Presently there was no more left. With a faint no-sound the path and all its apparatus that had waited on Clivorn since before the glaciers fell, went away.

As it went the winds raged back but he did not hear them. He was lying quite comfortably where the bones of his face and body would mingle one day with the golden pebbles on The Clivorn's empty rock.

FURTHER READINGS

Science Fiction Novels with Religious Themes

Blish, James. *A Case of Conscience*. New York: Ballantine Books, 1972.

Farmer, Philip José. *Night of Light*. New York: Berkley Publishing Corporation, 1972.

Heinlein, Robert A. *Stranger in a Strange Land*. New York: G. P. Putnam's Sons, 1961.

Herbert, Frank. *Dune*. Philadelphia: Chilton Book Company, 1965.

—————. *Dune Messiah*. New York: G. P. Putnam's Sons, 1969.

Hesse, Hermann. *Journey to the East*. New York: Farrar, Straus & Giroux, 1956.

Lewis, C. S. *Out of the Silent Planet*. New York: Macmillan, 1943.

————. *Perelandra*. New York: Macmillan, 1968.

————. *That Hideous Strength*. New York: Macmillan, 1968.

Vonnegut, Kurt, Jr. *Cat's Cradle*. New York: Delacorte Press, 1971.

Zelazny, Roger. *Lord of Light*. New York: Avon Books, 1971.

INDEX

Teilhard de Chardin, Pierre, 379, 431
Tillich, Paul, 2, 11
Tiptree, James, Jr.: "And I Have Come Upon This Place by Lost Ways," 450–77; introduction to, 447–49
transcendence, 4, 10
True Believer, The (Hoffer), 200

universe: creation of, 3, 298–99; exploration of, 12–13; medieval understanding of, 6–7; nature of, 1, 5; as process, 12; purpose of, 3, 9, 378; Renaissance understanding of, 7

"Waste Land, The" (Eliot), 324
Whitehead, Alfred North, 8

Yeats, William Butler, 299–300
yin/yang, 263

Zelazny, Roger: "A Rose for Ecclesiastes," 326–77; introduction to, 323–26
Zen Buddhism, 264
Zoroastrianism, 261